NO PLACE FOR A LADY

The Regency Rags to Riches Series
Book One

Jade Lee

Book design by eBook Prep
www.ebookprep.com

Cover design by The Killion Group Inc.
www.thekilliongroupinc.com

January, 2017
ISBN: 978-1-61417-889-7

ePublishing Works!
www.epublishingworks.com

DEDICATION

To the ladies who never hesitated to wade in when I
most needed them:
Pattie, Cindy, Elisabeth, and Dixie.
Thank you.

CHAPTER 1

London, England, February 1807

"Ey, Fanny! 'Ow bout a diddle wi' me?"

Fantine Delarive winked as she swiveled her hips past a group of leering men, her smile friendly as she focused on the biggest of them all. "Ye ain't got enough t' diddle wi', Tommy boy. Talk t' me when ye grow a mite more."

She tweaked his cheek as she served him his ale. Then she passed on through the dingy pub, trading insults and affectionate pats with the customers.

They all knew her here, recognized her face, called her Fanny, but not a one knew the truth. They would never guess she had played maid to a princess or caught a French spy. They would never believe she could speak Spanish or cook a goose fit for the king. Nor would they credit that she planned to do such things again and again until she was too old to blow a kiss at an aged lord.

They would never believe what she had done, and she could never tell. So she teased the clientele like a two-bit tart, playing her role with consummate skill, because deep inside she did not truly credit it herself.

"Fanny!" called the keep, his gravelly voice carrying easily over the din. "'E wants ye. Tomorrow. Tea."

Fantine hitched her hip up to the edge of a bar stool, allowing a near-blind old man to feel the curve of her knee, but no more. "Tomorrow, tea," she echoed. "Guess I better put on me fancy togs. Not that I keep 'em on fer long!"

Then she laughed as loudly as the rest at her crude joke.

"Good morning, my lord. I trust you slept well."

Marcus Kane, Lord Chadwick, looked up, a single bite of egg poised precisely on his silver spoon. "Whom would you trust with such information, Bentley?" he asked dryly.

"Not even my sainted mother," the dough-faced man replied with a bland expression.

"Just so long as it is not *my* sainted mother," Marcus responded. "I trust that you have seen Paolina safely transferred from my bed to her own."

"Safely settled in, my lord."

A dozen possible responses came to mind, but Marcus washed them down with a sip of tea. His secretary would not understand a one of them, and so he did not waste his breath. Instead, he opened the morning paper knowing he could easily divide his attention between the news and Bentley's itemized list of the coming day.

He was wrong.

"I have canceled your appointment for tea with your sister, citing urgent matters with the Scottish estate."

Marcus's eye caught on a column detailing William Wilberforce's latest speech to the House of Commons, but at his secretary's news, he lifted his gaze.

"Do I have urgent matters at the Scottish estate?"

"No, my lord. But you do have an invitation to Lord Penworthy's home. The tone appeared somewhat urgent."

Marcus arched his eyebrows. He had not spoken with Penworthy since Geoffrey's funeral nearly three years ago. They had, of course, corresponded over political matters and seen one another in the House of Lords, but this was something else entirely. To be invited to his former mentor's house, and so abruptly, indicated something of supreme import.

Marcus set his napkin aside and rose from his chair.

"Thank you, Bentley. I now recall why I pay you so exorbitantly."

Marcus barely felt the carriage slow as it pulled up before Lord Penworthy's home. Though not in exclusive Grosvenor Square, Penworthy's home was stately enough for a fellow Member of Parliament (MP) and secluded enough to accommodate the man's more secretive activities on behalf of the Crown.

In short, Marcus liked it and the owner, and therefore was in a congenial frame of mind as he alighted from his carriage.

The mood would not last. He knew that. Marcus was in the dubious position of having to refuse whatever task his friend would no doubt request of him. But the decision was already made. It was time for Marcus to assume his responsibilities as eldest son, and that included an end to his favorite pastime.

Especially now that there was no other son to take his place should he make another costly mistake. He had not made many errors in his short time as a British spy, but the one had been enough. And Geoffrey had died because of it.

Marcus lifted the knocker, pushing it down with the force of a hammer, slamming his memories with the motion. Time heals all wounds, he reminded himself. Then he smiled bitterly.

Some wounds never fully healed.

The door opened swiftly, held by a man who could have been Bentley's twin except that his voice was cavernous, as befitted a butler.

"Good afternoon, my lord. His lordship is expecting you in the library."

Marcus crossed the threshold and handed over his hat and coat without demur, trying to shed the February cold as easily. He moved automatically down the hall, not bothering to wait for a footman to precede him. Then he realized no one was about. Even the butler had disappeared. In fact, the whole atmosphere of the house was hushed and secretive.

What Penworthy wanted must be serious indeed.

Marcus sighed, already steeling himself to refuse. Skulking in doorways, waiting through the night in some freezing ditch, all these things were over for him now, and he did not yet know whether to regret it or rejoice.

He knocked softly on the library door.

"Come in."

Respecting the mood of the house, Marcus entered without sound, closing the door carefully behind him. He could not see deeply into the room, but he smiled at the soothing scent of leather books and a fire built with pine.

"Chadwick, old boy! Glad you could come."

Marcus navigated past two wingback chairs before he greeted his old friend. "I would not have missed it for the world," he said easily.

Then he stopped and tried not to stare. Good Lord, what had happened to the man? Rather than the sturdy if aging gentleman of barely two months ago, Penworthy looked more like a monk bent with the weight of time. As he rose from behind his desk, his white hair waved wildly and his eyes were red with fatigue. Though his steps were quick and steady, the hand he extended was slightly curled and arthritic, his body thin and aged.

Naturally, Marcus could not ask what had occurred, nor even reveal his startled thoughts. So he merely smiled, forcing himself to bring out some pleasantry. "Fine day, is it not?"

Penworthy grinned. "What? No polite lie about how well I look?"

Rather than answer directly, Marcus gestured toward the desk and the stacks of paper scattered about. "Do the affairs of state weigh heavily upon you?"

"Not that lot," responded Penworthy with a jerk of his head. "I am merely growing old and have developed a cough that will not end. Brandy?"

"Certainly. Pray, allow me." Marcus stepped to the sideboard, pouring with practiced ease. He had forgotten that Penworthy was nearing sixty. The thought that Marcus might lose his longtime friend to a cough disturbed him greatly. But his morbid thoughts were cut short by Penworthy.

"What concerns me is a far more serious matter."

Marcus allowed his expression to relax, focusing his attention on the coming information. Finally, he would know what all this secrecy was about.

"I am, of course, at your dispo—"

Suddenly, the library doors burst open with an explosion of air that extinguished the desk candles, splattering hot wax across any number of state papers. Then a high voice cut into the room's serene atmosphere.

"'Ello, luv. Sorry I'm late."

To his shock, a diminutive streetwalker strutted in, her dress a blazing swirl of colors, her bodice cut low enough to reveal tantalizing glimpses of her curves. In her hands, she carried the tea tray, and Marcus wondered that she could keep the items on the silver with her hips swaying so very much.

"Fantine!" Penworthy said the single word with a mixture of dismay and amusement that was not lost on the young whore.

"Aye, ducks," she said, straightening from where she set down the tray. "'Ey now! Wot's this?" she cried as she lifted the brandy snifter from Penworthy's hand. "This Frenchie stuff will rot yer innards, it will!" Then, before the man could object, she neatly emptied the glass down her own white throat. "Aye," she said huskily as she smacked her lips. "Rot yer innards, it will. Now come 'ave some tea like a good nob."

Penworthy sighed, slanting an expression at Marcus that was half apology, half surrender. "Marcus, may I present to you, Fantine Delarive. Fantine, this is Marcus Kane, Lord Chadwick."

"Auw!" she cried, her accent thick enough to crack glass. "Wot a pleasure, t' be sure." Then she leaned forward, her hand extended as her ragged dress slipped lower with her every breath. "But me name's Fanny."

Centuries of breeding warred within Marcus. Politeness demanded that he rise and kiss her hand like a gentleman, and yet those very rules of behavior required that he ignore invitations from a backstreet tart.

In the end, respect for his friend won out. He rose, albeit stiffly, and took her hand. "Fanny."

She clucked appreciatively, her hand still extended, clearly expecting him to kiss it. He waited, knowing what she wanted, but finding the act difficult to perform. She smelled almost overpoweringly of stale beer, and her hand, though small and perhaps pleasingly formed, was dirty, the nails cracked and blunt.

"Come on, luv. I won't bite, less'n ye pay," she cooed.

"Fantine!" cried Penworthy, clearly exasperated. "Cease torturing the man." He pushed between them, breaking their contact, neatly pushing the whore into a seat before the fire. She collapsed expertly, her legs extended before her, giving Marcus a full view of their delightful shape.

Really, he thought as he settled into the other chair, he could almost understand Penworthy's attraction to the woman. Despite the tattered clothing and coarse attitude, the dark-haired tart was well formed, both graceful and sensual in her own vulgar way.

He had thought her extremely young at first glance, but now, as the sunlight slanted across her face, he saw she was a lovely woman of perhaps twenty-five. Her hair, though cut haphazardly, appeared a lush dark chestnut, and her complexion beneath the smudges of dirt seemed not quite brown, not quite clear. "Golden" sprang to mind. And her eyes were a sparkling bronze beneath long, black lashes.

What a pity that such beauty was given to one so vulgar. That Penworthy had such questionable taste in bed partners was none of his affair. If only the man would make quick work of it and send her away. Unfortunately, the whore gleefully relaxed into her chair as if intending to remain.

Stifling his irritation, Marcus decided to opt for expediency over good manners. Reaching into his pocket, he produced a guinea and lifted it up to the light. As expected, her eyes were drawn to the flash of gold, though other than that, her expression remained curiously bland.

"I see your stockings are in need of repair," Marcus said coolly. "Perhaps you would like to go purchase another pair." Then he flicked the coin into the air, not in the least bit surprised when it disappeared into her dress faster than his eye could follow.

"Auw!" she cried again, and this time Marcus could not restrain his flinch at the sound. "Want t' talk man t' man, do ye? Well, don't ye worry, ducks," she said, reaching forward to pat his cheek like a fond old aunt. "Ye ain't got nothing wot I ain't seen or 'eard afore."

Marcus stiffened, his temper fraying by the second. But before he could give voice to any of the blistering responses that came to mind, Penworthy once again interrupted.

"Fantine, would you like some tea?"

"Why, thanks, luv, but no' now. Perhaps later."

Marcus shifted his gaze to his friend, surprised for the second time that day. Surely Penworthy meant to send her away. She could not be part of their discussion.

Almost as soon as the thought formed, Marcus answered his own question. No doubt the woman had discovered some information through her sordid life on the street. Penworthy wished Marcus to question her.

Marcus relaxed, his faith in the elderly man restored. What the MP had done was quite right, quite right indeed. Meanwhile, he glanced discreetly to his left, seeing that the tart waited as well, though her gaze fell disdainfully on himself.

Before he could return the scrutiny, Penworthy began speaking, his voice tired and hurried. "There has been an attempt on Wilberforce's life."

Marcus did not move, but his attention sharpened instantly. "Is he harmed?"

"No, thank God. We were saved by a lucky accident. We cannot expect such felicity in the future."

No, agreed Marcus silently, they certainly could not. William Wilberforce was a powerful member of the House of Commons, one of the nation's most influential leaders. A diminutive man with thin, crippled legs, he still maintained high moral and religious standards. When he spoke, it was with amazing power and eloquence. His life was an example of Christian intensity and political power. In short, Wilberforce was one of the few men Marcus openly admired.

The thought that someone had attempted to kill the famous MP sent chills down Marcus's spine. "It must be because of the antislavery bill."

"My thought exactly," said Penworthy. "If Wilberforce were to die now, his reform bill might expire with him. But who would want that so much as to kill him?"

Marcus frowned, shifting through Parliament's faces and names, searching for the one man whose guilt made sense. "Harris. It has to be him."

"Why?"

"He has loudly opposed the bill, fighting it with everything from bribes to threats, but it all stopped this last month."

"Almost as if he had found an alternate solution?"

"Such as murder."

Penworthy nodded, his gaze thoughtful, and Marcus felt a surge of pride that he could have been of assistance. Then a rude snort broke his mood.

"Precious little to 'ang a man fer murder," said the tart. "Me 'eart goes out t' this 'Arris."

He turned to her, not bothering to hide his annoyance. How like the lowbred woman to assume Harris would come to such a violent end. "Rest assured," he said coldly, "the matter shall be dealt with appropriately. Despite the joy and increased trade I am sure you enjoy at a hanging, I am afraid that is not the end for an MP, even if he is a cold-blooded killer."

"Ew, la-di-da," she cried, clearly mocking him, but he had already turned his shoulder to her, confident that his tone and attitude would more than silence the unwanted companion. Indeed, he regretted that he had not insisted the wench remain outside the room. He did not like that she had heard the matter at hand. By nightfall, every tavern keep in London would know of their suspicions.

But before he could more than lift his snifter, her voice cut through his thoughts. It was not the screeching dockside wail he expected, but something entirely different. Suddenly, her voice was low and husky, stiff with matronly outrage and a gossip's undertone. It was so different that he caught himself looking about the room for another person.

"You are quite correct, my lord," she said. "I, myself, cannot abide such blood sport. Truly it is an act for the masses, though I fear we stir their passions overmuch. Why just last month I attended a hanging, and I saw two filthy boys brawling over a ha'penny. Imagine!"

Marcus turned back to her, his jaw slack. Then she leaned forward, reaching for the tea service with smooth and maidenly modesty despite her ragged clothing.

"Would you care for some tea, Lord Penworthy? I find that good English tea always stimulates the mind and the digestion. Most beneficial for weighty matters of state, do you not agree?"

Penworthy nodded, clearly not in the least bit surprised. "Of course, Fantine. Thank you."

Marcus watched dumbfounded as she served his friend tea with sugar, clearly demonstrating that she had learned of his preference beforehand. She turned expectantly to Marcus.

"And you, my lord? Ah, never mind," she said with a mischievous smile. "I can tell you would prefer stronger spirits, especially as yours seems to have deserted you."

Marcus stiffened at the insult. He held back a scathing comment demanding Penworthy explain himself. He had no expectation that she would illuminate this odd situation. But even as he turned toward his mentor, the elderly man shrugged.

"Do not look at me for answers. If I had warned you in advance, she would have behaved the perfect society miss and then you would have thought my wits had gone begging—"

"Ah," interrupted the strange woman as she poured her own tea, "but I believe Lord Chadwick thought so in any event. Imagine," she said, slipping into her tart tone, "a peer o' the realm introducing a dockside fancy piece to 'is friends!"

Marcus winced at her abrupt shift in accent, only now realizing that she had read him perfectly, guessed his assumptions, and had, in fact, played upon them to make him feel all the more uncomfortable.

For the first time in three years, his blood began the slow simmer toward fury. But he kept it contained, purposely turning his shoulder to the woman as he addressed his friend in low tones as sharp as any blade. "Why is she here?"

Penworthy opened his mouth to respond, but once again she cut in, her voice tripping expertly over the accents of a dockside chippy. "Why, to catch yer thievin', murderin' aristocrat, ducky!"

Marcus felt his breath catch in his throat. It could not be true. Penworthy was not a foolish man. He would never employ such a woman.

But as the moments ticked by without a word from his associate, Marcus's confidence began to waver. As the seconds dragged into minutes, Marcus found himself studying Penworthy's guilty expression.

"You cannot be serious," Marcus finally exploded. "You cannot send this…this creature to apprehend a peer! Why, she would make a circus of the whole affair!"

"Aye, an' won't that be just peachy for th' masses?" she chimed in.

Marcus turned, his eyes critical as he rudely inspected her from top to bottom. He could not tell whether she was a smart miss playing the whore or a whore playing a society maid. But either way, she was not in the least bit qualified to stop a threat to one of the nation's leaders. Why, he would not trust her to black his boots properly!

But as he turned to Penworthy, he saw from his friend's set expression that he truly did intend just that. "Good God," Marcus sputtered, "but she is an *actress!*" He spat the word out like bad meat.

Finally, Penworthy spoke, and his voice sounded calm, albeit weary. "No, Marcus, Fantine is very much more than an actress, just as you are very much more than a rich peer." That last part was clearly directed at the woman, but she appeared to take no note of it. "In actual fact, I hoped the two of you would work together on this particular assignment."

"What?" he cried, surging to his feet.

"Impossible!" she exclaimed at exactly the same instant.

He spun around to glare at her though his words were aimed at his friend. "I have given up this skulking about, as you well know, Penworthy. But even if I had not, God himself could not make me teach this street rat what she needs to know."

"Teach me!" she cried, leaping to her own feet to match him glare for glare. "God Himself could not teach you what you need to learn." Then she spun back to Penworthy. "If you think I shall allow myself to be hampered by this spoiled flash, then your wits are addled by the pox!"

"The pox!" Marcus retorted. "Perhaps that is why you imagine you could possibly—"

"Do not even attempt to speak to me with that tone—"

Suddenly, a loud hacking cough interrupted both of them. They turned together, and Marcus's eyes widened at the sight of his dear friend coughing blood into a handkerchief.

"Have some tea, my lord," the woman said, as she deftly poured him another cup. But Penworthy merely shook his head, his face a dull gray.

"Brandy," he whispered.

"No..." she began, but Marcus was already at the sideboard, pouring a brandy. Penworthy accepted it with alacrity, gulping it down too quickly, then gesturing for more.

Marcus, however, hesitated. "Sir," he began slowly, "if your health is precarious—"

"Pray do not pretend concern now," interrupted the shrew. "Not after giving him the drink."

Marcus turned to her, using the motion to set aside the brandy, well away from Penworthy. He had not intended to respond to her gibe, but one look at her contemptuous expression had him pulling on his aristocratic bearing like a coat, words tumbling from his mouth without conscious thought. "His color is much better now," he said, his voice fairly reeking with hauteur.

She merely shook her head and mocked him with an inelegant snort. He responded silently, raising his eyebrow with an equally contemptuous sneer. Then she mimicked his pose, adding an extra measure of haughtiness by pretending to lift a quizzing glass to her eye, and suddenly he had the strongest desire to stick out his tongue at her.

Had he regressed to the point of infancy? he wondered as he struggled to control his baser instincts.

Meanwhile, Penworthy interrupted his thoughts. "Where were we?" he wheezed.

"Saving Wilberforce's life," supplied Marcus gently.

"Ah, yes," returned Penworthy. "Fantine, can you help me protect the MP, please?"

She straightened her shoulders, her expression sickeningly demure. "Of course, my lord. It would be my great honor to do my duty for England and my king."

Marcus merely rolled his eyes.

"Naturally, you will receive your standard pay," returned Penworthy.

Marcus shifted, his face pulling into an unholy grin. "Standard pay? For doing your patriotic duty?"

"Some o' us," she said, shifting into her dockside accent, "ain't paid just t' breathe an' dress fancy, ducks. It be this or on me back, spreading me thighs for the loikes of you. An' believe me," she added in an undertone, "I'd rather face a whole battalion o' Frenchies than spread for you."

Marcus felt his hands clench at the insult, but he kept his comments to himself. Despite his fury, he was still a man ruled by reason. He had no right to question or mock her method of earning a living, especially if those were indeed her only two choices.

"You have other choices than that, Fantine, as you well know," Penworthy said harshly. "If you would but—"

"No," she interrupted hastily. "I cannot."

"You can."

She merely shook her head, her mouth pressed tightly together, and Marcus frowned, wondering at the exchange. Did he sense an edge of fear from the raucous woman? A vulnerability, maybe, but to what? Penworthy? Or whatever Penworthy offered? He didn't know, and there was no time to ponder as his mentor turned to him.

"What of you, Marcus? Fantine could search through the rookeries while you investigate from Grosvenor Square. The Season will begin soon. There will be ample opportunity to mingle without raising comment."

"Merely the interest of every matchmaking mama from here to Scotland," he responded dryly as he crossed to the sideboard for more brandy.

"Ah, poor ducks," Fantine cut in. "All them laidies tossin' 'emselves at yer feet. Ain't it a pity they's all blind t' wot ye're really loike?"

He turned slowly, knowing his gaze was cold and cruel. "Quite true," was all he said, but he had the satisfaction of seeing her bronze eyes widen with surprise. Of course, she quickly shifted her expression into an exaggerated pout that perfectly mimicked any of a dozen society misses. The final touch came when she coyly began fluttering her eyelashes at him.

So exact was her imitation that he might have laughed out loud. As it was, he merely clenched his jaw and focused on Penworthy.

"There is nothing she can do from the docks," Marcus said curtly. "Harris does not go there."

"We do not know that Harris is the guilty one."

"He is the most likely candidate," Marcus returned.

Before Penworthy could speak, Fantine cut in again, apparently unable to keep silent for more than a few seconds. "Let him blunder after this Lord Harris, Penworthy. If my usual contacts cannot discover the culprit's identity, then I shall pay Ballast for the information. The worst Lord Chadwick can do is make the true villain more confident, thinking you have hired a bumbling idiot to chase him."

"Fantine," said Penworthy, his voice weary and soft, "you are not being helpful."

"And you are being ridiculous," she answered as she folded her arms. "You cannot think a starched-up popinjay could do more than bungle the entire affair."

Marcus held back a caustic retort, knowing she was baiting him. He was aware as well that despite the harpy's ramblings, Penworthy knew his true value. Still, he could not resist questioning the other man. "Do you seriously intend to allow her to investigate?"

Penworthy shrugged. "I know no one better."

"You know me."

"You have not said yes."

Marcus looked down, idly swirling the amber liquid in his glass. "My mother reminds me that when she was my age, her sons were entering Harrow."

Penworthy nodded. "An excellent school. I made many lifelong friends there."

Marcus did not respond, knowing that his mentor understood the problem, but was too polite to comment. The difficulty, of course, was that his mother wanted grandchildren. And his father wished Marcus would do his duty to continue the family name. That meant finding a wife and setting up his nursery, not embroiling himself in another sordid drama, especially one that might endanger his life, limb, and ability to procreate.

Then his eyes chanced to fall on Fantine's shapely leg. Her gown was in tatters, artfully designed to advertise her attributes without showing too much. She was clearly canny at her trade, whether actress or whore, and Penworthy would not put his faith in her for no reason. If she were remotely competent, he could refuse Penworthy with good conscience.

But the thought of William Wilberforce, a name synonymous with Christian piety, placing his life in her soiled hands frankly turned his stomach. At best, her blundering about would cause countless political embarrassments. At worst, she would expose herself to the villain.

The risks to Wilberforce and the nation aside, he could not allow her to take on the task. She would be killed within a week.

"Very well," he said. "I shall do it."

"Excellent," cried Penworthy, not nearly loud enough to drown out Fantine's groan. Then he returned to his desk, as if dismissing the entire matter from his mind. "I trust the two of you will not kill each other while coordinating your activities?"

Marcus looked up abruptly. "Coordinate? You cannot mean she will continue."

"Of course I shall continue!" she snapped. "I am your only hope of remaining alive." Then she was once again on her feet, stepping directly up to his friend. "Penworthy, please do not be a fool in this. He is a lord and an MP," she said, gesturing toward Marcus. "Surely he has someone who cares for him. His mother, if no one else. Do not put him into a situation he cannot handle. It is too dangerous."

It was some moments before Marcus understood she referred to him, and another moment before he realized that Penworthy appeared to be seriously considering her words.

It was too much, the perfect *coup de grace* on a ruined afternoon. It was bad enough to be insulted, harangued, and mocked by an actress who could not decide whether she was a strumpet or a lady, but to finally circumvent his principles in the interest of saving a cheap bawd only to have Penworthy think of pulling him off…It was insupportable!

"Penworthy," he said, setting down his glass with a click. "I will not work with her. I will not speak with her. In fact, I heartily intend never to look upon her again. Do not even think I shall budge on this."

"And I," she said, matching his bearing with her own arrogance, "will not risk either Wilberforce or myself with him strutting about!"

Her cry echoed through the room, but it did nothing to diminish his own position. It was now for Penworthy to decide who was the most appropriate person for the task.

Marcus had no doubt as to the outcome.

But Penworthy's response did not come immediately. He took his time, setting his hands on his desk with arthritic precision, slowly lifting his body from his chair until he stood and glared at them both. When he spoke, his voice vibrated with a low fury that seemed to come from deep within the aged frame.

"This matter has already taken up too much of my time. Hear me and hear me well. This is too important for the two of you to spend your time fighting. You *will* work together. You *will* coordinate your activities, and you bloody well *will* do it without botching or I shall have you both clapped in irons and locked in Newgate!"

Penworthy looked more fierce, more furious than Marcus had ever seen him before. But Marcus was not a future earl to no purpose. He had never been intimidated in his life, and he had no intention of starting now. He merely lounged backward against the sideboard and smiled at his dearest friend in the world.

"You would not dare," he said softly.

"Aye," she agreed, her own voice gentle. "You would not do that to me."

Penworthy, however, narrowed his gaze, his expression colder than Marcus had ever thought possible.

"Try me," was all he said.

For a long moment, all that could be heard was the nearly silent tick of the gilt clock on the mantel. Penworthy's glare shifted with measured pace between both Marcus and Fantine, his every muscle daring them to defy him.

It took less than a second for Marcus to realize that he had no prayer of winning this argument. Honor, duty, and loyalty all demanded he capitulate. If Penworthy persisted in the madness of using Fantine, and it certainly appeared that he intended to, then Marcus's only option was to try and mitigate the damages.

One look at Fantine's disgusted expression, and he knew she had come to the same conclusion. Although, apparently, in her arrogance, she thought it was he who would mismanage everything.

In short, the two of them would have to work together to save Wilberforce.

God help the poor MP.

CHAPTER 2

Fantine crouched low in the dirty gutter and cursed long and fluently, using words in as many different languages and cants as she could think of. When she was done, she made up new ones and gave them their own gruesome meanings. And every single one she rained down on Chadwick's head.

Too bad he was not there to hear her.

Lord Chadwick was late. And late in the rookeries could mean dead.

Fantine tugged at the dirty cap that covered her hair and silently wished she had not bound her breasts so tight. It was damned difficult to breathe. And her breeches were so thin they could split apart in a stiff breeze. She hated wearing these dull gray clothes and her street persona as the Rat, but it was the only way to meet with Ballast without risking being chained up in some dockside brothel. Of course, if his lordship did not show up soon, the entire affair with Ballast would go sour in any event.

But there was no help for it. She had agreed to work with him, so she folded her arms against the cold and continued to wait.

Long after her legs had gone numb and her face felt cracked with the cold, she finally spied him. Lord

Chadwick was following a small boy, barreling around the corner with as much subtlety as a runaway carriage.

Gawd, she thought with a groan, his lordship was still handsome despite the muck now staining his clothing. Ever since she had first seen him, she knew his looks would trouble her. Lean, like a sword, and tall, his body appealed to her baser instincts in a way no one ever had. She saw no fat on him, no softness of any sort. Even at this distance, his muscles were well defined, easily contracting and releasing with his movements. She had no doubt he would best most men in a fair fight.

But if his body was attractive, it was nothing compared to his face. She could not see him clearly yet, but she recalled every moment of their meeting yesterday, especially the hard aristocratic angles of his jaw as he turned away from her in disdain. She remembered the way his clear blue eyes had gazed down his straight nose at her. Why, even his dusky blond hair had seemed to mock her with its rich luster, far more beautiful than her own short brown locks.

In short, he was handsome in every way, a lord of the realm with the hauteur to match. And he annoyed her. So she had tormented him in their first meeting, teasing and harassing him merely to find out how much it would take before the self-contained Lord Chadwick lost control of himself.

It never happened.

That disturbed her more than she cared to admit. If she could not push him to an emotional outburst, then she very much feared she could not manage him. In the end, he might actually be more in control than she.

So she watched with almost gleeful satisfaction as Chadwick ran through the rookeries following a small boy with freckles whom everyone called Nameless.

"Gi'e it to 'im good, Nameless," she whispered into the dark. Then she raised her chilled hand, flashing it open and closed in a pulse of pale flesh, barely visible through the dark gloom. His lordship did not see it, but the boy did, ducking his head in acknowledgment.

Nameless stopped barely a foot away, standing just to one side of a dripping overhang. Eventually his lordship joined the boy, his breathing surprisingly steady given what Nameless had put him through. Nevertheless, his lordship appeared worse for wear as he softly cursed the drip that splattered his forehead every second and a half.

"Can you not stand to one side, boy?"

"No, guv," lied the child. "Ain't no room."

With a barely muffled grumble, Chadwick grasped the thin boy and lifted him up, setting him gently on a barrel. He then stepped into the added space beneath the overhang. But even with the extra room, the drip still fell on his broad shoulder, adding its own color to the smeared muck already on his tattered coat.

"So where is she?" Chadwick said to the boy.

"Right behind you," Fantine answered from her hiding place behind them. "And keep your voice down."

He spun around, scanning the gloom until his gaze found her face, his eyes widening in stunned surprise. She couldn't hide her grin. She knew that when she wore her Rat persona, not even her own mother would recognize her. Fantine had spent long years watching and imitating young boys so that even as she sat in the shadows, her entire slim frame radiated that peculiar mix of bristling arrogance and heartbreaking vulnerability typical of a street boy.

Then Nameless spoke, redirecting her thoughts to Chadwick's costume. "Oi took 'im ever' way Oi could, but 'e still looks loike fat flash t' me."

"That he does," Fantine agreed softly. The man had obviously made some attempt to dress crudely. The outfit fit him poorly. The coat pulled too tightly across his broad chest and the fawn breeches were much too fine, defining his muscular thighs with almost indecent precision. Nameless had done well to disguise the expensive fabric, and Fantine wrinkled her nose as she picked out the telltale odors. Clearly the boy had dragged Chadwick through every fish stall and sewer in London. Unfortunately, it appeared as surface dirt. Nothing had the threadbare look of neglect.

She sighed, thanking Nameless with a wink. "You did fine. Best disappear now before Ballast's men catch you." Then she glanced at Lord Chadwick. "Pay him, please."

The peer paused in the act of tugging irritably at the buttons of his tight coat. "Pay him? For what?"

"For leading you here."

Chadwick caught her eye, grimacing with annoyance at the entire affair, but he did not argue. He pulled a shilling out of his pocket and tossed it at the boy. "There was no need for this nonsense. I could have just met you here instead of finding the boy in Cheapside and having him lead me to you."

She lifted her face toward Chadwick, wishing the moon were not so bright on his still clean blond hair. "If you are too tired, my lord," she taunted, "I can handle the meeting without you."

"Pray do not be ridiculous," he responded curtly.

Fantine stood, then noticed that Nameless had yet to disappear. "Wot be ye still 'ere fer?" she said, lapsing into her street accent.

His young face wrinkled into a look that only a street boy could manage. It was half pathos, half stubborn pout as he held up his hand and glared at the peer. "Oi were promised two shillings."

Fantine did not even flinch at the lie. In truth, Nameless only expected a copper or two, but as he had said, Chadwick was fat flash, and that made him an easy cull.

To his credit, his lordship's frown said he recognized the lie for what it was, but for some reason, he chose not to argue. Instead he pressed a bright guinea into the child's hand. "Get some clothes, boy. It is cold out here."

Fantine gasped in horror at the flash of gold. Good Lord, if she had thought Chadwick would be that generous, she would have stopped the boy at the very beginning. Giving away a shilling was one thing. A guinea was another matter entirely. That one piece of gold marked them as a target for every thick-armed brute in the area. She'd lay odds that even Nameless was thinking about rounding up his friends for a gang attack.

"Off wi' ye," she said with a low growl. "And do not think t' betray me."

The boy disappeared in a blink of an eye, his movements too eager, making Fantine curse softly.

"Sweet Jesus," she muttered, "you have not the sense God gave a rat."

Chadwick glanced sharply at her. "I have enough sense not to try to lose my partner by giving the wrong directions."

"I did not give you the wrong directions," she said, her gaze slipping back to the pub across the alleyway. Ballast waited inside. "You found me right enough."

"Merely because I chanced to find that boy."

Fantine sighed, wondering at his arrogance. "You cannot believe that any boy, even Nameless, could find me if I chose to remain hidden." She turned to look at him, making sure he understood her meaning. "I sent Nameless to you. His job was to bring you to me and to help you with your…attire." She straightened, keeping her gaze steady, silently conveying that she was the one in control. He did what she said.

She saw his eyes narrow as he understood her message. She could tell he was not used to surrendering control to anyone, much less a woman, but she didn't care. This might be fun for him, but it was her livelihood. He would bloody well listen to her.

She waited a bit longer, making doubly sure he understood, and then she shifted her gaze away, back to the pub. "Ballast is in the back," she said softly as she started across the street.

She took no more than a half step before she was suddenly blocked by Chadwick's large frame. He had barely moved, but he quietly prevented her escape. She was trapped in the corner shadows behind him.

"What—"

"Listen carefully, Miss Delarive." His voice cut low through the chill air. "I agreed to work with you because

Penworthy wished it. You may know London's sordid underbelly, but I am here to keep Wilberforce alive, not scramble through the sewers for your amusement." He reached out and neatly caught her chin, lifting it up until she gazed directly into his hard blue eyes. "Do not play with me again, Fantine."

She swallowed, unable to answer. He was right. She could have met him at Cheapside and run him through the alleyways herself or even sent him more appropriate clothing. But she had wanted to add that extra measure of humiliation, establishing her superiority from the very beginning.

Except she was not the one truly in control. Even though she was smart and agile with contacts throughout London's dark streets, he was physically stronger, politically powerful, and had his own fair share of wits. She was not sure who would win a contest between them. She was not even sure she would survive one. She was too vulnerable in too many ways.

But neither was she willing to simply concede.

Jerking her chin out of his hand, she drew herself upright, trying as nearly as possible to match his size. "Despite all that Nameless could do, you still reek of French perfume—"

"We passed a bawdy house—"

"Distinctive, rich, French perfume that was no doubt sprinkled all over you by your mistress. It is one way the bawds have of identifying ownership of a man. Your breeches are too fine, your manner too proud. You will be marked within seconds of entering the pub, and my only hope is to pass you off as a mad peer playacting in the docks. Ballast does not play games, yer lordship, and neither do I. It would be best for us both if you turned around now and went home. This is not your world."

Fantine watched him closely, gauging his reaction and his intelligence, but he gave nothing away beyond a slight clench to his jaw. "I have been in alehouses worse than any you can find," he finally said.

"Alone?" she countered. "Or with another?" Then she rushed on before he could answer. "Alone, you make your own rules, you live or die by your own actions. With another there is added safety, but also more risk. What will you do when Ballast takes me into the back room and then you are surrounded by his men? Will you turn and run? Or will you try to be a gentleman hero and protect the woman?"

She watched his eyes, expecting to see the telltale flush of guilt as he admitted to himself that he would run. It did not appear. Instead, she saw a grim determination flatten his gaze, as if he would do anything, including a foolhardy rush against ridiculous odds to try and save her. And why? She did not make the mistake of thinking such idiocy was for her sake. Gentlemen worked on a code of honor, and apparently Chadwick had more than his measure.

"Cut and run, you halfwit," she snapped. "I can take care of myself."

His smile was slow in coming, but no less startling. "You would like that, hmmm?" he asked, his voice humming with the low throb of authority. "Perhaps you intend to betray me to Ballast, tip his hat to me only to rid yourself of an annoyance? Who is the halfwit, Fantine? I would not advise such an act."

Fantine swallowed, unnerved that he could think as deviously as she. "*I* will not betray you, Chadwick. You are a fish out of water, here. Your own ignorance will destroy you." Then she decided to end this debate, knowing she could return to it when she had more command of the situation. She jerked her head toward the pub. "We cannot waste any more time on this. If we wait much longer, Ballast will be too drunk to be of any use."

He shifted slightly, as if allowing the change in topic. "Perhaps we should wait until he is well into his cups."

Fantine shook her head. "Ballast is a mean drunk—suspicious and violent. Our best chance is to approach him when his brainpan is not awash with spirits." She did not add that her guise as a child would not protect her from a drunken Ballast. At such times, he was known to take boys to bed as well as girls.

Chadwick nodded once, as if he understood her silent concerns. That was impossible, of course, but for some silly reason, the gesture reassured her. She began to relax, making the mental shift into the persona of the Rat.

"Ye're me daft flash," she said softly, "who 'ired me to let ye peer at London's sordid underbelly." She repeated that last phrase again, seeking to imitate his wording as a boy would, mocking the man while trying out his large words. "If we be split," she added, looking directly at him to give weight to her words, "run like a craven mort. Oi can 'andle Ballast." Then she let herself smile. "'E ain't near as smart as 'e thinks."

She saw the question in his eyes, but she did not give him a chance to voice it. Instead, she sprang past him, scurrying through the damp street until she could duck into the pub doorway. She knew he would follow, no doubt cursing her all the way, and the thought made her smile grow even wider.

She was still grinning when she shook her damp clothes by the smoky fire. All around her, the patrons cursed as drops of sleet and mud flew about her, some landing with a hiss on the fire. She neatly ducked a fist thrown out to cuff her as she scampered to the opposite corner.

The pub was dark and dingy, filled with a sea of sweaty men and stale ale. Directly in front of her, Gilly the barmaid navigated tables, alternating curses with suggestive winks. Fantine took a moment to admire the way she handled the rough customers.

Then Chadwick burst in.

True to form, he did not slink in as she and all the other customers would. No, he let the wind throw open the door, gusting through his cloak so that it billowed about his large frame as he peered down his aristocratic nose at the clientele. Everyone looked up. Many began to grumble. And Fantine was hard-pressed to stifle a curse.

Then something happened. Chadwick did not strut in like an arrogant lord. Instead, he ogled the people.

"Are ye daft? Git out!" grumbled a thick-shouldered dockworker by the door.

Chadwick grinned. "Ooo, how positively delightful!" he drawled, effecting a dandy's nasal tone. Then he stepped in the door, his gaze unerringly picking out Fantine as she crouched in the shadows. "Come, boy, this is perfectly delicious. Charming. Marvelously dreadful. No need to hide in the corner. Fetch me some…some ale!"

Fantine could only gape. He was perfect! Her having told him to play a daft peer looking for some dockside excitement, he performed the role exquisitely. Which allowed Fantine to play her own part with equal nerve.

She groaned out loud. "Damned queer, 'e is," she muttered to the nearest man. "Wants t' see the local color, 'e says. Pay good money." Then she caught the avaricious gleam in the man's eye and shook her head, her grin cocky. "Ain't no use, wot yer thinkin'. I already cleaned 'im out. 'E's got enough for 'is drink and a diddle wi' Gilly, 'at's all."

She watched as the man narrowed his gaze, quickly evaluating the truth of her statement. Eventually he spat out a curse and turned back to his tankard of ale. Nearby, other men hunkered back down, their interest in the daft lord already gone.

"Boy!" Chadwick called again, his voice slightly roughened, as if he were trying to assume a dockside accent. "Come along now, I am parched. Uh, now, ye bugger!" Then he grinned as if he had just said something brilliant.

Fantine pushed herself up from the corner. "Gilly!" she called to the barmaid. "Entertain 'im fer a mite. I needs to talk wi' Ballast."

The barmaid nodded, her hips already shifting enough to catch Chadwick's eye. Not one to miss so obvious a cue, Chadwick returned the wink and patted his lap lasciviously. Gilly grinned, barely remembering to pass her tray to Rat.

"Ballast's in th' back room. Ye can take 'im 'is drink."

The barmaid extended the tray, and Fantine rushed forward to catch it. She barely made it in time, and she held her breath while the ale sloshed, but didn't spill. Lord, but she was slow tonight. Her joints ached, and she had yet to feel her toes after her hour's wait in the bitter cold. Ten years ago, she would have laughed at such minor discomforts, but at twenty-five, she could no longer move like the wind. How long before she would be too slow to outrun her pursuers?

She shuddered at the thought, pushing it away with the ease of long practice. Now was not the time to fight demons she could not conquer. So she straightened, pushing her way through the back door into a small, windowless room.

"Evenin', guv'nor," she said to Ballast, who sat counting his money at a scarred desk on the opposite side of the room. Beside him stood his son, a gangly youth with greasy black hair and eyes that studied everything and everyone. Lounging against the walls were two large brutes, one on either side.

Fantine sauntered forward, her gestures cocky as she kicked the door shut behind her. "'Ave a little rat's piss," she said as she sloshed the tankard down before Ballast, spilling drink over the coins and notes piled there. Then she grinned at Ballast's startled expression. He probably had already known she was in the pub. Ballast simply had not expected her to push her way into his back room without so much as a by-yer-leave.

Continuing her role as a cocksure youth, she perched insolently on the only other piece of furniture there—a rickety chair opposite the desk—then began swinging one foot back and forth as so many children do. Meanwhile, she studied her opponent.

Ballast had gained weight. Thickset and heavy by nature, his flesh now seemed to hang on him while his mouth drooped in a perpetual frown. But his fatty body was all that had gone soft. His narrowed black eyes and his meaty fist appeared just as hard as ever.

"Got a minute t' speak wi' an old, dear friend?" Fantine asked happily, pretending to a confidence she didn't feel.

"Humph!" snorted Ballast, his gaze returning to the pound notes before him.

Fantine was not fooled. She knew his attention was firmly fixed on her. And if she had any doubts, the actions of the other three would have tipped her off. The boy glared at her, his face a mirror image of his father's contempt, except that his gaze still held a lively intelligence that could be dangerous. As for the other two, Fantine's back prickled as they moved silently behind her, one on each side.

"Go' a tad bit o' business fer you, guv," Fantine said as she bounced slightly on the seat with boyish enthusiasm.

Ballast continued counting his coins with dogged determination. "Forty-eight. Nine. Fifty."

Fantine swallowed. Fifty pounds. Oh, the things she could do with such ready blunt. It had been a while since her last job with Penworthy, and her money was stretched painfully thin. Her empty stomach growled loudly.

Suddenly, the man looked up, his gaze intent."'Ave t' do wi' th' nob?"

Fantine blinked. "Wot?"

Ballast grinned as Fantine forced her thoughts into order. The man might be crude and slow, but he had not become a dockside force by being completely stupid. She had to remain sharp if she wanted to keep herself and Chadwick alive.

"Oh," she stammered. "Naw," she answered, her cockiness returning with each word. "'Is queer nibs jes wanted a night peeping at London's soirded underbelly. So naturally Oi thought o' you."

Ballast straightened slightly, clearly not catching the insult. "Oi've th' best drink on the docks."

Fantine had a lively retort ready until she caught the flash of annoyance in the boy's eye. He had understood the insult and was not pleased. She had best watch her tongue.

"'Is nibs is just an…an incidental," she said. "Oi've come about a matter fer another lord."

"Moving up, ain't ye, Rat?" That was from the boy, his tone as haughty as any peer's. "Two lords in one day? Comin' t' you? Oi don't believe it."

She turned to look at him, noting that he would grow to be as tall as his father, but at present was more gangly than broad. What was his name? Jack, but everyone called him Sprat. His father doted on him, and he was smart as a whip.

"Oi ain't nowhere's t' go but up," she said, her voice cheeky. "'Sides, it were a friend of 'is queerness. Wants t' buy information."

"On what?" asked the boy, stepping forward, his eyes narrowed. He was much too suspicious, and therefore the most dangerous person in the room.

"'Ey, who's running this meetin' anyway?" she asked, turning back to Ballast. "Ye give 'im all yer brains? Or do ye still 'ave some left t' negotiate wi' me?" She narrowed her eyes, leaning forward in as much of a challenge as she dared. "Or should I take me business t' Hurdy?" She named Ballast's primary rival.

True to form, Ballast took the bait. Cuffing his son back, he matched her glare for glare. "You deal wi' me, Rat. Tho' I ain't so sure I should trust ye after th' last time I saw ye, so keep yer tongue honest."

"Aw." Fantine laughed to disguise a tremor of fear. "'At were jes a big misunderstandin'." Actually, it was more than a big misunderstanding. She had downright stolen from Ballast, taken one of his new whores—a girl named Jenny—away from him. That was, in fact, one of the reasons "Rat" had disappeared from this area of town.

Jenny had sharp ears, hearing things that Penworthy found most valuable. In return for the information, Fantine had gotten the girl away from Ballast. She was now working happily as a maid/spy on one of Penworthy's political enemies.

"Wot's past is past," Fantine said, as she folded her arms across her chest. "'Sides, if ye kill me now, ye'll lose a fat lot o' gold. Now, do ye want t' do business, or shall I go out an diddle a little wi' Gilly?"

"You ain't got the balls to diddle a rat, Rat."

True enough, she thought with a grin. Then she leaned back and grasped her crotch in a typically male gesture of arrogance. "I got enough balls to offer ten guineas for the name o' the man who wants t' kill some cove named Wilberforce."

"Ten guineas." Ballast laughed. "Not after costin' me Jenny. You owe me a brand-new whore, Rat. Not ten lousy guineas."

Fantine winced. She had never truly expected Ballast to forget Jenny's disappearance. She simply hoped he would not be smart enough to connect her with the girl's escape. "Aw, ye cain't be blamin' that on me, Ballast!" she cried, full of righteous indignation. "I cain't 'elp it if ye lost yer whore!"

Ballast grasped the desk, his knuckles white with anger. "I saw ye meself, Rat. You an' me spankin' new whore!"

"It weren't Jenny. Ye saw Nameless dressin' up." Ballast nearly purpled in rage, so Fantine rushed on, speaking in a mollifying tone. "Tell ye what. I ain't had nothin't do with Jenny disappearin'," she lied, "but in t' name o' good relations, I'll double me offer. Twenty guineas fer that name. 'At's a fair deal, ain't it? An' now I ain't makin' so much as a copper from this 'ere transaction, so make yer mind up quick. It ain't worth me time no more."

Ballast paused. She had clearly gotten his attention, but he was not a man who thought with great ease. He grabbed his tankard of ale and drained it, then leaned back, crossing his arms over his massive chest as he stared at her.

Fantine held his gaze, working hard to maintain the false bravado that was so key to survival in the rookeries. Then Sprat made a gesture to one of the men behind her, and Fantine tensed as the brute quickly left the room. She wondered what was going on, but didn't dare lose eye contact with Ballast. It was her only show of strength.

"Come on, Ballast," Fantine said, all her instincts urging her to cut and run. "Wot be yer answer?"

Ballast merely smiled, and Fantine felt a chill settle into her belly. A moment later, her premonition was confirmed as she heard a sound that spelled disaster.

"I sssay, old boy." *Hic*. "What is the meaning of this?"

It was Chadwick, still playing the role of daft peer, only he now seemed slightly castaway. Looking back over her shoulder, she saw that his normally clear blue eyes were owlish and bleary, and she prayed this was pretense and not for real.

He would not have intended to get drunk, of course. She gave him that much credit. But Ballast's fare contained more punch than the finer stuff. He might have misjudged his abilities.

In which case, they were both in serious trouble.

"'Ey now!" she cried, jumping up to her feet. "There's no need to roust 'im. 'E's me cull, and I means t' keep 'im!"

She turned to Ballast, but it was his son who stepped forward, his eyes gleaming with excitement. "But you said you already cleaned 'im out. 'E's only got enough fer Gilly and a couple o' pints."

Fantine bit the inside of her lip, caught in her own lie. If what she had claimed was truly the case, then Rat would barely care what happened to her daft gent. Unless...

She straightened."'Ey now, 'e's got friends wot would come next time if'n I show 'im a good time. Don't be 'urting me future business."

Sprat's eyes narrowed with greed."'Ow many friends? 'Ow much future business?"

"Boy," cut in Chadwick, as he jerked awkwardly out of his captor's restraint. "Rat, what is going on here? I told you, you shall not receive a copper unless I return safe an' sound to Grosvenor Square."

Fantine breathed an internal sigh of relief. At least Chadwick retained enough wits to support her.

"Do not worry," said Ballast's son smoothly, adopting a cultured tone and friendly manner. "Rat 'as turned your care over to us. Me name is Sprat. I shall see you safely 'ome and collect wotever is due."

"'Ey now!" Fantine exclaimed, but she was quickly silenced by a knife at her back. The best she could do was turn slightly, enough to catch Chadwick's gaze and his slight nod as he flicked his gaze to the only door.

Fantine felt her breath catch in her chest. Chadwick wasn't drunk. He was, in fact, quite aware of the situation. So aware that he clearly expected her to follow her own advice: Cut and run. Just what she'd told him to do before this all began.

She glanced back at Ballast and his son, quickly considering her options. They would not kill Chadwick. It was too dangerous to finish off a peer. But they might hurt him. They would certainly steal everything he had on him, not to mention cleaning out his Grosvenor house. Good Lord, why did he have to mention such an exalted location?

"'Ey, Rat, ain't that so?" Sprat asked, cutting into her thoughts. "'Aven't you turned over his care to us?"

Fantine bit her lip. The situation was rapidly slipping out of her control. Rat would certainly cut his losses and escape, but could she? Much as she disliked Chadwick, she could not leave him to Ballast's tender mercies. He was her partner, after all.

She just did not see any good alternatives.

Taking a deep breath, she made her decision.

And heaven forgive her for her sins.

CHAPTER 3

Chadwick blinked, working to maintain the image of drunkenness while keeping his mind sharp. He knew he should never have let Fantine talk him into this ridiculous charade. Things were rapidly slipping out of control. He knew the brute behind her held a dagger to her back, just as the one behind him used his knife to tease Marcus's left shoulder blade.

They were both well and truly caught.

He could only pray that Fantine did the intelligent thing and escaped while she could. These bullies would not kill him. He was a peer. He might be somewhat bruised in the morning, probably robbed of everything he owned, but both he and Fantine would still be alive.

So why was she waiting? She had made it clear from the very beginning that she would cut and run at the first sign of trouble.

"Ye don't need 'im," she said as she straightened her back, presumably trying to distance herself from the knife pressed into her spine. "Ye got me, an' I be much more valuable."

The boy, Sprat, turned around, his face breaking into a mocking laugh. "You! What do we need you for? You are just a filthy little rat."

"Aye. A filthy rat oo can get ye twenty guineas."

"Keep yer stinking guineas," Ballast countered. "This cull gots 'undreds."

Marcus straightened, blinking a bit as if to brush away the drink. It was time he entered the negotiations, if only to tempt them to leave Fantine alone in favor of better game. "Yes, I can," he said softly and clearly. "Three hundred, but only if you let me and the boy go."

"Three 'undred!" gasped Ballast. "'Ear that. Sprat?" he cried, slapping the boy on the back. "The gent's got three 'undred at 'is 'ome jes waitin' for us."

Marcus frowned. That was not at all what he had meant to convey. Fortunately, the boy understood.

"He ain't got no three hundred at his 'ouse," he said. Then he spat at Marcus's feet, his cultured accent slipping with his rancor. "'E thinks we'll take 'is word that 'e'll send it t' us. 'E thinks we be that stupid."

"'E ain't got a hundred shillings," cried Fantine, refusing to be ignored. "Ye think a daft nob like 'im can manage 'is money? 'E gots markers spread all over town."

"Mebbe." That was Ballast as he leisurely toyed with another dagger. Where it had come from, Marcus could not guess, but it was long and sharp and gleamed dully in the light. "Bring Rat 'ere."

"Wait—" Marcus said, searching for something to say, anything that might forestall whatever Ballast intended to do. But the bully to his right stopped him from moving forward, and everyone else ignored his call.

"Aw, let go," Fantine cried impatiently, twisting away from her captor. She got nowhere until Ballast nodded, allowing her release. Then she stepped forward, her demeanor cocky despite the situation.

"Ye think I'm stupid," growled Ballast, "but I ain't." He lifted the point of his dagger to just beneath Fantine's white chin. "I can count, Rat," he continued, his voice low, almost husky. "An' I know how old ye be."

Then before anyone could react, he sliced his knife downward. The thin fabric of Fantine's shirt tore easily, as did the restraints that bound her chest. Then before everyone's startled eyes, Fantine's breasts pushed upward, the curve of each creamy mound lusciously outlined by the edges of the cut fabric.

"Gawd almighty," Sprat breathed. "Yo're a woman!"

"That I am," Fantine said, her voice suddenly as smooth as French silk. "Perhaps I am willing to deal, seeing as how you have seen through my disguise." Then she leaned down toward the thick-jowled leader. "Send your men away," she whispered.

Ballast had not taken his eyes from Fantine's chest, and in truth, Marcus found it hard to look away as well. She seemed to know just how to tease a man, how to breathe so the fabric nearly fell away, but did not, and how to shift her shoulders so that they...Marcus swallowed...so that they jiggled just right. Mentally, he chastised himself for such thoughts. This was not the time to be ogling Fantine or to be imagining how she would fit in his hands and the sounds she would make...

"Go on," she said in a husky voice. "You can touch them if you send your men away."

Ballast blinked. Apparently, he, too, was having difficulty focusing his thoughts, even though he was the one who began this little interlude. Then his eyes shifted away from Fantine for barely a second. "Sprat. Go 'ome t' yer mother."

The boy stiffened in outrage. "But—"

"Out! Now!"

The boy spun around, glaring at everyone in the room before stomping out. Then, as an apparent reward for sending the boy away, Fantine twisted, lifting one breeched leg up onto the desk. Smiling coyly at Ballast, she gently, easily removed the dagger from his hand. The villain surrendered it quietly, no doubt figuring that there was little one woman could do against him, even with a wicked-looking knife.

Then Fantine placed the knife at the base of her breeches before slowly, seductively, slicing the seam apart. Stitch by tiny stitch, the cloth fell away, exposing a single well-formed limb that seemed to go on forever.

Up and up the dagger went while four men tried not to pant. The room was so silent, Marcus could hear the soft tick as each stitch gave way. Fantine had started at her shin, but now she was exposing the curve of her knee, until finally her creamy thigh came into view.

Good God, she was gorgeous.

"What I got is just for you," she whispered, her accent still as cultured as a talented courtesan. She leaned down and her breasts pushed at the tattered edges of her shirt. "Send your men away."

Still Ballast hesitated, and in that moment Fantine struck, surprising everyone. Using the leg she had extended across the desk, she pulled it hard to her left, connecting painfully with Ballast's face, knocking him soundly in the temple. He reared back, his head cracking against the back wall, but he did not lose consciousness. Neither did she slacken her assault. Surging forward off the desk, she closed in on Ballast.

It took less than a moment for Ballast's men to react to Fantine's sudden attack, but that was all Marcus needed. The one just behind him was most vulnerable. Spinning around, Marcus landed a heavy blow to the man's chin. Pain sliced up Marcus's arm through his shoulder, but he still smirked as the unconscious lout slid down the wall.

Marcus had less than a second to stop the other cutthroat who was already aiming to throw his knife through Fantine's neck. Marcus didn't have time to grab him, so he took his only other option.

Reaching down, he grabbed the nearest item, a spittoon, and flung it across the room. By some miracle, the object was empty and therefore much easier to aim. A split second later, the heavy metal connected with the head of the second brute.

The man stumbled, coughed, and groaned, giving Marcus enough time to close in and finish the job. As for Fantine, she pinned Ballast against the wall, pushing the point of his own dagger against his neck. As Marcus straightened from the second unconscious thug, he saw a single drop of blood ease slowly down the sharp edge of the blade in Fantine's hand.

"Ye're dead, the both o' ye," said Ballast, his voice hoarse as Fantine pressed her forearm into his windpipe.

"Seems t' me," she said, her accent slipping as she discarded her seductive attitude, "I've 'eard that from you before."

Ballast's face turned nearly purple with outrage, but he never produced a sound. Not when a high-pitched voice near the door said all he needed to.

"But this time ye really are dead."

Marcus spun around, seeing the boy Sprat framed in the doorway. Reacting without thought, he snatched the child's arm, dragging him into the room before slamming the door shut. It was easily done, but it was also obvious— especially as the door thudded loudly into place.

Every man and woman on the other side of that door now knew something was amiss.

From across the room, Marcus could hear Fantine groan, and he could only echo the sentiment. They had been caught before. Now they were trapped, and unless they found something to bargain with fast, they would soon be dead. His name would not protect him now, especially if his body was never found, never traced back here.

He looked up, catching Fantine's eye and seeing fear and desperation there. Then suddenly she frowned, her gaze flicking speculatively between Marcus and the boy struggling in his arms.

She was planning something, but what he couldn't guess. Meanwhile, Fantine turned back to Ballast, continuing to press their rapidly shrinking advantage.

"I want that name, Ballast. Now."

"Wot name?" he croaked out.

"The name of the cove who wants Wilberforce dead."

Ballast screwed up his face as if to spit at her, but she pressed the knife point deeper into his throat. Finally he spoke, his words forced out between clenched teeth. "Ye ain't gettin' nuttin'."

"I got somethin'," she said on a low whisper. "An' I'm still willing t' deal if ye talk." She took a deep breath, shooting a silent plea to Marcus before turning back to Ballast. "I got a lord in me pocket," she said. "An' you got a boy abo' the right age fer Harrow."

Marcus had been listening closely, but it still took a moment for her words to penetrate his thoughts. Harrow? The elite school that he himself had attended so many years ago? She could not possibly be suggesting...

"What?" Marcus exploded, but no one was listening to him. Even the boy stilled, his agile mind no doubt absorbing what Fantine offered even faster than Marcus could.

"Think about it," continued Fantine. "Yer boy in Harrow, mixing with all them future earls and dukes. Think wot he could learn. Think wot he could do."

Ballast was considering it. As was the boy. As was Marcus himself, and it made him feel quite ill. The son of a dockside criminal...in Harrow!

"Do not even begin to suggest—" began Marcus in stiff accents, but then they ran out of time. Marcus was leaning against the door, using his weight to keep it shut, but it shook as a mighty fist banged against it.

"Ballast!" came a muffled voice from the other side. "Wot's up?"

"Kill us now," said Fantine in a low whisper, "and yer boy will never see the inside of Harrow, never collect gambling cits from an earl's son, never treat a future duke to 'is first diddle in yer fine establishment."

Marcus swallowed, both appalled and amazed by the things her mind could think up.

"Ballast!" called the voice with more urgency.

"Betray us," whispered Fantine, "and I will slit yer throat right 'ere." Then she let up on Ballast's windpipe just enough for him to take a deep breath.

"Let be, Corey," Ballast called. Then he lowered his voice, his face squeezed into a frown of concentration. "Let me think a minute."

Fantine did not give him a minute. She pushed against him hard with her shoulder, making him gasp for breath. "No more time, Ballast. I want that name."

Apparently coming to a decision, he lifted his head and glared at Fantine. "I ain't got no name. Just Teggie."

Marcus frowned. "Teggie? As in teeth?"

"Yeah," Ballast continued, his face cracking into a soundless laugh. "Seems some swell wi' three gold teg paid Hurdy t' pop Wilberforce."

Marcus needed a moment to unravel the man's cant, but he eventually figured it out. Some nobleman with three gold teeth paid Hurdy, Ballast's chief rival, to kill Wilberforce.

"Hurdy cain't decide," continued the man. "Do he pop th' swell for 'is teg?"

Does he kill the gentlemen for his gold teeth?

"Or do he take th' game?"

"He decided to take the job," said Fantine dully.

More's the pity, thought Marcus. If he had chosen to kill the culprit, then Marcus would right now be sitting by a warm fire with a brandy rather than having to choose between his own demise and sponsoring a thief into Harrow.

Sweet heaven, he still didn't know what he would decide. Did it have to be Harrow?

"More details, Ballast," Fantine said, cutting into Marcus's thoughts. "Was the swell tall? Fat? Ugly? Anything?"

"All I knows is that 'e gots three gold teggie."

"Are you sure it was three?" asked Marcus. "Not two or four?"

Ballast grimaced as if Marcus were an idiot, but he answered anyway. "It were three. Less, an' it ain't worth the pain o' killing a nob. Four, an' there ain't no question. Three, an' ye think an' think an' think."

"Wot about the gentlemen's clothes, hair, eyes?" demanded Fantine.

"I don't know nothing more!"

Marcus frowned, trying to gauge Ballast's expression. The man wasn't lying. He knew nothing more. Apparently, Fantine came to the same conclusion as she switched the topic.

"All right. 'Ave we got a deal? The daft and I leave safe, and Sprat gets an education?"

Ballast shook his head, the movement slight since Fantine still held the dagger at his throat. "The daft goes. You stay." His hands slid around her bottom for good measure. "Ye still owes me fer Jenny."

Fantine hesitated, and Marcus clenched his teeth in frustration. Nothing about this evening had gone as it should. First the grubbing through every Cheapside gutter and sewer hole, then having to choose between his life and sponsoring the boy into Harrow, and now this! Having Fantine sacrifice herself to this brute for him? The entire affair was humiliating, and he absolutely refused to allow it to continue even a moment longer!

He stepped forward, resolution knotting his shoulders and fists. His movements were awkward considering he had to keep one hand on the boy, but he managed nevertheless. With a single well-aimed blow, he smashed Ballast into unconsciousness.

Fantine jumped back from the villain's body, gasping with dismay as the portly man slumped to the floor.

"Nice hit," she said, and he was surprised to hear a note of admiration in her voice. "Next time, ye think ye could warn me?"

"He ain't dead, is he?" asked the boy in a small voice.

"Naw," said Fantine. "But I do not wish t' be 'ere when 'e wakes."

Both Fantine and Marcus turned toward the only door, but the boy, now reassured that his father still lived, found his courage again. Stepping before the door to block their way, he merely smiled at them. "Me father's men will stick ye as soon as ye step through that door."

Marcus sighed, his anger still simmering. "I will not be murdered in this hellhole," he said flatly. "It would kill my mother."

Fantine glanced at him, her expression unreadable, but her attention returned to the boy. "They cain't kill us if ye stop them. Tell them yer father is drunk. They'll believe that right enough."

The boy smirked back, his expression mimicking his father's earlier one. "An' why would I do that?"

"Because if you get us out safely, I swear t' see ye into Harrow."

Marcus stiffened. Good Lord, she could not be bringing that up again? Not when he thought he had just managed a narrow escape with Ballast. "Absolutely not!" he began, only to be cut off by the boy.

"'E won't do it," said Sprat, jerking his head toward Marcus.

"'E'll do it," returned Fantine. "Trust me." Then she crouched down far enough to look at the boy eye to eye. "It be your only chance, Sprat. Do you want to live like your father? Getting piss-eyed drunk every night and grabbing at anything what moves 'cause your life is too damned empty for anything else?"

Sprat paled at her bald assessment of Ballast, and Marcus feared she'd overplayed her hand. But the boy had intelligence. His gaze slipped to his father's slumped form, taking in the spittle that dribbled on the man's chin.

"Once in Harrow," Fantine continued, "you can create your own life. Become friends with the elite, learn what you need to know. Maybe one of them has a sister—"

"Do not even think it!" exploded Marcus. Then Sprat's gaze slipped to Marcus. He suddenly felt uncomfortable under the boy's scrutiny. Why, the lad was judging him, weighing his character! Yet, there was nothing he could do except hope he passed the test, because he had the feeling their very lives depended on it.

He failed.

Sprat spat at his feet. "'E won't do it."

"He will," returned Fantine. "If you cannot trust him, then trust me. I have never lied to you."

"Ye ain't never had to afore."

Marcus swallowed. Both Sprat and Fantine were staring at each other, measuring each other's worth in infinitesimal detail. Marcus himself had already been dismissed as unimportant, a mere detail in this game. He would have been insulted had it not been abundantly clear that he had no clue how to function in this dockside world. He could watch, readying himself for anything, but Fantine and this small boy were the true players.

Marcus almost smiled at the thought. Finally! A new game to learn!

And at that moment, Sprat made his decision.

"Best cover up," he said as he jerked his head at Fantine's clothing. "Less'n ye want everybody to know ye're a girl."

Fantine gasped as she glanced down at her clothing. Though her breasts were not exposed, they were handsomely apparent. She would not be able to repair that, Marcus realized. The damage was too extensive. So, rather than give in to temptation and watch her wiggling movements as she struggled with the torn fabric, he yanked the shirt off one of the unconscious thugs.

"Wear this. It will cover up most everything. With luck, people will only see what they want to see."

"They want to see a half-naked girl," muttered Fantine. But she did as he suggested. Within moments, she had tucked the overly large shirt into what was left of her breeches. There was nothing to do about the cut seam on her leg, but at least she looked vaguely like a boy.

"Let's get to it," said the boy. But before they could do more than take a deep breath, the boy pinned his steely gaze on Fantine. "Cross me an' I'll kill you."

Fantine nodded, her manner equally serious. "I know."

Apparently satisfied, Sprat raised his voice enough to carry though the door to any listeners. "Come on, ye buggers," he bellowed as he pushed open the door.

Marcus was just crossing the threshold into the main pub when Ballast began to revive. It started as a muffled groan, growing louder as consciousness returned. Fantine and the boy heard it too because they sped up their pace, pushing through the crowd almost before Marcus could shut the door behind them.

"Out o' me way," cried the boy as he weaved quickly through the crowd. "Ballast's got a special treat fer 'is lordship, and th' swell is anxious t' see it."

Picking up his cue, Marcus shifted quickly into the pose of a drunk peer too stupid to realize his own danger.

"Hurry up, boy," he said, slurring his words slightly. "I want to shee this woman with four breasts." He grinned as he made a drunken grab for the barmaid while stumbling past a thick-shouldered obstacle. "One for each hand, an' my lips, then another for spare."

The boy rolled his eyes for the crowd's benefit, tugging Marcus away from Gilly. "Come along, guv."

Marcus nodded and lurched forward, making sure his motions speeded up their progress. From behind, he heard Ballast's roar as the man fully regained consciousness. Fortunately, they made it out into the street before the noise died.

"Go that way," said Sprat, pointing. "An' around th' back."

Fantine nodded, grabbing the boy's arm before he could escape. "Will 'e hurt ye fer this?"

"Naw," he said with a grin. "I'll jes tell 'im ye knocked me out while I was taking ye to the stable."

"The stable?" asked Marcus.

"Ballast's place t' initiate girls into whoring," Fantine answered grimly.

Marcus gritted his teeth, wondering how she could speak of such things as if they were of no consequence. But there was no time to think as the sounds from within the pub grew louder. "We must be going," he said urgently.

Fantine nodded. "Do it," she said, turning toward Marcus.

He blinked. "Do what?"

"Hit the boy. But do not hurt 'im."

"What? Now?" It was not that he misunderstood her meaning or even the purpose of the act. It was simply that his mind could not grasp that he must actually hit a boy with the intent of knocking him unconscious. "But—"

"Hurry," urged Fantine as she began stacking debris in front of the pub door.

"Very well," he said, forcing himself to knot his fist despite his reluctance. Then he pulled back and swung.

His blow landed neatly on the boy's cheek, knocking the child's head to one side. Then the boy turned his head back to him with a grimace.

"'At's it?" he asked as he slapped disdainfully at his cheek. "Me own grandma cain do better than that. There ain't gonna be no bruise!"

Marcus gaped at the boy. Did he actually mean he was to hit him harder?

"Aw, never mind, guv," Sprat said, disgust plain on his small face. Then he grabbed a nearby piece of wood and raised it aloft. "Remember," he said urgently. "Yer deal is wi' me."

"I remember," answered Fantine softly.

Then the boy hit himself with his makeshift club. He had not enough strength to do more than bruise himself, but Marcus winced nevertheless. Then tossing the club away, Sprat looked at Fantine. "Good eno'?"

"Aye. Good enough."

With an impish grin, he sprang backward as if thrown, smashing bodily against the wall only to sprawl on his side in the dirty gutter.

Marcus stared at him in shock, amazed at the sight. "Do you think he is really injured?"

"No," she said with a smile. "He is good. Almost as good as I was at his age." Then, before she could say more, the pub door burst open and three very large men armed with long knives appeared, easily pushing through Fantine's stack of debris.

"They's right 'ere!" one of them bellowed.

Marcus and Fantine ran.

Jump, scramble, duck, run. No thoughts. No noise. Run.

Fantine scampered like the rat she took her nickname from. She scurried, she struggled, but most of all, she ran, searching through the black night for an escape.

Chadwick was right behind her, huffing and wheezing like an old dog. In truth, he had done remarkably well, especially given that Nameless had already run him for almost an hour before the evening began. But now they were racing for their lives. She had no doubts that if Ballast caught them...

Don't think, she admonished herself. *Run.*

She did. But with every turn, every street, she heard the heavy footfalls of her pursuers. Ballast's men were falling behind, but not nearly quickly enough. And she feared that Chadwick would soon give out.

Run. Quietly. Run.

Then Chadwick stopped.

She didn't notice at first, but then the steady huff of his breath disappeared. Spinning around, she saw him leaning against a brick wall, gasping for air.

"Not much farther," she lied. "We cannot rest. They are just two streets back."

He shook his head, pushing each word through his gasps. "I am...too slow. You go. They will not...hurt...a peer."

"Don't be a fool," she whispered urgently. "Your title is no protection. Bloody hell, you punched Ballast in the face! You may have disfigured him permanently. If he catches you, he will hurt you, then kill you, then toss your body where no one will ever find you."

He looked up at her, his expression bleak in the cold moonlight. He knew the truth, she suddenly realized. He knew his title was no protection.

"And what will he do to you?" he asked hoarsely. He pushed her down the street with surprising strength. "Go. I cannot run like you. Not through these streets." She watched him straighten his shoulders, his hands clenching into large, punishing fists. "I will hold them off as long as I can. Go to Penworthy. He will help you escape."

She stared at him, shock robbing her of words. Was he truly offering to sacrifice himself for her—*an actress*, as he had so contemptuously put it? Apparently, he was, and for the first time ever, her heart softened toward a peer.

"Blimey, you are a fool."

He lifted his head, a bitter smile on his lips. "Aye," was all he said.

Fantine looked down the alleyway. She knew she could escape their pursuers. There were any number of any holes and darkened corners that would hide her. But she had not abandoned him to Ballast before, and she could not do so now. No one, not even a rich, arrogant peer, deserved that fate.

"There must be some other choice," she said, more to herself than him. Then her thoughts were interrupted by a sudden burst of laughter from a pub across the street. The door had opened and an aged whore stumbled outside supporting a man obviously too drunk to know better than to wander outside with a desperate woman. Fantine turned away, knowing the whore would strip her cull of his valuables long before he relieved the itch that brought him outside.

Fantine dismissed the pair without a second thought. It was only one of the thousands of sins that occurred nightly in the rookeries. But Chadwick seemed inordinately interested in the sight.

"Come along, guv," she said, her irritation plain. "She be busy an' we ain't got time fer a diddle now."

He looked up, his eyes glittering slightly in the moonlight. "On the contrary," he said softly. "I think now is the perfect time."

Before she could react, he caught her about the waist and pressed her against the wall. The brick was cold against her back, and with half her breeches torn apart at the seam, the chill seeped directly into her bones. Then he pressed himself against her, his every hard angle heating her front with a devilish fire.

"What are you doing?" she gasped, alarm coursing through her.

His hands trapped her securely against the wall. To her left was a pile of refuse—a broken barrel, a shattered chair. To her right lay the open street. There was room and air about her, and yet she still felt surrounded by Chadwick, his body strong and heavy as he tried to shield her from view.

"You paid no attention to that other pair," he said, his breath a warm caress against her cheek. "You dismissed them without a second thought."

She tried to take a breath to calm herself, but that only pushed her breasts farther against the muscled wall of his chest. She closed her eyes, trying to block the memory of other hands, other chests pressed against herself, against her mother. Against all the actresses in the company.

She had always escaped before. As a child. But as Chadwick's hands wormed their way beneath her cap, discarding the item with a single flick of his wrist, she felt a strange languid heat weaken her body. It frightened her, and yet, she had no strength to fight as his nimble fingers burrowed deeper, pushing away the pins so her hair flowed freely.

"That is much better," he whispered. "Now no one can see your face."

She closed her eyes, mentally correcting his statement. No one could see her burning face except him, no one could see the flush that stained her skin except the man who was even now making her chest tighten with a tingling awareness that set her head spinning.

"This is wrong," she said, her voice too soft and breathy. She had meant to sound forceful, but she could not, not when she felt his breath hot on her skin as he trailed his lips over her shoulder, nuzzling along her neck until he found the sensitive curve of her ear.

"We are hiding in plain sight," he whispered as he settled harder against her pelvis, his desire a hot brand that made her squeak with alarm. "Shhhhh," he whispered, soothing her with more kisses, more heady touches along her arms and her neck. His hands slid beneath her shirt. "I am merely another customer doing his business against the wall."

"No," she gasped, wondering why she wasn't fighting. Why didn't she struggle as she had in her mother's greenroom? Why did the strength in his body seem a wonderful shield against the cold?

"Yes," he answered, as his fingers brushed apart the torn bindings over her breasts. She cried out, a low whimper of alarm, while her legs gave way, dropping her weight onto the corded muscles in his thighs.

Then, too swiftly for her reeling senses, he pulled back, dropping his hands to the bottom of her breeches, grasping the one untorn leg in both hands and ripping it open. Both sides now fluttered down to lie flat against her legs like parts of a shortened skirt.

"I run," she gasped, speaking to herself more than him. "Men never catch me." But he had caught her. He was even now settling himself even more securely against her. His hands dropped to her hips, curving beneath her bottom and pulling her up hard against his arousal.

"Wrap your legs around me," he said, his low voice reverberating through her body. "They are almost here. We must make this look real," he said as his mouth found hers.

The kiss was hard and heavy, draining the last of her thoughts away. He invaded her mouth with practiced ease, caressing her lips and then dueling with her tongue. She could taste him, strong and potent, and she felt as if she were being swept away in a storm—a heaving, surging flood of bodies and moans and guttural cries.

"No!" she whispered, feeling herself drown beneath the onslaught, even as her body arched into him. But it was too late. Through the haze that fogged her thoughts, she could hear their pursuers heavy bootfalls coming steadily closer.

She felt Chadwick's body clench, tensing as he began the motions of the act. Though clothing still separated them, she felt his hardness press deeply against her, felt herself open and moisten as the bawds said would happen.

No! Her mind screamed silently. It was too much. He was too much and she was afraid. So afraid, despite his whispers.

"A moment longer," he soothed against her cheek. "They're almost here."

She acted without thought, her movements coming from panic and fear. Grasping the broken leg of a chair, she lifted it up high and brought it down hard on Chadwick's temple.

He crumpled like a stone.

When Ballast's men searched their street, they saw only a filthy whore, calmly picking the pockets of her sotted cull. They could not see much of him as his face was turned into the wall. One of the men chuckled as he passed them by, thinking that drunken fools always got what they deserved.

CHAPTER 4

"She hit me!" Marcus spun on his heel, glared at Penworthy, then continued pacing off his fury within the confines of his friend's library. "I can barely credit that it happened!" he muttered. He, a peer of the realm, had been sprawled near naked in the sewer. "She clubbed me with a block of wood, robbed me of everything but my breeches, then left me there to rot!"

Penworthy did not respond. Much to Marcus's frustration, all his friend did was lean back against the winged chair and extend his stockinged feet toward the fire. And rather than outrage, Marcus read amusement in the man's gaze.

Marcus spun away, letting his gaze fall into the fire. "She is a menace. She should be locked up."

"Tell me," responded Penworthy. "How do you feel today?"

Marcus lifted his head and turned back to his friend. "Feel? Bruised, battered, and…"

"Alive?"

He stiffened, uncertainty making his voice sharp. "Alive? Of course, I am alive, though no thanks to her. Do you know she stole my pocket watch? My sister gave that to me for Christmas last year!"

"I see you have another already."

Marcus frowned, looking down self-consciously at the chain that held his current watch. "Well, yes. Mavenford sent me this for my birthday. Quite a handsome piece, actually."

"Hmmm," repeated Penworthy, though this time there was a wealth of meaning underlying the sound. It suggested all sorts of things, not the least of which that Marcus had half a dozen pocket watches that he could lose to Fantine without even noticing. And that, perhaps, it was his own fault for bringing a watch to the rookery in the first place.

"That is not the point!" Marcus exploded, coming around near the fire to confront his friend directly. "She knocked me flat and left me there to die. Good Lord, if you had seen Norton's face when he opened my front door. He nearly had a fit laughing. My own butler, whooping it up like the veriest hyena!"

Surprise widened Penworthy's eyes. "Norton laughed at you? Right there?"

Marcus lifted his drink, trying to hide the blush that heated his cheeks. "Well, not just then. It was afterward in the servants' quarters. I could hear the merriment two floors up!"

"Ah," said his friend as he turned back to the fire. "Decidedly uncomfortable, I do not doubt."

"Uncomfortable! I was visited this very morning by my mother and sister. The story has already spread throughout London that I was accosted and beaten by no less than five assailants. Five!"

"Yet it was my Fantine, a little slip of a girl, knocking you flat with a chair leg." Penworthy had the audacity to actually smile.

"Damn it, man!" Marcus exclaimed, dropping his fists onto his hips. "You are not listening to me!"

"Merely because you have said nothing to the point," responded the MP happily. "All I know is that you are furious, slightly bruised about the temple, have lost a pocket watch, and seem happier than I have seen you since your brother's death."

"Happier! I am furious!" Marcus glared down at his friend, who merely smiled and sipped his drink. Then a totally unexpected emotion came over him.

Humor. He began to laugh.

"Sink me," he said, finally collapsing into a chair beside his friend. "I have not been this exercised in years."

"It is a nice sight to see, you know. You are much too young to wrap yourself up in mothballs."

Marcus frowned. "Is that what I have been doing?" He did not need Penworthy's nod to realize the answer. Indeed, since the moment he had first received news of his brother's death in Spain, Marcus had felt wrapped in a shroud, his world and thoughts dulled by that protective shield. Now a single annoying woman had ripped the covering away, throwing him into heights of exhilaration, fury, and even lust.

"Very well," Marcus said finally. "I shall not beat your thoroughly aggravating Miss Fanny."

"Fantine does have a somewhat unique effect on a person. Would you care to know how I first met her?"

"More than my good breeding allows," Marcus responded dryly.

Penworthy's eyes grew distracted as he gazed into the fire, his glass forgotten in his hand. His posture was lax, and the lines of strain eased from his face as he spoke.

"She came here in the dead of winter. I had just come home from a session at Parliament and 'ill-tempered' is the kindest term that could apply to my mood."

Marcus leaned forward, his thoughts already leaping ahead in Penworthy's story. "You cannot mean to say she came here to this house? How was she dressed? I cannot think that your staff would allow her entrance."

Penworthy grinned. "She did not come in by the door." He glanced up, and his eyes were actually twinkling. "She climbed in my bedroom window and waited for me there."

Marcus felt his mouth grow slack. "In your bedchamber!"

"I did not notice her at first. You know how she can hide in shadows." He lifted his brandy and took a sip. "I did, however, notice an odor, but I could not locate it."

"When did she finally show herself?"

"Just as I sat down before the fire. She introduced herself with her knife applied directly to my throat."

Marcus swallowed, his own throat constricting at the thought. "She did not hurt you." It was as much a question as a statement.

"No. She said she wished to speak with me privately, and this was the only way to get my full attention and cooperation." Penworthy grinned as he set his brandy aside. "I assure you, she received that in full measure."

"I do not doubt it for a second."

"Understand, I could not see her. I merely felt her knife and had a vague impression of her height...and odor. I thought she was a street boy come to steal what he could." He took a deep breath. "So you see, you are not the only one to experience Fantine's somewhat violent side." Penworthy lapsed into silence, apparently content to end the conversation there.

Marcus nodded, knowing that good breeding demanded that he not press his friend for more details. But he could not let it rest. "Did she steal anything? How much did you offer her to spare your life?"

Penworthy started, as if woken from a reverie. "Hmmm? Oh! I offered her fifty pounds, my pocket watch, and a silver tray I had in the room."

"I wonder that she did not demand you summon tea so that she could take the service," Marcus commented dryly.

"Well." Penworthy chuckled. "Money has never been Fantine's primary motivation." Then he lapsed once again into his memories while Marcus tried not to give in to his frustration.

"Penworthy!" he cried. "What happened? What did she want?" Then he stopped. Bedroom. Night. Could Fantine have been looking for a rich protector? The very thought made his gut tighten painfully. It could not be possible. She had been too young to become Penworthy's mistress.

"You should see your face, old boy. I swear I have never seen you so anxious for information. Especially as it is about a woman you have vowed to hate until your dying day."

Marcus frowned, then shifted grumpily in his seat. "All right, I confess. I am acting particularly vulgar today. Now tell me what she wanted of you!"

"Why, certainly my dear boy," chortled Penworthy, apparently enjoying Marcus's discomfort. "It was quite odd really, or so I thought at the time. She wanted to know about me. Who were my parents, what did I do during my days, who graced my bed chambers—"

"No." It was more of a groan than a statement.

"Oh, yes," countered Penworthy. "She was barely twelve, but quite aware of the lascivious details of a gentleman's life. It took quite some time before she accepted that I did not spend my nights in debauchery. To this day, I thank God in heaven that I had no mistress."

Marcus stood and paced to the fire, using the time and motion to think. "But why would she be interested in all that?" he pressed. "In you in particular?"

"Because she is my daughter."

Not by a single flinch or flicker of an eye did Marcus betray the shock that reverberated through his system. He stood absolutely still, and when his muscles began to protest, he slowly, gingerly lifted his drink to his lips, but did not sip.

"Oh, good show, old boy," cheered Penworthy. "You would think we were discussing the weather."

Marcus drained his glass.

Penworthy merely laughed with good humor, then let his gaze wander back toward the fire as if patiently waiting for Marcus to take the lead.

Unfortunately, Marcus felt completely inadequate to the task. Fantine was Penworthy's daughter? A thousand questions crowded into Marcus's mind. Why was she living in the rookery? How could a man as decent and caring as Penworthy allow his own flesh and blood, and a woman no less, to exist in such a state? And to actually give her assignments that might endanger her life...It boggled his mind.

"Sit down, my boy," Penworthy urged. "That is fine French brandy, and I have no wish for you to waste it if you faint."

"I do not faint!" he cried, insulted to the core.

"Of course not," the older gentlemen reassured him as Marcus found his seat. "Fantine and I managed to come to an unusual bargain. We began trading information. She wanted to know about me, and I about her. So we traded questions and answers. Though it took a month's worth of visits—and at least half my food stock—I finally pieced the sordid truth together."

For the first time in the entire bizarre conversation, Penworthy sighed, betraying a regret that seemed to come from deep within.

"I had been very young, and Fantine's mother was a beautiful actress. Gabrielle Delarive. A petite woman with the most amazing agility. She was under my protection a very short time." Penworthy glanced up. "She was too expensive, you understand."

Marcus nodded. Penworthy's taste had always been exquisite. Any woman who caught his fancy would no doubt cost well beyond the means of a young man-about-town.

"I never even knew she was pregnant. Or at least, not until much later. I suppose I consoled myself with the thought that it could have been any number of gentlemen who had done the deed."

"Are you sure it was not?"

Penworthy shrugged. "Fantine says her mother named me as her father. That is enough." Then he glanced up, a self-conscious twist to his lips. "Besides, she has my eyes, I think. And my arrogance."

Mentally, Marcus constructed Fantine's face, analyzing it feature by feature to compare with his friend. Perhaps there was a family resemblance. Her bronze eyes were certainly as brilliant and lively as Penworthy's.

"I wished to care for her immediately. I cannot tell you how much I have longed for a child. I could never tolerate the thought of a wife, but I have missed the children. She was like the answer to my prayers."

"But where was her mother?" Marcus asked.

"Dead. Of the pox. Fantine was ten when her mother's death pushed her out onto the street."

"At ten years of age?" Marcus could hardly comprehend it, and yet he knew it happened every day.

"Even then she was smart. She knew there was no future in whoring." The older gentlemen glanced up. "Her words, not mine. So she dressed as a boy and picked pockets to survive, but even that was difficult. She could not ally herself with any one leader for fear that her sex would be discovered. So she remained independent, playing one leader off against the other."

Marcus nodded. "I saw her technique last night. She would mention Hurdy just to throw Ballast off balance."

"Those two have been fighting over the dockside territory for years. Their rivalry is easy to exploit."

Marcus twisted in his seat, not wishing to be distracted into discussing the previous night's events. "Did you let Fantine live here?"

Penworthy looked up, and for a moment Marcus thought his eyes were haunted. "I could not take her in here. You understand what it would look like, what it would do to my position."

Marcus frowned, thinking back. So many years ago, Penworthy was rapidly growing in political influence, rising up toward true power. To take in a child and sponsor her as his own would have been disastrous. Everyone would have known she was his bastard. The scandal could have destroyed his career.

Penworthy sighed again, the sound coming from deep within. "I sent her to a school under a fictional name and family. I knew the headmistress there would turn a lenient eye on Fantine's less polished attributes."

"And?"

Penworthy looked dolefully down into his empty glass. "She hated it. Think on it. She had lived on her own for two years. Probably making life-and-death choices every day. To expect her to quietly settle into the life of a pampered miss was too much."

"She ran away?"

"And right back to the rookeries."

Marcus shook his head. He understood the transition would have been difficult. But if she could have managed it, she could have had a decent marriage, a safe home, children, everything a woman wanted. Instead, she chose a dangerous existence, rife with poverty and crime.

"Do not judge her too harshly," said Penworthy softly. "Even you who were born to your position chafe at the constant restrictions. You cannot expect her to leap into a life more claustrophobic than your own."

Marcus sighed, acknowledging the truth. Still…"You must offer it again."

"I did. I have. Every way I can think of. But no lock holds her. No school could keep her. Always she returned to the world she knew and nothing I did swayed her." He paused, and again Penworthy seemed to carry the world upon his shoulders. "I give her what money she will take. I pay her generously for information. I do whatever she asks. I have even offered to acknowledge her as my own, but she is very proud. Like her mother. And, she distrusts the peerage. Even me."

Marcus did not doubt it. "Anyone raised in a greenroom would see the worst the aristocracy has to offer." Vice and debauchery ran rampant in the backstage world of an actress. "Still—" he began, only to be interrupted by his mentor.

"That is why I forced you to work with her. You must help me. There is no one else I trust more than you."

Marcus looked up to see Penworthy's brilliant eyes pinned on him, begging him for assistance. "Anything," he answered without thought.

"I cannot die with her on my conscience."

Penworthy's words echoed in the still library, chilling Marcus's bones even as his thoughts whirled. He wanted to deny his friend's illness, but they both knew the truth. Penworthy might not see another Christmas. But how did one help someone who did not seem to want or need help? Especially a woman as recalcitrant, spirited, and beautiful as Fantine?

In the end, he was saved from commenting. Before he could begin to frame his thoughts, the door burst open and once again candle wax splattered across the papers on Penworthy's desk.

"I knew I would find you gentlemen in here, steeped in brandy no doubt," called Fantine in her cultured voice.

Marcus turned, mentally steeling himself to see her in some new outrageous attire. He was not disappointed.

She wore a demure gray gown, so high in the collar it nearly covered her mouth. It was almost colorless, and its very blandness made the sparkle in her bronze eyes, the dark bow of her lips, and the rosy flush to her cheeks all the more vivid. Why, even the shapeless gown seemed to take on her curves at the most tantalizing moments, making her the visual fulfillment of any schoolboy's most lurid fantasies.

But that was not the worst. No, the absolute most horrible shock was that she entered the room on the arm of one of the most powerful gentlemen in the world: William Wilberforce.

Marcus was hard pressed to restrain his groan.

"Good afternoon, William," said Penworthy as he gained his feet. "Do come in."

Marcus was quick to follow, vacating his chair for the lame Wilberforce. The man nodded congenially, his dusky white hair whisper thin as he pushed his crippled form forward. Fantine remained by his side, no doubt ready to assist if the elderly man should stumble. He did not. Neither did he sit, choosing instead to wait politely for Fantine to seek a chair. She did so with alacrity, settling prettily into the seat Penworthy had occupied moments before.

Meanwhile, Penworthy settled down behind his desk. "I trust you two have introduced yourselves?"

"Why, yes," returned Fantine pleasantly. "It seemed the most appropriate thing to do when we met upon your doorstep." Then she turned to the aged man. "Shall I order tea or would you prefer something stronger?"

Marcus flinched at Fantine's mistake. He and Penworthy had already put aside their own drinks out of respect for the man's religious convictions. "Mr. Wilberforce does not drink, Fantine," he said smoothly. "He considers it sinful."

He saw Fantine's eyes widen at such a fanatical view. "I do beg your pardon—"

"Nonsense, nonsense," cut in Wilberforce. "You could not have known. Besides," he said with a wink, "you offered it so prettily I was tempted to accept."

Any other society miss would have dimpled up at such a nicely offered compliment, and to Fantine's credit, she managed a smile, but Marcus could tell the action was at odds with her true personality. Wilberforce had already relegated her to the role of an empty-headed miss. But if the MP maintained a condescending tone, Marcus feared Fantine's reaction.

How long could she restrain her fiery temperament? And how would Wilberforce react? Unfortunately, Fantine showed no inclination to leave, and given that she had been hired to protect Wilberforce's life, perhaps she had the right of it. So Marcus leaned against the bar, his muscles tense as he waited for whatever explosion might come.

"Are you here for the Season then, Miss Delarive?" the MP asked. "I am positive the gentlemen will be tripping over themselves to catch a glimpse of your face."

Fantine's smile appeared somewhat strained, and Marcus scrambled for something to say, but he never had the chance.

"In truth, sir," she said smoothly, "I am much too old for my coming-out. I am quite content to live in London and be of service to Lord Penworthy as needed. It is perhaps an unusual life, but one I value greatly."

Wilberforce raised his eyebrows in surprise. "Certainly, one must learn to be content with one's lot, my dear, but the Lord requires that we grasp the opportunities He presents to us. Do not be overly timid."

Marcus nearly choked. Timid? Fantine? Penworthy, apparently, had a similar reaction as he pushed almost rudely into the conversation.

"Fantine is the most untimid soul I know, William. She is, in fact, half of the team I have hired to keep your soul safely with us, still trapped in its mortal coil."

Wilberforce turned his keen gaze to Penworthy and his brow furrowed in concern. "Thomas, surely that cannot be wise. She is a woman."

"A quite competent one, I assure you." That comment came from Marcus's own mouth, and he was as startled by it as Fantine appeared to be. But once spoken, he realized the absolute truth of the statement. "You may safely entrust your life to her."

"I trust in the Lord God."

Marcus smiled. "Of course. Still, one must seize whatever opportunities the Lord presents," he said, echoing the older gentleman's earlier words. "No matter how strange it may appear," he added softly, his comment more for himself than anyone else as he shifted his gaze to Fantine.

"William," cut in Penworthy, "have you had any additional thoughts on who might be threatening your life?"

Wilberforce turned back to his friend with a stifled sound of disgust. "I have given no thought to it whatsoever. Truly, Thomas, you make too much of it. Threats to my life are commonplace."

"Yes, but not attempts on it."

The older man shrugged. His attention sharpened as he focused first on Penworthy and then on Marcus. He completely ignored Fantine. "What I have given a great deal of thought to is whether I can count on your support next month."

Now it was Penworthy's turn to be impatient as he casually dismissed Wilberforce's life goal—the abolishment of slavery. "Yes, yes, you know I support the antislavery bill. What I am more concerned with—"

"And you, Lord Chadwick, do I number you among my supporters?"

Marcus paused. He had every intention of lending his name and political power to the bill. It was, he knew, the right and moral thing to do. However, he could not give up the opportunity to bargain with Wilberforce.

Marcus leaned forward, matching Wilberforce in intensity. "That all depends," he began slowly. "A bill fostered by a dead man will go nowhere."

Wilberforce merely waved off the comment. "That is not a motive, my dear boy."

"But what about the bill?" That was Fantine, her lovely face pulled into a slight frown. "I thought if you died, the antislavery movement would end with you."

Wilberforce turned to her and actually had the audacity to pat her hand. "Nonsense, my dear. It shall become cause celebre when sponsored by a martyr."

Marcus nodded, knowing that was probably true. Still, he allowed doubt to color his voice. "Perhaps. Or perhaps not. I cannot but question the wisdom of a man who will not cooperate with the people trying to save his life."

"Tish tosh," returned the gentleman. "I have told you, such nonsense is commonplace, yet I am still here."

"Help us make sure you continue in that happy state."

Wilberforce sighed. It was the sound of a man forced into what he considered inanities for the sake of a greater cause. "Very well. I shall supply you with a list of my opponents, although I warn you, the account is rather large."

"Excellent," Marcus returned. "Then I shall fully support your bill."

That, at least, caused the older man to grin with wholehearted delight. "You will speak out at the next meeting?"

Marcus nodded. "Provided you supply Miss Delarive with your list and give her your complete cooperation."

Wilberforce blinked as if just recalling Fantine's presence. "Miss Delarive?"

Marcus smiled, only now realizing how right the action felt despite the tightening in his gut. "I am afraid the preparations for my speech will occupy much of my time. No, I fear I shall have to leave your safety to the professional." He glanced over to Fantine, relishing the look of total astonishment on her face.

"You are quitting?" she gasped. "Just like that?"

Wilberforce was also quick to notice her expression. "The young lady appears uncomfortable with the weight of responsibility."

"Nonsense," Marcus returned with a grin. "She is merely stunned that I would step aside." He watched with devilish amusement as a pink blush crept up her face. She had not thought him able to see past his pride. "Miss Delarive is quite capable of handling this particular task, is that not so, Fantine?"

"Uh, too roight..." she began in her Cockney accent. Then she flushed an even deeper crimson and began again in cultured tones. "Of course, my lord." She turned to Wilberforce. "I shall not fail you."

"Her credentials are quite impressive," put in Penworthy.

Wilberforce still looked unconvinced, but Marcus knew he was a man of his word. With a cordial smile and a last lingering look at Fantine, Marcus stood. "It appears I must begin work on a speech. If you will excuse me..."

"Of course, dear boy," Wilberforce said, standing up as well. "Pray allow me to accompany you. We can discuss the points you absolutely must stress." The older man linked arms with Marcus, leading him out the door as he spoke. "It is imperative that everyone understand..."

Marcus twisted around, trying not to be rude to the aged MP, but still wishing to speak with Fantine. He was only now realizing what he had done. By stepping down from the investigation, he might not ever see her again. She would have no need to contact him.

How would he find her again? How could he help his friend care for her, see to her future if he had no apparent reason to find her?

Then it was too late. Wilberforce succeeded in pulling him out of the room as the library door closed behind them.

Fantine stared at the closed library door, her thoughts a jumble of images and feelings. She saw Marcus, agile despite the grime, scrambling after Nameless. She recalled him playing the daft peer in Ballast's bar, pretending to be a castaway while his keen gaze missed nothing. And she remembered the lean strength of his body as he pressed her against a wall while his lips moved so potently over her own.

Through all those memories, one thought echoed in her mind.

"I cannot believe he would just walk away."

"Indeed," said Penworthy with a sigh. "I had thought you would be the one to break him of his fear."

Fantine swung her gaze to her father. "Fear?" She would never have applied that word to Chadwick.

"I told you Marcus was much more than a bored aristocrat. He was invaluable to the home office. Thwarted *le petit colonel* a dozen times over the years."

Fantine felt her jaw go slack in surprise. "He fought Napoleon?"

"Not overtly. Remember, he is the eldest son of an earl. He cannot actually fight, much though he might wish it."

"Then what exactly did he do?"

"He worked secretly. First as a messenger, then later as a spy." He turned and smiled at her. "Much like you do for me. He performed odd tasks that required stealth, a quick mind, and a cunning resourcefulness."

Fantine pushed up from her chair, stunned by this history. "What happened?"

Her father reached for a brandy, his expression sad. "He made a mistake. He discovered a French plan to invade

England, but it was incomplete. So he sent his partner back with what information he knew and went on to find the rest."

"And did he?"

Penworthy nodded. "I received the entire plan in time, but not before his partner was caught and killed."

Fantine looked away, knowing the pain of loss. "Who was his companion?"

"His brother."

Fantine sucked in her breath.

"He had no idea that Geoffrey would be apprehended. And we did need the entire invasion plan. Because of his actions, hundreds were saved, England was saved. If it were not for Marcus, we might even now be on French ground."

"But his own brother…" Her voice trailed away as the blood began to pound in her head. She knew she was overreacting, and yet she could still feel the emotions churning within her. He abandoned his own brother. Her mind created scenes of poor Geoffrey's death, using details that she did not have, pictures she knew were impossible. Yet they were there, right before her eyes, she saw a frightened youth left abandoned and alone.

It was nonsense. She knew that. More than that, she knew what Marcus had done was perfectly reasonable. He and his brother were spies for the Crown. One of them had died. It happened. Except the very thought shook her.

"He abandoned his own brother."

"He did no such thing!" exclaimed her father.

She spun away, the last sane part of her wondering why she was reacting so strongly. After all, she was not the one who had been left without aid, without Marcus's strong, comforting presence. It had been his brother. Yet she still felt it as keenly as if he had just walked away from her.

"Fantine, he received a commendation from the king."

She shook her head. "I do not care if he was blessed by the angel Gabriel. Had I a sibling, I do not care if all of England was at stake, I would not put him in the middle of a war!"

Penworthy shifted uneasily in his chair. "It was not like that. He thought Geoffrey was safe."

"I do not care what he thought," she shot back. "What is a man if not someone who protects those he loves?"

Penworthy stared at her, his jaw slack with astonishment. She could tell that he did not understand her reaction. In truth, she did not comprehend it herself.

"We are at war," he said firmly. "Surely you understand that everyone must make sacrifices."

Fantine shook her head. "Not those sacrifices. Not me. If I had someone, I would protect him, or her, with my life, no matter what. But then I do not have anyone, do I?"

Penworthy stiffened, and for the first time in years the old anger was back, heating the air between them. She thought she had made her peace with this, thought she had come to accept her life and her heritage. She understood her mother had not meant to abandon her. The woman had simply died. She knew that her father had not ignored her. He had not even known of her existence. And if she wished to come in from the rookeries, she need only ask and Penworthy would provide for her.

As for Marcus, he was merely her former partner. He had not left her. In fact, she had wished for him to quit. He had done exactly as she desired, turning over control of the investigation to her. Yet she was still so angry that her fists quivered in her lap.

"Fantine—" Penworthy began, his voice slow and unsure.

"No." Her word was sharp, cutting off anything her father might want to say. "I have to leave." She could not allow anyone to see her in this state. At least not until she understood why she was reacting this way.

"Stay here, Fantine. Let me take care of you."

"I will not be kept and then abandoned!" she cried. Then she bit her lip, appalled by her own nonsensical words. She moaned, her throat closing off as she struggled with demons she did not fully understand. Meanwhile, her father took a step closer to her.

"Fantine—" he began.

"He should have stayed with his brother," she said, as if that explained anything. Then she ran from the room.

CHAPTER 5

Fantine slipped through Lord Harris's glittering ballroom, her servant's clothing ensuring she was as invisible as a ghost. She took a deep breath, savoring the cooler air in the main room despite the press of bodies. The ladies' retiring room had been close and humid, and she was sure she would reek of expensive perfume for the next month at least.

She had been lucky to get the job for the evening. Luckier still to be assigned to the ladies' room. Good Lord, she had heard enough gossip in one hour to give her blackmail fodder for years to come. Not that she intended to use it, of course, but it never hurt to keep one's ears open.

Yet for all the wonderful eavesdropping opportunities, Fantine was grateful to slip away. Too many scents reminded her of her mother's greenroom and never failed to give her a headache. Too many grasping dandies then, too many viper-tongued women now.

So Fantine had stolen away, anxious to investigate Lord Harris while he was busy entertaining his many guests.

She was pushed to one side, pressed against the back wall. She did not object, taking the time instead to survey her surroundings. The room was typical for one of these affairs: The rich and the titled squeezed into the tiniest spaces, all vying to show themselves better than everyone else. Young misses flirted with abandon while the gentlemen tried to prove their manhood by wagering staggering sums of money on nonsense. It was really quite boring and more than a little sad.

So why did she so long to be among them?

The thought came as no surprise to her, much as she hated it. She had had such illogical, traitorous desires all her life. She blamed these on her mother, who had spent her short life trying to climb from one exalted bedroom to another. In the end, Gabrielle Delarive had died of the pox, alone except for Fantine, ugly, and afraid.

Definitely not the life Fantine wanted. So she wrinkled her nose in disgust even though the thought of putting on a golden gown and dancing until dawn made her knees go weak with a mute hunger.

She was a fool.

Stiffening her spine, Fantine pushed around the edge of the room, heading for the library. She would begin her search there. Men always hid the most damning evidence in the most obvious place, right where any good lock-pick could find it.

She was only halfway there when she saw him.

Chadwick.

Not ten feet beyond her, clear as a streak of sunlight in the rookeries and even more compelling. Dressed all in black, except for the white swath of his shirt, he shined in this crowd of overblown beauties and effeminate dandies.

He took her breath away.

Not because he was handsome. She already knew that.

But because he was here undoubtedly doing exactly what he had sworn not to do—investigating Lord Harris. Good Lord, she had just accustomed herself to working without him again, and yet here he was. True, they had only been together that one evening, but that time had left a permanent mark on her memory.

It had taken all week to stop thinking of him. And now that she had finally locked him out of her thoughts, here he was again, upsetting her composure.

She stood there nearly shaking with the need to scream her frustration at him. Impossible, of course. Still, the idea of leaving him free to interfere whenever he wished made her clench her fists. There had to be something she could do.

Then Chadwick bowed over the bejeweled hand of a statuesque blonde and her anger at last found a plan. She was one of the best pickpockets alive. It would take less than a moment to steal a signet ring here, a diamond bracelet there. The guests were too busy sniping at one another to notice if some tiny piece of adornment disappeared.

She could place a few items in his greatcoat and a few more on his person. She still had his pocket watch hidden beneath her shirt. She could attach most of the items on the chain and then plant it on him. Marcus would never know what had happened until it was too late.

Sometimes, she thought, life could be very, very good.

Marcus let his gaze travel over the various members of the political and social elite, first catching one person's eye, then another as he struggled to stifle a yawn. Whatever had induced him to come to this ridiculous affair?

He did not have to think twice to find the answer. It appeared before him in the form of a mental image, a picture of a dark elfin face with bright, mischievous eyes.

Fantine.

She wouldn't thank him for his help, but when he had received his invitation to Lord Harris's ball, he could not force himself to refuse. It had been a week since he'd left Penworthy's home with Wilberforce on his arm. A week of toying with his speech and staring out the window. A week of feeling at loose ends with nothing to occupy his time except memories of the oddest, most compelling woman he had ever met.

He imagined her at his breakfast table every morning, commenting delightfully on the morning's news. He pictured her in his bed every night, sliding her sensuous body along his. And during the day, he saw her in strangers and servants.

He was a man who relished a well-ordered life, and so Fantine ought to fill him with dread. Instead, he delighted himself by picturing Bentley's reaction to her sudden appearance on the doorstep. The poor man would be stupefied.

The thought was actually somewhat titillating.

So, he had come to Lord Harris's ball, hoping to stumble across something useful, thereby requiring him to seek her out to deliver the information. It did not hurt that he expected to find evidence of Harris's guilt. The memory of her scoffing at his suspicions still burned.

With that thought in place, he edged his way toward the library. He didn't notice the maid until he sauntered into the main hallway. Her hair was hidden beneath a tight cap, but the girl's size and form were familiar, and most especially, the walk. Who else wiggled just that way except Fantine? His blood heated at the possibility of seeing her so soon, but then he quickly dismissed it. He had been imagining Fantine everywhere from his own breakfast table to Hyde Park. Why not Harris's ball?

Still, the body seemed so familiar....

Changing directions, he followed her as she ducked into the cloakroom. Waiting in the shadows just beyond, he heard muted voices, then a low giggle.

A rendezvous. Which meant she couldn't be Fantine.

Marcus squelched his disappointment and turned back down the hallway. But before he could move beyond the tiny alcove, the serving maid left the cloakroom, a chocolate in one hand and a glass of champagne raised to her lips in the other.

So that was what the laughter was about, he guessed. A maid sampling the host's expensive dessert fare. Then, at the exact moment she passed in front of his hiding place, she lowered her glass. He finally got a clear look at her face.

It was Fantine! Probably investigating Lord Harris.

He glanced nervously around. Fortunately, the hall remained empty, but it was still not the time to perform a clandestine operation. Half the ton were here! She did not have the protection that invitation and his title gave him. If she was caught, nothing would prevent the full weight of the law from crashing down on her beautiful head.

He watched her move gracefully down the corridor before slipping quietly into the dark library. He followed her without a second thought, closing the door behind him.

"What are you doing here?" he demanded.

She spun around, her eyes wide with surprise, her body clearly outlined by the moonlight. But true to her quick wits, she straightened her shoulders and spoke with that grating cockney tone. "Auw, look wot the cat dragged in."

"Stop that!" he snapped, unsure why he was so angry except that the memory of her husky giggle in the cloakroom stood prominent in his memory. "You can speak like a lady, why do you insist on that backstreet caterwauling?"

"'Cause it makes ye mad, ducky," she said as she crossed behind Harris's desk. "It just burns in yer gut that ye had to work wi' the loikes of me—a thief an' a back-street whore."

"Ah," he said, adopting a casualness he did not feel. "Is that what you are?"

She frowned slightly as she maneuvered her lock-pick. "Wot, ducky?"

"A thief and a whore." He had no idea why he was asking, except that he had a desperate need to resolve at least one question about her.

"Oi ams what Oi ams," she responded glibly.

Marcus could only stare at her. She brushed him off as if he were of no account when he had spent the last week imagining her, thinking of her, even dreaming of her.

Suddenly his anger got the better of him. Stepping forward, he grabbed her wrist, pulling it up until she was forced to look at him. "What are you, Fantine? Actress? Whore? Thief?"

She glared at him, hatred clear in her beautiful eyes. "Go play wi' someone else, guv. I be busy jes now."

Rage burned within him. He knew his reaction was completely out of proportion, but that did not seem to matter. No one had ever toyed with him, dismissed him, infuriated him as much as she did. The feelings were as exciting as they were maddening, and he could not decide whether to kiss or throttle her. In the end, she took the choice away from him.

"Why are you here?" she asked, her voice as cultured as it was cold.

"I am making sure your pretty neck does not get stretched for thieving."

"My neck is quite safe as long as you stop bellowing." Then she twisted out of his grip and returned to Harris's desk.

He settled his fists onto his hips. "You cannot seriously expect to investigate his desk now," he said softly. "Anyone could walk in. The house is filled to the rafters with people."

She did not glance up as she inserted a long thin wire into the lock. "When should I do it? When there are servants loitering about? Or when everyone, including the host and hostess, is occupied with the myriad guests?"

"Perhaps when the servants are on holiday—"

"That will not happen until May."

"Or in the evening when the house is silent and asleep—"

"Noise is easier to cover now."

"Or rely on your friends to assist you. I have already furthered my acquaintance with Lord Harris. I could easily—"

She glanced up, her eyes steely and hard. "You are not my friend."

He paused, seeing again the seething hatred in her eyes and wondering at its origin. When had he offended her that deeply?

"I am not your enemy," he said softly.

Her only response was the quiet click of the desk lock as she finally released the catch. Pulling open the drawer, she gazed into the neat stacks of linen within.

"Ye're in me light, guv."

Glancing behind him, he saw that he was indeed blocking the moonlight. Stepping to one side, he lit a candle, placing it so that a stack of papers hid the light from anyone who happened to glance at the window from outside. Then he crossed to her side, his gaze drawn to the sight of her small, delicate hands rifling Harris's papers.

"Are you looking for anything specific?"

She glanced irritably at him. "You said you would leave this matter to me."

"And I have," he countered. "I merely wish to be of assistance."

"I do not need your help."

"You have it nonetheless."

She twisted away from him, pulling open another drawer and lifting out a large leather volume. "I do not want your help," she bit out through clenched teeth.

"Really?" he asked casually, as he reached for the open volume. "Can you decipher this?" He ran his hand down the neat rows of accounts, frowning as his attention followed the path of his fingers.

"Is it significant?"

He heard the note of uncertainty in her voice and nearly crowed out loud. "Do you admit that you need my help?"

He watched her closely, seeing the moonlight trace her lashes and illuminate the turmoil in her bronze eyes. What a difficult choice this must be for her: remain staunchly independent and lose a potentially significant clue or admit weakness and further her investigation. He could almost feel sympathy for her plight, but he was too interested in which direction she would choose.

In the end, her integrity won out. "Yes, I admit it. Now what does this mean?"

He quickly paged through the accounts, pointing out the relevant notations. "See all these companies and the money Harris has invested in them? It shows exactly what I knew originally. Lord Harris was deeply steeped in the slave trade."

"Was?" she asked softly.

Marcus grimaced. Trust Fantine to catch the most significant part of his explanation. "Yes," he said, even though it disproved his own theory. "He has been pulling his money away from those investments and putting them in more sound companies."

"Companies not threatened by Wilberforce's bill?"

"Yes."

"Which means he has no reason to kill Wilberforce."

Marcus nodded grimly. "This is why his objections to the bill have stopped. He merely wished to delay its passage until he could shift his money around. Now—"

"Now he can afford to embrace Wilberforce's Christian charity."

Marcus caught the hard note of cynicism in her voice and could not disagree with it. "So now our only lead is a man with three gold teeth."

She nodded grimly, and in that moment of silence came the sound of a female giggle. A woman was in the hallway and coming closer.

Marcus did not spare time to think. He immediately doused the candle. Beside him, Fantine was equally swift as she silently shoved the ledger back into its place. They had no idea if the woman intended to enter the library, but they had no wish to take the chance of being caught.

"We must leave," he whispered urgently.

She shook her head. "I have to lock the desk." Her hands were remarkably steady as she worked the lock-pick. Then the unknown woman's giggle was joined by the low tones of a man.

Marcus could have groaned out loud. This was exactly why he had not wanted Fantine to search during a rout. All too frequently, a couple would sneak off somewhere private. Some quiet place like the library.

"Hurry," he whispered as he scanned the room for an escape. He found none. The library windows were old and narrow. They would creak abominably when opened. The only other exit was through the door, but the unknown couple's voices were growing louder by the second.

"Done!"

She shot up from the chair while he reached for her wrist. Together, they dove into the only hiding place he could see—behind a leather couch, partially hidden by the curtains. It was a painful squeeze between the furniture and the wall, especially as Fantine had landed beneath Marcus, half twisted on her side, half turned face-up toward him. He did his best to keep his weight off her, but there was no room, and at that moment, the noisy couple entered.

"Why, this is scandalous!" said the woman, her voice breathy with excitement.

"Nonsense," returned the man. "You have been driving me mad since this morning."

It took a moment for Marcus to recognize the voices, but when he did, he felt his jaw drop. Good Lord, it was Harris and his wife!

Certainly, the man was prone to emotional displays. His political speeches alone exhibited more sentiment than refinement. But how vulgar to sneak off during one's own ball to cavort with one's wife!

And what cavorting it was.

Harris's ardor clearly outstripped his reason as he lowered his wife to the floor. She landed with a soft thud and the whisper of silk skirts, her slightly drunken giggles swiftly silenced by his kisses.

Marcus cringed, silently cursing the lecherous old man. Why must he take his wife now? And why on the floor, for God's sake, where the slightest turn of his head would reveal Marcus and Fantine? Sweet heaven, did not the man have the simplest decency to do the deed on the couch instead of beside it?

But there was no help for it. Marcus and Fantine were trapped for the duration, listening to soft moans that could not fail to arouse. The same dismay colored Fantine's eyes, but Marcus was more interested in the bright spots of color heating her cheeks and the soft curve of her breast against his arm.

The thoughts that heated his blood were inevitable, especially as he had only to turn his head slightly to see them acted out by another couple. But he did not turn his head. Instead, he let his gaze wander over Fantine's face, seeing moonlight spill across her pert nose and rosy cheek. Her dark lips parted and she shifted slightly, clearly aware of his arousal pressing against her thigh.

"Kiss me," Lady Harris moaned.

How could he resist?

With a shudder that came from deep within, he lowered his head to her mouth. He tasted refinement on her lips. The faint brush of champagne, the rich whisper of chocolate. He felt her body soften beneath him, shifting slightly as she clung to his kiss. On the other side of the couch, Lady Harris gasped in delight, while Marcus felt a shiver tremble through Fantine.

"I love the smell of you," mumbled Lord Harris, and Marcus lowered his face to Fantine's neck, inhaling the heavy fragrances of the ton, as well as the scent that was uniquely hers.

"Touch my breast," whispered Lady Harris. Marcus obeyed, shifting his hand to Fantine's soft bosom. He found the peak already erect, pushing into his fingers. He flicked his thumb over the hard nub, his nail scraping across the rough fabric that separated them. Beneath him, he heard Fantine gasp.

"Oh, yes," gasped Lady Harris. "Do that again. Harder."

The fabric was in his way, so he eased open the buttons of her maid's gown and slipped his hand beneath to hold her naked flesh. She was warm and soft, and Marcus thought he could feel the rapid beat of her pulse as she arched into him, both fitting herself better into his hand and tormenting him below.

"Oh, blimey," whispered Fantine, the words both a cry of distress and a plea, her breath hot and moist against his cheek.

He raised his head to trail his tongue over the curve of her ear, desperately wishing they had more room. There were so many things he wished to do to her, to explore with her. He had but one hand to tease and stroke her nipple, while he felt tension rise within her. He pulled, and she gasped. He circled, and she moaned.

Then he whispered, ever so softly. "You are perfect. So very, very perfect." And he pinched her nipple.

She cried out suddenly, and her hips pulsed upward in the most exquisitely torturous rhythm. Marcus groaned, his blood on fire despite the layers of fabric that separated them. All he could do was kiss her flushed cheeks, her dark red lips, her neck, her breast.

Then, a chance movement to his left drew his attention. He did not want to acknowledge it, but a cold dread began forming in his stomach. Turning his head, he encountered the accusing gazes of Lord and Lady Harris.

CHAPTER 6

Fantine noticed the change in Marcus immediately, but it was some moments before she could react. Never before had she felt so wonderfully strange, so encompassed and liberated all at once.

Always before, a man's touch repulsed her, pushing her to escape in any way possible. But not with Marcus. His touch warmed her, set her skin to tingling, and her heart to skipping with excitement. It was terrifying and consuming, but she had no time to absorb or even understand what was happening. Because as soon as she opened her eyes, she saw Marcus, his face set in rigid lines, his gaze fixed on the center of the room.

Turning her head, she encountered the horrified stares of Lord and Lady Harris. "Gawd almighty," she whispered, a mortifying blush burning in her face.

Marcus shifted his gaze to her, his expression both chagrined and apologetic as he buttoned up her bodice.

"My dear," said Lord Harris to his wife, "perhaps you had best return to our guests."

The plump woman nodded and pushed to her feet. She had already readjusted her clothing, and after a final reassuring smile from her husband, she left the room.

"You might as well come out of there, Chadwick. I cannot imagine your position is all that comfortable."

"On the contrary," drawled Marcus with a rueful glance at Fantine. "It has its advantages." Despite his words, Marcus gingerly struggled off of her. Unfortunately, Fantine's nerves seemed to have developed a hypersensitivity to the slightest touch. His movements left her quivering, gasping for breath, wanting nothing more than to curl into her side and die.

"Come along, miss. You, too," came her employer's gravelly voice.

"Give her a minute, Harris," returned Marcus, his tone almost bland. "I am somewhat heavy. No doubt it will take some time for the feeling to return to her legs."

Fantine stared at Marcus, stunned by his attitude. His face was the perfect aristocrat's mask of boredom. He looked as sated and as uninterested in her as the worst satyr in her mother's court. He cared nothing for her and even less for what feelings he had created in her. He used her!

Betrayal burned like acid within her. How dare he? How could he? And how could she have allowed him—with one single kiss—to turn her into her mother? She had no illusions about what would have happened if they had had more time and more privacy. She would have done anything for him, been anything for him, allowed him to do whatever he willed with her.

Suddenly everything she believed about herself was in doubt. Called into question by him. She could not hate him more if he had chained her around the neck and driven her naked through Hyde Park.

And at that precise moment Marcus leaned down, extending his hand with an expression of sympathy. "Come on out. There is no use hiding now."

She gaped at him. Hiding! Did he think she was hiding, when in truth she was fighting the urge to drive a knife straight into his lascivious heart?

He saw her expression and hesitated, clearly confused. Behind him, she caught a glimpse of Lord Harris, frowning at her, and realized that she did not need a dagger. She had a much more potent weapon at hand.

Above all things, the peerage prided themselves on the appearance of propriety, the show of poker-up-the-arse decency. She now had the opportunity to rip that veneer away, wounding Marcus in the most important aspect of his entire personality: his respectability.

Her lip began to tremble, and she drew away from Marcus's outstretched hand as if he were evil incarnate. She released a pitiful whimper akin to a tortured kitten. Then she turned pleading eyes toward Lord Harris.

"Don't let 'im touch me, guv. Please!"

"Fantine!" gasped Marcus, clearly angered by her reaction, but she pressed on, relishing his every squirming expression.

"He made me, an' it were sinful!" She knew she could not claim she had been completely forced. She had too obviously enjoyed what had happened. The memory of what she had done, what she had allowed him to do to her, spurred on her theatrics. "Please," she cried to Lord Harris. "Send me away. I won't cause no trouble. Let me go t' church an' pray for my soul."

"Fantine!" cried Marcus. "There was nothing sinful in what we did, and well you know it."

"Oh, no!" she responded, her eyes tearing as she pleaded with Lord Harris. "I'm a good girl. I swear it. I never—"

"This is outside of enough!" bellowed Marcus as he bodily hauled her out of the corner. But she was ready, using his motion to help her scramble away to cower behind Lord Harris.

"Save me," she cried. "He is evil! The things 'e said 'e'd do if I cried out."

Marcus planted his fists on his hips as he glared at her. "I threatened nothing, Fantine, but I do now. I swear to God—"

"Enough, Chadwick," cut in Lord Harris.

"What!" he exploded, suddenly turning on his host. "You cannot believe what she is saying!"

"What I believe," he said slowly, "is that Miss—"

"Fanny Smith, yer lordship," she offered in a trembling voice.

"That Miss Smith would be better off as far away from here as possible. I shall pay her wages and see her home."

"Oh, no!" Fantine gasped. She did not want anyone knowing where she lived. Not even Penworthy knew that. "Jes me wages, yer lordship. I can find a 'ackney t' take me 'ome."

Apparently seizing on anything to discomfit her, Marcus stepped forward, his voice dripping with sarcasm. "Oh, no, Fanny, not after the trauma you have just sustained. I insist that my own coachman drive you."

She shook her head vehemently, not needing to act her distress. "Do not let 'im know where I live," she cried.

"Why would I wish to visit you, Fanny?" Marcus's voice was cold, but his eyes fairly glittered with emotion. Though he pretended absolute disgust with her, she knew he would come see her at his first opportunity. Then he would exact his revenge.

The thought was as thrilling as it was terrifying, and for a moment she felt paralyzed with fear. Everything was happening so fast! She turned one last pleading eye to Lord Harris. "Please, yer lordship. I be sore afraid."

"Very well," Harris said with a sigh as he paid her triple wages. "Get your hackney."

She smiled gratefully, though she knew her relief would be short-lived. One look at Marcus told her that he had just made finding her home a priority. She had no doubt he would succeed, eventually. But for this moment, she need only leave without having him follow her. If only one of those society ladies would discover—

A piercing wail split the air, coming from the ballroom. It was an older lady, Fantine guessed. Probably the matron who had somehow lost a diamond and emerald bracelet. The very same bracelet that currently rested in Marcus's pocket.

She grinned, knowing she could now escape. "Thank ye, yer lordship. An' may God bless ye," she said as she bobbed her curtsey.

Harris barely noticed, his attention already shifted to the ballroom and the mayhem beginning there. Marcus, however, easily caught her arm.

"What have you done?" he demanded, his grip tightening as Harris pushed past them out the library door.

"It is just a distraction in case of trouble." Then she abruptly twisted out of his grip and made for the hall. At the last possible moment, though, she glanced backward. "Of course, you might want to check your pockets." With that parting shot, she made her escape, running as fast as her legs could carry her.

Marcus watched her leave, knowing he could catch her if he wanted. But there was no need. Slipping outside, he signaled to his own coachman, who was loitering nearby. He simply pointed at Fantine's retreating form, and Jacob nodded in complete understanding. Quick as a wink, Jacob's son, Giles, slipped into the darkness, following Fantine.

The two would be an even match, Marcus thought with a grin. Before he had hired Jacob, the coachman and his son had spent their own time in the rookeries. It had not taken long for Marcus to discover Giles was as valuable as his father. The boy was quick and well versed in exactly the kind of tricks Fantine used. With luck, Giles would soon get him a little more information about the mysterious Fantine.

But in the meantime, Marcus had other things to occupy his thoughts, not the least of which was the growing chaos from within the Harris household. Steeling himself for the worst, Marcus pushed his hand into his pocket and drew out his watch. Well, at least she had seen fit to return it.

It was not until he heard the gasp of a nearby footman that he thought to look at the base of the chain. There, glittering in the evening candlelight, was an heirloom diamond and emerald bracelet worth at least six thousand pounds.

* * *

Fantine settled into the hackney and released a sigh. Normally she would not have bothered with the expense, but she was too frazzled, too tired to walk all the way home. So she had hailed a hackney and now only wished to close her eyes.

Just as she rested her head back against the worn squabs, she felt a telltale dip as the vehicle picked up another passenger. A street child no doubt, jumping on the back. She didn't care. If he was not caught by the driver, she had no objection to sharing her ride. She had, after all, stolen quite a few rides herself at one time or another.

Releasing a heavy breath, she willed away the tension of the last few hours. She blocked out the anger, the frustration, and all the other tangled emotions she had no energy to examine. All that was left was one image, one face, smiling tenderly at her.

Marcus.

No big surprise there. He seemed to dog her footsteps during the day, why not torment her at night, too? But she need not dwell on him. He was merely another reality of her existence, a force to be measured and managed, like Penworthy and Ballast and Hurdy.

Or so she told herself.

The difference, of course, was that none of them had ever touched her, stripping away her reason with the tiniest press of his lips. A single heated look from Marcus weakened her with alarming speed. If she were superstitious, she would have said he had the evil eye.

Fantine sighed again, the sound echoing in the dark hackney. Age was making her vulnerable to one thing a man like Marcus could offer her: luxury.

She had scorned it as a child, but now, at twenty-five, she couldn't run the streets by day without feeling the ache by night. She longed for the warmth of a good fire, the ease of a comfortable bed, and the sweet scent of clean clothes.

But such pleasures came with a trap. It came with men like Marcus who cared for nothing except their own personal pleasure. Women like her mother were taken, exploited, then thrown away. Fantine was eight when she vowed never to let a man use her like that. And no one ever had.

No one, that is, except Marcus.

She should hate him for that, for bridging defenses she thought no one could conquer. Yet when he had pressed his weight into her, when he had touched her breast and trailed kisses along her face, she had wanted nothing more than to be used, to be enjoyed, to be touched however he willed.

Her face burned with humiliation even as her breasts tingled with the memory.

Biting her lip, Fantine finally faced the brutal truth. Marcus had somehow stumbled upon her one weakness, the one legacy from her mother that she had been unable to subjugate—her own body. And he had not hesitated to use it against her.

Self-recriminations did not help matters. What she needed was a plan, a course of action that would neutralize his threat. But what?

Marcus was nothing if not determined. He would find her home, seek out her various aliases, even ferret out her allies, if only to relieve the boredom in his life. Then, when he had her cornered and trapped, what would he do to her?

Delightful images sprang to mind: horrible, wonderful pictures of her mother kissing various lovers. She had never seen more than that, but she had heard things. She remembered tiny gasps, low moans, and then the final triumphant cry. Could he make her do that? Would she…Her mind balked at the thought, even as she grasped it, wondering how it would feel.

She swallowed, her mouth suddenly very dry.

She definitely needed a plan, but what? The hackney stopped long before she had an answer. She felt the boy disembark and run off. Then slowly, as if she were a hundred years old, she opened the carriage door and stepped out. She paid the coachman, feeling every ache of her tired muscles as she turned for her home.

She was not paying attention. She knew that. But tonight, she was simply too weary with herself to care. Which is why, when the blow came, she was not even aware of the man who struck it. It landed with numbing force on the back of her head.

She went down like a stone.

Two hours!

Marcus clenched the mahogany banister in his town residence and repeated the phrase like a silent litany.

Two hours!

Two hours of apologies and explanations and desperate repartee as he tried to explain why he had a countess's jewelry dangling from his watch fob. Two hours of finding other people's jewelry on his person or in his coat as he tried to convince his friends that it had all been a lark, a careless wager at whether he could be a successful pickpocket.

Then, when he had thought it all done, he had endured stern recitations about responsibility and ridiculous wagers from, God help him, his former suspect and host, Lord Harris.

Two hours, but it would take much longer before his political standing recovered, if it truly ever did.

He would kill Fantine for this!

He stepped into his chamber and stripped out of his jacket in one fluid movement. He had no more than pulled out his diamond stickpin when he heard the rapid tattoo of a boy's steps on the stairs.

"Yer lordship! Yer lordship!"

"Giles?" Marcus dashed out of his room. "What happened?"

"They got 'er!" he gasped out. "There was nothing…I could do! They just 'it 'er…an' she went down. No fight. She jes…went down!"

Marcus dropped to one knee before the boy, steadying the child's shoulders. "Who got her?"

"Urdy's men. They was waitin'!"

Marcus felt his chest squeeze into a painful knot. "How badly was she hurt?"

The boy shook his head. "Couldn't tell. She just went down!"

The knot in his chest suddenly grew, cutting off his breath.

"But I followed 'em," Giles continued. "To Hurdy's. They carried 'er inside, an' I came back here."

"Excellent," Marcus said grimly as he started down the steps. "Now take me there."

CHAPTER 7

Fantine knew what had happened long before she opened her eyes. She had far too much experience with being cuffed to miss the evidence now.

Forcing her body to remain relaxed, she concentrated on her other senses, cataloguing information with as much clarity as possible. The odors came first, telling her she was still in the rookeries, near the docks. She lay on a rough cot that smelled of old tick and unwashed bodies. Nearby, men's voices murmured. No women, thank God, so she was not in a brothel. The perfume she sensed came from herself, a remnant of her work in the ladies' retiring room…How long ago?

It could not have been long. The pain was not throbbingly intense. It was probably still the night of the ball, the evening when she had seen Marcus and he had…

She could not stifle a moan. Why would the world not just stop for five bloody minutes so she could get some rest? Too much, too fast. She could not keep up.

"She be awake!" called a man's rough voice.

"How long awake?" returned another voice that hovered on the edge of cultured without quite crossing over.

"Jes starting."

"She's been awake fer at least ten minutes, then. Bring her along."

Fantine restrained another sigh. The second voice was not only better educated, but its owner was canny, too.

Hurdy.

She opened her eyes. She barely saw the small, bare room before a huge brute of a man jerked her to her feet and dragged her into a hallway. She staggered, not needing to fake weakness. Her knees wobbled and her head lolled back and forth. Fortunately, her movements showed her enough that she recognized Hurdy's home. They were on the second floor, near the main staircase.

Then she was in the sitting room, stumbling toward a roaring fire in a very decadent room. Plush pillows abounded everywhere, heavy fabrics draped the walls and the single window, and a trio of fat couches stretched across the room. In the center of all this, in a large, ostentatious chaise, lounged Hurdy.

She recognized him immediately, even though this was their first meeting. With curly reddish brown hair and a sweet freckled face, he looked as innocent as a newborn babe. His green eyes were alive with intelligence, his expression welcoming. Even his body lay in negligent ease in a colorful silken wrap that seemed to shimmer in the firelight.

Most women would think him boyishly handsome. She thought him soft. Especially when compared to Marcus's rock-solid frame and chiseled features.

"Hello, Rat," he called cheerfully as two of his huge servants took positions on either side of the door. Then he frowned. "Or perhaps in that attire, I should call you Fanny."

Fantine glanced down, noting for the first time that her dress was somewhat the worse for wear. The buttons down the bodice had pulled wide, revealing a gaping expanse of bosom, while a tear in her muddy skirt showed a good portion of her right calf.

"What do you want with me, Hurdy?" she asked, her voice halfway between vulgar and cultured, exactly matching Hurdy's speech pattern.

"What I wanted, luv, is to meet the woman who could fool Ballast into thinking she was a boy. For years, in fact."

Fantine shrugged. "Ballast ain't known as a deep thinker."

Hurdy smiled. "True. But neither is he completely stupid." He set his brandy glass aside as he inspected her from head to toe. "Looking at you now, no one would ever think of Rat." He fell silent, still watching her. Fantine remained quiet, too. "I think," he continued, "that you are a good deal sharper than just about everyone in the rookeries."

"Excepting yourself, of course," she added, doing her best to sound sincere.

"Naturally." He reached forward and daintily rang a tiny silver bell. "I have just called for dinner. Care to join me?"

Fantine shook her head, allowing her tone to become surly. "My head still hurts from yer men."

"I do apologize for that," he drawled, "but I did not think you would come just for the asking."

Fantine folded her arms over her chest. She would have come, if only to see what she could discover about the Wilberforce job. "Next time, ask. I might jes be willing."

"Really?" he asked, his attention not on her, but on the doorway as he audibly sniffed the air.

Fantine turned slightly, mimicking his motion, catching the delightful scent of roast mutton wafting up the stairs. Sweet heaven, it smelled wonderful. To her mortification, her stomach growled.

"Truly, my dear, you must join me," he offered with a grin. "I assure you it ain't poisoned."

Fantine stepped forward, her hunger eating at her patience. Of course she wanted his dinner, but she knew she would be surrendering to him in some small measure if she joined him. She could not afford that vulnerability. She would eat when she felt safe enough to do so.

Shutting down all thought of the succulent smells, she concentrated on her enemy. "Look, Hurdy, you didn't knock me on the noggin jest to meet me. What do you want?"

He did not answer, not that Fantine expected him to. He merely folded his arms and watched her while a stocky cook set out his meal. She held his gaze, showing her irritation while secretly praying that her stomach did not rumble again.

Finally the servant was done, leaving the room as silently as he had entered, and still Hurdy did not speak, did not even move. And so it continued as the room filled with the heavenly aroma of mutton done to perfection, and Fantine had to clench her jaw shut as she tried not to drool.

Finally, he took a breath. "I understand you promised to get Sprat into Harrow."

Fantine frowned, her thoughts momentarily distracted from her stomach. She had expected that news of her run-in with Ballast would be common knowledge within moments of her escape, but she had hoped her deal with Sprat would remain secret.

"Well?" prompted Hurdy when she did not answer.

"Well wot?" she returned.

"Can you do it?"

Fantine shifted her pose into one of arrogant disdain. "I promised to."

"And can you?"

She hesitated, wondering how best to answer. She finally decided on a show of strength. "Yes, I can. For Sprat because I like him. I will not do it for anyone else."

He smiled. "That almost sounds like a challenge."

She shrugged. "Call it what you like. I will not be putting your bastards into 'Arrow."

"But you could if you wanted to," he pressed. "Or that daft peer of yours could."

She shook her head. "No." But despite her calm assertion, a shiver of fear chilled her blood at Hurdy's mention of Marcus. The last thing she needed was for

Hurdy to get Chadwick involved, especially when the mere thought of Marcus tangled her emotions anew. "The daft peer is simply that. Daft. My contact to Harrow was a onetime bit o' luck. Ain't no more where that came from."

She fell silent, hoping she had convinced him.

Apparently she had because suddenly she was done. Hurdy sighed and waved her away. "Very well. Go away."

Fantine blinked. Go away? She peered at Hurdy, her thoughts reeling. He had truly just wanted to get some child into Harrow? The thought was ludicrous. Especially since…"You ain't got no children." Or at least none that he appeared to care about, none that he would pull strings to get into an elite school. She stepped forward, frustration and exhaustion making her bold. "Now look here, what's this all about?"

Hurdy glanced up from his food. "It is about nothing. I find you are unimportant after all. Go away."

Fantine dropped her hands onto her hips. "What a bloody waste o' time!" she exclaimed. Not only had she been knocked on the head, but Hurdy had learned very little from her, and she had gotten nothing out of him at all! She didn't mind being dragged in here. That was all part of the game. But to get hit on the head for no point at all, to tell him something he could have found out on his own, and that he did not want anyway…Why, the whole situation was ludicrous.

"Bloody hell," she said, spinning on her heel as she went for the door. "No wonder neither you nor Ballast can gain control of the docks. Neither one o' you got enough brain to feed a rat!"

She should not have been surprised when one of the thugs suddenly slammed the door in her face. She should not have been, but she was. And that surprise made her even more angry.

And reckless.

She spun back and glared at Hurdy. "I thought you said I could leave."

Hurdy slowly picked up a thin silver fruit knife. "You have a remarkable amount of nerve for a woman in my house at my mercy. I could have you killed."

Fantine folded her arms, letting her voice becoming more cultured by the second. "Oooh, I am mightily impressed," she drawled. "You have big, burly brutes. Ballast has big, burly brutes. But do either of you use them for any good? No. Ballast drinks and diddles with anything that moves. You cannot even kill a lame MP. Why should I think either of you worthy o' me?"

For better or worse, she had his attention now. He was not dismissing her like an annoying puppy dog. What he was doing was standing slowly, fury knotting his brow. "What do you know about 'oo I kill and why?" Despite his attempts at culture, his accent slipped as his voice rose in power and fury.

Fantine shrugged. "I know you have tried to kill Wilberforce and have not even succeeded in scratching the man."

"'Oo told you that?"

"Don't matter. What does matter is that you are already doomed. Whether or not you succeed in killing the MP, there ain't a single gent who will hire you again. And you do not even see it."

She had expected him to bluster at her, trying to intimidate her without giving anything away. But for all his vulgarity, he was not stupid. Hurdy simply looked at her, like a dog sighting a really fat rabbit.

She knew what he was thinking. He needed her. He had not had the benefit of her early training, learning how the peerage worked in all its twisted nonsense. And that gave her the upper hand.

With a slow, lazy smile, Fantine settled in to enjoy her newfound position. It had been a long time since she had felt like she had an upper hand. The moment was temporary, she knew. But for now, she reigned, and she intended to exploit it to the fullest.

First and foremost, she decided to eat. After being tormented by the smell of his delectable dinner, she could not think of anything but filling her stomach. Easing herself down at his table, Fantine scanned the food. There was only one plate—Hurdy's—and she took it, heaping roast mutton onto it with singular abandon. For his part, Hurdy could only drop down opposite her with barely concealed impatience.

Too bad. She was ravenous. Savoring the smell, Fantine cut her first bite, lifting it delicately on her fork, intending to draw as much pleasure as possible out of this simple act.

"Right there," said Giles, pointing at what appeared to be a tall, comfortable-looking house in the middle of a long row of warehouses. "They took 'er right in the front, clear as day."

Marcus stared at the house, unable to hold back his surprise. "Hurdy lives there?"

"It were the talk o' the rookeries fer months."

Marcus nodded, still staring at the structure, clearly visible in the light of the full moon. It was a bloody castle. True, it was short and squished between the long rows of warehouses, but it was a castle nonetheless, complete with a central turret containing a single arched window. And the whole thing was right in the middle of the dark menace of the docks.

"That light up there." Giles pointed to the turret window where a light shone clear as a beacon. "Hurdy likes to sit there and watch wot goes on out 'ere. An' 'e likes us to see wot 'e does in there. She will be in that room. Less'n 'e's got 'er in 'is bedroom."

Marcus dismounted his horse, not wanting to consider what the child was suggesting, but unable to rid himself of the image. Fantine in Hurdy's bed? Brutalized in the worst possible ways? He could not allow it.

He focused his mind on his task, removing the rope he had brought with him and neatly looping it over his shoulder. "Can you ride back without me?"

"But—"

"No buts, Giles. You cannot help any more than you already have. Go home." He slapped the rear of his horse and watched with a silent dread as his only means of escape trotted back to home and safety. Then, with a grim fatalism, Marcus prepared to risk his life for the woman he had recently vowed to torture at the earliest possible moment.

He stepped into the shadows of a nearby warehouse, studying Hurdy's home with care. What kind of man would build a castle in the center of the docks? Only someone who thought himself a king, someone who wanted to rule the dockside Londoners as a medieval warlord ruled his serfs. And Marcus had to breech the castle walls like some knight errant of yore.

When had he gone completely insane?

Marcus shook his head. There was little time to think of such nonsense. He had to find a way into Hurdy's castle. Fortunately, Marcus had spent a good deal of his childhood climbing and exploring a castle near his family's Yorkshire estate. He knew just how to gain entrance thanks most especially to a stable hand named Ty who had spent a good deal of time in the American colonies. Marcus had never quite managed to handle the lasso like Ty had, but he had some basic proficiency.

Marcus turned, scanning the surrounding warehouses. They were all squat formless buildings, lined up like bricks pressed one against the other. It took half a block before he found what he needed: a warehouse with a lookout, a small tower in the middle of the roof where someone could watch the ships coming in and out and thereby predict the shift and flow of commodity prices. Quite intelligent, actually. And quite useful because along the outside of the building was a single rickety ladder designed to give access to the roof and the lookout post.

Readjusting the rope on his shoulder, Marcus climbed the ladder, gaining access to the roof. It was then a relatively easy run from one roof to the next, all along the row until he came to the one right next to Hurdy's castle.

While he looped the rope into a lasso, Marcus searched for his best option. His only choice was to anchor the rope to the top of Hurdy's tower, then swing into the lit room Giles had indicated. He would fly through that window like a suicidal bird, shattering the glass, and making enough noise to alert everyone in a ten-block radius.

Unfortunately, much as he tried, he could not see a better alternative. He could only hope Fantine was there, because if he was forced to search through the house for her, he was a dead man. Of course, if he missed this particular jump he would be worse off than dead. He'd be a bloody splat on the side of a castle turret.

With that image in mind, Marcus gripped the rope, gauged the wind, then prayed. He threw.

He missed.

Cursing under his breath, he pulled back the rope and tried again. It took two more tosses before the loop caught and held.

Now came the hard part—the jump. Assuming he gauged his rope and momentum correctly, he could burst through the window, grab Fantine, then jump out, sliding down the rope to the ground below. Hopefully, they would then make their escape through the rookery byways. Again.

If their luck held. If Fantine was indeed in that room. If he had lassoed the turret correctly. And if he did not kill himself on the jump.

Marcus took a deep breath, then relaxed. He'd already admitted to himself that he was completely insane. Everything would go as planned because everyone knew the feebleminded were protected by God. With that thought in mind, he ran and made his leap.

He knew from the moment he left the rooftop that he had figured correctly. His feet crashed through the glass window, shattering it inward with truly awesome force. Keeping one hand firmly gripped on the rope, he landed with only a small stumble even as he scanned the room for Fantine. He saw two people at a table and two guards near the door. Then he looked down, searching the floor for a crumpled body, a prostrate form, anything to indicate a bound prisoner.

Nothing.

What he saw instead was a diminutive virago in a torn frock push up from the remains of a sumptuous dinner and round on him in fury, fork waving like a dagger in his face.

"Good God, I did not even have time to eat it!" she screamed. "Not one measly, tiny bite. And now it is covered with glass! Glass! Damn it, I am hungry!"

Marcus blinked, first once, then twice, but the nightmare remained. It was indeed Fantine, the woman he had come to rescue, screeching at him like some shrew and waving...was that roast mutton? He sniffed appreciatively. It must have been a good one, too.

Then all thought was cut off as the door burst open, neatly flattening one large person who had been standing there, but admitting three more big men all running straight for Marcus.

"Come on!" he cried, making a grab for Fantine, intending to snare her around the waist and leap out the window to safety. That was his plan, but she eluded him, stepping directly into the path of the oncoming men.

"Don't you dare!" she said, brandishing her fork. The men skidded to a halt, looking uncertainly at her, then at him, then at a third man who still sat at the opposite side of the makeshift table. "He is mine," she practically hissed. Then she spun back toward Marcus, her eyes blazing with fury as she threw her fork straight at his face.

"What?" he gasped, barely eluding the projectile. It sailed out the window, no doubt landing on the very place he had thought to carry her. "Fantine—" he began, but she cut him off.

"Why are you here? Why is it that everywhere I go, suddenly you are there? Sweet heaven, will you be in the privy too?"

Marcus stared at her, his breath stolen by her fury. Her chestnut curls whipped about her face while her bronze eyes burned him where he stood. Good Lord, she was beautiful. But she was also contrary. And exasperating. And absolutely fascinating.

He decided he would bed her. If he did not kill her first.

"Could we possibly discuss this later?" he asked, as much to himself as to her. "I am trying to rescue you, you know."

"Not a prayer," she shot back.

It was at that moment that the other man pushed leisurely to his feet. He was quite handsome in a boyish sort of way. His redhead and freckles gave him an endearing look, but Marcus had no illusions that the man would be easy to handle. Noticing the man's expensive clothes and his confident air, Marcus deduced that he was looking at none other than Hurdy, dockside warlord and Ballast's main rival.

At Hurdy's nod, the guards retreated to strategic points in the room. Two of them went to either side of the window and firmly pulled the rope out of Marcus's hands. He did not want to relinquish his one faint hope of escape, but he had no choice. Not only was he severely outnumbered, but one of the men by the door had a sharp, wicked-looking knife, ready to embed hilt-deep in his throat.

Then Hurdy turned to Fantine while gesturing toward Marcus. "The daft lord, I presume?" he asked in cordial tones.

"Yes," snapped Fantine.

"No!" Marcus said at the exact same instant. He was not sure why he objected. Perhaps he was simply feeling contrary. Whatever the reason, for this moment, he wanted to be someone else. Someone with some measure of authority over Fantine.

So he said the first thing that came to mind.

"I am her guardian."

Fantine gasped and spun around, but Marcus was prepared for her. He folded his arms across his chest and glared at her. "I know you do not like it, my dear, but it is the sad truth. Barely two weeks ago, our sainted father on his deathbed charged me to care for you, annoying and difficult though you are."

"We most certainly are not related!"

"We are, Fantine. I insist you leave with me immediately. You cannot continue in these godforsaken ways!"

"This is ridiculous!" she cried.

"Shall I have him removed?" That was from Hurdy, his voice soothing.

"Yes!" Fantine was already waving toward the guards, urging them to haul him away.

"You do," cut in Marcus, "and I shall bring in the watch, Bow Street, all the holy men I can find, and any lord available to harass you for..." He struggled for some charge, however absurd. "For corrupting my sister!"

Fantine snorted her disgust and one of the guards joined her in a stifled chuckle, but Hurdy did not respond. He eyed both Fantine and Marcus in a way that made Marcus distinctly nervous. Then the man abruptly leaned down and brushed aside the glass shards before resuming his seat.

"Fanny was about to explain how I am doomed."

Fantine blinked, apparently having difficulty coming to grips with what had transpired. "But what about dinner?" she asked softly.

"I have eaten my full," responded Hurdy congenially.

"I will serve you all you want at home," said Marcus.

Fantine groaned. "You cannot wish me to explain while he is here." She jerked her head contemptuously at Marcus.

Marcus folded his arms and made sure his determination showed on his face. "I will not leave without her."

"Oh, go away, old man!" she said. Then she swung back to Hurdy. "Toss him out on his ear!"

Once again Hurdy looked at them, his light green eyes studying them with an unnerving intensity. Suddenly, he grinned. "No. He stays."

"But why?" gasped Fantine, clearly outraged.

"Because he annoys you."

She gaped at him. She turned and glared at Marcus, who did his best to look smug. She took a deep breath, brushed the glass shards off the other chair, and plopped down, muttering with every movement.

"Idiots, amateurs, every one of them!" She twisted to pin Marcus with her stare. "My guardian! Paugh!" She turned back to Hurdy. "Cannot even eat one lousy morsel. Harumph!"

Marcus grinned. He could not help it. She was indeed quite delightful when riled. Then his smile quickly faded as she began speaking, her voice growing stronger with each word. Her irritation was still plain, but it was apparently fading as she warmed to her topic.

"Very well, Hurdy, here is the problem. A lord comes to you and asks you to kill someone. The two of you agree on a price, and he goes away. You do not think to ask why he wants the man buried. You do not even think if killing the man will accomplish his purpose—"

"That is his business."

"No. The moment you accept the job, it is your business." Suddenly she leaned forward, her eyes alight with cunning. "Do you not see it? What happens if you kill Wilberforce and it turns out to ruin the man who hired you? Who will he blame?"

Hurdy frowned, the expression sulky on his boyish face.

"He will blame you, that's who," continued Fantine. "Then he will not pay you. Neither will he come back to you when he wants another cove killed."

Hurdy fidgeted in his seat, clearly understanding the value of repeat customers. "But how am I t' know what the gent needs? All he said was he wanted Wilberforce dead."

"You must think!" Fantine took a deep breath, sounding exasperated. She folded her arms, looking like a tutor outlining the simplest task for an inept student. "Let us start at the beginning. Who hired you to kill Wilberforce?"

At those words, Marcus suddenly felt his body relax.

Now he understood why Fantine had refused to escape with him. Whatever the reason she was first brought here, she had now turned the situation to her advantage. She intended to get the name of the man who had hired Hurdy to kill Wilberforce. Unfortunately, Hurdy was not stupid enough to give away such information easily.

"What does Ballast call him?" he asked.

Fantine hesitated only a moment. "He said you were hired by a man with three gold teggie," she said.

"Then Teggie it is."

Marcus kept his disappointment carefully hidden as Fantine continued, her expression still severe. "Very well. Now think. Why does Teggie want Wilberforce dead? Did you even ask?"

Hurdy poured himself a new brandy, his expression carefully guarded. "Why do you think he does?"

In other words, Marcus translated silently, he does not have the slightest idea.

"Because of the bill against slavery, of course. Have you not read the broadsides?"

Hurdy narrowed his eyes, but did not comment. Was it possible that the man could not read? Marcus wondered.

"It will come to a vote soon, and Teggie probably thinks that if Wilberforce dies, the bill will fail miserably."

Now it was Hurdy's turn to shrug. "So?"

Fantine sighed, clearly exasperated. "So, he is wrong."

Hurdy frowned. "Why?"

"Why? Because he will simply turn Wilberforce into a martyr, everyone will vote for the bill or look like they had part of killing the poor sot, and who will the man blame? You, that's who." Fantine leaned forward again, gripping her knees as she pressed her last point home. "You will never see another quid from the man. He will take his business to Ballast instead."

Hurdy's eyes glittered ominously as his cultured accent slipped. "I cannot 'elp it if the sod buys the wrong job."

"No, but you can help show him the right job. Or rather," she added, leaning back in her chair, "I can."

"No." Hurdy shook his head, his expression adamant. "You ain't gettin' in that easily."

"Why not, Hurdy?" she asked softly, and suddenly Marcus noticed that she had shifted position. All she had done was subtly stretched out her legs, maybe turned her shoulders, but suddenly the curve of Fantine's breasts pressed more tightly against the fabric of her scandalous bodice.

Marcus swallowed, remembering all too clearly how perfectly those breasts had fit in his hands not more than four hours ago. He saw Hurdy swallow as well, his gaze drawn to Fantine's assets. Then the lout's expression hardened as he pushed out of his chair.

"I ain't no backstreet cull, Fanny," he snapped, his back to her. "If I wanted you, I could 'ave your legs spread right now."

Though still wary, something inside Marcus relaxed at Hurdy's words. The criminal had not done Fantine any violence.

"Yes, you could do a lot of things to me," Fantine countered. "But then I would never, ever help you."

Hurdy spun around, his eyes like sharp chips of ice. "What do you want, Fanny?"

"I want in," she answered. "You are right. Rat is unimportant. But me, now, I am different. I am looking to my future. You and Ballast have been fighting over the docks for years, and nobody is getting stronger. You both need someone who can help you expand your business."

"You are that someone?" Hurdy asked.

"Who else do you know with a daft lord in her pocket, a rich guardian willing to go through windows for her—"

"'E is not yer guardian," cut in Hurdy.

"He is whoever I say he is," returned Fantine, her voice equally cold. Then she continued speaking before Marcus could object. "I know the peers, the rich nobs, and the easy culls. I know what to ask, when, and how." She stood, stepping around the table to confront Hurdy eye-to-eye. "You need me, Hurdy. And I need a new start."

Marcus stared at her, temporarily stunned. He had not expected this type of offer, and neither, apparently, had Hurdy. But both were considering it now, and well they should. From Hurdy's perspective, it was a good proposition, well reasoned and dead on the mark. The man did need some way to move up on Ballast, to expand beyond the rookeries to the real money of the upper crust. As for Fantine, anyone could see that her life as Rat would lead nowhere. She did need other options.

The main question now was whether Fantine was sincere. She certainly seemed so, but she was an excellent actress. Of course she would seem sincere. Her life depended on it.

The problem was that she seemed a little too sincere for Marcus. He wanted to believe she was simply finding out Teggie's identity. What better way than by infiltrating Hurdy's operations? But she was right. A connection between Hurdy and Fantine would be incredibly potent. As far as he could see, the only reason neither Hurdy nor Ballast had progressed in his crimes was that neither possessed the brainpower to do so.

With Fantine's help, that would no longer be a problem.

Marcus shook his head. She would not do that, he told himself. If nothing else, she would not betray Penworthy that way. But a little voice in his head questioned his conclusion.

In short, he simply did not know. And that thought terrified him.

For the first time since this began, Marcus lost the feeling that this was a game. A woman spy, an attempt on an MP, even their mad dash through Ballast's rookery had seemed more like a lark. Now it was real to him, perhaps because for the first time, Fantine seemed real.

After all, what were her choices? An honest living in hell's kitchen, scraping by off whatever government jobs Penworthy could find for her? Or a very wealthy, easy life with Hurdy?

Things did not look good for Penworthy or Wilberforce.

Marcus had to give her another option. He had to offer her wealth and comfort without having her sell herself to Hurdy.

He would have to make her his mistress.

Then there was no more time for thought as Hurdy turned his attention to Marcus, pushing Fantine aside as he crossed the room. "Wot about you? Wot do you think?" he asked brusquely.

Marcus frowned, not at all sure what he should answer. His own position here was tenuous. So he fell back on noblesse oblige.

"I forbid it," he said flatly.

"You cannot forbid anything," shot back Fantine.

"I shall lock you in…" His voice trailed away at her arch look. True, she could pick any lock and escape any prison he was likely to devise. "It is sinful, Fantine," he said sternly. "Your immortal soul will burn in hell forever."

"I be sore afraid," she mocked.

He had not expected her to listen. Everything he said was pure nonsense, made up for Hurdy's benefit, and to give Marcus time to think. But his best thought was inept at best. He stepped forward and grasped Fantine's arms in an earnest plea. "You have other options," he said softly. "Come away with me."

She looked up, and for a moment he detected a softening within her bronze eyes. Then it was gone. Her jaw firmed, her eyes grew cold, and she shoved him away.

"I choose Hurdy," she said, her voice angry and curt. She turned to the criminal. "As a test, let me meet with Teggie, explain a better solution."

"What solution?" That came from both Hurdy and Marcus at the same instant.

"It is better to discredit Wilberforce. Then he cannot be a martyr and the bill will fail. Let me get him in a compromising position, set him up in my bed with…with Nameless and a couple of others. Think of it. The upstanding and moral Wilberforce caught diddling a couple o' boys."

Marcus was thinking of it, and he cringed at the image. It would ruin the man, and that, he supposed, was exactly the point.

"I could do it," she pressed. "And I am the only one you know who could."

Hurdy frowned, apparently thinking hard. He reached for his brandy glass, but then it dangled forgotten from his fingertips. "Perhaps I could speak with him. Not right away. Ever'body is watching ever'body right now. But soon. I will talk with Teggie."

Fantine nodded. "It will work, Hurdy. I never go wrong."

His gaze sharped on Fantine. "Wot if it does go wrong or if Teggie does not change his mind? If you want in, you must prove yourself to me."

She lifted her chin, her manner as implacable as a winter storm. "How?"

"Kill Wilberforce yourself."

CHAPTER 8

"Agreed."

Fantine's one word seemed to echo in the night air, and she swallowed, wondering what she had just committed to. Playing with Ballast was one thing. Hurdy was an entirely new game. Without a son or any other obvious weaknesses, Hurdy was a lot trickier to manipulate. Despite what she had just said about him needing her, the truth was that he had the power. She didn't.

And his next words underscored the truth. "Betray me, Fanny, and there will not be enough o' you for even the fishes."

Fanny grimaced in a false show of bravado. "Ye break me bones, smash me face, rip me from for t' aft." Then she folded her arms and shifted into her cultured accent as she pushed her only advantage. "So when do I meet Teggie to explain my idea?"

Hurdy snorted his disdain. "You do not meet him at all. I will tell you what we decide."

Fantine shrugged. "Very well." Then she turned to leave, but Hurdy caught her arm, pulling her back. "What about 'im?" He gestured to Marcus, who stood stoically beside her. She almost smiled. Marcus was arrogant, naive, and foolhardy to boot, but he had risked his life to rescue her. No one had ever done that for her before, and she found herself softening toward him.

"Aw," she groaned, "leave the prig t' me. I'll see 'e gets wot 'e deserves."

She saw Marcus's eyes widen with apprehension, and this time she did smile. Just what tortures was he envisioning?

"Very well," returned Hurdy, echoing her earlier cultured phrasing and intonation. "Make sure he does not interfere again."

Fantine nodded and, smart man that he was, Marcus appeared appropriately frightened. She knew that was a lie. The man was too arrogant to understand his danger. Still, he made a good show of grabbing her arm and pulling her out the door.

Much to Fantine's relief, Hurdy let them leave, and soon she and Marcus were breathing deeply of the fetid dockside air. But she did not have much time to enjoy the dubious scents of the outside as Marcus began pushing her into a run.

"Slow down," she gasped. "I've had a long day."

"I don't want Hurdy to change his mind."

Fantine shrugged, even as she picked up her pace. "He won't stop us. But he will follow us."

There was a slight hitch in Marcus's step, but not enough to slow them down. "To see what our true relationship is?"

"To see what I do with you." She glanced sideways at his grim expression. "If I cannot control one daft lord, then I am of no use to him."

"Then we will both be killed. My title can't protect us from a knife in the dark."

Fantine nodded, surprised by his quick grasp of the situation. Then she abruptly slowed, turning to peer through the dark at him. "This is no longer a game to you, is it?"

She heard his soft inhale of surprise, and she knew she had guessed correctly. Then he began speaking, his words slow as if he were groping for them. "It has never been a game so much as a challenge."

"And now?" she prompted.

"Now it is important to me." He took a deep breath. "You are important to me."

Fantine felt her breath catch, wondering at his meaning. But then they were interrupted by a loud shout.

"Yer lordship!"

They both turned to see a light, unmarked coach pulling out of a narrow alleyway.

"Jacob!" Marcus cried, rushing toward the conveyance and pulling Fantine along with him. "How did you find me?"

"Giles told me. I thought ye might need a bit o' help."

"Bless you, Jacob, we do. Take us home."

"Home—" Fantine began, but he ignored her, pushing her inside the carriage without another word. Then he dropped down beside her and released a relieved sigh.

Though annoyed at his peremptory treatment, Fantine could not help but echo his sound. Marcus's carriage, though small, had cushions that could ease an angel's arse. The rich velvet seemed to enfold her in softness, and the bricks, though nearly cold, provided some warmth to her toes.

Still, she had to voice her fear. "Hurdy will know where you live and who you are."

"Good," responded Marcus flatly. "Then perhaps he will think twice about killing me."

Fantine nodded, agreeing with the sentiment. Then, as Marcus settled a rug about her legs, she allowed herself to close her eyes, relishing the unaccustomed feel of luxury.

"If only you had waited ten minutes," she said softly. "Then I would at least have eaten."

"You will eat with me." It was not a question or even an invitation, but a simple statement of fact. "It is the least I can do after ruining your meal."

There was a note of irony in his words as he subtly reminded her that he had risked his life to save her. The least she could do was accept the meal he offered.

"You are tired," he continued.

"My head hurts," she returned without opening her eyes. "They clubbed me pretty good, and I didn't even hear them."

"You cannot be alert all the time." He was a disembodied voice, drifting easily past her defenses, easing her soul. "You are safe now." Then he settled her head against his shoulder. She went willingly, too tired to argue. "Rest," he urged.

And she did.

Roast mutton.

It could not be. She could not be smelling roast mutton.

But she was.

Then her stomach growled as if underlining the thought.

Fantine roused herself, pushing upright on...a bed? A bed with silk sheets and a feather down pillow. She dropped back down, rolling over and burying her face in the wondrous softness with a groan of pure delight.

"You need not get up now," drawled a voice from behind her. "My cupboards are well stocked. There will be plenty of food when you wake."

Fantine edged around the coverings, peering through one eye at Marcus. He looked so handsome. The glow of the fire bathed his face in a gentle light, softening his harsh angles. Glancing around, she saw a large and airy room filled with the colors of spring—green and gold. She lay in a huge four-poster bed and to her right, just between the bed and the fire, sat Marcus at a table. A well-stocked table. A table covered with more succulent dishes than she could eat in a week.

Her mouth watered.

"Where am I?" Her voice felt coarse in her throat, and she swallowed, grimacing at the bitter taste in her mouth.

Marcus stood up, poured water into a glass, and brought it to her. "This is a guest room in my house. How is your head?"

She sat up, taking the water from him and swallowing it down greedily. "Much better," she lied. In truth, it pounded like the very devil.

"Would you like some more water?"

She shook her head and pointed to a bottle near the roast mutton. "Wine, please."

He nodded and filled her glass to the top. His compassionate expression told her he knew she wanted to dull the pain. She didn't care. This was one time when drink would clear her head, assuming it took away some of the throbbing.

"Would you care for something to eat?"

She nodded dumbly, hating herself for how slowly her wits were returning. She slid her feet out from under the covers, only now realizing she was not in her maid's uniform. Instead she wore a negligee of rich burgundy satin. It was a cool, sensuous delight as it moved with her, but all she could do was frown at it.

"My housekeeper changed your clothing." He gestured to a large closed wardrobe. "My sister also keeps some things there if you wish something different." When she did not respond, he held out a chair for her at the low table near the fire. "You should eat something."

She shook her head and held out her glass. "More wine, please."

He took her glass, refilled it, then set it near her plate on the table. The implication was clear. She would not be allowed to drink any more until she sat down at the table.

She grimaced. "You are being manipulative."

He smiled at her, his expression too innocent. "I thought I was being a gracious host."

"You are that, too." She spoke grudgingly, not meaning to be surly, but she felt too disoriented to match wits with him. Yet here she was, drinking his wine and about to eat at his table when she had no control over the situation whatsoever.

As if reading her thoughts, he smiled as he helped her to her seat. "You are quite safe, you know. I will not harm you."

She wrinkled her nose. "I never trust anyone who says that."

He leaned forward, cutting up the succulent meat with a steady hand. She nearly groaned at his excruciatingly slow movements, especially since she wanted to rip at the food with her bare hands.

"I doubt you trust anyone," he said.

She shrugged. "Actually, I trust a great number of people."

"Like?"

"Nameless, for one. And his friends. As long as I keep feeding them. As long as they keep supplying me with information for Penworthy."

As she spoke, Marcus served her a huge portion of mutton along with healthy measures of every other sumptuous dish. Fantine could do little more than smile her gratitude as she picked up her fork.

They spoke little as she ate. In fact, Fantine spoke not at all, spending her time totally on her meal. She took care to maintain her manners, but it was a strain. After her first bite, she became absolutely ravenous, and she could barely keep herself from shoveling the food in like a starveling.

Meanwhile, Marcus kept up a leisurely prattle of no consequence until finally lapsing into silence. It took her embarrassingly long to notice the silence.

"I'm afraid I'm not much company tonight," she apologized.

"On the contrary, you are a perfect companion—beautiful and appreciative."

She sent him a wry glance. "That sounds like a lapdog."

"Certainly not," he said, obviously insulted. Then he reached for her, tracing the curve of her cheek with a long, slow stroke. "You are the most beautiful woman in the world."

Fantine wanted to laugh. How many men said the same thing every night to a thousand different women? The least he could be was original. But she did not laugh. She couldn't. Because the way he said it made her believe it was true.

She swallowed, nervous and excited. "Marcus—"

"You fascinate me, Fantine. I do not know why or how, but I can think of nothing but you."

He pulled her close for a kiss. She went easily, mesmerized by the clear blue light of his eyes. When their lips met, his touch was tender, but no less powerful, robbing her of breath as he tasted first her lips, then deeper within her mouth. When he pulled away, he gazed down at her, and she could only stare back in a daze.

"I do not like the way you live," he whispered. "Buying friendship, scurrying about the sewers, in constant danger from thieves and curs." He stroked her face, tracing the edge of her lips. "I want you as my mistress. You will live like a queen, have servants, a luxurious home, whatever you want."

Fantine blinked at him. The wine, the food, even the peaceful surroundings had lulled her. But she should have known. Men like Marcus thought of her in only one way.

She pulled away in disgust, angry with him for asking and with herself for not seeing it coming.

"No." The word fell like a dead weight from her lips, but she said it nevertheless. Then she pushed him away with enough strength to rock him backward in his chair.

That he seemed totally shocked by her refusal only added to the insult. "But why?" he asked.

She lifted her chin, remembering the sweaty men in her mother's greenroom. The hands, the smells, and the heat still repulsed her. "I will not become my mother," she said, her voice firm, her gaze steady. "And I do not trust you."

He matched her gaze, silently testing her statement. When she did not waver, he suddenly thrust himself away from the table, the scrape of his chair loud in the room. "Hell and damnation, Fantine, I have mucked through the sewers with you, flown through a window for you, even sat through hours of inquisition at Lord Harris's because of you. If I meant you harm, don't you think I would have throttled you by now?"

"I am sure your brother trusted you and look what happened."

He froze where he stood, and Fantine bit her lip, realizing she'd been unfair. Yes, he had insulted her, but she should not have struck back so viciously.

"I am sorry," she whispered. "I should not have said that."

"No," he agreed, "you shouldn't have."

She sighed. "Bloody hell, Marcus, I am tired, but I am not blind. I do not wish to be your mistress, and no amount of excellent food and beautiful clothes will change that. Why can you not accept that?"

Suddenly, he leaned down over her, large and dominating. "Because I wish to know why."

She shrugged and looked away. She had nothing more to say.

As if sensing her thoughts, he changed his posture. Sitting back down, he poured himself more wine. "What do you know about Geoffrey?"

"That you sacrificed…" She bit her lip, knowing that was not true. "That you sent your brother back to England, alone and unprotected. That you saved England, but Geoffrey died."

He was prepared for her answer. The clench of his jaw told her that much. But he still reacted to her bald statement, bringing his glass to his lips with a shaky hand. Even seeing how effected he was, she could not leave it alone.

"Do you not understand my fears? Your loyalty to your country supersedes your feelings for anyone, even your brother. I am less than nothing to you."

His eyes widened in surprise. "My loyalty to England has nothing to do with you."

"Given the choice, you will always choose England. Those I trust will sacrifice everything for me, and I for them. No vague loyalty to king and country interferes with that."

Suddenly she felt the weight of his keen stare. "Do you intend to make me choose? Do you plan to join Boney in France?"

She toyed with the food on her plate. "England has given me precious little to revere. If one is not rich or titled, there is little to respect."

"How can you say that?" he asked. Shock echoed in every line of his face.

"Do not misunderstand," she continued. "I am fond of England. She is the land of my birth. But England also allows Ballast and Hurdy to rule the rookeries, ignores poor girls forced into whoring, and abandons boys to thievery."

"You have other options!"

"As your mistress? Penworthy's salvation? Why must I sell myself to the highest bidder? Why can I not have an education in medicine or shipbuilding?"

"Do you wish to build ships? To be a doctor?" The thought clearly astounded him. "But you are a woman!"

"And why should I be loyal to a country that so limits me?"

He set down his glass with a click. "It is the same the world over, Fantine. You cannot think that England should change just because you wish it."

She nearly laughed. "No, I am not that naive. But you think everything is just as it should be. You and I see the world through very different eyes, my lord."

There. She had explained as clearly as she could. But inside her heart, she wept. She already knew she would regret her choice. She was giving up wealth, comfort, and passion. For what?

"You are throwing everything away because you will not see the world as it is." Marcus's expression was fierce. "You are throwing me away because you wish to be a man."

"I do not want what you offer. I do not trust you." Once again, her words remained firm, but inside she crumbled. Was she so angry to give up, out of pride, everything she could have?

His eyes narrowed as he studied her. "Whom are you trying to convince?" he challenged.

Herself, of course. But she would not admit it to him. So she pushed away from the table, turning her back as she searched for something else to focus her energies on. But there was nothing else, no one except Marcus. Then she felt him behind her, like a flame, heating her body from behind.

"You are right," he whispered, heating her ear. "I should not have pressed you now. Come." He started leading her forward, and she took two steps before she thought to resist.

"Where are we going?"

He turned, a mischievous look on his face. "To teach you that I am not the ogre you have painted me." Then, before she could object, he scooped her up in his arms and carried her to the bed, impatiently pushing the blankets aside.

Fantine released a surprised squeak, but he silenced her with a swift, fierce kiss on the lips. "Hush. I have no designs on your virtue."

She raised her eyebrows, knowing he lied, but did not have time to object as he settled her down on the bed.

"Come now. Turn over," he said as he pressed her downward.

Fantine tensed, knowing her burgundy negligee was a flimsy barrier at best. "What do you want?"

"Lie on your stomach. Trust me."

His smile was so reassuring that she did as he bade. She told herself it was because she felt too tired to fight, but she knew the real reason was to escape the lazy heat that warmed his eyes. She could not think when he looked at her that way.

"I warn you," she said, her voice muffled by the thick pillows. "I am not defenseless." She was bluffing, of course. The wine, the food, and the stresses of the day were already taking their toll. Lying flat on the bed, she felt too boneless to raise a finger, much less fight him.

Still, he must have taken her comment at face value because he responded sincerely, his voice rich with amusement. "Believe me, I know you have claws."

She smiled. Image was half the battle. Then he did something that forced all thoughts from her head. He put his hands on her shoulders and began kneading the muscles there.

"What are you doing?" she whispered.

"It is medicinal. My valet learned it in India."

His touch deepened, probing into her flesh, pushing out her pain as easily as if he lifted away a stone. His hands were most thorough as he worked down her spine before easing around her hips, his thumbs pressing deeply into the small of her back. She groaned, feeling both nervous and wonderful.

"Relax," he coaxed. "I will stop any time you wish."

She did not want him to stop. She knew what he intended. He could not seduce her with words, but he could with his touch. She had refused his cold business offer, but she was powerless against the sensuous textures of silk and heated flesh.

So she succumbed. Without even a token objection, she closed her eyes and accepted whatever would come. Before long, time ceased to have any meaning. He rubbed her legs and her feet, his touch firm and assured. When he gently rolled her onto her back, she helped him. When he began rubbing her shoulders, easing the nightgown down her arms, she made no demur. The silk slipped lower and lower until finally her breasts sprang free of the material, seemingly eager for his ministrations.

He continued as he had been doing, focusing on the muscles beneath the skin, using his thumbs to elongate the sinews. But as he worked, his fingers brushed ever closer to her taut nipples, until finally, he stroked over them.

She gasped, but it was only a small sound, lost amid the feelings he stirred. He repeated the motion, this time pinching the tender flesh slightly with his fingers. She moaned and arched her back slightly, hoping he would do it again.

He did. Again and again, his hands becoming firmer, more bold as he caressed her breasts.

Then he slid lower.

Though her breasts ached with longing he kept up the assault, spanning her waist with his hands before completely divesting her of her gown.

He spoke not a word, and neither did she. The only sound was her tiny gasps, her soft whimpers of hunger. Then he pressed his thumbs to the top of her thighs, barely brushing the secret folds between.

She bucked beneath him, feeling as if a spring had been released. Her legs were already open and hungry for his touch, so he leaned down to kiss her, not on her mouth, but on her belly, which trembled beneath his lips. She felt his body, lean and hard, as he stretched up along the left side of her. It was not until she felt the ticklish brush of his chest hairs that she realized he had stripped off his shirt.

Opening her eyes in surprise, she gazed at the broad expanse of his shoulders. The candlelight sculpted his lean form with golden light and shadows. Unable to stop herself, she touched his body gently. His skin was soft beneath the dusting of blond hair, and she gloried in the different textures over the corded strength of his muscles.

She looked up at him then, trying to meet his gaze, but seeing only dark pools of shadow. She moved her hand higher, tracing the coarse line of his chin, the hard lift to his cheek, until finally resting on the dark blush of his lips. Never before had she been able to simply touch a man as she willed.

Then he lowered his head and kissed her mouth.

His kiss was slow, measured, patient, but she could feel the tension that gripped him, the power he restrained for her sake. He wanted more. She felt his desire like a hot brand against her thigh, and without conscious thought, she rubbed against him.

A groan rumbled through his body as his tongue pushed deep within her. She allowed his entrance, absorbing him, reveling in him with a wild abandon completely foreign to her nature.

Then he pulled back. It was a momentary pause, a second or two when he looked down at her, his eyes hungry, his lips curled in a triumphant smile. In that instant, she remembered other looks, other men. The creaking rhythm of her mother's bed echoed in her thoughts. Over and over, night after night, while Fantine hated her. Hated him. Hated every part of that life.

Yet here she was lying naked beneath Marcus, her body still wet and aching. Twenty minutes ago, she'd flatly refused to be his mistress. Twelve hours before, she'd sworn never to let him touch her again. Yet here she lay, a whore just like her mother.

Marcus lowered his lips to her, kissing her neck with tiny bites that sizzled along her skin. But everything was different.

"Now I know why my mother was so eager to sell herself," she said, her voice crude.

He reared backward, his body jerking as if slapped. "Is that what this is to you? Just a…" His words stopped as if choked off.

"A dockside diddle?" she asked in her coarsest accent. "Wot else could it be? Ye ain't about t' offer marriage. Oi suppose ye ain't expecting t' pay, but then ye gave me dinner an' wine. Oi's guessin' this'll make us abo' even."

If she thought he was angry before, it was nothing compared to now. She felt his fist twist on her belly. Never before had she seen such dark and potent anger, and suddenly she was afraid as she never had been around Ballast or Hurdy.

"Marcus?" She hated the tremor in her voice, but she could not stop it.

"Do not cringe from me now," he said softly. "You have stated the rules here, not I." Then he reached forward, grabbing a handful of her hair. "If a dockside diddle is all you want, then it shall be all you get."

She had no time to react as he suddenly threw himself on top of her. She gasped as his weight pushed her into the mattress. His hips were hard, his desire blatant as he unerringly found her center despite the barrier of his clothing.

It was both terrifying and wonderful, and she spread her legs without thought, drawing up her knees to pull him deeper.

He groaned, the sound guttural and anguished. He thrust against her once, hard and fast. She met the motion with a push of her own, unable to stop herself.

Then suddenly, he spun away. He threw himself off of her to land with a thud on his feet, his back to her. She heard his breathing, heavy in the still night, and it was matched by her own shuddering inhalation.

"I want you, Fantine," he said harshly. "I want to bury myself in you every night until you stop haunting my dreams." He slammed his fist against the table, rattling the cutlery. "But I cannot buy you. God help me, I cannot do it that way."

Fantine pulled her legs together, pulling the blanket over her body as she stared at his rigid back. "What is it you want?" Her cockney accent had slipped away, but she did not care. "You cannot wish for marriage. Not with me."

Suddenly he turned around, his expression like that of a wolf, lean and hungry, but he held back, and she saw the muscles in his arms ripple with the effort.

"I already told you. I want you as my mistress, Fantine. Let me find you a place to live. I will shower you with finery, jewels, anything. I will come to you whenever I can."

She looked at him, shaking her head, not in answer, but as she fought to understand. "And that is not buying me? How is that different from tonight? From a tumble against a wet wall in the rookeries?"

"I do not know!" he cried out. "I only know that it is different."

"No," she returned. "It is not." She pushed the hair out of her eyes, ashamed of the tears that wet her fingertips. "Why do you want me so badly, Marcus? You are everywhere I go, touching me, using my body against me like some conqueror. I am not a disease to be purged from your body. Nor am I a salve for your pain. Why can you not just leave me alone?"

"Because I need you. I do not know why, but I do."

She stared at him, blinking away the tears that made her

vision hazy. "Why cannot someone want me for just me? I am not Penworthy's passport to heaven or Wilberforce's savior or even your escape from pain. I am merely myself. Until someone can see me as I am, I shall stay in the rookeries and make my own life as my own mistress."

He stepped toward her, dropping to one knee as he grasped her hand. The posture was heartfelt and lover-like, and Fantine flinched at the sight. He looked as if he would propose, and yet she knew the truth.

"You deserve a better life," he urged.

Fantine lifted her chin, her memories of her mother's life clear in her mind. "So I should become your slave, imprisoned in lush finery, dependent upon your beck and call, forced to submit to whatever you wish, whenever you wish?"

"It would not be like that!"

She shrugged, her feelings dying away as she heard the familiar words. Every protector, every man who wished to enter her mother's bed, had said the same words, voiced the same thought. With me, they claimed, it will be different.

Except that it never was different. Unless it was worse.

"I will not be owned by anyone."

"Sweet heaven, Fantine—"

"No!" She jerked out of the bed, pulling open the wardrobe and snatching up her newly pressed and repaired maid's clothing. She pulled it on with quick, efficient movements. "I cannot do it. You are cruel to ask me to."

She did not look up until she was fully clothed.

And alone.

CHAPTER 9

Marcus heard her leave. He doubted anyone else could have heard her steps or the soft thud of the door as she left. She was as silent as a whisper, but he seemed to be attuned to her every movement, seeing it in his mind even if she was not before his eyes.

Her skin would be flushed, not with passion now, but anger. At herself for offering him her body. At him for wanting to have it all the time.

He had his own full supply of fury as well. He should have just taken her. She would have enjoyed it. Sweet heaven, her legs had been wrapped around him, drawing him to her. He closed his eyes, groaning at the memory of her body gripping him tight.

He was a fool. A besotted fool because he still wanted her even though she had left him, laughed off his money and his passion. And for what? A life in the rookeries.

Until someone can see me as I am, I shall stay in the rookeries and make my own life as my own mistress.

He didn't understand her at all. Whom did he want but her? Whom did he see but her? What did she want? It was not money. He had offered to shower her with jewels. It was not his title. She knew he couldn't marry her. He couldn't do that to his family. And yet she didn't even want passion. She'd had to be cornered, threatened, and seduced before her desire flowed like a river.

Damn! Why had he stopped? Perhaps it was vanity, but he wanted her to choose him, to knowingly come into his arms.

But how? What power did he have over her that she would pick him over her current life? What could he do that would bring her to him?

"Just 'ow long do you intends t' sleep, Fanny?"

Fantine rolled over in her bed and groaned, refusing to look at the redheaded girl pestering her.

"Aw, please, Fanny. Jes a little time. Please?"

Fantine grimaced as she peered out from under her pillow. She had made it home just before dawn and had collapsed on her bed. Her sleep had been restless, haunted by sultry dreams that left her achy, uncomfortable, and randy. Now only a few hours later, the window in her tiny room was filled with sunshine and Louise, a pesky twelve-year-old, was intent on rousting.

She sighed, stretching underneath her covers.

"Feelin' stiff?" asked the girl.

Fantine shook her head, cataloguing her ailments with morbid curiosity. Firmly ignoring aches associated with her erotic dreams, she landed on three identifiable and acceptable pains: Her feet hurt, her head ached, and she was very, very thirsty.

"Water." She croaked out the word, and Louise was quick to accommodate. Her tiny body leaped across the room to a pitcher of tepid water on the floor. She pirouetted once, then filled a cup before bounding back. Anyone else would have spilled liquid from here to the docks, but Louise balanced the cup flawlessly before presenting it to Fantine.

"Master Fouchet wants more money," Louise said.

Fantine let her head drop back onto her pillow, understanding now why her friend had woken her this morning. "Cannot your father pay the dancing master for once?" she said. "He must see how good you are."

Louise shook her head. "All 'e sees is that you ain't paid yer bill in months an' Fanny ain't been working in the pub neither. The last thing 'e wants is to lose me too. Somebody's got t' serve the drinks."

"What happened to the money you made in the last show?"

"It went t' make the costume fer the new performance. Remember?"

"I remember," Fantine said dully. In truth, she did not recall a thing about it, but Louise was the most practical girl she'd even known. If she spent her money on something other than a costume, it was probably more dance training or as a bribe to get into another ballet. Either way, it was money well spent.

"Take the money in the pocket of the maid's dress," Fantine said. "And tell your father I will work tonight." She would have to, she thought sadly as her stomach rumbled in hunger. It was the only way she would eat tonight.

Louise wandered over to the maid's gown and made a show of rooting through the pockets. Fantine sighed, seeing through her friend's deception. The girl had probably already pocketed the money while Fantine slept.

"Never mind, Louise. Come tell me what you have heard."

"Aw!" she cried with an excited little hop. "It be all over the rookeries that Rat is a girl! I figure a week afore Ballast figures you as Fanny the barmaid too, an' then wot? Father won't 'elp you. He's got enough trouble wi'out fighting Ballast."

Fantine let her eyes drift shut. The walls were closing in, her options slowly dwindling. Ballast would kill her because she'd escaped him one too many times, and Sprat would not help until she got him into Harrow. Hurdy had given her a few days' grace, but that was all. If he found out that she'd been doing work for the Crown, he would kill her for sure. He would know she was using him to discover Teggie's identity.

She could go to Penworthy. Her father could get her out of London if necessary, but the rookeries were her life. What would she do if she was not here? Gardening and stitchery were not for her. Plus, how would Louise pay for dance lessons or Nameless and his gang get food?

Then there was her obligation to Wilberforce. She had promised to stop Teggie. She could not just run off and leave the MP to his fate.

"Tell me about the ball."

Fantine blinked. She had forgotten Louise's presence. "Hmm? Oh, it was nice," she said blandly. "There were lots of beautiful ladies and handsome gentlemen. They danced the night away." She pushed aside the covers, groaning as her muscles protested the movement.

"Fanny!" Louise exclaimed. "Tell me it all."

Fantine spun around, exhaustion making her curt. "It was the same as every other ball."

Louise narrowed her eyes. "No," she said slowly, "it was not. The daft lord was there." Louise sashayed over, her face dimpled with delight. "Do you like 'im? Does 'e make yer toes curl when you kiss?"

"What would you know of toes curling, missy?"

Louise's face became dreamy. "Only wot I see and 'ear. Aw, come on, tell me about it."

Fantine sighed, knowing she would have no peace until she explained reality to her romantic friend. So she plopped back on her bed and stated the facts baldly. "He kissed me and he touched me, and then he asked me to be his mistress."

"Coo!" Louise's eyes were filled with wonder. "Imagine! A lord's fancy piece!"

Fantine gritted her teeth, appalled by her friend's reaction. "But I cannot do that! He wants to keep me in a room, always at his beck and call. Think, Louise, what if you got a protector who wanted to keep you from dancing. What would you do?"

The girl's face split into a sudden impish grin. "Why, but that be part o' the deal from the outset. Coo, love, jes make it clear from the beginning wot you want. Then milk 'im fer the jewels an' rent, an' in a few months you'll be rich!"

Fantine shook her head. "I cannot."

"Wot else can ye do? Ballast will be 'ere soon and wi'out money for a new place—"

"No!" Fantine pushed off of the bed. "I will think of something else." As she paced the room, she felt the girl's gaze following her. The feeling became heavier until finally Fantine spun in anger. "What?"

Louise's gaze did not waver. "You be in love with 'im."

"Pray do not be ridiculous," she snapped.

"Well, you like 'im a lot." Louise fell forward on the bed, kicking up her heels behind her and dropping her head on her hands. "Did 'e bring you to completion?"

Fantine actually stumbled, she was so shocked. "What?"

Louise smiled. "You said 'e touched you, an' Mary says a girl always falls fer the man 'oo brings 'er t' completion for the first time."

Fantine did not know how to respond, so she turned away. "You spend too much time with Mary."

Louise stiffened. "Mary is a good whore, an' she says I cain learn a lot from 'er."

"You will be a dancer."

"An' unless I get more money t' bribe me way into the company, I will 'ave to whore too."

"But—"

"Coo, Fanny!" interrupted the girl, clearly exasperated. "Whoring is th' only thing for girls like us. Might as well be wi' someone rich 'oo can make us 'appy."

Fantine dropped into her only chair and stared at the cold fire grate. "You are too cynical for your age," she said softly.

Louise snorted in disgust. "An' I never thought you were this foolish. 'Oo is the daft lord? 'As 'e got a title?"

"Chadwick will be an earl some day."

"Coo," she said, shaking her head. "An earl." Then she abruptly hopped up off the bed, her expression canny. "Do not forget Father wants 'is rent," she called.

Fanny sat up, warning bells ringing in her head. "Louise?" But it was too late. The girl was gone.

"My lord, a young…miss wishes an audience."

Marcus handed his hat to his butler and scanned the empty drawing room to his right. "Who is it?"

Norton merely raised one impeccable eyebrow. "As to that, sir, she would not say. I have put her in the rose parlor." He gestured to the parlor in the back of the house.

Marcus frowned, impatient with this latest distraction. He had just spent the last two hours with his sister, alternately begging, cajoling, and threatening, only to be met with grudging success. It had been exhausting and had cost him quite a bit of his pride, but with luck, his plan would succeed.

Now all he wanted was to find Fantine, not waste time on some lost miss. But there was no hope for it. The girl was here, and the sooner he removed her from his home, the better.

"Very well," he said as he headed for the parlor.

"Shall I send for tea?" Norton inquired.

"Heavens, no," Marcus exclaimed. "I doubt the lady will be staying that long."

He strode purposefully toward the back of the house, schooling his expression into a severe frown. But as he pushed open the door, he felt his jaw go slack with astonishment.

There, silently spinning in his parlor, was a young girl with a diminutive figure and shocking red hair. She stopped as soon as the door opened, dropping lightly to her feet. She had taken pains with her attire, no doubt dressing up in her mother's clothing since the bodice gaped above her modest chest. Her skirt was hiked up to reveal trim, youthful ankles nearly blue with the chill.

"Good Lord, girl, where are your stockings?" he asked.

She flushed slightly, then stepped forward, watching him with bright hazel eyes. "Hello, guv," she said in what would have been a low, sultry voice had she been a few years older. As it was, it sounded more like a girl with a cold than an alluring woman. "I understand you are in need o' a mistress."

Marcus frowned. He had sent Paolina her congè the very day he'd met Fantine. But that did not explain how this...urchin knew of his circumstances. He stepped farther into the room, settling himself on a leather chair as he spoke.

"What makes you think I am seeking someone?"

He had no more than sunk into the cushion when the child literally bounded across the room to drop neatly into his lap. "Wot does it matter, ducks? I be 'ere an' you be wantin'." Then she began wiggling in a most inappropriate manner.

"Please!" He nearly shot straight up out of his chair. As it was, he simply threw her off his lap. She landed sweetly on her feet in an oddly balletic maneuver, then turned coyly and gave him a wink. "Fanny said yer might loike me."

Marcus leaned forward. "Fantine sent you?"

"Oh!" she exclaimed, blushing a pure innocent red that was quite becoming despite the layers of powder. "Yes, Fantine sent me." She made an effort to smooth out her accent. "But, why should we speak o' 'er? Tell me wot you loike in bed, ducks."

"What!" he exclaimed, though the sound came out more as a squeak than a word.

"I cain do wotever you wants." She stretched one leg above her. Then, in an amazing feat of agility, she spun around and would have landed on his lap if he had not jumped out of the way.

"Guv!" she exclaimed in dismay. Marcus ignored her, moving to the sideboard. He definitely needed a brandy. She started toward him again, but he held up a hand, his expression stern.

"What is your name?"

"Louise," she answered.

"Very well, Louise, despite what Fantine may have told you, I am not in need of a mistress just now."

He could see the disappointment in her whole body. She drooped, her entire frame melting in disappointment.

"But," he hastened, "I do need some information. Perhaps we could make an arrangement."

She straightened, and he caught the flash of interest in her eyes. "Wot does you need? I knows all sorts o' things."

"I am sure you do," he said. He took a step forward, intending to return to his chair, but on second thought decided to remain standing. She was much too quick and way too determined. The last thing he wanted was for anyone else to see him being fondled by a girl barely into puberty.

"What do you know of Fantine?" he asked.

She wrinkled her pert nose. "Aw, she will no' be yer mistress, guv. I talked and talked to 'er, but she ain't never wanted that sort o' life."

"Never?" Marcus pressed.

Louise shook her head. "Never." Then she hopped off the couch and pirouetted toward him. "I, on the other 'and—"

"Stay right there, young lady!" Marcus cringed at his own tone. He sounded just like his father. Louise merely shrugged, then minced about the room in tiny, intricate steps while Marcus tried to keep a large piece of furniture between himself and her.

"How do you know Fantine?"

"She lives wi' me."

Marcus took a deep breath. At last, someone who knew exactly where he could find Fantine. "Could you take me to her?"

Louise turned her shrug into a stylized gesture to the sky. "Fer a price."

Marcus nodded, already reaching into his pocket for some coins. He tossed her a guinea. "Where and when?"

"Depends on wot you want 'er for."

"I do not understand."

"If you wants 'er as Rat, she be out an' about wi' Nameless now. If you wants 'er as Fanny, she'll be at me father's pub tonight 'elping wi' the customers. If you wants 'er in yer bed..." Louise did a shimmy that slipped her bodice lower on one shoulder. "Then, you best think about me."

Marcus shook his head and used two fingers stretched across the back of a chair to gingerly slip her clothing back onto her shoulder. "I want to see Fantine. Alone."

"Awake or asleep?" She moved abruptly so that he suddenly found his fingers brushing the side of the padding that was supposed to be her breast. He pulled back as if burned.

"Awake," he said firmly.

She shrugged. "She ain't never alone an' awake."

Marcus frowned. Never alone except when she slept? She did not seem as if she would crave constant company. In fact, he got the distinct impression that, like him, she valued silence. "What is she doing all that time?"

Louise twisted sideways, folding her arms irritably across her chest before balancing up on her toes. "An' when is she supposed t' be alone wi'out workin'? She be two months late on t' rent now an' I swear Nameless an' 'is boys eat more than a brigade. 'Ow she going t' pay fer that wi'out working?"

Marcus leaned forward, resting his arms against the back of the leather chair while his mind raced. "Is Fantine in debt?"

"Everyone be in debt in the rookeries."

"How much does she owe? Is it more than she has?" He stepped around the chair. "Take me to her room."

Finally, for the first time, Louise froze. "Why should I?"

"What do you want?"

She grinned. "More than you 'ave, guv. But for now I will settle for dance lessons. Lots an' lots an' lots o' lessons!"

"Done," he said despite his surprise. He'd expected demands for money, jewelry, even pretty clothing. But dance lessons? That was so very...practical. Money would eventually disappear, but the training he could buy her might save her from a hard and harsh life. "Were dance lessons Fantine's idea?"

The girl's nod turned into a stylized bow. "Father does no' know, but she 'as been paying for lessons with Master Fouchot. She says I should look for something other than whoring."

"She is right."

Louise lifted up on her toes before arching into a back-bend. "I think I'd like being a mistress—all them fancy jewels an' the like. Though I cain't think I would want the men about the pub. Mary, she be the pub whore, she says it be easy money, an' they ain't so bad if'n ye plug yer nose...."

She continued to chat while Marcus discovered he quite liked the girl. He even bargained over her fee with relish. It was not until he opened the door and nearly tripped over Bentley that he realized his staff was likely agog at the thought of their priggish master bargaining with a child prostitute. He ought to be mortified.

Instead, he grinned at his secretary's austere expression. "Bentley. Excellent. Please cancel all my appointments for the next few days. I find I shall be quite occupied. Good day."

Then he did something entirely foreign to his nature. He winked at his man of affairs. When that stiff gentleman forgot himself so much as to let his jaw drop, Marcus actually laughed.

Out loud.

CHAPTER 10

Nothing.

Five hours of trudging through the London streets. Five hours of Rat talking with every whore, sot, and street rat. Five long, wearisome hours, and Fantine had learned absolutely nothing about Teggie. Waiting for word from Hurdy would drive her mad, but her own investigation had proved fruitless.

And now she had another nine hours of work in the pub beneath her flat.

She groaned as she sidestepped a retching drunkard. Right now, life as a pampered mistress tempted her as nothing else. Just the thought of resting in a hot, perfumed bath made her knees go weak. She would have a glass of expensive champagne nearby and a maid holding a heated towel. Then Marcus would come kiss her, caressing her face, her shoulders, her...

She slammed down hard on her thoughts. She knew where they led. Before long, she would be running straight toward Marcus and the life he offered, despite what it would cost her. It was a useless path and a useless life, and she would not do it.

No matter how much part of her longed for it.

With a dispirited sigh, she climbed the steps to her tiny room on the third floor. She pushed open the door and encountered both her greatest wish and her deepest fear.

Marcus.

He was real this time, not some vivid image brought up from her overactive imagination. His broad shoulders and warm smile dominated her tiny room, and she was relieved to finally confront him in the flesh rather than as a ghost in her thoughts. Still, she dealt with the living man the same way she handled the specter.

"Go away."

"'Ello, Rat," chirped Louise, as she rooted through Fantine's stack of whore's clothing. The girl held up a particularly thin dress of brilliant scarlet. "Guess wot. I am t' be 'is lordship's mistress!"

Fantine did not respond except to feel a chill invade her body. Marcus and Louise? The cold fury was enough to shake her out of her stupor. But then Marcus abruptly spun around.

"You are not, and well you know it!" he snapped at the girl.

"We 'ave an arrangement," continued Louise to Fantine. "'E will pay for me lessons!"

Fantine turned her gaze to Marcus, noting his flushed cheeks and his agitated expression, while Louise sashayed about, the scarlet dress swinging with her movements.

"It were just a one-timer. Or maybe…" Louise shot a coy glance at Marcus. "Whenever 'e 'as something 'e wants. But for that, I gets a year o' lessons!"

"Louise!" Marcus snapped as he hastily turned toward Fantine. "Do not even think that I would take this…this child as my mistress—"

"Child!" exploded Louise, thoroughly insulted.

Fantine closed her eyes, relief mixing with weariness. She dropped heavily onto her bed. "Go away."

"Yes, Louise," Marcus said firmly. "Go away."

The girl huffed as only a preadolescent can, then did a pirouette out the door.

"Good Lord," he said, as he firmly closed the door behind her, "is she always so energetic?"

"Actually," Fantine responded dully, "she seems a little tired today."

"As do you."

Fantine opened her eyes. "Oh, la," she said in her dockside accent. "You do know 'ow t' turn a girl's 'ead." She stood up slowly, pulling a long dagger from her shirtsleeve. "Now get out."

Marcus did not move. "I need to talk to you."

"Out!" She waved her knife threateningly at him. She did not want him so near. Not when she felt so tired, so vulnerable.

"I have been many things around you," Marcus said casually as he leaned against the door. "Amazed, outraged, embarrassed, even horrified. But I have never been frightened. Not by you. I do not think you will hurt me. You would have done so long before now."

"Do not be so sure, guv," she said. He moved for her, intending to grab the knife. It was a quick movement, but she had seen it coming. Without thinking, she threw and had the satisfaction of seeing her knife sink just where she aimed.

In the wall, a bare inch from his nose.

She smiled, expecting to hear an outraged diatribe from him. Then he would storm out of her room without a backward glance.

Instead, he grinned at her as he pulled the dagger out of the wall. "I knew you would not hurt me. Now, may we discuss a few things, please?"

Fantine looked at him with surprise. Could he truly have read her so well? She studied him, seeing determination in the hard set to his jaw and the implacable gaze in his blue eyes. How much could she fight him?

The answer was painfully clear. She could not. It was not that he was so handsome he made her knees go weak. He was, but he had always been so. It was not that he had come through their adventures together stronger, more

noble, and more human than any of the peerage had a right
to be. He had, but she had given him her grudging respect a
long time ago.

It was simply that he was too determined, too unwilling
to leave her alone. Expediency suggested she should let
him have his say.

At least that is what she told herself. It could not possibly
be that his presence, his voice, even the gentleness in his
gestures were comforting on a day when she felt she had
not a prayer of solving half the problems she faced.

"What do you wish to say, Marcus?"

"Only that you are in trouble. Louise told me you owe
rent. How long have you been feeding Nameless and his
gang of boys?"

She shrugged. "As long as they needed food, and I
needed information. It is a good trade."

"Yes. Penworthy told me when you're desperate enough,
you accept money from him. Neither of us understands this
stubbornness, you know."

"He pays me for my services," she said stiffly. Then she
recoiled, knowing her mother used to claim the same thing
regarding entirely different services. Did everything come
back to whoring?

"But you cannot go to Penworthy now," Marcus
continued. "He is in Bath recuperating in the waters there."

Fantine felt her stomach clench. "He's gone?" She had
already planned to ask for an advance on her payment for
protecting Wilberforce. "When will he return?"

"At least a fortnight. Maybe more."

Fourteen days? She had given her last copper to
Nameless this morning. What would she do for fourteen
days?

Then Marcus continued, his voice compassionate even as
he delineated her problems with the cold efficiency of a
tally sheet. "Let us not forget Ballast," he said. "Even if you
do get Sprat into Harrow, he may not forgive you. What
will you do if Sprat fails or is sent down? Ballast will kill
you then, and we both know it."

Fantine stood, feeling vulnerable sitting still. "I can handle Ballast," she said with false bravado. "And Sprat will not get sent down. He is too smart." Still, Marcus had just added another fear to her growing list, and she was mortified to see her hands tremble.

"All right then," Marcus said as he stepped up behind her, "what about Hurdy? You will have to prove yourself to him. There are worse things than whoring. A lot worse. He will ask you to do one of them."

She spun around, her eyes burning with unshed tears. "Have you come to offer me money? In exchange for what? You already know I would rather die than be trapped by any master."

He dropped his hands onto her shoulders, his touch firm, his heat welcome, but Fantine did not make the mistake of thinking it a lover's touch. This was something more harsh, more businesslike than ever before. She was both disappointed and relieved by the change.

"You need to leave the rookeries," he said. "For a while. You can gather your resources against Ballast and prepare for Hurdy. More importantly, it will give you time to find Teggie."

"I—" she began, but he was quicker.

"Just listen," he said. "You won't be my mistress. Very well. But your father wants you to have a Season. He has even provided an acceptable portion for you."

"No…" Fantine whispered. No one beyond Penworthy and her mother had ever used the word "father" to her before. To hear Marcus use the word—and so easily— reverberated deep inside her.

He continued as if unaware of what he was doing to her. "My sister has agreed to bring you out as a genteel family friend. As a debutante, you will be able to move about society. Neither Ballast nor Hurdy will look for you there." He touched her chin, lifting her gaze up to his. "You will be safe."

She shook her head, but no words formed. Everything moved too fast. She couldn't think. Could barely breathe.

And yet everything he said made sense.

Suddenly releasing her, Marcus stepped away, leaving her feeling bereft. "You have done all you can in the rookeries. It is time to move your investigations elsewhere. Unless…" He paused. "Will you allow me to take over the investigation?"

"No."

"Then a coming-out is your only choice."

Fantine sank back against the cold, damp wall, the truth choking her even as she whispered it. "I can't."

"Why?"

She took a deep breath. Dare she tell him the truth? She turned away, forcing herself to admit something she tried to hide from even herself.

"I am not one of you," she said. "I have tried, but I can't be. Penworthy sent me to schools. Many of them. All with beautiful flowers and good food and coal in the winter." She fell silent, remembering those days. She had been so young, so hopeful that at last she had a life she could trust.

"What happened?"

"I was hated and miserable every minute of every day."

Marcus frowned. "I beg your pardon?"

She sat down heavily on the edge of the bed, the memories twisting together in her mind. She looked down at her rough hands, seeing the dirt and the calluses, the cracks in her skin from the cold. "They laughed at my hands," she said softly. "They mocked everything about me. I did not speak correctly. I walked like a farmhand and ate like a pig. I could not even brush my hair as a lady did. Nothing about me was right."

Not even her name.

She heard Marcus sigh as he settled down beside her on the mattress. "Surely there was something you enjoyed there, someone you befriended." His words were as much a hope as a statement, and she nodded, remembering the one person she had talked with.

"There was a girl. Phoebe. She was quiet and shy and nearly as tormented as I. I thought we would be friends."

She lifted her gaze from her lap, seeing not the damp walls of her room but a tiny blond girl, as delicate as a china doll. "She was the only one who made my life bearable."

"What happened?"

Fantine closed her eyes. It had been so small a thing. Nothing important. "One day she asked me about my name. She thought it was so unusual, and so I told her. In truth, it was not her fault that the others found out. She was never strong and could not keep silent when the others pressed her for my secrets."

She felt Marcus shift uneasily. "I do not understand. What secret? Fantine is a lovely name."

She shook her head. "But Fantine is not really my name." She pushed up from the bed, needing to walk as she spoke. "My mother was an actress with little time for a child. Her pregnancy was merely an interruption in her career, a time when it was nearly impossible to make any money. When I was finally born, she left me in care of a servant and returned immediately to the stage."

She glanced back at Marcus, shrugging as if it were of little importance. He simply watched her, his blue eyes steady, his expression sympathetic.

Eventually she found the strength to continue.

"She called me Enfant. 'Infant' in French. When I was six, I demanded a real name. I wasn't just her nameless baby."

"So you picked Fantine?"

"I picked Christina, but she could not remember it. In the end, we settled on Fantine because it was close enough to enfant for her to remember." She heard the bitterness in her own voice, but she could not stop it. She turned away, rubbing her hands against her arms. She felt so cold.

Beside her, she heard Marcus stir, but she drew away. She had to finish before she let him touch her.

"You told Phoebe," he said, his voice gentle. "And she told the others." He sighed. "Children can be so cruel."

She nodded, hearing the compassion in his voice. "I stood it as long as I could, but in the end I came back to the rookeries. Names mean less than nothing here."

She fell silent, closing her eyes against the memories, blocking them from her mind as best she could. It was over. It no longer mattered.

"And the other schools?"

"I never stayed long enough to find out."

Marcus enfolded her in his arms, his touch gentle, his warmth so comforting. She let her head settle against his chest, listening to the steady beat of his heart and relishing the feeling of his arms about her.

Then he spoke, his words low and angry with a suppressed violence that surprised her. "Penworthy should have claimed you. No matter what it did to his career." He took a deep breath that shuddered as he released it. "I am glad he is in Bath, now. I think I would kill him if he were here."

Fantine twisted in his arms, turning to look at him, and marveling at the vehemence in his expression. He understood. She could see it in his eyes, feel it in his caress. He knew why she chose to live in the rookeries, why she stubbornly clung to her independence here. And why she feared returning to the very society that had tormented her so before.

She touched his face, still awed that he could be enraged for her sake. He caught her fingers in one hand, drawing them to his lips for a kiss.

"I will do anything to protect you," he vowed, his very tone of voice sending chills through her. "You will not go through that again. I swear it."

She did not answer, but inside she felt a change. It was as if his words brought a release she had not expected. Her childhood anger dissipated. The hatred was brushed away with his touch, and at last she believed her own words.

It *was* over. Her childhood no longer mattered.

"Thank you," she said softly. She leaned forward, breathing deeply of his scent and closing her eyes. He held her there, cradling her in his arms, giving her more comfort than she thought possible. But in the end, even he could not change the truth.

"Dress me any way you like," she said. "I will still be a bastard reared in the rookeries. I cannot act the part of a brainless debutante." She reached forward, spreading her hands across his chest as she spoke, letting her desperation fill her expression. "Can you not simply give me the resources to cover my debts? That will buy me the time I need. I will repay you as soon as Penworthy pays me."

She felt his shuddering inhale. "I cannot."

His words hit her like a physical blow. "But why?"

"Because your father wants you to have a Season. He wants to atone for his sins. You cannot have a better life if I give you the means to stay in the rookeries."

Fantine gritted her teeth in frustration. She had thought she had settled this with Penworthy years ago. "You cannot think that a nameless bastard will find a place in society."

"But this time Penworthy has given you his name."

Fantine jerked, her jaw going slack in astonishment. Could it be true? "He intends to acknowledge me?"

Then she saw the regret on Marcus's face and knew it was not so. "He would, if you wish it. But you know it will destroy his career. And it will not help you to be labeled a bastard."

She swallowed bitter tears, knowing Marcus told the truth.

"He has put about that you are his niece, the only child of his brother and sister-in-law."

Fantine frowned. "The couple who died from a lung ailment years ago?"

"Yes. You will be Miss Fantine Drake."

Fantine pushed away, kicking absently at her pile of Rat's clothing. "More lies. More make-believe parents."

He did not answer at first. When he did speak, his tone was more forceful, more urgent. "You have promised Hurdy you know the rules of the upper crust. Perhaps now would be a good time to learn them."

She hesitated, silently acknowledging his point. "You will teach me?"

"Yes."

"You will help me establish an identity, a means of traveling about through the ton?"

"Absolutely."

She took a deep breath, mulling over her options once again. If she went with Marcus, she would create a new identity for herself, someone to become after Ballast discovered Fanny. Perhaps she could not maintain the persona for long. It was quite possible that the haute ton would see through her charade in a moment. But she could not afford to let the opportunity disappear. Especially as her two identities as Rat and Fanny were nearly played out.

But before she agreed, she had to be sure. She pinned Marcus with her steady regard. "What do you want in return?"

She felt him hesitate. She knew what he wanted—her in his bed. But she would not make it part of their arrangement. Perhaps, she thought, she was learning from Louise. Establish what you want from the beginning.

"Come, Marcus. What do you expect in return?" she repeated.

"You must let me be your guide. You must listen explicitly to what my sister and I tell you and not disobey us. We will explain as best we can, but there are many things that are simply nonsense, but must be performed nevertheless. Do you understand? You must listen to me."

"I will not go to your bed."

Once again, he touched her face, leaving a trail of fire wherever his finger wandered. "I am done seeking answers where there are none. You are not a disease for me to purge or a salve for my pain," he said, repeating the very words she had used against him last night.

"Then what am I to you?"

He shook his head as if even he did not know. "You are more than I ever expected, and I wish to learn more of you than can be found in a bedroom." He frowned, struggling with his words. "I swear I will not ask for more than you are willing to give."

She smiled, relieved by his words even though she barely understood them. "Then I agree. I will go to your sister's."

He smiled his relief, his shoulders easing down while his eyes began to sparkle. He looked so handsome that she was not at all surprised when she found herself stretching up for his kiss.

CHAPTER 11

She wasn't surprised to find herself asking for his kiss, but he apparently was. His eyes widened and he tilted his head in confusion. She smiled, unable to resist teasing him.

"Are you refusing me?" she asked.

"Good God, no!" he exclaimed. Then he leaned down, but he did not take her lips. He lifted his hand, brushing his fingertips across her jaw. She felt the whisper of heat along her cheek. "You constantly surprise me," he whispered. "No soul—man or woman—has ever fascinated me so."

She stretched up to meet him, opening herself to his invasion. Arching into his embrace, she ran her hands through his silky curls and pressed herself against the muscular wall of his chest.

Even through the barriers of their clothing, she felt his shudder. As she reveled in the stroke and parry of his tongue, his hands pulled at her shirt, lifting it out of her breeches so that he could touch beneath the fabric, stroking her lower back. But above her belly, her breasts were bound, and when he reached higher, all he could do was stroke across her tips. She moaned softly, feeling her body tighten beneath the rough fabric.

She barely even noticed when he opened her shirt. Then she was the one who stripped it away, revealing the tight swath of fabric that restricted her breathing. Breaking from her lips, Marcus tugged at the edge of her binding, tucked in the flattened valley between her breasts. Then he unwound her slowly, kissing her shoulders, her collarbone, and even lower, as inch by inch her body was revealed to him.

"Marcus..." she began, but he silenced her with a kiss. Abandoning the binding, he pressed her backward into the bed, and she sank willingly into the thin mattress. The cloth was loose enough that he could torment her with every movement, as he pulled and pushed it across her breasts.

She had meant to say something. Something about timing and location and how she had just said she would not be his mistress, but she lost those words now. She was beyond caring for her problems or his plans, beyond thought other than the need to feel his hands on her breasts, his lips across their peaks, his body between her thighs.

She wanted him. And from the ardor in his touch, his need was equally strong.

"Fine bit o' attention from a guardian, I'd say."

Fantine froze, forcibly expanding her attention beyond herself and the man on her bed. Shifting her gaze, she saw Sprat leaning against the wall, an adolescent leer on his face.

Above her, Marcus cursed audibly, rolling off of her in a single lithe movement, landing easily in a defensive posture. Fantine would have done the same if it had not been for the loosened bindings. As it was, she scrambled to her feet, the cloth gripped in one hand.

"What do you want, Sprat?" she asked, as she quickly rewound the fabric.

"Merely wot you promised. When do I go t' Arrow?"

Fantine sighed. "Be reasonable, Sprat. You cannot go in the middle of the term. You must wait for the next session."

It was only when she finished speaking, after she had pulled on her shirt, that she chanced to look closely at Sprat. The boy's face was discolored from repeated beatings. Though many marks had faded, one eye was still slightly swollen, the skin livid and purple.

"Has Ballast been beating you?"

She saw his jaw clench, his chin lifting slightly in pride. "Wot me father does ain't yer business."

She opened her mouth to argue, but Marcus forestalled her. "No, but how you do at Harrow is my business."

Fantine shifted her attention to Marcus, noting that he was standing straighter, no longer on the defensive. His arms were folded across his massive chest, and he looked as stern as any taskmaster in the rookeries.

"If I am to sponsor you to Harrow," Marcus continued, "you will have to leave immediately for Yorkshire."

"York!" exclaimed Fantine. "But that is—"

"All the way across England," finished Marcus. "So far, in fact, that it would be quite a problem for Ballast to follow or Sprat to run away." He pinned the boy with his heavy gaze. "If you mean to go to Harrow, you must do it completely. There is a good deal for you to learn before you even enter those hallowed doors. I have a tutor and a housekeeper there who can teach you all you need to know. Neither will take any nonsense."

Sprat's eyes narrowed, but he never said a word.

"If and only if they give a good account of you by summer's end, I shall sponsor you to Harrow."

Fantine clenched her jaw shut. She wanted to interfere, but knew better. There was a great deal for the boy to learn, and this was the only way. And to Sprat's credit, he seemed to understand that as well. His expression was guarded, but his eyes were steady as he considered Marcus's words.

Finally he straightened in a clear challenge. "Your word as a gentleman? You will sponsor me?"

"Provided Mrs. Grindley and Mr. Harwood agree." At the flicker in the boy's expression, Marcus continued. "They are fair people. They will not sabotage you."

Sprat stuck out his hand. "Your word as a gentleman."

Marcus stepped forward, taking it with equal gravity. "My word as a gentlemen to a future gentleman. I will sponsor you."

Fantine exhaled in relief, knowing that one of her problems had been solved. Sprat would get his chance at Harrow.

"But we must leave now," continued Marcus. Glancing toward Fantine, he lowered his voice. "If Sprat has found you, then his father cannot be far behind."

"He's on 'is way now," put in Sprat. "That's why I came. He found out that you live 'ere as Fanny the barmaid, and he means to come get even fer the bruise on 'is face and fer Jenny."

Fantine closed her eyes on a groan. Would Ballast never forget about Jenny?

"We must go," Marcus said, and Fantine agreed. Without so much as a backward glance, she left her home and everything she owned. They were Fanny's and Rat's, not hers. And so she abandoned them as she hoped to abandon both those personas. When that thought had entered her head, she hadn't a clue. But it was there now, and for the first time in her life, she embraced it wholeheartedly. Perhaps she could leave the rookeries behind. Perhaps she could try to become more than she was now.

Perhaps her father and Marcus were right.

She was so caught up in those thoughts that she did not think about Sprat's words until after they had climbed into Marcus's carriage.

Turning to Sprat, she frowned. "How did you know that Chadwick posed as my guardian? That was told to Hurdy, not Ballast."

Sprat shrugged as he stroked the rich velvet squabs. "I know wot the boys know, an' the boys know about Hurdy an' Ballast both."

Fantine nodded. That was, in fact, why her guise as Rat was so useful. "But if Hurdy and Ballast know the daft peer and my guardian are both Chadwick..."

"An' they know Rat and Fanny are the same," added Sprat.

"Then," cut in Marcus, "I got you away just in time."

"But to where?" Fantine asked. "They know who you are."

Marcus shrugged. "It takes timing and nerve to attack a peer. Besides, Hurdy will do nothing as yet, and Ballast will not move against either of us as long as Sprat is with me. Or rather in Yorkshire getting his education. Remember, I am his only hope of a sponsorship to Harrow."

Fantine looked straight at Sprat. "Will that be enough to keep your father away?"

The boy did not respond at first, but then he shook his head. "He will no' touch Chadwick. 'E figures the deal's with the nob."

"But what about Fantine?" asked Marcus.

Sprat turned to her, his expression almost apologetic. "Rat has tweaked 'im awful bad. 'E can't let that go an' still keep 'is men."

Fantine squeezed Marcus's hand, taking strength from his heat even as she tried to reassure him. "I can duck Ballast. Besides," she added with a smile, "Sprat will write his father from Yorkshire saying how happy and wonderful things are, and Ballast may forgive me some."

Sprat looked doubtful, but he did not say anything until Marcus looked at him sternly. "You will write your father?"

"O' course. But I will write the truth, guv. If'n I ain't being treated right, then I'll tell. And 'e'll go fer Fantine an' you both."

Marcus folded his arms across his chest, his expression hard. "*He*," Marcus corrected, emphasizing the "h" sound. "And if you intend to write the truth, then I shall make sure you understand it."

Sprat stiffened. "I understands that…."

Fantine groaned, tuning out the boy's words. With Marcus and Sprat sparing, the threat of Ballast coming to kill her, the difficulty of negotiating with Hurdy, not to mention her debts, Wilberforce's looming murder, and, God help her, the fear of meeting Marcus's family, she felt completely exhausted. "Gawd, when did me life get so bloody complicated?"

Then for the second time that day, she was surprised by the sight of Marcus's grin.

Ballast slammed his hand into the wall of Fanny's tiny room and cursed until he wore out his breath. She was gone. He had missed the wench by less than five minutes.

He drew breath, intent on venting his spleen some more, but stopped when his gaze snagged on the cap. It was tucked away behind the door, but the item was unmistakable.

Sprat's cap. His boy was with Fanny/Rat.

Ballast picked up the ragged thing and smoothed it over his fist. Everything was all right then, he told himself. His son was smart. Sprat would know just how to handle one stupid woman and her daft lord. He would set things up so that Ballast could make mincemeat out of both the girl and her lord.

Jerking his head at his men, Ballast motioned them out of Rat's tiny room. He would give Sprat a few days to explain what was going on.

The whore just better not hurt his boy. If anything happened to Sprat, he would tear her from limb to limb.

Marcus shoved his hands in his pockets and tried not to fidget. Nothing in his life had ever prepared him for the delicacy of this moment. After all, how *did* one introduce a friend's secret bastard to one's sister?

In the end, he need not have worried. His sister was the consummate hostess. She did not care that he arrived on her doorstep with a filthy boy and an equally dirty woman dressed as a boy. Charlotte took one look, ordered a huge tray of food and baths. It was not until Sprat and Fantine were immersed in hot water that she cornered her brother and demanded an explanation.

"All right, brother dear, who are they, why were they dressed like that, and why am I bringing her out?"

He did not even blink an eye. "Because I am your brother and you love me."

"Hah!"

"Because you already promised."

"I promised to bring out Penworthy's niece, not a bedraggled woman in torn breeches."

"They are one and the same."

"But why? What does all this mean?"

He did not answer. She folded her arms and frowned at him. And they remained that way for a very long time.

In the end, he won. He always did with Charlotte because, deep down, she adored him almost as much as she once adored their brother Geoffrey.

"Very well," she finally huffed. "I shall make my peace with her. As for you," she said as she dropped her hands on her hips, "you can open your purse to all sorts of expenses. If I hear a single objection, I shall tell everyone you used to chase goats in your underwear!"

Marcus stiffened in horror. "I was five years old!"

"Does not matter in the least. I shall tell everyone. Perhaps I shall even commission a painting of it. Are we in agreement?"

Marcus pressed his lips together and tried to stare her down. This time he lost. "Very well," he said. "You have carte blanche, but do try not to beggar me. I am to inherit the title one day. It would be nice if I could support it."

She narrowed her eyes. "Then you are to pay, not Penworthy?"

He sighed. They both knew his mentor did not have the funds to support a Season. And now Charlotte knew that her brother had more than a casual interest in her new charge.

"If you will excuse me, I need to compose a letter to go with Sprat to Yorkshire." And so he slipped away before Charlotte's quick mind figured anything else out.

Fantine sighed deeply. Once again, she was clean and well fed thanks to Marcus. Was she thankful? Yes. Was she nervous and wary? Very much so. Did she wish he was here kissing her so that she could not remember to be nervous or wary or even disoriented? Absolutely. But he was not here.

Hence the sigh.

She closed her eyes, trying to capture a sense of blissful contentment without worrying, but she couldn't. There were too many unknowns in this place, too many things that could go wrong. She did not like the feeling, and so she could not sit peacefully in a bathtub no matter how delightful the perfumed fragrance.

She stood up, then hastily grabbed a towel just as a knock sounded. A moment later, a maid's shadow appeared on the other side of the screen. "Milady wishes to speak with you and wonders if she could interrupt your bath," she said.

"Uh, yes," Fantine responded, carefully schooling her voice to keep out all traces of Cockney. "Tell Lady Charlotte she may come in." She spoke quickly, too quickly.

This is ridiculous! she scolded herself. There was no reason to be nervous. She had faced a good deal worse than Marcus's relations. But despite the chiding she gave herself, she was still nervous and anxious, and completely ill prepared for the woman who peeked around the screen.

"Do you need any help, Fantine?"

Fantine shook her head, cursing the lank of wet hair that flopped into her eye. "No, I am fine," she lied as she quickly dried herself and reached for some undergarments.

They were soft and clean and Fantine could not help pausing to appreciate their texture as she pulled them on.

"Do come out from behind the screen," Lady Charlotte urged. "I've found some clothes that may fit you."

Fantine did as she was bidden, slipping closer to the fire in the beautiful violet and white bedchamber. As she moved, she studied her hostess, noticing the family resemblance between Lady Charlotte and Marcus. Both were tall and strong, their hair light, their eyes alert and keen, though Lady Charlotte's eyes were more hazel than

Marcus's clear blue. Looking at her hostess now, Fantine realized it would be easy for the woman to adopt the same haughty disdain that she had seen so often from Marcus, but apparently, she had chosen not to. Ever polite, she smiled often, maintaining a concerned aspect rather than a critical one.

Fantine found the effect rather disconcerting. Even her mother had never seemed so…so maternal.

"Do you like them?"

Fantine followed the lady's gesture to see three exquisite day gowns spread out over the large bed. The first was a bright canary yellow, the others of colorful patterns, one of pink and lavender, the other of green and gold.

"They will be a trifle large for you, I fear. I am somewhat taller than you, but they shall have to do until we can get you some of your own."

"My own?" Fantine echoed.

"Why, yes. You cannot have a Season in my cast-off gowns."

"A Season?" Up until that moment, she had blissfully forgotten that Marcus planned for her to make a debut in society. She had been focusing her thoughts on what she would learn and how she would find the mysterious Teggie.

Lady Charlotte frowned and folded her arms across her chest, and Fantine had to steel herself against shying backward. "What has Marcus told you?" Charlotte asked.

Fantine took a deep breath, forcibly bringing her thoughts into focus. "Marcus has a lot of strange ideas, my lady."

"Please call me Lottie. I cannot be easy with someone who is always milady this and milady that-ing me."

Fantine blinked, her thoughts stumbling. "You do not wish me to use your tide?" But everyone with a tide wanted people to use it. Everyone including Marcus, which was, of course, exactly why she used his Christian name.

"Oh, my," Lady Charlotte continued blithely. "You have some terrible bruises on your legs. Shall I call for a doctor?"

"For bruises?" Fantine blinked in confusion.

"My physician can be here in a twinkling."

"No. No, thank you." Fantine shook her head, her thoughts still reeling. A physician, she thought dazedly, not a surgeon. Physicians were for the upper crust. People like her had surgeons.

"Come, come," chided the woman gently. "We cannot have you standing about in your shift. Try the canary yellow."

Then before she could so much as blink, Fantine found herself pulling on a gown of the finest silk. It was the softest material that had ever touched her skin, and yet she could only stare awkwardly down at it.

The last time she had touched anything like this had been when she was in school. In a flash, all her memories came back to her—each cruel remark, each cutting act. She could not go through that again. She could not.

"This is a mistake," she said as she pulled at the skirt, trying to take it off.

But Lady Charlotte pushed her hands away. "Give me just a minute to button the back."

Fantine's anxieties began to build. She should never have come here. Marcus had confused her, getting her to agree against her better judgment. She belonged in the rookeries and no good would come of taking her out of the one place she understood.

"I think I should go home," she said, reaching behind her to undo the buttons. "Thank you so much for all you have done. If you could send my other clothes, then I shall be off."

"Oh!" the woman exclaimed. "But Marcus ordered them burned."

Fantine turned, her hands dropping down to her sides. "He burned my clothes?"

"Yes," she said slowly. "In fact, he made sure it was done immediately, and then he warned me that it might make you angry."

"Too roight, it does!" Fantine said, forgetting her accent and slipping into Cockney. "'E 'ad no right!"

"Yes, I know. I think that is exactly why he did it."

"Why, the bloody nob!" Fantine folded her arms across her bodice and spun around, staring into the fire as if it would give her some answers or at least calm her nerves. It did not. It only reminded her that Marcus had burned her clothes.

"Dirty high-handed bloody nob," she muttered. Then she sneezed, her damp hair chilling her despite the fire. "He burned my clothes so I could not leave. He knows I cannot go to the rookery in your clothing. I would stick out like a sore thumb."

She heard a rustle as Lady Charlotte stepped toward her. "But why would you wish to go there?"

"Because that is where I belong," she snapped. It was some moments more before Fantine got control of herself enough to regret her rudeness. Whatever else had happened, Lady Charlotte was blameless. The woman was kind in the best sense of the word. She did not deserve Fantine's ill humor.

Turning around, Fantine tried to apologize. "Please forgive me. Your brother brings out the worst in me. You have been most generous, and I have no wish to offend you."

The woman smiled, the gesture warm and friendly despite her words. "But you have offended me," she said. "I think you do not wish me to bring you out."

"I do not wish for a coming-out at all," Fantine said, her voice rough as her fears found an outlet in her voice. "But your brother seems to think—"

"Yes, my brother," interrupted Lady Charlotte. "I have struck a bargain with him, you know. I am to bring you out, and he is to be forever in my debt. I thought it most unfair at first, but I begin to think I have gotten the better of it. I shall be watching you very closely, you see."

Fantine bristled, sensing another high-handed nob. "I have no need of a nursemaid!"

"Oh, I have no intention of being one. What I want to know is what you have done to my brother. And that, I believe, can only be learned by watching you. I have the feeling your tactics have been most unorthodox."

"I have done nothing but hit him over the head when he most deserved it." Fantine spoke without thinking, releasing more of her pent-up frustration.

"Ah," returned Lady Charlotte. "As I said, unorthodox. I shall have to try it sometime."

Fantine frowned. "I do not understand."

Lady Charlotte grinned at her. "Bentley tells me Marcus actually laughed out loud today. We think he either told a joke or has taken up with a child mistress. And he smiled at me just this morning."

"This is unusual?"

"Most unusual. Mother and I have been racking our brains trying to discover the reason for the change. And now I find it literally on my doorstep."

Fantine shook her head, putting her arms out in a gesture of defense. "Oh, no, my lady. You cannot blame me for Marcus! He was domineering, arrogant, and as mad as a bedlamite when I first met him. I cannot help it if you have only now discovered it."

"Well, the domineering and arrogant part is common knowledge. I merely wish to know how he became crazy—"

"My, you do look lovely in yellow," drawled a low voice from the door.

Lady Charlotte and Fantine spun around, indignation radiating from both of them.

"Marcus!" cried his sister. "Where are you manners?"

"I am afraid I have had to discard them where Fantine is concerned." He spoke to Lady Charlotte, but his eyes remained fixed on Fantine.

"Then find them again! You cannot just walk into a lady's dressing room."

"But that is just the point," said Fantine softly. "He does not think of me as a lady. He wants me as his mistress."

Lady Charlotte pressed her hand to her bodice in shock. "It cannot be true!"

Marcus merely smiled as he let his gaze travel the length
of Fantine's gown, returning slowly to her face. "Could any
man resist such loveliness?"

Fantine bit her lip, her face heating with embarrassment
and excitement both. She had never seen a man look at her
with such naked hunger, and she felt the heat of a blush
burn all the way down to her toes.

Lady Charlotte, however, had an entirely different
reaction. Stepping directly in front of her brother, she
placed her hands on her hips and glared up at him. "You
are a pig, Marcus! An oinking, dirty, smelly pig!"

Marcus's eyes widened in surprise. "Why, Lottie, I
bathed this very morning."

"Nevertheless," she said primly, "you stink. Now get out
of my house before I punch you." Then she made an
awkward fist and raised it to his nose.

His lips twitched. Fantine distinctly saw the glimmerings
of humor pull at his cheeks, but he responded with absolute
gravity. "Please, I beg of you not to hurt me, sister dear. I
merely wished to insure—"

"Insure this, brother dear. Fantine will stay. You will go."
Then she pushed her brother square in the chest.

"But you cannot wish me to stay now!" Fantine
exclaimed. "Not...not now that you know..." Her voice
trailed away.

Lady Charlotte turn around. "Know what? That my
brother is a pig? I knew that already. That he would have
designs on your virtue? Well, he is a man, after all, and
there is only so much maturity one can expect from them."

Fantine shook her head, unable to understand this bizarre
situation. Why, the woman had threatened to punch Marcus!
"You do not understand. I am..." Her voice faded away.

This time Marcus was the one to speak, his eyes suddenly
grave, all traces of humor gone. "You are what, Fantine?"

She shook her head, uncertain what she had meant to say.
"I do not belong here."

She did not hear him step away from his sister, neither
did she hear his approach, but before long, she felt his arms

around her, drawing her into his embrace. "You are right," he said softly. "Fanny does not belong here. Neither does Rat. But what about Fantine Delarive?"

She pulled out of his arms. "I am Rat and Fanny."

He shook his head. "No. You playact Rat and Fanny. But you are Fantine Delarive. I think you have been pretending to be someone else for so long that you do not know who you are anymore."

"You are being ridiculous." She tried to speak firmly, but her voice was high and nervous as she sensed the truth in his words. "Besides, I am supposed to be Fantine Drake," she said, reminding him that he was merely pushing a new role and a new history on her.

But he simply shook his head. "Fantine Drake and Fantine Delarive can become the same person. Make them the same. Choose your future. From where I stand, Miss Drake is not my mistress. Neither is she a child or a strumpet. But what do you see? Who do you want to be?"

She pushed away from him, hating the entire conversation, hating the way he made her think of things she wished safely buried. "It makes no difference!"

He did not follow her, but neither did he stop pressing her. "Fantine, you resist the role of mistress because you believe it will make you into your mother. Yet that could never be you. You will never be the woman who reared you."

She shook her head. "You do not understand."

"I think I do. Your life in the rookeries has forced you to playact one role after another to survive. You never had time to discover what you thought, what you wanted, what you need. It was always the daily fight to survive."

"That is how it is there."

"Exactly. But part of you wants to know, wants to find out more. That is why you searched out your father so many years ago. That is why you stubbornly refuse any type of aid now. You do not want to be thrust into a role until you discover who you are. But you cannot discover that without the time to think. Who will you become when you no longer struggle to find your next meal? I vow I am almost as curious as you."

Fantine bit her lip, her thoughts and emotions knotted together. Then she felt him step up behind her, his presence warmer than the fire.

"You are here now," he said softly as he rested his hands on her shoulders. "Be anything you wish. Pick the life you want and make it your own."

She shook her head, feeling tears blur her sight. "I do not know how."

He turned her around and lifted her chin until she looked directly at him, her entire vision filled with his smile. "That is why I am here. And Lottie. And, God help you, my mother. We will all show you how to go on, if only you will let us."

Fantine looked away, unable to bear the burning intensity of his blue eyes. She knew what he was asking of her, knew he wanted her to commit to learning the ways of a lady. It was a frightening thought. She knew how to pretend for an hour or two, knew also how to laugh in the face of the spiteful women of society. But to actually seek to be one of them? To be accepted into their ranks? She had tried in school and had been crushed.

As if reading her thoughts, Marcus lowered his head, whispering into her ear, "You can do it. And you promised you would try. If nothing else, I thought I could count on your word."

Fantine closed her eyes. Surrounded by his arms, she felt oddly powerful, as if his very presence would prevent her from saying or doing the wrong thing. His arms were so strong, she could almost fancy them a shield against acid-tongued women. With him beside her, she believed it was possible.

She could become Miss Fantine Drake, highborn lady.

Lifting her chin, she met his gaze, drawing strength from his steady gaze. "Very well. I will do it," she said.

He grinned at her. The change in expression was so sudden and so complete, she was momentarily taken aback.

His eyes crinkled slightly at the corners, his teeth, though even and white, looked almost too large for his jaw. All in all, he looked...boyish.

And even more charming than before.

"Lawks," she suddenly drawled in her worst cant. "Oi'm to be a member o' the ton."

"God help the aristocracy," returned Marcus, still grinning.

"No," put in his sister as she came up to hug them both. "God help me, for I shall have to control you both."

CHAPTER 12

Marcus tried not to pace the small parlor in his sister's home. It had been a week, perhaps the longest week of his life, but he had stayed away. Lottie had insisted Fantine would adjust better without his interference, so he had remained scrupulously absent. But she had been in his thoughts constantly. Not even the search for the mysterious Teggie had provided distraction.

How was she faring? Did she hate him for abandoning her? Was Lottie being too hard on her? Or the reverse? The questions churned in his mind, anxious for resolution.

The parlor door opened, and Marcus spun around.

It was only tea, served by the butler, Fitzhugh. Marcus cursed and turned back toward the window. Good Lord, could women never keep an appointment? Lottie had distinctly said to come for tea. Tea was at four o'clock. It was four now, and she was not here. He slapped his gloves against his palm.

"Goodness, brother, you look as fierce as a bear."

Marcus twisted around, his gaze skipping right over his sister to scan the hallway behind her.

It was empty. No Fantine.

"Where is she? Did you explain to her that you absolutely insisted I stay away? Does she understand that?"

"Marcus! Contain yourself." Then her eyes widened in surprise. "To think that I would ever have to say that to you. Why, Marcus, I do believe you have changed."

Muttering a curse that reddened his sister's ears, he dropped unceremoniously into a chair. "Just tell me what has been happening here in the last week."

Lottie settled gracefully into a nearby chair, carefully serving tea. "What do you think has been happening? We have had dress fittings, dance lessons, deportment lessons, French lessons, shopping, and basic instruction in things I thought everyone knew. Did you know she had not the least clue what an oyster was or what one did with them?"

Marcus took his tea from his sister and immediately set it down. "Yes, yes, I could have guessed that. But how has she been faring? Is she happy? And where is she?"

"My goodness! She is upstairs practicing her curtsies. You can see her at her first ball and not before."

Marcus ground his teeth, but his sister was firm.

"I have precious little time to bring her up to scratch, Marcus, and I do not want you upsetting the balance. There is still a lot for her to learn."

Marcus grumbled into his teacup, understanding the wisdom of not distracting Fantine, but resenting it nonetheless. Finally he turned his sour expression on his sister. "But is she happy? Have you told her why I have stayed away?"

Lottie nodded. "I have explained it, and she seemed to understand. She also appears happy. Lord knows the servants adore her. She always seems to know just what to say to them."

Marcus sighed, somewhat reassured. "What about her manners? Was there a great deal for her to learn?"

"No, not learn. But these things must become habit. She cannot forever be slipping into Cockney when she is frustrated. Though I must say she handled Mr. Thompson quite well."

Marcus straightened his spine as he focused almost painfully on his sister. "Mr. Thompson? Mr. Edwin

Thompson whose father is Baron Thompson of Birmingham? She has seen him but not me?"

Lottie set down her own cup of tea with a frown. "He merely came by to speak with Christopher. You know our estates border one another."

Marcus waved away the history. "Yes, yes, but what happened?"

"Nothing happened! He stayed for tea. And Fantine was quite charming." Marcus watched as a slight smile formed on his sister's face. "In fact, he seemed quite taken with her. He is in London hunting for a wife, you know. I begin to think that he and Fantine would do quite well."

"Good God, Lottie," gasped Marcus, "she has only been here a week, and you already have her walking down the aisle!"

His sister's smile broadened. "It is not I who would have her walking down the aisle, but Mr. Thompson."

Marcus shifted irritably, nearly knocking over his teacup with his movements. "It is much too early to be thinking of Mr. Thompson," he snapped. "Let her go to some balls and parties—"

"Well, of course I shall!" she responded with a grin. "I was merely commenting that Mr. Thompson seemed quite taken with her. And she with him, for that matter. He has already returned for tea twice more, and we are having him to dinner tomorrow night. And no, you cannot come," she said before he could ask. "I do not think you are in the appropriate mood for such an event."

Marcus would have said something scathing, but he held his tongue. Lottie was enjoying his ill humor too much for him to indulge it further. But Mr. Thompson! It was not that the man was objectionable. In fact, he was the epitome of stalwart English fare, as moral and upright as they came. "He simply will not do for Fantine," Marcus groused.

He had not realized that he had spoken aloud until his sister cut into his thoughts, her voice soft with reprimand. "I believe that is for Fantine to decide, is it not?"

Marcus pressed his lips together, refusing to be drawn into an argument. He pushed out of his chair instead, pacing to the cold fire grate as he spoke. "What about her dancing and deportment and such? Is she doing well with that?"

Glancing back, he saw Lottie shrug, her manner slightly guarded. "She has thrown herself into it like a woman possessed."

"So she is doing well? She is learning."

Lottie sighed. "She is constantly watching me, learning heaven alone knows what. I swear she mimics me in her sleep."

Marcus nodded as he carefully studied his sister's expression. "But that is all to the best, is it not?"

"Of course," she said slowly. "I am perfectly pleased with her progress." But her voice belied her statement.

"Tell me, Lottie. What is it?"

She took her time answering, and Marcus had to wait as she sipped her tea. Finally, she set down her cup. "Fantine and I have been in each other's company almost constantly, you know. Yet, after all this time, I still know nothing about her." She reached for a tea cake, then set it back down again and fussed with the crumbs on her fingers. "Marcus, she has thrown herself into her lessons like a woman studying a role. She has become a model of behavior. But I do not know if it is part of her." She frowned, her expression awkward. "Do you understand what I am trying to say?"

"I believe so," he said with a sigh. "Fantine's manners are like everything else, like a gown put on and easily taken off again. They are not her."

"Exactly!"

Marcus took a few steps, found himself in front of his seat, and then awkwardly settled back into it. "I know too well the uncomfortable position you are in. You want to know more about her, to share with her, to find out who she truly is—"

"You do understand!"

"Only too well." He picked up his teacup and stared pensively into the dark water. "Unfortunately, Fantine does not reveal herself easily to anyone. Even her own father is not very sure of her."

Lottie leaned forward to add a bit more hot water to his teacup. When she spoke, her tone was casual. "Who is her father? Why has he not brought her out? Fantine has never spoken of her family."

Marcus shook his head. "And neither can I. But to answer your question in part, she is of noble blood, but he cannot bring her out. Circumstances prevent it."

"A bastard then. I feared it was so," Lottie said.

Marcus's breath caught in his chest. His family could be rather prim in their notions. Was Lottie about to cancel their arrangement? She could with perfect propriety, and as the seconds ticked by, Marcus became positively alarmed.

Finally, he shifted in his seat so that he could take hold of her hand in an earnest plea if necessary. "Lottie?"

"Hmmm? Oh! Pray do not look so terrified. I was merely trying to guess her father's identity. She has such distinctive features, but I suppose she got them from her mother."

"Then you will bring her out?"

"Of course I will." Lottie gave him her most mischievous smile. "I tell you, it is a sister's fondest dreams to see her brother tortured. And tortured, my dear brother, is exactly what you appear. Good Lord, I have not seen you fidget so much since you were still in leading strings."

"I have not fidgeted!" Marcus returned, firmly planting his hands by his sides. But then he realized he needed his tea and had to reach forward for it, which necessitated a shift in the position of his legs. Then when he balanced the teacup on his knee, it began to tilt, and he…

His sister's laughter reddened his ears with mortification. In the end, he put the teacup back on the table and tried, quite unsuccessfully, to appear stern. "Well, Lottie, you may be used to this nonsense of bringing out a girl, but I have never done it before. It is somewhat wearing on the nerves."

"Clearly," responded Lottie, her voice still brimming over with mirth. "Well, dear brother," she added in a more serious tone, "one thing you can cease doing is your nightly rendezvous with Fantine. Aside from the impropriety of the situation, she has been destroying the ivy beneath her window. It is most unsightly, even if it is the back of the house."

If he had been fidgeting before, Marcus was suddenly very still. "Midnight rendezvous?"

"Oh, you cannot fool me. I know she climbs out of her window nearly every night. Who else would she visit but you?"

"Who, indeed?" he responded dryly, a number of possibilities running through his mind.

Lottie was quick to pick up on his tone. "Do you mean you have not been meeting her?"

He shook his head. "I have not seen her in a week."

"Good Lord, I thought it must be you. I even gave her a key and told her she could come and go by the front door. It was not necessary to risk her neck climbing the brick."

Marcus pushed out of his chair, suddenly alarmed. "You encouraged her in this madness?"

"I thought she went to see you! It has been hard enough on her these days, I thought I could count on your good sense not to abuse the poor girl. It never occurred to me—"

"That she was off with someone else?"

"But who?"

Marcus took a quick turn about the room, his thoughts churning with possibilities. "It is not a lover," he said harshly. "Fantine cannot have found one so quickly."

"Do not be too sure, brother dear," responded Lottie. "She is quite lovely. No doubt the men find her."

Marcus clenched his teeth, his thoughts grim. "You are no doubt correct. Still..." He shook his head. "There is no help for it. I shall have to follow her." He spun back to face his sister. "She goes out every night?"

Lottie nodded. "I believe so."

"Very well."

"No," she snapped, "it is not well at all. I had thought to attend our first party tomorrow night. Mother is due back any day and was to help me sponsor Fantine." She looked up, her expression fierce. "I will help her, Marcus, but do not forget she is your responsibility. Whatever she does at night, you must end it now."

"Believe me," he answered, "I have no intention of allowing any such nonsense to continue."

His sister nodded, apparently satisfied. "Now if only you could do something about her eating."

Marcus lifted an eyebrow. "Her eating?"

"I swear, she consumes enough for ten people. Why Cook took three extra trips to the market last week. Three! Yet, the girl is as skinny as a rail. I cannot understand it."

Neither could he. Then he frowned into his teacup. "I do not comprehend now, but I will before the night is over."

Marcus shifted his stance against the building and cursed as a lock of his hair caught on the rough brick. He despised this aspect of spy work—standing around in dark, uncomfortable places for hours on end. His feet had swollen, the wet had soaked clean through his trousers, and despite the coming spring, it was still damned cold.

But worst of all was the nagging suspicion that Fantine had discovered his presence and intended to forgo her midnight excursion. Or worse yet, had already given him the slip.

He should leave. He should go home to a warm fire and a brandy. But he did not. He remained by her window, wondering if the clouds would clear away from the nearly full moon. Even in the half-light, he could see how the ivy beneath Fantine's window had been torn or broken. Someone had certainly been climbing in and out of her bedroom, and he was determined to discover who.

Then came a thump. Not a loud thump, but a soft thud as a side of mutton dropped to the ground. It was followed by a rope and then a most darling derriere clad in tight breeches. It was Fantine, of course, climbing backward out of her window. She had a huge canvas satchel slung over one shoulder and banging awkwardly against her side.

The sight was quite delightful. The satchel caused her to wiggle in the most interesting ways as she descended, and Marcus nearly forget to move. Then when he did, it was hastily, without the subtlety he intended, as he half tripped, half jumped over the mutton to stand beneath her.

Fortunately, she was too busy cursing the awkward sack to listen for him. So when she finally dropped to the earth, he easily circled her with his arms, pulling her luscious body against his own.

"Sink me!" he drawled. "I say a burglar has robbed my sister's home! Shall I call the watch?"

Her body was tense, already beginning to fight him, but at his words, she relaxed, her back settling against him with erotic familiarity. "Marcus! You startled me."

"Oh, no!" he said as he shifted her, turning her to face him before pressing her back against the wall. "I shall not call the watch," he continued. "I should punish her."

He could see her eyes widen at his husky tone. Indeed, he could not blame her. He was as startled as she. But over the last hour, a strange anger had taken hold of him. He was Lord Chadwick, a future earl, and yet he waited for hours in a damp alley for a street girl who had not the brains to take the opportunities offered to her.

So when she dropped so unceremoniously into his arms, he wanted to punish her—just a little—for the damage to his dignity. Or perhaps he simply liked the feel of her in his arms. And against his chest. And pressed hot against his groin.

"Marc—!" Her word was cut off as he claimed her mouth.

His kiss was hard and hot, and though she began stiff and unyielding, she soon softened. A heartbeat later, she returned his passion. The more he demanded of her, the more she struggled, not against him, but with him, taking what he could give her, and urging him on.

Her pelvis rocked against him, and he groaned. He pushed his arm beneath the satchel and took her breast, pinching her nipple as she wrapped her hands around his back. Her shirt was a rough fabric that he could easily rip apart, but he did not bother. He lifted it up, letting both his hands slide beneath the shirt to grope and explore like the veriest cad.

She was the one who pulled the shirt open, exposing her flesh to the silvery moonlight. Then she arched against him, her own hands slipping down his back until she gripped his hips and ground him against her. He could not help thrusting, again and again, in a movement that was as hungry as it was frustrated. There were too many clothes between them, they were too exposed.

And the damned sack kept bouncing against his elbow, as if trying to push him away.

"I want you, Fantine," he gasped, in a desperate bid to regain his thoughts. "God, I need you." Then he dropped to one knee before her and began kissing her breast, teasing the nipple until her breathing came in loud pants.

The sack rolled with her movements, bumping him in the head. He heard a crack, but it barely registered in his thoughts. Pushing irritably at it, he resumed his place, using his hands to mold and shape her tender flesh.

Then he felt her knees spread, and he let his hands slide lower, over her belly, and down.

Thud. The sack again, landing against his temple. He pulled angrily at it, but she had wrapped it securely about her. If he ripped it off her, he risked choking her with the rope. He had no patience with the knot, indeed he had no patience with anything but her body, still writhing enticingly.

He leaned forward to take her breast again.

Thud. Only this time the thud felt more like a wet splat.

"Fantine," he gasped, pushing the sack away.

Splat. It returned harder against his temple.

"What the devil—"

His words were cut off as the sack again rolled against him. He reared away, wiping some sort of slime from his forehead.

"Marcus?" Her voice was low and husky, a siren call despite the confusion in the word.

"What the devil is in that sack? Can you not put it down?"

"The sack?" She straightened, pulling away from the wall as she inspected the offensive item. "Ugh! You have broken the eggs. Damn, Marcus, they are all over everything!"

"I have broken the eggs!" he cried, unsuccessfully trying to wipe the slime from his hands onto the nearby brick. "I was not the one who packed eggs in a ridiculous sachel! My word, it is all over me! Take the damned thing off!"

She twisted against him, her face flushed, even in the silvery moonlight. "Take it off! But then what am I to do with the eggs? I need those eggs!"

"Well, you cannot have them," he retorted hotly. "They are all over me! My entire coat is ruined!"

"Your coat? What do I care about your coat. The eggs—"

"Hang the eggs!"

"Hang your coat!"

They stared at each other, frustration and anger tightening their expressions, while shadows chased across their bodies.

Then suddenly Marcus laughed. It was not a full bellied laugh. It was more a snort as he looked down at the slick goo all over his hands. Fantine let her gaze slide away, but he saw the pull to her lips as she too fought a smile. It was all he needed for his snort to become a guffaw.

"Shhh," she said urgently, though the sound was cut off by her own giggle. "We shall wake the entire neighborhood."

"Let them wake," he said, unable to contain himself.

"Hush!" she admonished. "Your reputation will be ruined."

That sobered his laugh into chuckles. "Since when do you care about my reputation?"

"Since it is your family sponsoring my coming-out!"

He straightened, though he still felt mischief like a potent liquor in his blood. "Is your coming-out so important to you?"

She nodded, a curt slash of her chin as her smile faded.

"Good. Then get back in the house with your ridiculous bag of smashed eggs and do not come out again."

"But—"

"Go!"

He had not expected her to obey. She was nothing if not contrary. But she surprised him. With a smile, she pulled off her satchel, dropping it heavily on his foot. "Very well. Please be sure to give these to Nameless. Thank you for taking on this task for me. And do not forget the mutton." She gestured to the meat still lying in the middle of the alley. Then with a nod, she began to scale the wall.

"What? Fantine!"

She paused, barely two feet off the ground. "Yes?"

He groped for something to say. The lust had dulled somewhat, dispelled by their sudden humor, but still the erotic tension remained. She needed to go before he succumbed to his baser instincts.

"Marcus?"

"Uh," he stammered, wondering what he had intended to say. Finally, his gaze fell on the heavy satchel. "You take Nameless food every night?"

She shrugged, an amazingly graceful movement considering she was still hanging by a rope. "Him and the other boys. But Lottie says my evenings will be busy soon. I thought to take enough to tide him and his boys over." Then she paused. "I also have them listening for news of Teggie or Wilberforce, but they have found nothing."

He nodded. "My efforts have yielded nothing as well." Then he hefted the bag, wincing as it landed heavily on his back. "Very well," he groaned. "Go back to bed."

She frowned at him. He saw it quite clearly. Then she dropped nimbly back to the ground. "You cannot mean to deliver this."

"I cannot?"

"Of course not. You are…"

"Too stiff? Too arrogant?"

"Yes."

"Ah, well," he said with a grin. "You have changed me, Fantine. Or I have succumbed to some mental disorder." He started walking away, and she scrambled to follow him, snatching up the mutton he had forgotten.

"But you do not know where to go."

"I expect Nameless will find me."

"But—"

He stopped abruptly, turning to face her. "Fantine, I brought you to my sister's house to protect you. Ballast still wants to hurt you, and Hurdy—"

"I am in no danger from Hurdy. He has not discussed matters with Teggie yet."

He paused, frowning at her. "How do you know that?" It frightened him to think she might have seen the villain alone.

"The boys," she repeated firmly. "So far, they say Hurdy has done nothing but the usual rookery games."

Marcus nodded, somewhat reassured. "Still, Ballast will be watching your associates, including Nameless and Louise."

"He will be watching for you, too."

He smiled at the clear note of worry in her voice. "I thank you for your concern." Marcus reached forward and tweaked an errant curl. Lottie had done wonders with Fantine's short mop and the style looked entirely fetching. "Now go back to your room. Ladies do not wander about at night."

Then he folded his arms across his chest and looked absolutely firm as he watched rebelliousness war with resignation on her face. In the end, reason won out.

"Very well," she said softly. Then with a nimbleness that surprised him, she climbed her rope and disappeared inside.

He did not make the mistake of leaving immediately. Instead, he waited in the dark for another ten minutes. Long enough for him to see her rope disappear into the confines of her room and to hear the creak of her bed as she settled into it. He was not sure he actually heard it, but his imagination did, just as it supplied graphic images of her in bed.

In the end, he resolutely turned to his task, wishing he could turn his back on his thoughts as well.

That was the moment he realized what he had just agreed to do. Sweet heaven, had he, a future earl, actually agreed to deliver a sackload of broken eggs and slimy foodstuffs in the middle of the night to a group of street urchins in the rookeries? It was not possible. But then he hoisted the sack and her blasted mutton and began trudging away toward his carriage, realizing that he had indeed changed.

And he was not at all sure he appreciated the new him.

"Take me near that pub beneath Fantine's home, Jacob," he said drearily as he unceremoniously tossed the satchel and mutton onto the floorboards of his conveyance.

"Milord?"

"I am to play Lady Bountiful and feed a bunch of starving urchins in the middle of the night."

"Of course, milord," the coachman responded evenly, as if this were the most normal thing for a peer to do.

Marcus climbed inside his carriage and pulled out his pistols, making sure they were primed. He might have nothing to fear from Nameless and his cohorts, but Ballast was still out there. Sprat would not have written his father yet, so Ballast would still be looking to take his revenge on both Marcus and Fantine. Marcus had no intention of making another trip to the back room of that dockside pub.

He had just finished his task when he felt the carriage dip. He would not have noticed if he had not been thinking of Fantine and street urchins and what she might have learned as a child. But he was thinking of it, and the thought brought an image of children stealing rides on the back of carriages.

Fantine would not…But of course she would.

Heedless of the still-moving carriage, Marcus flung open the side door and bellowed toward the rear.

"Fantine!"

At first there was no response except from Jacob as the coachman gently reined in the horses.

"Fantine, come in here or I shall be forced to haul you around by your hair!"

This time his bellow was rewarded by a cherubic face suddenly appearing around the corner of his carriage. Fantine. And with an expression that could charm a bird down from a tree.

"Was you wantin' me, guv?" she asked in her street voice.

"Fantine!" he exclaimed, more exasperated than angry. "I am trying to save your life."

"Ain't mine wot needs saving."

Marcus sighed. "Why do I get the feeling that we keep having the same argument over and over to no avail?"

Fantine shrugged. "Cain't really say. Perhaps you are a mite thickheaded."

He did not dare answer. So he addressed his coachman instead. "Turn us around, Jacob. I must take a miscreant home."

"Do not bother, Jacob," cried Fantine, as she blithely jumped off the carriage. "I can make it t' Nameless now without yer help."

Marcus jumped down as well, grabbing hold of her arm as quickly as possible. "You cannot possibly go wandering about the streets of London alone at this time of night." But even as he said the words, he realized how ridiculous they were. Of course she could wander about. She had done so for many years. Indeed, if Fantine chose to risk her life, then nothing short of clapping her in irons would prevent her. And he was not so sure about the irons.

"Oh, very well." He gestured toward the carriage. "Get in. I might as well have you where I can see you."

"Thank 'ee," she said with a beaming smile. "It be ever so much easier t' protect you when we are together."

He opened his mouth to respond with some scathing retort, but then he stopped. She was baiting him. "Just get in," he muttered, "before I strangle you."

"Thank you, sir," she responded sweetly, switching to her society voice. "It is ever so nice to travel with so kind and mannerly a gentleman."

He would have throttled her then if it had not been for Jacob's barely muffled snort. The sound did not stop the murderous thoughts that went rampaging through Marcus's mind, but it did remind him that his own coachman would be a witness to any nefarious deed he might commit.

Still, that did not keep him from planning some sort of revenge. And he knew just what he would do....

CHAPTER 13

Fantine sprang lightly up to the carriage, gave Jacob directions, then settled onto the squabs with a giddy sense of freedom. She knew it was dangerous for her to go to the rookeries, but she needed this last evening. Lottie had already warned her that everything would change the moment she made her debut tomorrow night. She would become immersed in the social whirl, and who knew when her next free night would be?

That she had made no progress on her investigations bothered her. But not as much as she expected. She could do no more until Hurdy met with Teggie or she entered the social world. And Marcus—through Lottie—had kept her apprised of his measures to protect Wilberforce. Everything was proceeding as planned, and yet she often felt a pang of longing for her familiar world in the rookeries.

So even if she had not needed to deliver food to the boys, she would have escaped anyway. That Marcus had suddenly appeared to be her companion was merely a happy accident.

She looked across the carriage at him. He stared at her grumpily. He was plotting something. Revenge, no doubt. She wondered briefly if she had pushed him too far. A man could only take so much frustration.

Then she pushed the thought aside. He had promised to take only what she offered and no more. That included accepting her as she was. Besides, whether he realized it or not, she had to come along. It would take all her persuasive powers to convince the boys to trust Marcus.

Lord, she had missed him. She still felt like she wanted to throw herself into his arms, even knowing where it might lead and that she would be throwing away what tiny bit of independence she had. But when he had appeared out of the darkness to kiss her like that, it had been like a dream come true.

Everything she did these days was with him in mind. Every time she practiced eating with a fork, she wondered if Marcus would appreciate her dainty bites. Every time she executed some intricate dance step, she pretended she was dancing with Marcus. Sweet heaven, she even went to bed with a smile on her face because she knew she would dream about him.

Her whole attitude was inexcusable, and yet she could not stop herself. She was finally with him again, and she felt happy. She did not care that he glared at her or that it would be a long time until he released his anger enough to kiss her. Nothing mattered for now, because she was going back into the rookeries. Finally, she would not have to think about how she walked or talked or moved.

And she was with Marcus.

"Tell me about your mother."

Fantine blinked and stared at Marcus. "What?"

"I said, tell me about your mother. Do you look like her? Was she a dancer? Did she sing?"

Fantine frowned, her happiness fading. "Why?"

He shrugged. "No reason. You are meeting my family. I thought it would be nice to know about yours."

"You know about Penworthy."

"And now I want to know about your mother."

Fantine twisted in her seat, looking out the window. "We are getting close. Help me watch for Nameless."

"Does talking about your mother make you nervous?"

She glanced back at him, determined not to show her surprise. "Of course not."

"Then tell me about her."

Fantine took a deep breath. "Yes, I do look a little like her. She sang a little, danced a little, but her best skills were in acting."

"Did you like living with her?"

"She was my mother," she snapped. "I had to live there."

"Yes, but was it fun or horrid or just boring?"

"What does it matter?" she snapped as she turned away from him again. She planted her face against the window, staring out at the passing shadows.

She thought she had escaped Marcus's questioning, but she should have known better. He was determined to understand her, and that meant questions. Bloody painful questions that probed into thoughts that she had no wish to remember.

"Why does talking about your mother upset you so?" he continued.

"It doesn't upset me," she shot back.

"I do not believe you."

"You are getting even with me for coming along."

"Yes."

"But you are not going to stop, are you?"

"No."

Fantine sighed. He would ferret out the truth whether she fought him or not, whether she wanted him to know or not. She closed her eyes, giving up with little grace. What did she remember of Gabrielle Delarive? "She always smelled good. I know that is a silly thing to say, but it is true. There are so many odors about the stage and the rookeries. Even among the ton. But I could always find her just by closing my eyes."

"What was her favorite scent?"

Fantine opened her eyes, not needing to search her memory. "Gardenias. But we could not always afford them. Lilacs and roses were more common."

"Which do you like best?"

She frowned. His expression was unreadable in the dark.

"Why do you ask?" she finally said.

He shrugged. "It is a simple enough question. I was curious. What scent do you like best?"

She frowned. "I do not know." In truth, no one had ever asked her such a thing before, and it had never occurred to her to wonder. Was there a scent she preferred? She could identify any number of odors, picking out the type of rotting fish, the different perfumes of the ton. But did she prefer one over the other?

The question made no sense to her.

She was grateful when Jacob pulled the carriage to a stop. She was out the door and melting into the night before the horses stopped snorting. They were in a choked alleyway, so like all the other streets in the rookeries. Except this one hid the boys.

She did not wait to see if Marcus followed her. She knew he would, but she wanted to get to the boys first, warning them about her companion before they bolted.

She need not have worried.

They tumbled out of their hiding places, slipping into the moonlight like tiny creatures disturbed from their resting places.

"'Ello, Rat," they cried. "'Ello, Daft," Nameless added, patting Marcus on the shoulders as he and the other boys grabbed the mutton and sack of food.

"'Ello, Nameless," Fantine said. "I thought to bring Chadwick. 'E may be makin' the deliveries if'n I cannot come."

"'At's fine," quipped Nameless as he rooted about in the sack. "The eggs be broke!"

"I know—"

"But Oi were looking forward t' eating an egg."

"I am sorry, Nameless. I ran into a bit o' trouble—"

"A bit o' bouncing, Oi'd say," he quipped, making a crude gesture at Marcus.

"No..." she began to say. But then she stopped. That was exactly what had happened and the boys' raucous laughter told her they knew it.

"Ain't no news," Nameless said as he took a bite from a loaf of bread. His other words were swallowed down with the food. Then there was no more information as the satchel passed from child to child and the bickering over morsels began.

Fantine took the moment to pull Nameless aside. "Look, I know this is awkward about Chadwick and all—"

"Aw, ain't no trouble at all," interrupted the boy. "Oi'll keep somebody 'ere ever' night fer 'im." He glanced over at Chadwick. "At midnight, 'ere. Ever' night at midnight." Then he squinted, stepping up to inspect the peer. "You ain't daft," he said firmly, poking Marcus in the chest.

Chadwick smiled and shook his head as if in amazement. "Sometimes I wonder." Then he poked the boy back, lightly at first, but before long, the two were twisted in combat, joined by the other boys of the gang. Fantine was left standing on the side, watching as if in the audience while the boys initiated Marcus into the gang.

It was nothing significant. Merely a wrestling match on the ground with lots of little fists and feet and one big man laughing and roaring in the middle. It was simple fun, and she had seen it dozens of times over her years in the rookeries.

But never once had she been in the middle of one as Marcus was now.

"Don't worry none," said a voice beside her. Fantine spun around to see Jacob grinning from ear to ear. "They's just playing as boys do."

"I know what it is," she snapped. Then she stormed off to the carriage, kicking at trash on the street as she went. She climbed in, shut the door, and pouted. She knew what she was doing, was well aware of the childishness of the act, but she could not stop herself.

She was alone, and that made her mad.

It took a full ten minutes before Marcus joined her. When he climbed into the carriage, his face was grimed, his clothing torn, and his grin nearly blinded her. Then, to top it off, he took a bite of an enormous red apple.

"That was for Nameless!" she cried. "Do you know the trouble I went through to get that for him?"

"Do you know what I have to pay my sister for this food you are pilfering from her?"

"She does not know! The servants and I—"

"She does know!" he interrupted with a grin. "She knows exactly how much her food bill has risen since your appearance. And she is charging me for every groat."

She folded her arms across her chest. "Well, if I am such a burden, then perhaps I should go back to my old rooms!" She made to leave, but he was blocking the door. "Get out of my way!"

But he merely sat there, staring at her. "Good Lord, you have become surly."

"I am nothing of the sort," she huffed. "Now please—"

"Fantine…" Whatever he was going to say, he stopped. He merely latched the door and settled in across from her.

"You stink."

He looked mournfully at his attire. "Between standing beneath your window and your friends, I am afraid these clothes will have to be burned."

"Well, do not lay the blame for that at my door. I certainly did not ask you to stand beneath my window."

He did not answer, merely watched her while he ate his apple and the carriage started up. "You are furious," he finally commented. "Sweet heaven, I thought you would be pleased that the boys accepted me so well."

Fantine looked away. She had thought she would be happy. But then she'd expected to wheedle their trust, to convince them to accept Marcus. Instead, the boys had transferred their loyalty to him without a blink of their collective eyes. In fact, they had already given Marcus a great deal more friendship than they had ever given her.

"Devil take it, Fantine," Marcus cursed, surprise coloring his tone. "When I think of all I have gone through to learn about the rookeries…And now you are jealous!"

"I am not!"

"Then why are you so angry?"

She turned away, unable to stop her own childishness.

"Fantine?"

"I do not know!" she finally retorted. "I do not know why they suddenly wish to tumble in the dirt with you. They have never done so with me. I do not know why Hurdy is taking so long to speak with Teggie or why your sister suddenly does not like me and has to charge you for my upkeep. I do not know anymore, and I do not like it!"

He stayed silent for a long time, and all she could do was sit there and stew, hating him for making her reveal her thoughts, hating herself for saying them in the first place. But most of all, she simply felt lost. Alone. Miserable.

"I know why they wrestled in the dirt with me."

His words came to her softly, surrounding her in the darkness when she least wished to listen.

"They wished to show me that seven boys could overpower me. They wished to pile on top of me and prove to me that they could hurt me if they so chose."

She glanced up, caught by the wry note in his tone.

"And when they had me facedown in the dirt, half of them sitting on me, the other half showing me their knives, do you know what they said to me?"

She bit her lip. She wanted to know. Of course she wanted to know, but she could not bring herself to ask.

"They told me what they would do to me if I hurt you."

"You cannot be serious," she gasped.

"On the contrary, I am quite serious. And so were they."

Then he abruptly moved over so he could pull her stiff form into his arms. She resisted at first, but it was only a token protest and they both knew it. She needed his touch right now, needed to feel that someone cared.

"Fantine, the only reason they accept me is that you brought me here."

"You do not know that."

"I do. Nameless said so quite explicitly."

She did not know how to answer. "I suppose I was being foolish," she said softly.

He shook his head, then reached over and turned her face to his. "For the first time, you have shown me that something is important to you. The boys are important to you, as you are to them. I am honored you would trust me with such knowledge."

Fantine averted her eyes. She had not realized she had revealed so much or that he would be so astute at seeing it. But now that she had, she did not regret it. He would not hurt the boys.

As for hurting her, it had already begun.

Because at that moment she realized she loved him.

CHAPTER 14

He felt her stiffen in his arms, heard the catch of her breath. Marcus tried not to groan, wondering what he had said wrong now. She was such an unpredictable woman, angry one moment, giddy the next, and now, from the sound of her breathing, she seemed nearly panic-stricken.

"I must go," she said softly.

"What?"

"I have to go."

"But why? And where?"

But there was no more time. She was already out of his arms, flinging open the carriage door and jumping out of the moving vehicle.

He scrambled forward, grabbing hold of the sides as Jacob drew tight on the reins.

"Fantine!" he cried, but there was no answer. Only the dark shadows of buildings outlined by the moon. He twisted, searching for Jacob's dark silhouette. "Where did she go?"

The form shrugged. "Could be anywheres in this lot. Good thing I was going slow or she might 'ave 'urt 'erself."

Marcus shook his head. "I do not understand."

"Aye, guv. That is just wot me wife says."

"About me?"

"About men."

"Damn!" He slammed his fist against the carriage hard enough to startle the horses. Then he stepped down, still scanning the darkness for some hint of her form. "Do you know I stood in the alley for three hours, three bloody hours, waiting for her. And now she runs off!"

"Aye."

"It makes no sense. She makes no sense."

"Aye."

Marcus sighed. There was nothing to see out here, nothing that would tell him where she had gone. "We should leave. She is more than capable of handling herself."

Jacob did not answer.

"You do not think she hurt herself? Jumping out like that?"

"She be more agile than a cat, yer lordship. She's not hurt."

"True," Marcus agreed. But that did not stop him from worrying. And wondering. Why had she run off?

Eventually, he chose to climb up on top with his coachman, his gaze constantly scanning the darkness. "We will wait here for a bit. Just in case."

"Very well," Jacob answered as he offered up a brandy flask.

Marcus accepted it with a grateful smile, taking a long pull before handing it back. "Tell me what else your wife says."

Jacob grinned. "I will try, but I cannot think it will make sense to anyone but 'er."

Marcus nodded and reached for the flask again. "Women."

In the end, they waited for over an hour. They waited long after the brandy was gone. Long enough for the horses to get restless and for a fine drizzle to begin.

But not long enough for Fantine to come back.

"I guess we best be getting home," Marcus finally said. "It is too cold to sit out here. And it is not good for the horses."

"Aye," answered Jacob, but he did not take up the reins.

"No, I mean it this time."

"Aye." But still they sat there.

"Go ahead. I have a better brandy for us at home."

That was all his man needed. Jacob had them moving at a spanking pace before Marcus could change his mind.

Still, he had to check one last place before he became thoroughly cup-shot. "But take me to my sister's home first."

Though Jacob tried to stifle it, Marcus heard the man's groan.

"One little stop," Marcus said. "I swear. Then you may have a full bottle of my best brandy."

"One little stop," Jacob grumbled, as much to himself as to Marcus. "One little stop an' we will be waiting there for 'er too. Hours and hours while me nice bed gets colder an' colder."

In the end, Marcus had to promise the man a full bottle of brandy and ten of his best cigars before Jacob would stop grumbling. He did not mind the sacrifice. He knew Jacob was right about how long they would have to wait. But despite everything he told himself, he could not go to bed without first knowing Fantine was safe.

It was not until they finally arrived at his sister's home that he realized disaster had struck. The house was ablaze with lights and commotion. Servants scurried about carrying in luggage from a very distinctive coach.

Staring at it, Marcus had to accept the brutal truth.

Fantine was not safe. She was, in fact, in more danger than she ever had been before.

His mother had arrived.

He cursed with singular determination and fluency, but it did nothing to ease his mind or illuminate what he most wanted to know. Had Fantine returned to her bedchamber? There had been ample time for her to walk home, but only if she went directly here with little wandering.

There was only one solution, much though he hated to admit it. One way to check on Fantine without alarming his mother. He had to climb the wall to Fantine's chamber. If she were there, then everything was well. If not, then he would have to distract his mother long enough for Fantine to come to her senses and return.

"Best go on home, Jacob," he said with a sigh as he dropped to the ground. "I do not approve of servants watching their employers make fools of themselves."

"I could close me eyes," he offered with a grin.

"Go home, Jacob," he said dryly, then watched as his coachman set off at a brisk trot toward a warm, dry bed. His own destination was the small patch of mud beneath Fantine's window.

It was difficult to slip around to the back of the house without being seen by the many servants still hauling his mother's baggage. He had to walk down the street, then come up the back row, cursing the cold and the mud and women in general. By the time he made it to the back of his sister's house, he was thoroughly disgruntled.

"Fantine," he called softly as he scanned her dark window.

Nothing.

He sighed. He dared not call louder, but he had to see if she was up there. That meant climbing the wall.

Putting one hand to the ivy, he began to pull himself up. Unfortunately, the leaves were damp and his boots were not suited to finding toeholds where there were none. With a muffled curse, he dropped back down to the ground and stripped off his footwear. Then, with another heartfelt curse, he began to climb.

He made it to her window despite the wet leaves that kept slapping him in the face. Then he twisted his large frame into position on her very narrow windowsill and leaned down to open the window.

It did not budge.

He worked harder, nearly lost his footing, and still nothing. It was locked.

He did not know whether to scream in frustration or kick through the window in anger. In the end, he did neither. He grabbed hold of two solidly placed bits of greenery, planted his feet on the sill, and stuck his buttocks far out over the ground. The position was undignified, but it allowed him to push his face against the window to peer inside.

Someone had to have locked the window. He could only hope it was Fantine. Pressing his cheek against the freezing pane he frowned. He thought he saw movement inside, but he could not be positive.

"Fantine!" he called again. "Fantine!" Then, he took the ultimate risk. He released one hand and used it to tap lightly on the glass.

The response was immediate. A dark shadow moved and came directly to the window. Then, before he could catch hold, the window flew open and he came face-to-face with his own mother.

"Marcus!"

"Moth—aieeee!"

It was not his fault. Even with one hand, he was in a stable position on the sill. Except the vine that anchored him chose that moment to pull away from the wall. And though he gripped it with all his strength, it was still wet and it slid right out of his hand. In the end, the vine merely slowed his descent.

He fell. Painfully. Twisting his ankle in the mud, then slipping onto his behind with a final, undignified splat. And all the while, his mother watched him, an expression of horror on her face.

"Marcus! Are you quite insane?"

"Yes, Mother," he groaned from his position, flat and spread-eagled on the ground.

"Are you hurt?"

"Yes, Mother. But not seriously."

"Well!" she huffed.

Then Marcus looked up to see Fantine, wearing a high-necked, canary gown, poke her head out beside his mother.

"You see, Fantine," his mother said, "even the best of families have at least one odd fish." Then they both pulled back into the room and shut the window with a resounding snap.

Marcus would have gone home right then and there if he could have. He would have crawled on his hands and knees if need be, but there was no opportunity for escape. The servants, alerted by his scream, scrambled outside, each one to gawk and pretend to assist him to his feet. When he found he could not move without groaning, they immediately lifted him up and carried him inside, gingerly depositing him in the parlor settee as if he were some crazy great-uncle. In fact, he nearly bared his teeth and growled at them just to see them scurry.

He would have if his mother had not chosen that moment to sail into the room, disappointment clear on her face.

"Very well, Marcus, acquaint me with the particulars. How desperately are you injured? Will you be able to dance? Can you stand? If you cannot escort us tomorrow night, I must know immediately so as to find your replacement. Your father will not be in town for another two weeks at the earliest, so tell me now if you intend to leave me in the lurch."

Marcus waited, making sure she had indeed finished speaking. When she spun back around, staring at him impatiently, he deigned to answer. "You are looking quite lovely this evening."

She did, in fact, appear magnificent. Though a somewhat stout woman, she carried her weight with grace and style. Her dark traveling gown was stately despite the wrinkles, and her pinned white hair was still striking.

"Marcus!"

"Hmm? Oh, I was merely admiring your new hairstyle. Last time I saw you, you were still doing that..." He gestured toward his ears. "Ringlet thing. I much prefer this."

His mother gaped at him, her jaw slack. Then suddenly, she spun on her heel and threw open the parlor door.

"Lottie! Lottie, come quick! He has lost his wits!" Then she came back and settled beside him on the settee, the whoosh of her skirts nearly enough to topple him over the arm.

Marcus merely grinned, knowing that at last he had accomplished his task. His mother's statement would no doubt rouse the entire household, including Fantine. He would be able to see her and finally judge for himself if she was all right.

At their mother's command, Lottie came rushing in, closely followed by her husband. Both she and Christopher looked hastily dressed and somewhat bleary-eyed, but both were able to nod in his direction. He smiled congenially back.

"Sorry about the ivy and the mud," he said, gesturing to the soiled settee and his filthy bare feet.

"Not at all, not at all," boomed his brother-in-law with a welcoming smile. "Brandy?"

"Please."

Lottie rushed over to him, brushing some of the mud off his face with her handkerchief. "Really, Chris, brandy? I do not think that is at all wise."

"Nonsense," returned her husband. "Seems like the perfect response to having a muddy, barefoot man in one's parlor. Come to think of it, sounds like the perfect response if one *is* the barefoot muddy chap, right, old boy?"

"Right," responded Marcus, but his eyes were still on the parlor door. Where was Fantine?

"He is frozen through!" gasped his mother, as she pressed her hand to his cheek. Unfortunately, the lace of her sleeve tickled his nose, and he was forced to release a prodigious sneeze. "He has taken a chill! Quick, we must warm him."

"Absolutely," cut in Christopher in his booming voice. "Your brandy—"

"Thank you—"

"Brandy!" gasped his mother. "We need blankets and boiling water for his feet."

"And tonic," continued Lottie, gesturing to the butler.

"Tonic!" snorted his brother-in-law. "Bother, but that is nasty stuff. Here, Marcus, have some more brandy."

"Much obliged," Marcus answered as Chris topped off his glass.

"Thank heaven," exclaimed his mother, as the butler preceded a veritable army of servants carrying blankets and hot water. "Lottie, help me take care of his feet—"

"Yes, Mother—"

"And what kind of tonic is it?" his mother continued without pause. "Pray, not that vile potion I sent you last year? It killed the rooster, you know. Cook gave him just a spoonful...."

Marcus never truly listened to his mother. Not closely at least, but her words faded into nothing when he saw Fantine step into the room. She still wore the demure canary gown. In fact, it was the very brightness of the fabric that caught his attention in the first place. But what robbed him of speech was something entirely different.

She looked terrible. Quite dull, in fact.

Her eyes were keen as they took in the scene. Lottie was at his feet carefully smearing the mud on his toes. His mother nearly stretched across his lap as she buried him beneath three heavy blankets. His brother-in-law stood two steps away, trying hard to stifle his laughter in his brandy glass.

But though she seemed to see the tableau, she did not react to it. Instead, she settled quietly into a corner, folded her hands into her lap, and lowered her head.

Something was most definitely wrong.

He leaned forward, trying to catch her gaze, but it was lowered to her lap. He had to do something.

Pushing away his mother, he stripped off the blankets.

"Marcus—"

"Hush, Mother. I am quite well," he said curtly, then stepped over his sister, set aside the brandy, and went directly to Fantine. "But are you?" he asked as he knelt before her.

It took an agonizingly long time for her to look at him. Then, when she did, her eyes were wide and confused, as if she was torn between fear and panic.

The sight alarmed him. He did not know what to do or say, especially since the wrong word might send her fleeing.

"I am quite well, my lord." Her voice was soft, cultured, and so restrained as to be almost nonexistent. Definitely not what he had come to expect from her. "It is kind of you to ask."

Marcus frowned, his fear escalating. "You do not sound at all fine. You sound..." He could not find the correct word. "So...demure."

She tilted her head slightly, her expression unreadable. She could have been any of a hundred different society girls, just another face in the crowd of debutantes. "I am behaving inappropriately?"

"Yes!" Then he shook his head. "I mean, no, but—"

"Stop it, Marcus!" his mother cut in. "You are upsetting the girl!"

Marcus shifted to stare at his mother. "Me? I upset Fantine?" The thought boggled his mind. But one look at Fantine's face, and he knew it was true. He did frighten her. And he had not the least clue why.

Then his mother was standing before him, her hands on her hips, her expression as severe as he had ever seen before. "Exactly what are your intentions here, Marcus?"

He shifted to look at her, but the movement strained his injured ankle, and for the second time that night, he fell flat on his behind with a rather loud thud. His mother merely stepped forward, as much the protective hen as ever. "Come, Marcus. Surely this is not a difficult question. Exactly what are your intentions regarding Miss Drake?"

He frowned, momentarily forgetting that Drake was Fantine's new surname. Then, when he did remember, he glanced at her, looking for help. But there was nothing to see, no expression on her face.

"Marcus!"

"I have no intentions whatsoever!" he snapped, not really knowing what he said. His only thought was to pacify his mother so that he could concentrate on Fantine. "I am concerned for Fantine's well-being. She is not acting right."

"Nonsense," his mother returned. "She is behaving perfectly."

Marcus shook his head. "No, you do not understand."

"On the contrary, I believe I do. Lottie tells me you want her as your mistress."

There was no safe means of responding to this statement, so Marcus remained silent, choosing to shoot his sister an angry glare. She merely shrugged while Christopher silently refilled Marcus's brandy glass.

"Well, you cannot have her," continued his mother undaunted. "We are bringing her out. That makes her a well-bred young lady in all respects, whether or not she is technically a bastard."

"Mother!" Marcus exclaimed. He could not help himself, as he glanced fearfully at Fantine.

"Do not feign worry now, my boy," she continued. "Fantine has been most honest with us."

"Fantine was honest?" The words slipped out without his conscious thought, and he regretted them almost immediately.

"Of course she was! Shame on you for even thinking that she would not be! Really, I am most disappointed in you."

Marcus had no response to this except to take his brandy glass from Christopher.

"Now you listen to me, young man, and you listen well. Despite her parentage, Fantine is a well-bred young lady. She will not be anyone's mistress, least of all yours. She is here for her coming-out, sponsored by me. There will be no more midnight climbs up to her window, no more furtive glances or attempts to be private with her. Whatever your political or private motivation, you have asked Lottie and me to bring her out, and we will. As of this instant, your responsibilities are at an end."

Then she paused, took a breath, and pinned him with her most imperious stare. "I believe it would be best for you to remove yourself from London for a while. Yes, in fact, I am quite sure of it. Christopher can be our escort. You may go away." She made tiny shooing motions at him.

He gaped at her. "But—"

"And now," she continued, "I feel in need of a rest. Good night, everyone." Then she strode out of the room leaving a deafening silence behind her.

Marcus gritted his teeth. It took him a moment to collect his wits enough to address Fantine. But just as he took a breath, his mother interrupted again—in the form of a disembodied voice from the stairs.

"Come along, Fantine. You need your rest, too." The woman did not even have the grace to stick her head through the parlor door, but her voice echoed through the room nevertheless.

Fantine immediately rose to her feet. "Yes, Lady Anne," she called. Then, neatly eluding Marcus's outstretched hand, she slipped out of the room.

"I'd best go as well," said Lottie as she too gained her feet. "It will take some time getting Mother's room just right, and I still hope to get some sleep."

Just before leaving the room she paused, turning to her brother with an expression she had no doubt learned from their mother. "She is right, Marcus. You cannot be seducing the girl we are bringing out, no matter what her background. It is bad ton, you know. And rather crude besides." Then she slipped away.

Marcus stared at the empty doorway, wondering if it too would begin reproaching him. Then he turned toward his brother-in-law, almost afraid to hear what the man would say.

But Christopher did not say a thing. He merely crossed the room, brandy bottle in hand, and settled his large frame into the chair recently abandoned by Fantine. He did not speak again until the two had nearly finished off the bottle.

When he did finally offer a suggestion, it was with all the hearty goodwill of a longtime drinking companion.

"Take my advice, old boy," he said cheerfully. "Find that maid you had at Harris's ball, buy her some bauble, and enjoy yourself. It will take your mind off Fantine."

Marcus just stared at him, words failing him completely.

CHAPTER 15

Fantine sat on her bed and tugged at the high neck of her
night rail. It was pristine white, covered with lace, and
made her feel like a doll in a shop display. Add a blank
smile and eventually some customer would buy her.
Unless, of course, no one wanted her and she was tossed
out on the rubbish heap.

But she refused to consider that possibility.

Flopping down on her pillow, Fantine resolved to focus
on the future. She loved him, but what of it? Marcus had no
intentions regarding her. Good. Because, as she and now
his mother had firmly said, she would not be his mistress.
The man had obviously never even thought of marriage,
and given the circumstances, there were no other options.
She was free of Marcus.

Forever.

Fantine forced her face into an empty smile and told
herself she was glad of it. But if Marcus had failed in his
goal to make her his mistress, he had succeeded in
something else entirely. He had reminded her what it was
like to live without constant struggle. She had discovered
that she liked hot food and warm rooms. She enjoyed nice
clothing and a soft bed. And she wanted such comforts to
continue.

She would indeed compromise so she could continue to have a warm bed, good food, and clean undergarments. So she could continue to feed Nameless and the boys. She still refused to become Marcus's mistress, but she would now consider a loveless marriage to some other man. Especially if she chose a husband whom she could tolerate, even like.

Mr. Edwin Thompson sprang to mind. He was a tall man with short brown hair and serious brown eyes. He was polite, intelligent, and after three teas and a dinner in his company, she felt quite at ease with him. Perhaps she could marry him.

Or perhaps not. After all, he was the only eligible gentleman besides Marcus that she knew. She still had a whole month and a half worth of balls and parties in which to discover potential husbands. Perhaps she would choose one of them.

True, this was not why she had decided to have her Season. She was intent on exposing Teggie. But she was a capable girl. She could perform her job for her father and still find a husband. That was, after all, just what Penworthy wanted.

And it was what she wanted too.

Especially now that Marcus would no longer be interfering, constantly tempting her away with his kisses. His mother had made that quite clear. She had even told him to remove himself completely from London. Fantine would be free of his distractions. She could meet the men of the ton and perhaps be snatched up in days.

Part of her still cringed at the thought. She had spent the last ten years throwing Penworthy's upper-crust heritage right back at his face. She had taunted and tortured him, saying she would live her own life on her own terms, not his.

But the thought of returning to the rookeries, of scrounging for enough to eat while the cold seeped into her bones, made her realize just how much of a fool she had been. Life required compromise. She could no longer stick to her principles when all they gave her was an empty belly and a cold hearth.

She was tired. And old.

How mortifying to discover that her father had been right all along. It was time to settle into a comfortable life with a husband. Even that was better than starving to death. And if she once viewed marriage as whoring, albeit in a respectable manner with a single customer, well then, she had begun to think that Louise had the right of it. Whoring was the only option for girls like her.

Marcus's words echoed again in her mind. *I have no intentions whatsoever.*

Fantine curled onto her side and cried.

"You look delightful. Simply delightful. Lottie, you have an excellent eye. That burgundy silk is perfect. It brings out the red in her hair. And the white lace overskirt conveys just the right amount of modesty for a girl in her coming out. Perfect, child. You are perfect."

Fantine nodded as she had been nodding for the last hour.

"You must remember not to catch the skirt in the mud. It can be ruinous. A pity your hair is so short. It is a beautiful shade, especially as that dress brings it out to perfection. Still it is so short, but I believe we have made it fetching."

"Yes, my lady."

"Remember not to dance with any gentleman more than twice—"

"Mother!" Lottie cut in. "Fantine knows all this."

"What about the story we have put about? She is Penworthy's niece, yes, but that she is also a dear friend of a dear friend of mine? A companion to my neighbor's neighbor, so to speak."

"She knows all of it."

Both women turned to inspect Fantine. "I remember everything," she responded dutifully.

"Oh, my," Lady Anne continued, "I must attend to my own gown. Now do not be nervous, Fantine. You shall be splendid."

"Yes, my lady."

Lady Anne hesitated a moment more, but then she

scurried off to her own room. Only Lottie remained, and she shot Fantine a tiny worried frown.

"Fantine—"

"I am quite well. Truly. Both you and your mother have been most kind. I have learned my lessons well, and I swear I will not shame you."

Lottie's frown deepened as she toyed with her fan. "You misunderstand. I know you shall be absolutely perfect. But I am worried nonetheless."

Fantine turned. Her legs already ached from standing, but she did not dare sit down for fear of rumpling her ball gown. She merely frowned at her companion. "I do not understand."

"Hang it!" cried Lottie, dropping onto the bed, completely heedless of creasing her own gown. "Just look at you!"

Fantine looked down, wondering what she had done amiss.

"No, not at your gown. At you!" Then Lottie stood up and turned Fantine around to stare at herself in the mirror. Her face was fashionably pale, her eyes appeared large and dark from the kohl, and her expression remained cool. She looked like any of the other debutantes she could recall.

"When Marcus first brought you to my door, your cheeks were rosy, your eyes sparkled, you seemed to bring an energy to everyone and everything about you. But now..." She shook her head. "Now I do not know what I have done to you. All last night and today, you have been like a marionette."

Fantine bit her lip. Had her thoughts been so apparent? "Is it my mother?" pressed Lottie. "Does she frighten you?"

Fantine spun around. "Oh, no! You and your mother have been perfectly kind. She is merely used to getting her own way."

Lottie nodded sagely, as if that were just the answer she expected. Then she stood up from the bed, crossing her arms and looking so reproachful, Fantine once again checked her gown. "Then it is just as I suspected. Very well, Fantine, you might as well tell me. What has my wretched brother done now?"

"Marcus?"

"Well, of course, Marcus. If it is not the ball, my mother, or myself, then it must be Marcus."

"Blimey, Lottie," she snapped, "the world does not revolve around your brother. There are any number of things that could upset me, all of which have nothing to do with Marcus!"

"Very well then, what are they?"

Fantine threw up her hands, turning away from both Lottie and their reflection in the mirror. But the only direction that remained was toward the door. And it was at that moment that she saw the one man she had tried to force from her thoughts for the last twenty-four hours.

Marcus.

He looked as handsome as ever. She had seen him in his ballroom attire before: black coat and pants, single diamond pin that sparkled almost as brilliantly as his eyes.

All was as it had been before, except for one thing. This time, he lounged against her bedroom door, a hungry look heating his expression, heating her body until her very blood seem to burn with it.

"What are you doing here?" cried Lottie. "I thought Mother sent you off to Scotland."

"I do not always go where Mother sends me."

"So you chose instead to come around here, cutting up Fantine's peace just when she most needs it. Really, brother, I had thought you—"

"Enough, Lottie," he interrupted, his gaze still locked on Fantine. "You and Mother cannot keep me from Fantine no matter how much you screech. So why not bow to the inevitable and leave gracefully, hmm?"

"You overbearing, arrogant pig!" That came from Fantine, and it startled everyone, including herself.

Lottie stared at her. "That is the most feeling you have shown all day."

"Then perhaps I should stay," cut in Marcus, "and see what other miracles I can achieve."

Fantine opened her mouth to deny him, but she did not get the chance. Lottie was there before her. "She will see you in the library." Then she firmly slammed the door in Marcus's face.

"But—" began Fantine; then she stopped. Lottie was turning around, a fiercely maternal look on her face.

"No, Fantine. It is my turn to speak." Lottie stepped forward, taking Fantine's hands and pulling her over to sit on the bed. "You have fallen in love with him."

If her face was overheated a moment ago, it suddenly felt very cold and clammy.

"Oh, Lord, do not faint on me!"

Fantine stiffened, insulted to the core. "I never faint!"

"Of course, you would not. My apologies. Goodness, I am handling this very badly."

Fantine closed her eyes, fighting to gain control of her thoughts. But nothing was stable, and the world shifted too quickly for her to keep up. "Lottie—"

"No, pray do not say it. Whether you deny it or not, I can see the answer on your face."

Fantine opened her eyes. Bloody hell, but she was slipping. Taking another deep breath, she clamped down on her thoughts and riotous emotions. Through sheer force of will, she changed the subject. "I am going to my first ball. That is what I am thinking about. And I am delighted."

"Good. Excellent." Lottie, too, appeared to be struggling, but soon her expression settled. "Now, listen carefully. Marcus is drawn to you, but if he has not offered you marriage by now, he will never do so. It has nothing to do with your parentage or his. If he truly loved you, he would brave everything—including social ruin—for you. But he has not. And that tells me that only his...er...his unmentionables are affected. Not his heart."

Fantine looked away, clenching her jaw to keep from reacting. Lottie had not said anything new. She had merely put voice to the very words that had haunted Fantine for the last day. But to finally hear them from someone else…

It hurt terribly.

"I am sorry." Lottie's words were soft and her touch gentle as she squeezed Fantine's hands. "I did not wish to say it so baldly, but you must know it to be true. If you are to make the most of your Season now, you cannot spend the rest—"

"I know. I have resolved to get a husband, Lottie. A respectable one." Fantine raised her gaze, pleased that her voice sounded steady and firm.

She was rewarded by Lottie's smile. "Excellent. You shall make a brilliant match. You have the makings of a countess or better. I am sure of it."

Fantine shook her head, her determination becoming firmer by the second. "My mother counted titles. I will not. I merely want a kind man. No more, no less. I can be content with that. In fact, I was thinking of Mr. Thompson."

Lottie grinned, pulling Fantine to her feet. "He is a good choice, but do not be too hasty. I shall be sure to introduce you to a dozen or more kind men." She leaned forward, her voice laced with humor. "I shall especially look for kind, rich ones."

Fantine raised her gaze, looking for the first time at Lottie as a person. As a friend.

The thought astounded her. Never before had she known another female friend of her own age. Lottie wanted nothing from her, no food, no money, nothing but her happiness. It was a novel concept, and one that she did not quite trust. But at that moment, it was more precious to her than all the husbands in England. And with a sudden impulsive gesture, Fantine surged forward to hug her.

The movement was awkward. She had never given another woman a hug. Her arms went too far around, and she feared creasing Lottie's gown. But Lottie did not seem to mind. She returned the gesture enthusiastically, and Fantine felt both bolstered and embarrassed by it.

"Lottie—" she began, not knowing at all what to say.

"Oh, never mind," whispered her friend. "Come, if we do not hurry, Mother will be barging in here with a new set of instructions."

Fantine nodded, taking her cue from Lottie. When Lottie bent forward to check her own appearance, Fantine did the same. Soon, Lottie pronounced them both ready, but she still hesitated.

"Are you sure you wish to see Marcus?" she asked.

"I am beginning to learn that my wishes do not matter significantly to your brother. He will do exactly as he wishes and tell himself that it is what I require as well."

Lottie smiled. "Good. You have seen that fault in him. Keep looking. He has more."

Then, for the first time that day, Fantine felt her lips curve in a true smile. "Dozens, I should not doubt."

"At the very least," returned Lottie.

Marcus paced the small library, his long strides crossing the room in less than four steps. He had traversed the same area eighty-seven times by the time he heard them come down the stairs. What had kept them so long? It did not matter. Not so long as he could finally see her.

He stopped moving, placing himself in a casual pose, leaning against the desk. But he did not like leaning, especially since the edge of the desk cut painfully into his buttocks. So he stood again, but he could not find the correct placement for his feet. Perhaps he should stand by the window.

He crossed the room to the window.

No, the evening light slanted across his left eye. He did not wish to disrupt his vision or appear to her with an odd-colored stripe across his face. By the bar would be better.

He crossed the room again.

But he did not wish her to think he was forever drinking brandy. Especially as he felt in need of a drink. Putting his body next to temptation was not a wise idea.

He should move away. But where?

He took a step. He could not stand in the middle of the room like some statue. Perhaps—

The door scraped open, and he spun around.

Good God, she was beautiful. He had seen her upstairs. But now she held her head a little higher. Her movements were graceful, her dark beauty enriched by the burgundy silk.

He stood almost mute with wonder. There was no comparison between this goddess and the filthy urchin Rat or even the teasing barmaid Fanny. Or perhaps there was, because they were all Fantine, his changeable, enchanting, delightful Fantine.

"You have never looked lovelier," he said, his voice husky.

"Thank you, my lord." Even her voice was intoxicating—refined and smooth like the brandy he had craved only moments before. Only now, all he wanted was her.

"I am besotted."

He saw her flinch at his statement and could not understand why. Whatever the reason, he had to make amends. Fumbling briefly with his pocket, he pulled out an awkwardly wrapped box. He groaned inwardly at the inexpert folds. He had been angry with the lazy way the clerk had creased the paper, and so he had tried to redo it himself.

He should have known better. The paper looked as if it had been crumpled by a child.

"I, uh, I bought you a gift for tonight," he said. "I hope you like it. I tried to wrap it myself, but as you can see, I am not very skilled with such matters. I apologize—"

"Thank you, my lord. It was most kind of you."

"Do not think it is improper to accept it. It is merely a token. Most appropriate from any gentleman, although I hope you do not get too many. That is, I hope you are quite a success tonight, just not so much that…But I am being silly. Of course, you will get many such gifts. I should have brought you jewelry. But my mother would make you give it back, and I—"

"Thank you, my lord," she said firmly, a slight smile about her lips. "Do you think I could have the package now?"

"Hmmm? Oh!" He had not realized he had a death grip on the gift. Would nothing with Fantine ever go right? "Here," he said awkwardly. "I hope you like it."

She opened the box. It was nothing special, he knew.

But he had seen the decanter and thought of her. Then he had spent hours searching for just the right scent to fill it. He had any number of other tasks, and yet he had taken an entire day finding this for her.

"It is perfume," he said unnecessarily as she lifted the decanter out of the velvet-lined box. She held up the elegant crystal to the light, tracing the cut edges of the bird's wings. "That is you," he said softly. "Just beginning tonight to soar. You shall be brilliant." He invested all his feelings into his words.

"It is beautiful."

"You mentioned that your mother always smelled special. I hope you like the fragrance." He had wanted something sweet, but instead, had been captivated by an exotic scent. It was subtle, slipping beneath a man's defenses, until it suddenly overwhelmed him and he could think of nothing and no one else.

"It is wonderful," she said, and he thought she meant it. It certainly sounded like she did. But then again…"I shall wear it tonight and think of you."

Then she delicately touched the stopper to her wrists and the flawless arch of her neck. He watched her, mesmerized, remembering the feel of her hands across his chest, knowing that he had tasted the curve of her neck.

He swallowed. "I must be mad," he said softly. "I could have had you all to myself, and yet instead I give you over to my sister and mother. They will not let me see you, and tonight they show you to the world. Very soon, you will have no time for me, no memory of our moments together."

She looked up at him, her expression somber, her eyes impossibly large.

"I could never forget you, Marcus. You have been part of my life so completely that I will always remember you. But I think your mother and sister were right. You should leave London now."

He smiled at her, watching the way her lips moved as she spoke. What a perfect color they were: a dark red meant for kissing. They were perfectly shaped as well, not too full, nor too narrow. Lord, he admonished himself. He was acting the mooncalf. What had she just said?

He replayed her words in his mind, this time listening for their meaning. The jolt he received was enough to snap his wits back into place.

"What did you say?"

She turned away, and he noticed her movements were not as smooth as he had thought. In fact, she appeared nervous, as if she wished to put distance between them.

"When I look at you...No, when you look at me, I see what you see."

"I beg your pardon?" He reached for her, but she spun around, confronting him as she had so many times before.

"When you look at me, you see a mistress. A whore."

He pulled back, appalled. "Nonsense!"

"Would you seek to be private with any other debutante? Would you lounge in her doorway or climb up her window?"

"Of course not! But you are not just any debutante—"

"That is correct. I am your woman, your quarry in some idiotic mistress hunt. When you look at me, you do not see a girl in her coming-out, but Rat and Fanny in some bizarre combination that is not at all respectable."

He frowned, unable to understand her. "I see only you."

"Well, I do not want you to see me!" she snapped. "How can I be a debutante with you constantly looking over my shoulder reminding me that I am nothing more than a street rat?"

"But you are not—"

"Exactly. But you look at me as if I were one. You treat me as if I were one."

He took her arms in his, pulling her close to his body. "Listen to me, Fantine, I do not know if this is simply nerves or some nonsense of my mother's, but it will not fadge. I arranged for this coming-out. I *paid* for it, for God's sake. You cannot throw me away now as if I counted for nothing!"

Then he drew her into his arms, waiting for her to soften toward him. It came within seconds. Her body fit itself to him, heating his blood as he lowered his mouth to hers.

Their kiss was heady, dark, powerful. Her arms wrapped around him as he leaned over her, arching her back into him. "We were meant for each other, Fantine."

Bang!

Marcus lifted his head, startled at the noise of the library door slamming hard against the wall. Blinking to clear the haze from his mind, he focused on the imposing figures of his sister and mother.

"Marcus! Step away from her!"

He did. A step. But he kept a hand on her shoulder. It was time his relatives understood the reality of the situation. He would not be denied Fantine.

His mother stepped forward. "I am simply appalled—"

"No."

That was Fantine, and Marcus could not help smiling at her cold tone. It effectively silenced everyone in the room. Then he relaxed, waiting for her to explain the situation to his family. They would listen to her.

"I thank you for your protection, Lottie, Lady Anne, but in this I must be the one to express myself. Not you."

"But—"

"Please, Lady Anne. A few moments more."

His mother pursed her lips, clearly annoyed, but it was Lottie who nodded, giving Fantine an encouraging smile. "Come along. Mother. Fantine can handle this."

"But—"

"Please." That was Fantine, and eventually Lady Anne gave way.

"Five minutes," she said. "And I shall watch the clock."

"Five minutes," Marcus echoed, as he sketched a bow. Then he stepped forward and firmly closed the door on his interfering family. After the reassuring thud, he turned to take his reward from Fantine's lips. But she had moved to the opposite side of the room.

"I told you," she said softly.

Marcus blinked. "I beg your pardon?"

"How am I to act the lady when you constantly treat me as your mistress?"

He pulled up short. "I have never treated you—"

"Then you often kiss unwilling women in their guardian's library?"

"You were most willing!" he shot back.

"Of course, I was!" she returned, her own voice becoming heated. "All you do is touch me, and I am at your mercy! Good God, Marcus, you have proved your power over me time and time again. But that doesn't mean I wish it to happen!"

"I have never forced you," he stated. But his tone was less firm. Did he truly have that devastating an effect on her? The thought was quite appealing.

"Gawd!" she drawled in her thickest Cockney. "Is this wot yer want, guv? Me breasts in yer 'ands and me nasties open? Then let's get to it." She made to rip open her gown at the bodice.

"Fantine! Stop that this instant!"

"Then which is it, Marcus? Am I to be your whore or a lady?"

He frowned, moving forward until he stood directly in front of her. "You are to be whatever you wish. That was our arrangement. I told you I would not force you, and I have not."

"I wish to be a lady, Marcus. I wish to have my coming out and dance in a beautiful gown and have gentlemen treat me as a respectable lady." Her voice quavered slightly. He was startled to realize the strength of her desire. "This is my moment, Marcus. Everything my mother dreamed of. And now I find I want it as well. Why must you ruin it?"

He pulled back. "I am not ruining anything! It is I who made all this possible."

"Yet you still wish to claim me. You bring me into a darkened library to kiss me and remind me that you *paid* for all of it. What is that, Marcus, but treating me as your whore?"

He swallowed, her words finally seeping in. Had he been treating her as a courtesan? All this time? When all he wished was to be with her. To talk with her. To show her how…

How what? How delightful it was to be a mistress in the ton? He should have locked her in a tiny room, given her a servant, and showered her with jewels until she succumbed to him. But he had not done that. He had brought her to his sister to make her respectable. Yet, the very next moment, he had attempted to seduce her.

Good God, she was right. If he wished for her to have a coming-out, then he should treat her as a highborn woman, with all the restrictions and formalities that entailed.

"I want you to be as you wish," he said slowly. "I want you to choose your life."

"Prove it," she challenged. "Leave London. Let me have a Season and see what happens."

He shook his head. "I want to guide you. There are many dangers—"

"Your sister and mother are adequate to the task."

Marcus clenched his jaw. Yes, they certainly were. "What about Teggie—"

"You have already relinquished your part in the investigations."

Yes, he had. "And Hurdy? Should I not wait until we know Sprat has written to his father?"

"Sprat's letter will only change Hurdy's attitude toward you. Hurdy will still come for me."

"Then—"

"But I can handle him. I have for many years until now and shall for many years to come."

Marcus remained silent. He had no more objections, nothing else he could say. She was right. He could not expect her to be a lady and yet treat her as a courtesan. It was not fair. To either of them.

He looked up, pleading with her. "Can you not see that I simply wish to be with you? I can stop kissing you," he said, fearing that he lied. "I can be your silent escort. But do not exile me. The week when I could not see you was torture." He stepped forward, wishing he knew the words to express his feelings. "I want so much more from you than just your body. I want—"

"My soul."

His mind rebelled at such a thought, but he knew deep down that she was right. He did want her soul. Her body, her mind, her heart. Her soul. He did not want to examine his motives. He could not believe he had already relinquished his heart to her, and so it was only fair she return the favor. But to deny the truth would be fruitless.

"If you care for me," she continued relentlessly, "please let me find my way. Alone."

Marcus looked away, his breath abruptly squeezed from his throat. She could not know how her words effected him. And yet apparently she did, for a moment later she was at his side exclaiming in horror.

"Marcus!"

She grabbed his hand, and he saw himself trembling.

How odd that now of all times, those particular words would come back to haunt him.

Fantine pushed him toward a chair and he went without a struggle, settling quietly down with her beside him. But even as her touch remained a balm, her voice hardened with demand. "What is happening, Marcus? Why are you so pale?"

He did not intend to answer, and yet the words came nonetheless. "Geoffrey said that. My brother. Those exact words."

She frowned, trying to remember, and in the end, he repeated them, giving voice to his darkest nightmare."'If you care for me, let me find my way. Alone.'"

God, how the words burned his throat. He squeezed his eyes shut, wishing he could cut off the memory as easily. "We both knew what was needed. One of us had to stay, the other had to return to England with the information. We both knew." He swallowed, remembering the taste of dust on his tongue, the icy chill that froze his soul. Even then, he had felt frozen. Immobile. Helpless.

"But you chose," Fantine whispered from his side. "You told him to go alone."

Marcus shook his head, though his neck ached with tears long suppressed. "He chose. I couldn't. It was too dangerous. I wanted us to stay together, but he insisted. How would he ever become a man if I was always hovering about?" Oh, God. He groaned; the pain was unbearable. "I should have kept us together. He would still be alive."

"But you chose," Fantine repeated. "You picked duty and honor and England over your brother. And he died because of it."

He looked at her, seeing the fear on her face, realizing she must have repeated those words to herself. But they simply weren't true. "Geoffrey wanted the risk. And God knows I thought he would be safe." His voice broke as he repeated the words, "I thought he would be safe."

She didn't respond, merely sat, her face drained of color. Unable to resist, he clasped her cold body to him, needing to feel her skin against his, her breath mixing with his own. Her life a part of his own.

"Cannot you understand?" he whispered against her cheek. "If I leave and something happened to you, it would be Geoffrey all over again. I could never forgive myself. Please, Fantine, let me stay."

He felt her body tremble against his, felt her struggle. And then, finally, he felt her body relax, slowly drawing away from him as her emotions quieted. He smiled, though the movement felt shaky at best. He had won. He had not intended his revelation as a weapon in his argument with her, the words had simply tumbled out. But as he looked into her shimmering eyes, he knew she understood. He could see her acceptance of the truth in her steady gaze.

"You did the right thing," she whispered, and he knew it cost her because she gripped his fingers until they went numb. "I have been blaming you, thinking you knowingly sent your brother to his death. But you didn't. It was his choice." She swallowed. "You acted correctly. His death is not on your shoulders."

She closed her eyes, a single tear slipping free.

He reached forward, gently wiping her face with his thumb. And as he did so, a great lightness filled his heart. She was right. Geoffrey chose his own path, and though he would always mourn his brother's passing, Marcus's guilt faded the moment Fantine forgave him. That she had such power over his emotions frightened him, and yet there was no other soul he would trust with such intimacy. Only Fantine.

"So, you will let me stay," he said, kissing the path his thumb had taken across her cheek. "You will let me remain in London with you?"

He knew what she would say the moment she touched his face, firmly setting him away from her. He knew, and if God had given him the power, he would have stopped her before she drew breath.

But he had not the strength, and her words landed with the finality of a gunshot. "You must go, Marcus. You must let me do this. Alone."

"No," he whispered, his denial immediate. "What if—"

"Then it will be my fault," she interrupted. "My choice. And you must not suffer for it."

As well ask the sun to remain set on the morrow. "I could not survive it," he gasped. Not another death. Not Fantine.

"I swear I will not die." Then, for the first time ever, she kissed him. Not because he cajoled or teased or begged it from her, but because she chose to taste him, to stroke the seam between his lips, and to at last allow him deep into the recesses of her mouth.

He took her offer greedily, trying to brand himself upon her, but when it was over he knew he had lost. In that kiss, he had felt the delight of her love given freely to him. More than happiness, it was a miracle that filled his soul. And he knew he would never again feel such joy unless he did as she asked—allowed her to become her own person. Without him.

"I will leave in the morning." How he spoke the words, he hadn't a clue. But they continued, flowing past the tightening in his throat as if his own wishes meant nothing beside hers. "Chris has already left for his club, so I must escort you tonight. After that, I swear upon my honor, I will leave."

She hesitated, her eyes dark with an emotion he could not name. "Thank you," she finally whispered.

He nodded, then turned the movement into a formal bow such as he would give the Queen of England. He lifted his arm, offering to escort her out, but she declined with a quick shake of her head. Instead, she stood by the fire, as far from him as possible. He watched her there, seeing her proud carriage, the classic lines of her face, even her lifted chin as she seemed to challenge the world.

She had never seemed more beautiful to him. Or more distant.

He had to release her. He knew that now. It was the honorable thing to do.

Gritting his teeth, he opened the library door for her. He had barely turned from his task when she slipped past him, darting quickly out of the room, careful to let nothing of hers touch him. Not even the edge of her gown.

But her perfume did.

It lingered in the air long after she had disappeared. Marcus inhaled deeply, closing his eyes to savor the scent.

Rich. Dark. Exotic.

His Fantine.

It had been a good choice, a good gift. And it was the last thing of hers he would ever have.

CHAPTER 16

"Lady Anne, Countess of Woodford; Marcus Kane, Lord Chadwick…"

One by one, their party was introduced, while Fantine waited impatiently in the rear. Lady Anne and Marcus stepped forward, then Lottie as Lady Charlotte.

"Miss Fantine Drake."

She stepped forward. Actually, she was pushed forward by the crush of people behind her. A good thing, as it turned out, since she could not have taken that first step alone.

Then she was there, at the top of an enormous stair, looking down on a throng of the glittering ton. Not a one looked at her. None of them truly cared who she was or why she was there. But Fantine could not suppress a shiver of excitement.

She was here. One of the rich elite.

For the first time in her life, she knew that both her mother and her father would be proud of her. The thought was astounding, and it brought forth a natural smile.

Then suddenly, she was not alone on the dais. Marcus stepped forward and offered her his arm as escort. She looked at him, seeing the caressing warmth of his gaze, the smile that softened his features.

He was proud of her.

In that instant, the scene in the library vanished from her thoughts. Their stilted conversation in the carriage, even her hurt that he would never truly love her, disappeared as if blown away by the wind.

All that mattered was his smile and his touch as he escorted her down the stairs. He treated her as royalty, and with him beside her, she believed it.

They reached the bottom of the stairs. She had been introduced, he had performed his duty, and now he turned to her, lifting her hand in the most elegant of kisses. His fingers lingered against her palm, his lips pressed the back of her hand with devotion. Then he released her.

"I was a fool," he said, emotion vibrating in his low tones. "I blundered heinously with you, and I shall always regret it." She tried to think of a response, but he shook his head. "Do not say anything. I think I finally understand." The pain in his eyes was enough to make her change her mind. Suddenly, she wanted nothing more than to throw her arms around him and tell him that everything was forgiven. She would be his mistress, she would be anything he wished, if only he did not leave her.

But it was too late.

He looked away from her, scanning the crowd even as he drew her gently forward, farther into the ballroom. She barely had time to draw her breath before a familiar red-haired gentlemen with light green eyes appeared before her.

"Ah, yes, Edwin," drawled Marcus. "I believe you and Miss Drake are acquainted."

"We are indeed," returned Mr. Thompson with a warm smile as he bowed over her hand. As always, Fantine appreciated his handsome features and easy manner. With his dark brown eyes and his slightly ragged haircut, he reminded her of a friendly dog. His expression was one of good-willed devotion, but his eyes were still bright with intelligence.

Fantine executed her curtsy and was surprised to feel the movement natural and graceful. "It is always a pleasure to see you, Mr. Thompson," she said as modestly as possible.

"I have been waiting for you, hoping you would honor me with a waltz this evening," he said.

"I would like that exceedingly well," she answered as she offered him her card. Then Marcus cut in, his voice stiff and slightly hoarse.

"Edwin, I am afraid I have a commitment in the card room. Could you stay near Miss Drake for me? Just as long as she needs a friend at hand?"

Mr. Thompson looked up from her card, and Fantine realized a message passed between the two men. It did not take her long to interpret the gesture. She had seen it before in the rookeries any time a man passed a woman off to another.

Neither one thought to ask her.

"I shall be honored," said Mr. Thompson smoothly.

"Yes, quite," drawled Marcus. Then with a curt bow to her, he left her for the card room.

She watched him go, his back broad and straight as he sifted through the crowd. She was free of Marcus at last, she told herself. She could finally go about the business of finding both Teggie and a husband without his interference. She had wanted this moment to come, but now that it was actually here, she could only clench her fists, wondering at the myriad emotions that washed through her. She recognized anger, sadness, and the too-familiar pain of abandonment. She searched for elation. She'd finally beaten Marcus, but instead she felt as if her chest were an open, bleeding sore. A pistol shot could not hurt more.

"Would you care for some lemonade, Miss Drake?"

Fantine blinked, only now remembering Mr. Thompson. "What?"

"Lemonade? The dancing will not begin for another hour. It is not necessary, of course. I am a little parched, but not desperately so. If you—"

"Actually, I am not at all thirsty. I would much rather talk with you."

His smile grew warmer. "I shall endeavor to be charming"

She smiled back, determined to distract herself from thoughts of Marcus. Taking Mr. Thompson's arm, she gave him her most devastating smile. "You know, you never did finish telling me about your south pastures. Something about corn, I believe?"

Mr. Thompson grinned and within moments was deep in his plans. Though many would have found the discussion dull, Fantine appreciated his careful thought and honest devotion to hard work. She knew this man would be faithful to his wife, providing both food and shelter with stalwart determination. He would never abandon her to the gutter or fritter away his money.

That put him at the top of her potential husband list.

"Fantine!" called Lottie as she stepped up beside them. "I thought for a moment I had lost you. Hello, Mr. Thompson, I am so pleased to see you. I see you have claimed Fantine's very first dance. An honor indeed." Then she began tugging slightly on Fantine's arm. "Come, my dear, there are a number of gentlemen who particularly wish to meet you."

Then began a long series of introductions that had Fantine's head spinning. Really, the variety of choices was beginning to give her a headache.

When Mr. Thompson came to claim her first dance, she nearly flew into his arms out of gratitude. So many men, so many faces. She wondered that she would keep them all straight. But as the music began, her feet took over, her mind closed down, and soon she was moving as easily as if she were practicing with her instructor. A few moments later, and she lost all thought beyond the simple joy of dancing.

It was at that moment that she gave Mr. Thompson a brilliant smile. He returned it with alacrity, his expression livening to one of pure happiness.

And she caught a flash of gold in his mouth.

He had a gold tooth.

Fantine stumbled, recovered her footing, and managed to rescue her position in the quadrille, but her equilibrium was sadly off. Could she have found Teggie so quickly? Could this very nice man actually be plotting to kill one of the greatest leaders of their time?

She had to get him to smile again. Had to actually count the number of gold teeth in his mouth.

She gave him another dazzling smile.

He returned it, but this one was not as wholehearted as the first. She caught the same flash of gold as before, but could not see the rest of his teeth.

What now? She realized with a slight sigh of frustration that she would have to make him laugh. Uproariously. Loud enough and long enough that he kept his mouth open so that she could count his teeth.

She set about being so charming as to be astounding. She flirted, she teased, she laughed, she even minced about on the dancing floor. She was stunning, and just as she was about to succeed, disaster struck.

Another gentleman smiled at her. He too had a gold tooth.

Now what? she wondered. In a flash, she memorized the gentleman's face and clothing, resolving to manage an introduction. It was just as well, she told herself. She was not at all happy with the thought of Mr. Thompson being Teggie. She was glad to have another suspect even if it meant a good deal more work. She would have to isolate the man, manage an introduction, then find a way for him to open his mouth.

Perhaps she ought to spend the rest of the evening in the dining area watching people eat. At least then she would be assured of them opening their mouths.

The steps of the dance took her back to Mr. Thompson. "You dance divinely, Miss Drake," he said.

"Thank you, Mr. Thompson. Pray, do you know who that gentleman is? The one over there in the dark green?"

"Who, Foxworthy?"

Fantine nodded, adding the name to her list of suspects. But then, as she turned to address her companion, she caught sight of another man, a portly gentleman of uncertain years who was laughing at some remark. She was almost sure she caught sight of two gold teeth in his mouth. Or perhaps it was merely a trick of the light.

"And that gentleman there?" she asked. "Who is he?"

"Which one?"

"Why, the one with…" She frowned. She had lost sight of him, and she knew nothing of the man except he was portly and fashionably dressed. "It does not matter."

"Are you quite well, Miss Drake?"

Fantine started, belatedly realizing that her behavior must seem rather odd. "My apologies, Mr. Thompson. I fear I am being most vulgar to be staring about me like this."

"Nonsense," he responded. "This is your first ball. I vow I spent my first two with my mouth hanging open and my eyes swiveling about like a broken top."

Fantine laughed at the image and was finally, mercifully rewarded. Mr. Thompson released an openmouthed laugh.

One. He had one gold tooth and no more. He was not Teggie, and she was inordinately pleased.

Then they were back beside Lottie, who very quickly began introducing her to a number of new gentlemen.

And the whole business began again. Fantine smiled, she simpered, she did everything but stand on her head so that her partner would laugh enough for her to count his gold teeth.

One gold tooth in this man, no gold teeth but three missing ones in that one. One gold tooth on that gentleman, although he fairly dripped with gold jewelry. She even found a baron with two gold teeth. But no one with three.

And none seemed as if they wished the slavery bill blocked. In short, though she had charmed half the gentlemen here, was becoming quite popular, and was even starting to enjoy herself, she counted the evening as a total loss.

She had been reminded of her mission. And she was not in the least bit nearer to finding Teggie.

Soon after that realization, Fantine began to get a headache. All this time spent being charming was draining, especially as she spent the rest of her time trying to look inconspicuous as she peered into gentlemen's mouths.

If it were not for Mr. Thompson, she would have gone mad. He remained faithfully by her side, providing steady company and a measuring stick with which to judge the other gentlemen.

She compared everyone she met to him, categorizing them according to their ability to care for her and her future children, including how likely they were to stray from their responsibilities. Many were easy to dismiss. Like the men in her mother's greenroom, they seemed merely to want a woman to own. She ignored them as soon as she had counted their gold teeth. The rest were ranked in descending order, factoring in age, general appearance, and likely companionship.

None scored as highly as Mr. Thompson.

As for touching her heart, only Marcus intrigued her, only he seemed like a man among all these boys. But he was in the card room, assiduously avoiding her at her own request.

If only she had met Mr. Thompson first, before Marcus. Perhaps he would have captured her heart. But then, if it were not for Marcus, she would still be back in the rookery slogging drinks, and Mr. Thompson would not so much as look at her.

What a difference a simple ball gown could make.

In her heart, she still felt alien to this glittering world. She did not belong here. But neither did she truly belong in the rookeries.

In short, Fantine felt depressed. And alone. And no nearer to finding Teggie. Which was exactly the moment she saw Hurdy.

He was there, plain as day, his red hair and boyish face a beacon despite his guise as a footman. Then he was gone.

At first, she thought she had imagined him in a nostalgic moment of longing for the familiar surroundings of

Southwark. Then she discarded the thought. She knew much too much to romanticize anything about the rookeries, familiar or not.

Hurdy must be here. But he could not be here. What would he be doing at her ball?

She answered her own question immediately. He was here to meet Teggie. Or perhaps to kill Wilberforce. The very thought made her shudder. Especially since she was not dressed to prevent a murder. She was, in fact, dressed to be quite conspicuous if she suddenly started wandering about the ballroom looking for an assassin.

But first things first, she reminded herself. She had to determine Hurdy's exact plans.

She stood up from her seat and scanned the crowd. "Is Mr. Wilberforce here?"

The gentleman who had been speaking to her, the one with two gold teeth but not a brain in his head, stopped in mid-word. "I was telling you about your most sensuous eyebrows."

"Yes, yes," she said impatiently. "They fairly bristle with allure. Now tell me, is Mr. Wilberforce here tonight?" She turned to the nearest gentleman who could be counted on to give her a straight answer. "Mr. Thompson, have you seen—"

"He is just over there, Miss Drake."

Fantine followed the line of his gesture and sighed with relief. The MP was indeed there, alive and well, the center of a circle of politicals in earnest discussion. Unfortunately, she could not guarantee that his happy existence would continue. Especially since she could not both guard Wilberforce and search for Hurdy at the same time.

She needed help.

"Mr. Thompson, would you please give a message to Lord Chadwick?"

"Of course," he said, straightening to almost military correctness.

"Please tell him that Mr. Wilberforce needs his attention directly."

The young man frowned at her, clearly wondering how Fantine could be in the slightest bit aware of the MP's needs.

"Trust me, sir. Lord Chadwick will understand."

"Of course." Then he disappeared with a speed that she found wholly gratifying. She would have to find some sort of explanation for him later. He was too intelligent to allow this sort of strange behavior to pass without some comment. But that was later. For the moment, he had performed without protest.

She found that a most attractive quality in a man.

Turning to her circle of admirers, she selected the most stupid, most self-involved, and most easily manipulated man. A future viscount with a very prominent gold tooth. She could not tell if he had more as the man had never smiled wide enough.

"Lord Baylor, I would like to take a tour of the ballroom. Do you think you could accompany me? I would like to hear more of your marvelous poetry."

The other gentlemen groaned while Lord Baylor preened and fondled his gold snuff box. He offered her his arm, and she gave him a closemouthed smile before she completely dismissed him from her thoughts. Or at least she tried.

"How long have you been friends with Lord Chadwick?"

Fantine blinked. She was consumed with searching throughout the ballroom while trying to appear completely casual. She had no wish to alert Hurdy of her presence, especially if he planned to speak with Teggie. She had to find Hurdy and follow him. But she could not do all that while maintaining a conversation with Lord Baylor.

"Miss Drake, how long have you known Chadwick? Were you children together?"

Fantine frowned. "No. I am friends with Lady Charlotte."

"Oh, but surely you must have been aware of Lord Chadwick. After all, what woman could not be?"

"Yes, he is a handsome man." She spoke slowly, wondering what the man was getting at.

"Tell me, was he a scamp? He is too lively to have been perfectly innocent. Was he ever sent down from school?"

It took a moment for her reason to take hold, but once it did, she was frankly appalled. "Sweet heaven, you are looking for scandal on Chadwick! You must think me dim-witted indeed if you think I could so betray the very family sponsoring me!"

Baylor was quick to placate her. "Nonsense, nonsense. I was merely trying to ascertain if you knew of his lordship's childish misdemeanor. I am sure you understand that it was a delicate affair. I just wished your comments—"

"There is no 'it,'" she snapped. "No delicate affair and no childish misdemeanor, and well you know it, my lord. You are merely searching for something on Chadwick and doing a very bad job to boot!" She shook her head. "Now, if you please, I suggest you return to reciting your poetry before I decide a scene would be better than remaining in your company."

Lord Baylor's prominent gold tooth disappeared from sight as he pressed his lips together in fury. The man clearly had a bad temper, Fantine realized. Unless he learned how to go about his business more intelligently, he was doomed to frequent fits of temper.

So as he pouted in an angry silence, she began looking about in earnest, searching for Hurdy.

She did not find him anywhere.

Then she saw the footmen.

She slowed her steps, narrowing her eyes as she studied the two men loitering by the champagne, refilling glasses. They did not appear the least bit odd, except that their gazes were on Wilberforce, some ten feet away.

Then one of them spoke to the other, his accent clear even over the chaos of the ball. She sighed. There was no doubt about it. They were Hurdy's men. And if she was not mistaken, one of them was toying with a dagger and no doubt ready to throw it straight into Wilberforce's throat.

Fantine frowned, trying to decide what to do. She could pretend Hurdy's men had insulted her and have them thrown out, but that would only take care of those two. What if there were others? Besides, she still hoped Hurdy was ignorant of her presence. Her only hope of finding Teggie was to follow him. That meant leaving Hurdy's men alone.

She would have to think of something else.

"Oh!" she cried in mock pain. "I have twisted my ankle!"

Lord Baylor was quick to respond, especially as she gripped his arm, wrenching him back a step.

"I say, careful of the coat!"

"My lord, I have hurt my ankle," she repeated. "Perhaps you could assist me to a seat. Over there?" She pointed to a chair close to Wilberforce. It was the best she could do. She could not push her way into the gentlemen's discussion. She was a woman at a ball. Such an act would be odd to say the least.

"Where is Chadwick?" she grumbled.

"You are not going to cry or anything, are you? You said you would not create a scene."

Fantine summoned up an acidic smile. "I have no wish to endanger your reputation as an escort. Please, if you would just find Chadwick, I will attempt to remain calm."

"Very well," he simpered, clearly unhappy with the entire situation. Fortunately, he left quickly, allowing her to act.

She stood and began walking forward, planning her steps so that she could fall directly upon the MP. She hated doing this to a lame gentleman, but she had to get him low to the floor, away from any hurled knives.

Stepping into position, she faked a tumble. "Oh!" she cried, barreling directly into Wilberforce, knocking both herself and him to the floor.

He landed with a soft cry of pain, and once again Fantine winced, but remained determined to keep him on the floor. In the guise of struggling to her feet, she managed to twist both Wilberforce and herself up in her skirt. She heard an ominous rip in the process, but she did not have time to regard it.

"Oh, oh," she cried. "My deepest apologies, sir, but I cannot stand. Oh!" Then she fell back, neatly trapping the MP.

Wilberforce was frowning in consternation, an expression that did not lighten when he finally recognized her.

"Miss—"

"Drake," she cut in, wondering if he had been apprised of her new name. Apparently he had not. Then, thankfully, they were interrupted before Mr. Wilberforce could say anything more.

"Fantine! Are you all right?"

Fantine looked up at the sound of Marcus's rich tones. He stood beside her, his hands gentle as he cupped her elbows, his eyes wide as he scanned her body for injury.

"I—I am fine," she said, her voice breathy. Then she recalled herself to the situation. "It is merely my ankle. I am afraid I twisted it and fell on Mr. Wilberforce."

Then she turned to the MP. The man had given up his struggle to stand and now tried to untwist himself from her gown.

"I am afraid I hurt you," she said.

He turned his head. "Nonsense. I am quite—"

"No, no," she said firmly. "I am sure of it. I have hurt you." Then she turned to Marcus. "Please, I insist we take Mr. Wilberforce home immediately. It is the least we can do."

"But I am quite well—"

"No, sir," interrupted Marcus. "I am afraid I must insist." Fantine smiled her relief, grateful that he had quickly understood the situation. "Miss Drake is quite right that she has injured you," he continued. "Why, I can see the pain you are in. Pray, allow me to offer you the use of our carriage."

"But Miss Drake—"

"Oh, no," cut in Fantine. "I shall wait here at the ball. I would simply die if you came to harm because of my clumsiness."

It was then that Wilberforce finally gave in. In truth, Fantine suspected he understood from the first what was happening, but the man was nothing if not dedicated to his cause. He would risk his life if he could convince one more person to support his crusade.

Marcus, it appeared, was equally determined. He turned to her, all the while making sure his large bulk shielded the small MP. "I shall see him safe—"

"Take an unusual route," she whispered.

"Then I will return directly for you and an explanation."

She nodded.

"And do something about your gown!"

It was not until that moment that she thought to look down. Her skirt was ripped to nearly halfway up her thigh. Fortunately, her undertunic remained only partially damaged so that merely her calf and ankle were exposed. Still, there was more than one gentleman taking an interest in the sight.

"Oh!" she exclaimed, feeling a blush heat her face. She quickly twitched the remains of her skirt over her leg while a gentleman with no gold teeth at all helped her to her feet. By the time she was situated, Marcus and Wilberforce were long gone.

Lottie and Lady Anne descended almost immediately thereafter, and Fantine had to spend the next few minutes assuring them she was quite well while trying to explain why Marcus had taken their carriage, thereby stranding the three of them.

And all the while, Hurdy lurked somewhere nearby.

Wilberforce grimaced as he settled into the carriage, throwing Marcus a reproachful glance.

"Really," he said, "I understand that bringing out a girl is a touchy affair, but were such dramatics truly necessary?"

Marcus frowned as he peered out the carriage window. "We are attempting to save your life, sir. Fantine no doubt saw something that concerned her at the ball. I will escort you to a property I recently acquired. You shall be perfectly safe there."

"Of course. Of course," the older man moaned, his tone mocking. "You are trying to save me."

Marcus squinted into the darkness outside, trying to sift form from shadow. "That is what Penworthy wished."

"And this has nothing to do with casting Mr. Thompson in the role of a heroic rescuer," the MP drawled.

Marcus pulled away from the window, finally allowing his attention to center on his companion. "I beg your pardon?"

"No need to sound so insulted," responded Wilberforce rather cheerfully. "I may be obsessed with my bill, but I am not blind. And I have taken particular interest in your Miss Dela—er, Drake." The gentleman paused and frowned. "Incidentally, why did you change her name?"

"It was necessary," Marcus responded, his voice curt.

"Hmmm. Anyway, I gather you needed an important reason to leave so that Thompson could gallantly escort the injured Fantine home. Quite neat, actually. I congratulate you. I think he is an excellent choice for her."

"So does my sister," Marcus grumbled.

Then Mr. Wilberforce touched his chin, his expression pensive. "I do hope Thompson carries her to the carriage. Women do so love grand romantic gestures."

Marcus was suddenly assaulted by a vision of Fantine in young Thompson's arms, her eyes misty, her arms wrapped around his neck, her red lips slightly parted...

"Good heavens!" he exclaimed, heedless of how the expression offended the devout man. "You cannot be serious."

"Why ever not? From what I understand, they would make an excellent match. In fact, I have been doing my best to encourage Mr. Thompson. Why, just yesterday in White's, he asked about her, and I mentioned that I found her everything that is charming."

"What!" The word echoed loudly in the dark carriage.

Wilberforce had the audacity to laugh. "Well, it can

hardly be surprising that I have taken an interest in her future. Penworthy has hired her to save my life. Besides," he said with a slight chuckle, "I think I may have had some small part in encouraging her to try a Season. You do recall that I told her to grasp the opportunities God presents to us, do you not?"

Marcus recalled nothing of the sort. His mind was too caught up with the thought that with the famous MP's endorsement, Fantine could not fail to make a splash this Season.

Then Wilberforce leaned forward and patted Marcus's knee in a paternal gesture. "You need not worry about her. Mr. Thompson is a good man and clearly intrigued. Given his limited time in London, I would not doubt he makes an offer within the week."

"A week?" Marcus echoed, his thoughts suddenly spinning. A week before Fantine received a proposal of marriage? It could not be possible. Why, the idea was...was...what?

Up until now, Marcus had comforted himself that there was plenty of time before the end of the Season. He had not thought she would receive a marriage proposal so soon.

But of course she would, he admonished himself. That was, in fact, exactly what his mother and sister had been trying to tell him. She was an eligible woman on the Marriage Mart. She was beautiful, smart, and had a way of moving that drew all sorts of thoughts from a man. It did not matter that her dowry was somewhat modest. A man like Thompson had enough money to make a comfortable living for the two of them.

Suddenly a marriage proposal did not sound so farfetched. Marcus groaned and let his head drop against the carriage window.

"I see you are not quite comfortable with the match," commented Wilberforce dryly.

Marcus opened his eyes. "Thompson will not be able to manage Fantine. She will run wild within a week."

The older gentleman stiffened in outrage. "Not Miss Drake! Her? Run wild? How dare you insult the lady that way! Recall that your family is bringing the girl out. If you continue spouting such nonsense, you shall ruin her chances entirely!"

Marcus felt his anger rise. He was not accustomed to being lectured by anyone, and lately it seemed that everyone from his sister to his carriage companions had taken to the task with a vengeance. "I believe I am more aware of Fantine's nature than you," he said stiffly.

"On the contrary. I believe you still see a young hoyden or some such." The MP leaned forward in earnestness. "Open your eyes, man. She is an attractive, well-mannered woman. If you did not think so at the beginning, then why do you sponsor her?"

Marcus opened his mouth to respond, various scathing responses ready on his tongue. Not a one came forth. Instead, he could only swallow, doing his best to adjust his thinking. "She cannot abide a quiet life. I practically forced this Season upon her so she could learn that wealth and peace need not mean tedium."

"You believe she would be quickly bored with Mr. Thompson?"

"I believe she would drive him and herself mad."

Wilberforce frowned and shook his head. "She must have some hobbies, something that would occupy her mind and her time. At least until the children arrive."

Marcus flinched as if he had been struck. Fantine? Pregnant with Thompson's child? The thought was nauseating. "Her...side interest is not entirely proper. Recall that she practically thrives on tasks such as protecting your life."

Wilberforce merely shrugged. "Then let her do them. If she is indeed as good as you claim—"

"She is." The words came out without thought. Ever since their first escapade with Ballast, Marcus had known she was quite skilled at the work Penworthy assigned her.

"Well, then," continued Wilberforce, "I do not see why her God-given talent would make her any less respectable. I imagine she is quite discreet about it. Indeed, she would have to be in order to perform her task. At least until the children arrive."

Marcus rubbed his face. He had been so settled in the notion of her as his mistress that the shift to thinking of her as a proper maiden required quite a mental adjustment. It was not that he thought her disreputable. It was merely that young ladies of the ton—young wives and mothers—did not perform such dangerous tasks as Fantine clearly adored. If she were his mistress, he would allow her to do what she loved and what he loved, all at the same time.

But if she could do such and still be happy as a married woman…"If William Wilberforce," Marcus continued, speaking his thoughts aloud, "the moral center of the ton, thinks her actions entirely proper, then everyone else will too."

The thought rocked him down to the foundations of his soul. Fantine was respectable. And marriageable.

"And I just agreed to leave London!" With a blistering oath, Marcus pushed his head out the window and called to his coachman. "Whip them up, Jacob. I must return to the ballroom immediately!"

CHAPTER 17

She heard Hurdy's voice before she saw him. Like her, he was able to hide in a crowd. Somehow he suppressed his natural arrogance so much that one could look straight at him and not see him at all.

Much as she tried, the chaos around her prevented an active search. It was not until she heard his nearly cultured voice, talking in a subservient undertone, that she finally knew where to look for him—right beside her, speaking with Mr. Thompson.

"Excuse me, sir. Message fer the miss," said Hurdy.

"A message? For Miss Drake?" Mr. Thompson sounded as disapproving as he did confused.

"Aye, sir."

"Thank you—" Fantine said, but Mr. Thompson ignored her, being more intent on interviewing Hurdy.

"But who could be sending her a message now? Right here?"

"A message?" That was Lady Anne, spinning around to confront the footman. "Give it to me at once."

Hurdy sneered. "Naw, ducks. It be fer the miss."

"Now just one minute, you impertinent—"

"Please, Lady Anne," interrupted Fantine. "It is all quite proper, I assure you." This last was for Mr. Thompson's benefit. The man looked as if he was about to take some protective stance. "You may give it to me."

She reached up and Hurdy, dressed as a footman, stepped forward with alacrity. She took the pristine piece of linen, not even bothering to look at it. The message was in Hurdy's eyes. He wanted to speak with her. Immediately.

"But there is nothing written on it." That was from Lottie, who had been peering at the note from over Fantine's shoulder.

Fantine merely smiled. "Of course not. But I understand it nevertheless." She spoke directly to Hurdy, and the man bowed insolently before turning on his heel.

"What is this?" hissed Lady Anne, coming to stand directly in front of Fantine. "Messages with nothing on them from horrible sneering footmen? This is not—"

"It is eminently proper." This was from Lottie, her voice low and cool, effectively cutting off her mother's growing tirade. "I assure you. Mother." Then she glanced significantly around, bringing Lady Anne's attention to the numerous people obviously listening in. "It has to do with repairing her dress so she can leave properly!"

The older woman's eyes widened as she recognized the lie for what it was: a convenient excuse until they could discuss matters in private. "Very well, Lottie. Perhaps we should give Fantine our arms so she can manage on her ankle."

But before she could fit action to her words, Mr. Thompson stepped forward. "Please," he said, his voice steady and low. "Allow me."

Then he leaned over and scooped her up in his arms.

Fantine was so startled, she let out a squeak of alarm. She had not expected this, certainly never thought she would be carried in the arms of a gentleman, her body pressed firmly against the solid wall of his chest. She lifted her gaze, seeing his strong jaw, his tender smile, his dark brown eyes...

And felt a jolt of surprise.

She did not wish to see brown eyes, but clear blue ones.

Fantine could have kicked herself for her stupidity. Unfortunately, her heart was not listening. It did not appear to care that Mr. Thompson was strong and smart, that he was a gentleman and thought her respectable. Her heart only knew that he was not Marcus, and the disappointment was so keen it robbed her of breath.

"Oh, Mr. Thompson!" said Lottie. "How very kind of you."

"Not at all," he responded gravely. "I am only too happy to oblige." Then he did the oddest thing. He looked significantly at Fantine, not as a potential lover, but as a man who meant to have answers. Clearly, he knew something odd was in the wind and wanted an explanation.

It was an awkward moment. She had not thought that gentlemen of the ton could be so astute, and now suddenly she was scrambling for something to say. He was already striding through the ballroom, heading for the ladies' retiring room, but there was enough time for Fantine to redirect him.

"I know you wish for an explanation," she said, her voice low. "But—"

"You do not owe me anything. I have no claim on you. Yet."

Fantine glanced up, her hands suddenly trembling at his statement. It was a clear declaration of intent. But there was no time for this. Hurdy was waiting to speak with her.

She bit her lip, taking a desperate moment to pray for divine inspiration. None came. None of her usual glib lies, nothing that would satisfy Mr. Thompson without actually revealing anything. What could she say?

"I do not wish to start our relationship with a lie, Mr. Thompson," she whispered softly. "But I cannot take the time to explain matters right now. Please, I can only ask that you trust me. Could you take Lottie and her mother home for me?"

She felt the shift in his step immediately. He did not even pause as he turned from the ladies' retiring room toward the door.

"You wish to go home?"

"An excellent idea!" That was from Lottie, hurrying her steps to keep up with Mr. Thompson's longer ones.

But Fantine merely shook her head. "I cannot go yet, but they must. There...there is nothing wrong with my ankle. I have to speak with someone alone." She felt his arms tighten about her, and she rushed into her words. "It is not anything amorous, I assure you. Why, the very thought is nauseating," she said truthfully. "But I cannot do this with Lady Anne and Lottie constantly hovering about."

She felt him hesitate, his steps slowing with each second. "Chadwick released you to my care. Now I believe he meant more than just as a dancing partner." He shook his head. "I am sorry, but I cannot leave you alone."

They had reached the door, and Mr. Thompson called for his carriage. Lady Anne and her daughter caught up to them, both a bit breathless from their rapid pace.

"Oh, excellent," gasped the older woman. "I do thank you, Mr. Thompson, for your assistance. Are we to use your carriage?"

"It is my great pleasure to assist you." He looked significantly at Fantine. "I will take all of you home." His breath was on her face, but Fantine barely noticed. She saw instead the dark form of one of Hurdy's men around the corner. That was her destination. And she had to get there soon.

The carriage was brought around. Lottie and Lady Anne stepped forward, quickly easing themselves into the dark interior, both complaining of the chill. Then Mr. Thompson turned his attention to Fantine.

"Tell me who you must meet and where," he said softly. "I shall explain matters."

Fantine smiled, lifting her hand to touch his cheek. It was smooth and somewhat soft, and Fantine wondered if she would spend the rest of her life with this man. Indeed, she could think of worse fates. In fact, given the situation, he might very well be the best she could expect.

"You are a very kind and considerate man," she said softly.

"You sound as if you are surprised."

She grinned. "I suppose I am. I am especially glad that you do not have three gold teeth." Then impulsively, she leaned forward and kissed him on the lips. He did not expect the gesture. Indeed, she had not expected to make it. But he responded quickly enough, slanting his mouth over hers with an intensity she found startling.

And somewhat dull. It was a press of flesh to flesh in all its unglorious, mundane, not at all interesting possibilities.

Nothing. Except another sharp stab of loss.

Fantine pulled away, the last remnant of joy drained from the evening. Despite everything. Despite the interest from numerous gentlemen, despite her success in finally ridding herself of Marcus, despite all the changes she had accomplished in her time with Lottie, one single inalienable fact remained.

She was alone. And would always be.

Even if she married this man, slept in his bed, and bore his children, she would still be alone. She did not love him.

With a sudden twist, she slipped out of Mr. Thompson's arms. She did not speak. She did not know what to say, and she would not trust her voice even if she did. So before he could react, she ran away, her feet flying over the stones.

Toward Hurdy.

Moments later she heard the sound of Mr. Thompson's carriage moving away. He had left. Lottie and Lady Anne were safely out of the way, and now she could concentrate on Hurdy.

By herself. Again.

"Where is he?" she demanded abruptly of the dark figure by the side of the building.

"Waitin' fer ye. Come on."

It was just as well that they had come to a ball thrown by one of the wealthiest families in London. They had a huge home and an extensive garden path behind it. The area was lit with glowing colored lanterns that lent a magical quality to the greenery without overly illuminating anything.

It was an enchanted walk for couples and a perfect rendezvous for her and Hurdy, especially as he and his men were still dressed as footmen. They could all wander though the area without appearing conspicuous.

Her guide brought her to a dark corner secluded by a hedgerow. In truth, it was no more than a small, dank clearing for refuse, and it smelled horribly, but it was likely the most private location.

"Well, well," she quipped, "fancy meeting you here."

Hurdy was leaning against the fence, inscrutable as he cleaned his nails with the point of a long thin knife. Around him stood three of his men.

Then Hurdy spoke. He did not even look up, merely addressed his long fingers, inspecting them with studied casualness. "Tell me why I should not kill you right now."

Fantine smiled. Part of her thrilled to the knowledge that she was no longer playing with amateurs. Hurdy was one of the best, and it was a pleasure matching wits with him. If only her life were not on the line.

"You cannot kill me because you still need me."

"You betrayed me."

"Me?" Fantine laughed fully for the first time. She had not realized how restricted her life with Lottie had been until this moment. She had finally returned to her element. "I did not betray anyone. We had a bargain. You do not move on Wilberforce until I speak with Teggie."

He shot forward, his knife at the ready, but she did not flinch. "We had nothing. And I am the only one what speaks with Teggie."

Fantine smirked, putting on a false show of bravado. "As if you could present my thoughts as well as I." She shifted, pushing his knife down and away from her as much as he would allow. It was still well within easy reach of her throat. But she continued as if he had dropped his guard completely. "What Teggie truly wants is to discredit Wilberforce, and only I can do that for you." She took another step forward. "Let me meet with Teggie, explain things."

His response was swift and final. "No."

Fantine shook her head. "Until I speak with Teggie myself, I will act as the MP's personal protector. You will get nowhere without me."

"Then I will kill you now."

She shrugged. "You cannot think I will go down without a fight. And I assure you, I shall make as much noise as possible. Whom do you think the nearby people will believe? Me, a pure and innocent member of the ton, or a hired footman who turns out to be a dockside criminal? Your neck will be stretched before you can say Jack Dandy."

She grinned, forcing a cockiness she knew was not warranted. And, in fact, her nervousness was soon proved true. Before she could do more than take a breath, one of Hurdy's men slipped forward to hold her securely from behind. She didn't even have the time to struggle before her arms were pinned behind her back, her own neck stretched as Hurdy's knife teased her throat.

"You will not have time to make a sound."

"No, but I will."

Everyone spun at the low voice, but it was Fantine who groaned at the sight.

There, silhouetted by a dark red lantern, stood Mr. Thompson, a pistol in his hand. He pointed it unerringly at Hurdy's chest, and he looked as if he was a crack shot.

"Sweet Jesus!" cursed Hurdy. "How many daft lords do you 'ave?"

"More and more every day, it appears," Fantine said.

Hurdy stepped forward, adding his own hand to her throat and squeezing in his frustration. "But 'ow? There is nothing special about you. You charms are barely above a street tart."

Fantine merely smiled, knowing that she was making headway with Hurdy, if only he would release his hold on her neck. "Let go an' I will tell you," she croaked out.

"But—" Hurdy cursed.

"I suggest you do as she says," said Mr. Thompson, raising his pistol.

The seconds ticked by as Hurdy measured Mr. Thompson's determination. Then he looked down at her, and she saw fury in his eyes. Had she pushed him too far?

Not yet. After an interminable wait, Hurdy cursed and stepped away. Though she was still held captive, she could at least breathe.

"Tell me now," Hurdy growled. "Who is this daft?"

"My friend," she gasped out. "'Tis easy, Hurdy. I know what they like, and I know how to give it to them." Then she lifted her head, her breathing at last evened out. "I do not know if I can teach it to you, but I can certainly tell you how to do it."

She spoke quickly. Despite Hurdy's concession, she knew the danger remained. She and Mr. Thompson could not easily defeat Hurdy and his men, especially as the henchmen had already spread out, preparing to take down the newest interloper.

"Come on, luv," she continued soothingly to Hurdy. "Let me go so we can talk." Then she glanced significantly at Mr. Thompson. "If he fires now, you will have dozens of daft lords here, all clamoring for your head."

Hurdy groaned, his expression one of resignation. "Very well." With a swift wave of his hand, he gestured for the one brute to release Fantine and the others to stop their menacing advance on Mr. Thompson.

"Very wise," returned Mr. Thompson. "Now, Fantine, if you would please come over here."

Fantine smiled, wishing she could explain. "I am sorry, Mr. Thompson. You have been very brave, and I am extraordinarily grateful. Unfortunately, Hurdy and I have not finished our discussion."

"Do not be ridiculous!" he snapped. "He was about to kill you."

"It is all part of a rather complex…um, negotiation. Now please just stand there looking threatening while I finish my business."

"But—"

"Trust me, Mr. Thompson. I can only keep them from killing you once, and I am afraid I just used up that allotment." Then she returned her attention to Hurdy. "Can you not see it? I am much better at this than you. Gentlemen fairly fall over themselves to save me. I know them, you see. And I know I am right about Teggie."

Hurdy folded his arms, his expression fierce. "The man hired me to do a job," he said firmly. "And I intend to do it."

"No, the man hired you to take care of a problem. Unfortunately, both you and Teggie lack enough imagination to see that murder is not the best answer right now." Fantine peered through the darkness, seeing hesitation in Hurdy's undisguised frown. "Look at him," she suddenly said, gesturing to Mr. Thompson. "He is as respectable as they come. Yet, he is here, risking life and limb to protect me. He is acting so gallantly, in fact, that I believe I shall marry him."

She could see Mr. Thompson's gaze dart to her in surprise before quickly hopping right back to Hurdy's thugs. Very good, she commended silently. He knew to keep his comments to himself until a more auspicious moment. So she turned her attention back to Hurdy, pressing her point as best she could.

"You cannot think you could engender such support on your own. Only I can do this. And that makes me extremely valuable."

Hurdy shook his head. "'E will never want you after all this."

"Then I will have lost the best one," she said as much to herself as to the others. "But there will be others."

"You are too cocky."

"I am bright, beautiful, and very sure of myself."

"Aye," Hurdy said, his frown so pronounced it seemed to take over his entire face. "Cocky means dead. You can never deliver what you promise."

"I can," she returned. "And if you do not snatch up my services, then I may have to make my bargain with Ballast."

That comment was the final straw for Hurdy, as she knew it would be. He cursed loudly and fluently, but the sound was his surrender and they both knew it. "Very well," he finally said, his words grudging. "You are in."

"Excellent!"

"But *I* talk to Teggie first. I will see if 'e wants to speak with you. If not, then you will 'ave to do what I say, as I say it."

"I want to meet him, explain—"

"You do as I say!" Then before she could react, he once again reached out and gripped her throat, cutting off her breath as surely as any vise. "I am still the leader here. Do not ever forget that!"

Fantine lowered her eyes in acknowledgment, nodding her head when he allowed her to. Then he released her, throwing her away from him so that she stumbled.

"Fantine!" cried Mr. Thompson as he stepped toward her.

That was a mistake. He should have let her be, but he was a hero at heart and thought he could rescue her.

He could not. In that moment of inattention, Hurdy reached out and snatched away his pistol. Then he shoved her erstwhile rescuer into her. She had just regained her footing and was forced to catch Mr. Thompson to prevent him from tumbling them both back into the mud.

"Watch 'em," Hurdy snapped to his men. Then he stomped out of their tiny alcove, presumably to find Teggie.

It took a moment before she and Mr. Thompson regained their balance, but when she did, Fantine nearly kicked herself in frustration. Good Lord, she had muddled the whole affair again! She had not discovered Teggie's identity, and now she had dragged yet another unpredictable aristocrat into the entire mess.

She knew how to handle men like Hurdy and Ballast. They were known quantities. But these bizarre heroic gentlemen were wild cards, as dangerous to themselves as to her because they were unpredictable. Truly, what possessed a man to think he could simply arm himself with a gun and win out over lifelong players reared in the dangerous rookeries?

Fools, every one of them. Yet, she could not help feeling affection for them. Sighing, she turned toward Mr. Thompson with a rueful smile.

"I am sorry you were pulled into this nonsense."

"I am sorry I did not throw you into the carriage when I had the chance," he returned irritably.

"But then you would have missed your chance to meet one of the leading criminal figures in Southwark," she said blithely.

He turned toward her, his expression fierce. "I do not find this a time for humor."

She raised her eyebrows at his sour tone. "Mr. Thomp—"

"This nonsense cannot continue! You realize that, do you not?"

She shrugged to cover her annoyance. He was not taking this situation very well. Not very well at all. She gestured to the four thugs cutting off their exit. "Perhaps you could use your money and your title to order them to leave us alone."

"Your humor is entirely misplaced! I take great comfort in the fact that there is little of this in Birmingham. You will have much less opportunity for this…this dangerous game after we are married."

Fantine turned slowly, torn between conflicting emotions. Elation and anger coiled within her, but neither found an outlet. Instead she focused on his fundamental assumption. "You still expect to marry me?" Then she shook her head. "No, I mean you still wish to marry me?"

He hesitated, as if he too was surprised by his own thoughts. "Despite this, uh, diversion, you are still the most intelligent female I have met. You appeared to take great interest in my plans. I am an honest, kind gentleman and the best you can hope for given your particular situation."

"And what situation is that?" she said, her irritation growing by the second.

"Your modest dowry, your unremarkable bloodline." Then he cast a significant glance about him. "Your unusual hobby."

"Hobby! You make this sound as if I were playing with dolls!"

"And are you not?" he shot back. "What is this but a dangerous game to you? Something to alleviate your boredom? Why else would a gently bred female begin consorting with felons?"

"Why—" She cut off her own words. Her anger had grown to a boiling fury, but Mr. Thompson was not the appropriate outlet. The most appropriate receptacles were standing nearby, smirking as they followed her spat with her possible fiancé.

But she still had to disguise her intentions. With that in mind, she let her hostility clench her fists and heat her words as she advanced on Mr. Thompson, simultaneously moving closer to the nearest thug.

"Now listen here, you rich aristocrat. Yes, I do like you. And yes, I support your plans for your land. But this is no game to me, and I am no gently bred poppet with too much time on my hands! And furthermore…"

She did not bother to finish. Instead, she planted her fist square between the nearest brute's eyes. He went down like a stone, while she turned on the next.

It took barely two seconds before Mr. Thompson joined in the fray. He was perhaps not as quick as Chadwick, but she was grateful nonetheless. After all, they were fighting professional killers, and they were still outnumbered.

CHAPTER 18

Marcus rushed into the ballroom with unseemly haste. Or rather, it would have been unseemly haste if he were not stopped every few inches by another person asking what had happened to Mr. Wilberforce. Was he quite well? Had the strain of his new bill finally caught up with him? After all, it was coming to a vote next week.

He dealt with them as quickly as possible without seeming to rush. Yes, Mr. Wilberforce was quite well. Yes, Marcus supported the bill and hoped that it would pass unanimously. No, the MP was not injured, merely tired, and could someone please direct him to his mother, his sister, and Lottie's young charge?

But when he got to that question, the answers became both specific and vague. Everyone had seen them. In fact, he was told over and over that Mr. Thompson had been quite dashing as he carried poor Miss Drake across the ballroom. An announcement was expected within hours.

But as to Miss Drake's specific location, no one knew exactly. Some said the ladies' rearing room. Others said their host had found her a room upstairs. Some said they had left. In short, the only thing that everyone knew was that they thought it an excellent match.

"Oh, there are you are, Chadwick. How is Mr. Wilberforce?"

"He is fine. Only a little tired," Marcus responded without thinking, his gaze still scanning the ballroom. He had intended to find the host or hostess to discover if Fantine was upstairs, but neither person appeared.

"So you took him home?"

"Hmmm?" Marcus shifted suddenly, thinking he had caught a glimpse of Fantine, but it turned out to be another young lady, her dress garish, her gaze rather vapid. Definitely not Fantine.

"Wilberforce. Did you take him to his home?"

Marcus frowned, finally turning his attention to the gentlemen addressing him. "Lord Baylor, why are you so interested in Mr. Wilberforce's whereabouts?"

The younger gentlemen pulled his lips taut over his teeth in a semblance of a smile. "Wilberforce and I have been working closely together on his bill."

Marcus nodded. He had heard as much, but somehow he found it hard to believe. The two had been bitter rivals for Mr. Wilberforce's seat in the House of Commons. In fact, Baylor had nearly beggared himself during the campaign, but to no avail. Wilberforce had triumphed, and Baylor had not disguised his hatred of the man.

Now they were working side by side on the same bill? The thought was ludicrous, but Marcus himself had seen the two together on more than one occasion.

"I have something urgent to discuss with him," pressed Baylor. "We may lose support from Mr. Woods and his friends. I fear that only Wilberforce can keep them on our side. They have been wavering from the outset and will not listen to me."

Marcus nodded. True, that was a serious matter. But not serious enough for Marcus to reveal Wilberforce's location. At least not until he spoke with Fantine and understood the exact nature of the danger.

"You have not seen Miss Drake, have you? Do you know for certain if she has left?"

Baylor frowned. "I was with her when she hurt her ankle. She asked me to locate you, but you discovered her directly after. Beyond your spiriting Mr. Wilberforce away, I do not know what happened."

Marcus sighed. He would simply have to go to Lottie's home and hope that she was there.

"So Wilberforce is at home then? I can speak to him there?"

Marcus was about to answer when he saw a dark-haired man wander outside with a petite woman on his arms. He had forgotten that the ballroom spilled onto an extensive garden.

Could she be out there? He tried to think logically. Something had happened here, something that required Wilberforce's swift departure. If Marcus knew anything about Fantine, it was that she would not run home to safety. She would stay here to investigate. She would probably make sure the MP was out of danger, then would pretend to leave, before returning in secret. After all, she was a master at fading into the background. Why not slip away and change into a maid's gown?

But if that was true, then she could be anywhere!

He began to scan the servants, ignoring the footmen to concentrate on the maids. There were few in sight, but he peered closely at those he could see. Lord Baylor was completely dismissed from his thoughts until he felt a strong arm pull him around.

"Chadwick! Please, I must know where Wilberforce is. The bill is at stake!"

Marcus sighed. "You cannot see him tonight, but I believe he intends to dine at White's at one o'clock."

"Excellent," Baylor said, his voice filled with relief. "Woods will be there, too." Then before Marcus could respond, Baylor was distracted by a footman who offered him a single white sheet of linen paper. "Excuse me, Chadwick," said Baylor as he turned toward the servant.

Marcus was only too happy to oblige. Stepping away, he dismissed everything from his thoughts except locating

Fantine. At the moment, he cared little for politics, little even for Wilberforce. He only had thoughts of finding Fantine. He had no idea what he would say to her when he found her. He merely intended to locate her immediately, assure himself that she was well and unmarried, and then decide what to do next.

With that goal firmly fixed, he headed for the garden.

Once there, he found nothing but beautiful globes of colored lights and a number of couples engaged in various stages of seduction. Most were quite proper, but he surprised two couples who had moved well beyond the edge of decency. It was nothing more than what he had expected, but the sight irritated him nonetheless. He kept imagining Fantine and Thompson engaged in such matters, and the very thought was enough to make him clench his fists in impotent anger.

He had nearly given up when he heard it. Soon, it came again.

"Mumph!"

Someone had just been hit. Hard. Marcus moved for the sound, and as he walked, the noises became more distinct.

A fight.

He looked around. It was the darkest area of the garden and completely deserted as far as he could see. Ahead lurked a dark alcove, shielded from view by tall hedges and a fence. Fantine had to be there. Who else would fight in the middle of a ball?

He nearly broke into a run. The urge to jump straight into the fray was overwhelming. But he could do more harm than good by throwing himself into the battle without assessing the situation first.

He had to move cautiously. He peered around the corner.

Even with his being prepared, the sight held him transfixed in horror for a moment. One man lay stretched out on the ground, groaning. Nearby, Fantine fought in the center of three brutes. She was a hellcat, raining blows with lethal fury. Next to her, Mr. Thompson added his own skill, but it was clear that his fighting style was too refined to triumph. He was a gentleman, used to boxing in a ring with polite opponents. These were street fighters using every dirty trick known to thief or criminal.

Fantine and Thompson were holding their own for the moment, but if the fourth regained his feet, they would soon be overpowered. Therefore, the woozy brute was Marcus's first destination. He crossed to the man in three short steps and knocked him unconscious with a single blow. Then he pushed his way straight into the fight.

"About bloody time," grumbled Fantine as she ducked a massive fist. "Is Wilberforce safe?"

"Yes," gasped Marcus, struggling to get his fighting wind. "Damn, this coat is tight," he muttered as he swung. Then, simultaneous with his blow, he heard the telltale rip of fabric. Lord, his valet was going to be furious.

"Good God, Chadwick," gasped Thompson from where he sparred with another villain. "You cannot mean that you support her nonsensical activities!"

"Support?" he responded, as he barely avoided a well-aimed blow. "No—"

"Yes!" That was Fantine as she grasped some mud and threw it at her attacker's eyes.

"No," Marcus repeated firmly. "I merely, er, surrender to the inevitable."

Fantine released an inelegant snort as she finished off her opponent. Thompson, on the other hand, appeared thoroughly incensed.

"It is unconscionable of you…to allow…such activities. That Hurdy character…said she was in. In what?" He punctuated his words with heavy blows to his opponent's shoulder and chest, but the man merely shuddered and continued his advance.

"I allow nothing!" gasped Marcus, landing his own blows, double time. "Fantine does as she wills. All I do…is mitigate…the damages." Marcus tripped over one of the fallen men, then quickly regained his balance. It took a moment more before the rest of Thompson's comments registered. "She is in with Hurdy? What exactly does that mean?" He dodged a meaty fist only to be caught on the side by the other.

"Do not be ridiculous!" gasped Thompson as he took his own blow right in the stomach. Fortunately, he used the movement to roll aside, and the next blows landed in the shrubbery. "You are a man, and she the woman. Take charge!" Then he stepped forward and began a furious assault on his villain.

"Take charge," muttered Marcus, too involved with his own fight to respond directly to Thompson. "Be the man. Obviously he was not reared...by any female...I know."

Then, adopting a new strategy, Marcus abruptly pulled back and waited, and waited, and waited until his opponent committed to a punch. Only then did he strike. He threw his whole body into a blow aimed at the man's chin. It landed with a horrible crunch, snapping the man's head backward, and dropping him like a stone.

Marcus turned to see Thompson finally finishing off his own brute.

"Well done," he commented, impressed by the man's fighting skill.

"It would not have had to be done at all," responded Thompson irritably, "if you kept better control of Fantine."

"I! I assure you, you overestimate the power men have over women. Truly, they do not need us as much as they pretend."

"That is merely the excuse of a man who cannot instill good discipline."

Marcus started to respond. Indeed, he had the words at the ready, prepared to eviscerate the man. But then he stopped. He remembered voicing similar thoughts not too many years before. Thompson was only speaking as young men did, young men who had not yet learned that people, especially women like Fantine, would not be dictated to by anyone.

"Someday," he said softly, "a young woman will come along and teach you exactly how wrong you are. Until then, believe in your own power as a man. It is as much a part of youth as scraped knees and bloody noses."

"And someday soon," Thompson retorted hotly, "you will see Fantine curb her wild ways and perform to my dictates as a lady! As her husband, indeed as her fiancé, I declare this type of folly to be at an end!"

Marcus merely shook his head. "Then you will have destroyed the very part of Fantine that you love." And with that, he turned, searching for the woman in question, wondering what she thought of her suitor now.

He scanned the darkness, thinking that she was resting against a tree. But the figure he spotted was her felled opponent. A further search of the area revealed nothing of her whatsoever.

"Damn! She is gone!"

Thompson groaned. "Now what game is she playing?"

Marcus whipped around, finding his temper much too short. "This is no game," he said darkly. "And if it were, she is a much better player than both you and I." When he saw the man's disdainful expression, Marcus cursed again. Thompson would never understand. He was too young.

"We will have to look for her," Marcus continued. "She is probably still nearby. You search in front of the house. Try to catch her if she is leaving. I will go through the gardens. If you have not heard from me within a half hour, assume I have found her and taken her home."

Thompson nodded, moving off with a speed and conviction that Marcus envied. What he would give to be that sure of himself again. But he was not. Indeed, ever since Fantine had come into his life, he was not sure of anything or anyone, least of all himself.

Two months ago, he had seen his entire future stretched before him in an endless series of tedious days. Now, he was newly emerged from a fistfight at a ball to slip through the shadows, straining for any sign of a woman who might be joining forces with a criminal leader.

At least he was not bored.

Perhaps that was the best explanation why Fantine held such desperate fascination for him. Or could it be that his feelings had changed from fascination to something deeper? Marcus paused in mid-step, not sure he should pursue that particular thought. No, he decided. Now was definitely not the time to think about that.

Especially as he had just found Fantine.

She was in the main portion of the garden, shielded from view by the night's gloom. But even in the dark, he recognized her silhouette. Never before had he responded so completely to anyone, seeing not only the outline of her lithe form, but sensing her absolute stillness, knowing she was listening to a conversation on the other side of the greenery.

Then she moved. Her head turned slightly, and he knew she saw him. With a nod, she acknowledged his presence, then turned her attention back to the conversation.

He listened too, though he heard very little—only snatches of words spoken by two men. It had to be Hurdy and Teggie.

Finally, their quarry was at hand.

So he slipped closer, easing his body alongside hers, feeling her presence as a palpable, erotic force despite the seriousness of the situation.

She turned once again and raised her finger to her lips, her expression both fierce and beautiful in the moonlight. She wanted him to be quiet. He wanted nothing more than to lay her down on the rich, fertile ground and bury himself in her.

Good Lord, he was insane!

Then someone spoke loud enough for him to understand the words, effectively distracting him.

"Good God, I did not pay you to think!"

"But—"

"I want the man dead! If you cannot do it—"

"Oi can, Oi just thought—"

"Enough." The voice had dropped to a low murmur, but Marcus still managed to pick out enough to understand the meaning. "…White's. One tomorrow…. Then…. Or never."

Marcus held his breath, his thoughts reeling. Anyone could have learned of Wilberforce's plan to be at White's tomorrow afternoon. The fact that he had told Lord Baylor about the MP's movements meant nothing. Or at least it would mean nothing if he did not recognize the voice.

But he did. Lord Baylor was Teggie.

Marcus nearly kicked himself in frustration. Instead, he held completely still, quietly considering his options. He could take care of it now. He could leap over the greenery, confront Teggie, and be done with the whole matter. Even with Hurdy there, he still could accomplish it. Surprise would even the odds.

Except for one thing. Fantine.

She still sat beside him, a silent spectator, no doubt trying to identify Teggie's voice. She would recognize it, but might not be able to place it. After all, Baylor had no doubt played a dandy with her, but had abandoned that affectation here.

It did not matter. Marcus could not allow her to end the business now. If Hurdy discovered she had betrayed him, if he discovered that her true goal was to capture Teggie, her life would be forfeit. There would be no place for her to hide from him or his men.

And even if they could somehow maintain her aura of innocence before Hurdy, this was still a public place. An altercation would certainly attract attention, especially once Teggie was arrested. If Fantine was in the middle of it, her reputation would be in tatters.

Fantine would count it a small matter, he knew, but he could not. Her life and her reputation meant a great deal to him, even if she ended up married to Thompson. He would not allow her to throw herself away.

Even if that meant risking Wilberforce's life.

So he stayed silent, his hand on her arm to keep her from doing anything rash. She made to brush it away, but he would not release her, and she could not risk the noise of an argument.

Moments later, Hurdy and Teggie separated. Marcus could hear their heavy footfalls as they slipped away.

"Damn it, Marcus," hissed Fantine. "Let me go! I can follow—"

"No. We must get you home."

"Do not be ridiculous." She tried to push to her feet, but he held her still. "I must discover—"

"We must make sure Wilberforce does not go to White's tomorrow at one."

Fantine took a deep breath, clearly trying to hold on to her temper. "Well, of course, but—"

"It is too late to follow Teggie."

Suddenly, she jerked her arm out of his grip and pushed to her feet. He followed quickly, but she did not move. Instead, she stood silent, pushing up on her tiptoes to try and see over the shrubbery. It was another few moments before her shoulders slumped in defeat.

"I could have followed him."

He shook his head. "Not as you are dressed. It would raise too much comment and alert Teggie as well."

She looked down at her attire, only now realizing just how torn and dirty it was. In addition to the great rent that exposed part of her right leg, her bodice and shift now showed a jagged V between her breasts. For the moment, everything was covered properly, but a single breeze or careless movement would bring the whole thing down to her ankles. As it was, delicious whispers of creamy white skin gleamed in the moonlight.

"Marcus! You are staring!" Then to his eternal amusement, he saw a blush creep up the skin between her breasts.

"I did not think you so modest."

"I am not. But the way you stare would make anyone embarrassed."

Marcus looked up, scanning her features in the moonlight. She had turned slightly away, but her lips were parted with excitement.

He could barely contain his joy. She was excited. By him. By his single heated stare, she was so affected as to become obviously nervous.

He reached out, his touch nearly reverent as he stroked her chin. Her gaze flew to his, and for a moment she reminded him of a deer, both vulnerable and infinitely beautiful.

"We can catch Teggie tomorrow," he said softly. "Nothing will happen before then. Right now, you are my chief concern. Come, let us get home."

Fantine nodded slowly, but her gaze remained locked with his, her eyes wide, her mouth so inviting. "Home?" she said, her word breathless; then suddenly her eyes widened. "Home! Blimey, Lady Anne will kill me. Just look at my gown!"

He smiled at her horrified expression. The woman had just fought hand-to-hand with killers, followed a murderer, and solved her case, though she did not realize it yet. After all that, she was terrified of what his mother would say?

"Never mind," he said softly. "I can take you to my home. You may clean up and get a new gown there while I send a message to Lottie. This way at least you will not present yourself in complete disarray."

Fantine frowned. "Will they not think it odd?"

Marcus shrugged. "Of course they will think it odd, but Lottie is used to it by now, I am sure. As for Mother, she will be discreet, though she may ring a peal over you in private."

"Wonderful," she said, her voice heavy with dread.

"You will survive," he said with a chuckle. "I always did."

CHAPTER 19

S he had to get out of the area quietly. Fantine knew that if anyone saw her in her current attire, her reputation would be in tatters within an hour. A few weeks ago, that thought would not have bothered her. After all, what need did she have for a chaste reputation? One could move about much more freely when one was thought a tart. That was, in fact, one of the reasons she adopted her persona as Fanny.

But for the first time, her reputation did matter to her. She wanted to be thought of as pure, as respectable, if not for herself, then for Lottie and Lady Anne, not to mention Marcus. They were bringing her out. Any misbehavior on her part reflected as much on them as it did on her.

So with a nod to Marcus, she allowed him to guide her through the bushes and around the house. They encountered no one, slipping through the shadows, avoiding the street, until they came up behind Marcus's carriage.

Then he pushed her inside, pulling the door shut before she had time to catch her breath, shutting out the light as thoroughly as if he had drawn a cloak of secrecy about them.

"My reputation is safe?" she asked anxiously.

"Yes," he said as the carriage began to move. "As long as you stay out of sight until you are properly attired. A torn and muddied dress is too much to keep secret."

"But if I am clean and decently covered?"

"Then Lottie and Mother will act as if everything is as it should be. Perhaps I should send a message to Lottie. She could escort you home."

Fantine worried at her lip, thinking through the events of the evening. Guilt ate at her for allowing the danger to Wilberforce to escalate so badly. If she had not attended the ball tonight, then the MP might very well have died. And she would be to blame. She had been sorely neglecting her investigative duties, though in truth she had no idea what she could have done differently.

Looking back at Marcus, she shook her head. "Have Lottie say that I have been called home unexpectedly. That my great-aunt is ill."

"But why?"

"Hurdy is going to act soon. I should stay close to Wilberforce. Act as his bodyguard."

Marcus shook his head. She could barely see him in the darkness, but his movements were as definite as his words. "Absolutely not. It is too dangerous. Hurdy will be furious at what you did to his men."

Fantine almost laughed. "Yes, but I can smooth that over. After all, it is a matter of pride with me that no one, not even Hurdy, can keep me locked up for long. Friend or foe, he no doubt expected me to try to escape."

"It is still too dangerous."

"It is all we can do until we learn Teggie's identity." She sighed and let her head drop back against the cushion. "If only you had let me follow him."

"Not as you were dressed."

Fantine knew he was right. Still, all she wanted was one glimpse of the man. "I have spoken with him. I know it. Did you recognize his voice at all?"

He hesitated a moment, but his answer was definite. "No. Not at all."

"I thought not. You would have said something by now." Then she shook her head. "I have handled this very badly."

"You have handled this excellently," he admonished her. "You cannot do everything, Fantine. I thought you understood that."

Fantine sighed. "I do. Indeed, I feel more vulnerable every day." Vulnerable to Marcus's husky voice surrounding her in the dark, warm carriage.

"You shall have a hot bath and fresh clothes. Then we can address other matters."

Fantine smiled and let herself relax. "I rely upon you, my lord." It was amazing how easy it was to say those words. She did trust Marcus. Completely. Throughout all their misadventures, despite their animosity and the insults to his dignity, he had always behaved with her best interest at heart. Certainly, he could be domineering and opinionated, but she never doubted his true intentions.

He might not love her, but he certainly cared about her. Perhaps that was enough. Not for a lifelong commitment. Not for her to become his mistress. But enough to warm her through and through on this cold night of failures. And in that moment, she allowed herself to feel the tension that crackled through the darkness, setting her skin and her heart to tingling.

She could barely make out his figure across from her, but she need not see it to picture him. Handsome as the devil with broad shoulders and a wicked smile, his features were often stiff and autocratic. But with her, he softened, his expression mellowing until he surprised her with a smile so enchanting it made her toes curl.

She thought of Mr. Thompson and his earnest defense of her. Certainly she cared for him. In fact, she still intended to marry him should he offer. But compared to Marcus, he was merely a sweet young man. She could make a life with Mr. Thompson, but her heart longed for Marcus.

The carriage stopped, and Marcus pulled aside the curtain to look outside, scanning the street. "There is someone out there. We will have to wait a moment."

Fantine nodded, grabbing hold of her skirt in preparation.

"Keep your head down," he continued, "and walk quickly inside. Go straight upstairs and do not reveal yourself until you have closed the door to the upstairs bedroom."

Fantine frowned. "Can your servants be trusted?"

"Of course," he said stiffly. "But I try not to tempt their loyalty." Then suddenly he grinned. "Besides, I have just raised all their wages. Pray do not give them an excuse to demand even more."

"Perhaps you could give them another holiday," she said, responding easily to his teasing tone. "That was what you did last time, is it not?"

"Yes, but you cannot believe how much my fellow MPs hated it. Once one lord's servants receive time off, they all want it. Harris even claimed I was undermining England's social fabric."

"Goodness," she gasped in mock outrage. "How dreadful of you."

"Yes. So dreadful that I think I shall do it again."

Their entire conversation was nonsensical. It was merely play talk, used to dispel the growing tension between them. Unfortunately, it did not work.

She could see his face, outlined by the moonlight. His eyes were dark pools focused on her and her alone. She saw him swallow, his jaw clenched, and she knew he held himself in check.

Suddenly, desire rushed over her. She felt a hunger beyond reason. Her skin felt scorched, and her lips painfully dry. She licked them, and heard his sharp inhale.

"Fantine…" he said, his words a low groan.

She did not know how to answer, did not know what to think. So she ran. She pushed past him out the door, rushing up his steps as the door opened before her. She heard his heavy footfalls behind her as she rushed into his home.

Then she was up the stairs and into her room, the one she had used so many nights before. The one where they had almost…

She shut the door fast, leaned against it, and closed her eyes tight. Downstairs, she heard Marcus speak with his butler. His voice was indistinct, but her body seemed to hum with the sound of his low tones.

She did not want this, did not want to respond this way to him, to think about him, to remember the feel of his body alongside hers. But she did. She wanted him.

Then a troubling thought came to her. It was a soft whisper in her mind, but its effect was like thunder. Two simple words:

Why not?

Why not give in to Marcus, why not welcome him into her bed this one night? The answer was clear. She was a virgin. In fact, she had guarded her virginity as closely as she would have guarded a hundred bars of gold. It was the one proof that she was nothing like her mother and never would be.

She looked up, seeing her moonlit reflection in the mirror. Her dress was in tatters, her face dirty, and a half-crumpled leaf stuck out from her hair. The very sight made her grin, not because she enjoyed being filthy, but because her mother would have been horrified by the sight.

Her mother had cared for nothing except herself. She became an actress so that people would look at her. She became a courtesan for the jewels and beautiful clothing she could wear. Her greatest dream was to live in a big house with a carriage to drive her around Hyde Park where everyone would say how beautiful and rich she was.

But Fantine cared nothing for those thing and never had. She wanted an easier life than the rookeries offered. She wanted a man to love her, one who would never, ever abandon her.

So she was nothing like her mother. The thought was so liberating that she nearly laughed out loud. She was not her mother! Marcus was right. No matter what she did, she was herself. And she was in love with Marcus.

Why not finally express that love for one night? For one precious moment before committing herself to a loveless marriage with Mr. Thompson?

Why not?

There was no reason not to. She knew how to prevent pregnancy. For that matter, she knew how to simulate virginity for her wedding night. So when she heard Marcus's measured tread outside the door, she opened it willingly, quickly, and allowed him to come in.

He looked nervous, his hands fumbling and his eyes dark and hungry. "My servants will bring a bath as soon as the water is heated."

She shook her head, the implications of her decision still too new for her to act on just yet. "N-no. A small pot and a cloth will do. There is no need to wake the entire staff."

Marcus nodded. "I have sent a message to Wilberforce, so there is no need to be uneasy about that. He will not go to White's tomorrow."

"Good, good," Fantine answered, her hands twisting uneasily in the remains of her skirt.

"And I sent a message to Lottie telling her you are safe. I said you were visiting a sick friend."

"Good, good."

They stared at each other a moment; then Marcus abruptly turned and left. Fantine could hear his curt tones through the door as he gave instructions to his servant.

Chastising herself for her nerves, Fantine quickly lit a small fire. Though it was spring, the night was chill, and the mundane task occupied her hands.

But it was not enough to occupy her thoughts, so when Marcus returned, she still felt jittery, anxious, unprepared. But then she saw something she had never thought to witness in her life. Marcus came in carrying a large pot of water.

Fantine gaped at the strange sight. "Marcus?"

"As you said, there was no need to wake the staff." His words were breathless as he set down the large cooking pot of hot water. "I think my sister left some gowns in the wardrobe."

Fantine glanced at the huge armoire. "Yes. Several." Her words came out in a breathless whisper.

"She sometimes stays here when I am away. Shopping trips, you know. Easier to stay here than rent a house."

"Of course."

Their conversation was awkward, their words stilted as they stood and stared at each other. Then suddenly Marcus frowned and looked down at the cloth in his hand. "Oh, and here is this." He handed it to her as she reached for it.

She would have touched him just then, but he dropped it in her hand and drew abruptly away. Then he ducked his head and made to leave.

"Marcus?" she asked, confused by his new, awkward side.

He stopped moving, his back to her. She could see how his shoulders bunched, the muscles of his back shifting beneath the linen shirt.

"I cannot stay, Fantine," he said, his voice hoarse. "I want you more than life itself right now. I will do anything, risk anything to have you in my bed this night."

She felt her breath catch. Could he feel the same hunger as she? Was it as strange for him—both exhilarating and terrifying all at once?

There was only one way to find out.

She stepped forward and gently laid her hand on his shoulder. She felt his muscles ripple beneath her touch, felt the tension he restrained for her sake.

"I am not used to gowns," she said, her voice husky and low. "Could you not stay and help me change?"

He whirled around, his expression fierce. "Damn it, Fantine, can you not understand? I am trying to keep my promise!"

He would have said more, but she reached up and pressed her fingers to his lips. His skin felt hot, his mouth even more so.

"I understand," she whispered. "But do you?"

She moved her fingers into a long caress of his face, starting with his mouth, curving across his roughened cheek, then brushing downward until she passed over his shoulder.

Then she stepped away.

She saw his dumbfounded expression and smiled. What power this was to so completely flabbergast a man!

She turned around, showing him her back as she pulled her hair across one shoulder. Then, as she walked toward the heated water and the fire, she released the last of the catches on her torn bodice, shrugging so that both gown and shift slipped off her shoulders. With each step she took, her clothing fell away until she stood naked, outlined by the fire.

Behind her, Marcus groaned. She turned her head slightly and peeked at him. He stood as if rooted to the spot, his hands clenching and unclenching by his side.

Then she did the most blatantly sexual thing she could think of. She slowly extended one leg, raising it up until it rested on a chest. She made sure Marcus had a full view in profile of her limb. Then she leaned down, wet the cloth, and slowly began washing herself. She started at her foot, dripping water across her ankle and toes. Then began the long slide up her leg to the top of her thigh.

She stopped and glanced coyly at him before leaning down and wetting the cloth again. She took her time, stretching and twisting so that she presented a variety of profiles. And all the while, he just stood there, his breath a low rasp.

When she was done with her legs, she once again reached down and wet the cloth. She stood up, arching her back and raising the fabric until water dripped across her breasts.

His groan reverberated in the still room.

Suddenly he was behind her, his large frame surrounding her as he reached around and gently pulled her backward. His touch sizzled across her skin, and for the first time she noticed that her own breathing was none too steady.

"Here," he said, "allow me to help."

He pulled her backward until she leaned against his chest. He wore no coat. Instead, she felt the silken swatch of his cravat, and beneath that, the cool press of each one of his pearl buttons. But the fabric could not mask the heat of his body or the fire in his touch.

He took the cloth from her, his palms large and powerful as he brushed against the back of her hands. Then, drip, drip, he allowed the water to slide onto her chest, slipping in long, wet rivulets over her breasts.

She gasped at the sensation. She felt her nipples tighten, and her body arch in response.

It took him a long time before he lowered his hand, brushing the cloth over her collarbone, circling around a breast, then leisurely stroking across a nipple. His touch was feather soft at first, then firmer, then torturous as he teased her peaks with the softest of strokes. She moaned, shocked by what they were doing, yet thrilled as well.

"Marcus." His name was more whisper than word, and beside her temple, she felt his lips curve into a smile.

"You are so beautiful," he said, and for the first time in her life, she believed it. She was beautiful. He made her so. "I cannot believe you are finally mine."

She smiled and made to kiss him, twisting in his hold, but he would not allow her to.

"No," he whispered. "Stay this way for me a moment longer."

He continued to stroke her body, brushing the cloth in random patterns, moving across her body where and how he willed. He pulled her arms up over her head, draping them over his shoulders, and with her stretched against him, he stroked the underside of her breasts.

She moved against him, wanting to turn to kiss him, and yet wanting more of this exquisite torture. It did not matter. He would not release her as his other hand joined the cloth, first pulling her hips hard against him, then roaming on its own.

Soon he discarded the cloth altogether, and his two hands cupped her breasts while she rocked her buttocks against him. As he held her, his fingers ever moving, he bent his head to kiss her along the side of her neck. His tongue made slow circles that were echoed by his fingers, and her legs began to tremble.

Marcus lowered his hands to her belly, then her hips as she rocked against him. He responded in kind, thrusting upward.

It was too much and too little. Turning in his hold, she lifted her face for his kiss. He claimed her mouth with a swift possession, and all too soon they were both gasping for breath.

Her fingers fumbled with his shirt, tearing at the buttons and peeling off the wet fabric from his slick body. He helped her as best he could, all the while raining kisses across her face, her neck, whatever part of her he could reach.

Then when she had at last stripped away his shirt, he leaned over and lifted her. In two strides, he was beside the bed, laying her down on the mattress with amazing gentleness.

Abruptly he stood back. His body was a powerful silhouette, broad and strong, but his eyes were dark, his face shadowed.

"Marcus?" she asked softly.

"I swore to leave you. To let you be a lady."

"But I am a lady," she answered easily. "And nothing you ever do or say can change that. I understand that now. I choose my life. And I choose you." She stretched up, catching his lips with her own. Then she pulled him down with her onto the bed. He went reluctantly, as if still doubting her, but soon she overpowered his restraint. His hands touched her, his tongue stroked her, and his weight began to shift on top of her.

She reached for his trousers, but he brushed her fingers away, breaking off their kiss. He disrobed quickly, with an efficiency she could not have managed. When he returned to her, he went not for her lips, but lower, to her breasts, tasting her as no one but him had ever done before.

She gasped, feeling the erotic swirl of his tongue, the slight nip of his teeth, even the heated brush of his breath.

She cried out, feeling the tension coil almost unbearably within her, but still he went on, tormenting her while she writhed.

"Marcus," she cried, "please." She didn't know what she asked for, only knew that she needed him more than ever. She felt him shift on the mattress, settling his weight over her as she opened up to him. She stroked his back, letting her hands slide down his lean form until they settled on his hips.

She felt the brush of his legs—corded muscles, taut on the inside of her thighs. Then she pulled him toward her.

His thrust was swift and powerful, and she cried out at the swift pierce of pain. He stopped, holding himself still, his eyes wide with astonishment.

"My God, Fantine, I never thought—"

"It is nothing," she whispered, except that it was everything, and yet she did not mind in the least. It felt right that he should be the one to take her virginity.

Marcus shook his head. "You should have told me."

"I chose this. I chose you." Then to emphasize her words, she began to move. Her body stretched for him, her hips pressed against him.

With a groan, he lowered his head and kissed her, taking her mouth while below he drove into her again.

And again.

The tension within her built and she gasped with each powerful stroke. She felt his hands, firm and hard on her body, pulling her against him.

Again.

And again.

Until with a final thrust, her world splintered into a thousand glittering diamonds. She heard voices crying out and knew one was hers. She felt Marcus, joined with her in joy, his own ecstasy as triumphant as her own.

CHAPTER 20

Marcus was grinning.

He knew he was grinning because his cheek muscles ached. In fact, his whole body ached, but he was so happy, he did not care. He could not believe what had happened. After thinking he had lost Fantine forever, she had come to him. She had offered herself to him in a seduction that still had the power to arouse him. If he closed his eyes, he could see her once again, outlined by the firelight, slowly extending one long, sleek leg to be washed.

Looking at her now, curled on her side in sleep, no one would guess at the passion she contained inside. How many times had they come together last night? How many times had she cried out his name in her joy?

She was his, and he could hardly believe his luck.

He reached out and stroked her cheek. Her skin was a soft rose, innocent and pure. He leaned forward, pressing his lips to the pink blush of her mouth.

Did they have time? Could he lose himself in her again?

From a long way away, he heard the downstairs clock strike eleven. There was no more time. Yet as she stirred, a smile of welcome curving across her lush mouth, how could he resist her?

* * *

"I must go." Marcus was feeling languid and sleepy and altogether too happy to stir. But he had to. "The servants will bring you anything you need."

"What if I need you?" Her words were soft and seductive as she stretched her arms across his shoulders and drew him down for a tantalizing kiss.

He nearly succumbed, but he could not. "Lord, Fantine, you do not know how much you tempt me." His words were nearly a groan, but he pushed away from her.

"Where are you going in such a hurry?" She sat up, letting the sheet pool about her waist. Her glorious breasts were revealed in the sunlight, and he had to clench his hands into fists to keep from touching her.

"I must talk with someone." He took a deep breath, then tore his gaze away from her. "And I must send Jacob to Wilberforce to make sure the man does not go to White's this afternoon."

Fantine frowned, remembering last night's events. "I swear I have heard Teggie's voice before. Why did you stop me from following him? I could have ended this."

"You know full well why," he said as he extricated himself from the bedsheets. "You would have drawn a great deal of attention. I shudder to think what Hurdy would do if he discovered you betrayed him."

Fantine shrugged, though he heard a slight tremor of nervousness in her voice. "I can handle Hurdy."

"No doubt you can. But I will not risk you. Not when I can handle the situation just as well today."

She had been shifting her position on the bed, but at his words she stilled, her gaze cooling even as she questioned him. "What do you mean? How can you resolve things?"

He knew he should have waited to tell her. He should have held his tongue until the entire affair was completed to his satisfaction. But he hated keeping things from her, hated that he had lied to her.

Their relationship had changed last night, and he did not want to begin the morning less than honest. So he settled back onto the bed and took her hands, trying to soften the blow as much as possible.

"I lied to you. I did recognize Teggie's voice. I know who he is."

She did not react immediately. In fact, she was completely still. Then he saw the fury blaze in her eyes as she jerked her hands out of his and leaped out of bed. She whirled around to confront him.

"You know who he is?"

"Yes."

"And you did not tell me! How could you?" She was shaking in her rage.

"Fantine, you must let me handle this—"

"I will not!"

He pushed to his feet, using his superior height to advantage as he gripped her shoulders. "Listen to me. I know you are loathe to relinquish any part of this investigation, but in this you must!"

"Bloody hell, do you think me too incompetent to—"

"Of course not!" His explosion was enough to temporarily silence her. "He is a lord and an influential one at that."

"That means nothing—"

"It means something to me. Fantine, aside from the risk from Hurdy, remember that we are dealing with the peerage, not some dockside criminal. There are rules. We must be discreet."

She shoved him away from her, her movement so sudden his hands slipped off her shoulders as if they had never been there. "He is a murderer. You would not be this merciful if we discovered Ballast or Hurdy at the bottom of this."

Marcus shook his head, wishing she would understand. "We cannot allow the British people to think our leaders are corrupt. We would have mass unrest. Good Lord, we might plunge the entire country into a revolution like France. Do you want that?"

She stared at him, her fists clenched. "You still think us idiots."

"I beg your pardon?"

She threw up her hands. "If the lower class is angry, perhaps we have a reason."

"Of course, but—"

"No, it is my turn." She stepped forward, pulling on a wrap as she moved. "We do not want to revolt like the mad French. We do not want a leader like Napoleon. We wish to be dealt with honesty. We wish a chance at a decent life."

Marcus nodded, his thoughts and emotions tangled together in an indecipherable knot. "Of course you do," he said slowly. "But what has that to do with Lord—with Teggie?"

"Can you not see it, Marcus? How are we to trust you if you hide your frailties?"

"How are you to trust us if we expose ourselves as less than perfect?" Marcus shot back. "The nation must be run smoothly or we shall be attacked from within as well as without. Napoleon is waiting for just such an event. Show him that our government is unstable, and he shall attack within days! I cannot allow that to happen."

"What will you do? Lock me up rather than let me finish what I was hired to do?"

Marcus looked at her clenched fists, wondering how events had slipped out of his control. "Be reasonable, Fantine. He will be more cooperative if it is handled quietly, between peers."

She threw up her hands. "Quietly! Between peers! My God, Marcus, he has tried to have a man killed. Expose him and be done with it."

"That is not how things are done!"

There was a long, taut silence as they stared at each other. They were barely two paces apart, and yet he felt as if they stood on opposite sides of a wide gulf.

"Fantine, it is the way things are done. We have discussed this before. You cannot change the world merely by wishing."

"So you will lock me inside and handle Teggie between peers. What does that mean? Does he go free?"

"Yes. To the Colonies."

She began to laugh, the sound not at all pleasant. "So you send the problem away, push him off onto other people."

"He will not be nearly so dangerous there."

"A murderer will remain a murderer, Marcus. He will not change just because you have sent him away from your exalted presence."

He sighed. "He will be leaving everything he has—his family, his title, his income, everything. Is that not punishment enough?"

She shook her head. "I do not know. And neither do you. Expose him, Marcus. Let a judge decide."

He was tempted. He nearly gave in. But in the end, he could not. "This is the way things are done. Gentleman to gentleman. I am sorry you do not understand that."

"Oh, I do understand." Her voice was filled with contempt. "All too well, Lord Chadwick." His title came out as a sneer.

He sighed, commiserating in part with her frustration, but unwilling to change his mind. This was the best way to handle the situation, and they both knew it. It was only her pride that kept her from accepting it.

He stepped to her. She would not want him to touch her, but he did anyway, taking her hands in his. She did not struggle long. She needed his caress as much as he needed to touch her. In the end, he drew her hands up to his face, kissing them with tenderness. "I will return shortly. We can discuss this as much as you like then."

"But it will be too late. You will have already dealt with Teggie."

"True. But I am willing to learn from you, listen to your opinions." He hesitated, then finally chose total honesty. "You may have a point, Fantine. Unfortunately, we do not have the time for you to convince me. It is nearly noon. I must speak with Teggie before he realizes that his latest attempt has failed."

"I will go with you." Her words were firm and determined.

"You cannot. The man has a great deal of pride. This must be done between gentlemen." He pulled her close, cherishing the feel of her body. "We will speak more tonight. When you can use all your skills to persuade me."

He felt her stiffen, and she jerked out of his arms. "You cannot think that I will grace your bed this night."

"Why ever not? Surely you cannot mean this disagreement will destroy what we mean to one another. Last night was…" He struggled for a way to express the splendor of their night together. "It was…"

"It is over." She stepped away. "Marcus, I shared your bed because I love you, because I wanted to spend a final night with you before committing myself to Mr. Thompson. This was never meant to be more."

He gaped at her. He blinked, he frowned, he even had to remind himself to breathe. He wanted to speak, wanted to express his outrage, but he could manage no more than one startled, horrified exclamation. "Mr. Thompson!"

"Yes. He is kind and intelligent and a good match. He has promised to ask for my hand, and I intend to accept."

His mind whirled. "But you love me!"

"Yes, I do. And I intend to marry Mr. Thompson."

"But we just…" He could not say it. He could merely point mutely at the rumpled bed. "You love me!" Then he frowned. That was not at all what he intended to say, but his mind kept returning to that fact. "You love me?"

"Yes."

He stepped forward, anger starting to sear through his mind. "You love me!" His tongue twisted out of his control. "Me!"

"You have said that!" she exclaimed, clearly as exasperated as he with his inability to express himself.

"But I never thought you would love me. I didn't think…"

"Well, I do." She was clearly upset with the notion.

He stepped forward, joy shimmering along his skin like fire. "I think…I think it is wonderful!"

"Of course you do," she snapped. "You are a man!"

She would not allow him to hold her, but neither could he stay away. So he hovered near her, his hands outstretched. "You cannot marry Mr. Thompson," he said firmly. "Not if you truly love me."

She bit her lip, and for a short moment, he saw all the fear, all the insecurities that haunted her. Then all was wiped away by a resolve as firm as any he had ever witnessed. "Understand this, Marcus, I do love you. I always will. We shared a night I shall treasure for the rest of my life. But I will marry Mr. Thompson, and nothing you can do will prevent it."

He shook his head. "I do not understand."

"Do you not? Think of the women of your class. They marry for position all the time."

"Of course, they do," he snapped, his anger once again outstripping his reason. "But you are not one of them."

She lifted her head, her eyes blazing, and he knew he had said the wrong thing. "On the contrary," she said, her voice colder than he could ever imagine. "I am one of them now. Or I will be the moment I marry Mr. Thompson."

"I forbid it!"

She merely laughed, and suddenly he was glaring at her, furious enough to shake her, angry enough to hurt her. But not with his fists. He lashed out against her smug certainty, positive he could puncture it with a single statement.

"What if you now carry my child?"

She shook her head. "I took steps to prevent it."

"What steps?" he exploded.

She shrugged. "It does not matter. There is no child. There never will be. At least not yours."

She said it so firmly, her words so matter-of-fact that he had no choice but to accept it. Still his mind rebelled. He had not even imagined a child between them until barely a moment before, yet now that he had, the fact that she would never carry one infuriated him. The thought that she might one day carry Edwin's…

"You cannot marry Edwin!"

She lifted her chin. "Do you intend to throw me in jail?"

"Of course not!"

"Publicly disgrace me or disown any association with me?"

"No!"

"Then you cannot stop me." She turned away from him and began dressing.

He would have stayed to fight with her. He would have spent as much time as it took even if it meant throwing her on the bed now and making love with her until she relinquished her ridiculous plans. In fact, he intended to do just that, but at that moment the clock struck twelve.

Noon.

And it would take some time for him to dress and prepare to confront Teggie. He had to go now.

He took one last look at Fantine. Her head was bent, her hair falling over her face as she pulled on her stockings. He was somewhat reassured when he saw that her hands shook. At least she was not unaffected, at least the thought of leaving him was painful to her. He still had some hope.

But he could not stay. Wilberforce's life rested in his hands.

"This is not over, Fantine," he said softly, part of him begging with her, part of him demanding that she listen. "We will discuss this again."

She looked up, and he read a kind of empty resignation in her face. "You may talk all you wish, my lord, but I shall be planning my wedding."

He looked at her, feeling torn between pulling her into his arms and his duties to England. "Fantine," he said, his voice nearly breaking on her name, "I must go."

"And I must marry Mr. Thompson."

Then she turned away from him, pulling open the wardrobe as she searched for an appropriate gown. He hesitated a moment longer, but what could he say? What was between them was too complex, too knotted to examine in a moment. It had to wait.

A man's life was at stake. His country's stability.

With a sharp curse, he stomped away, nearly slamming

the bedroom door in his haste. The sooner he dealt with
Teggie, the sooner he could return to Fantine.

He would deal with her. He could never allow her to
marry Mr. Thompson. Or anyone else for that matter.

She was his.

Fantine stared unseeing into the wardrobe. Her hand
touched costly silks, beautiful cambric, the soft muslin of
his sister's gowns, but all she felt was the empty room.

He had left her. As she had once predicted, Marcus had
chosen England over her. She understood his choice.
Indeed, she did not wish to sacrifice Wilberforce just so she
and Marcus could bandy the same argument back and
forth.

Still his absence cut at her. As did his lack of faith in her
ability to handle Teggie. He had not trusted her last night,
and this morning he had rubbed her nose in her
powerlessness.

Gentleman to gentleman. Rich man to rich man.

Fantine let her hand *drop* to her side. She could follow
Marcus. Indeed, that had been her intention when she
began dressing. But suddenly, she felt very tired. It seemed
as if she had spent her entire life running. Sometimes she
was chasing someone like Teggie, but usually she was
running away. Her childhood had been spent avoiding her
mother's lovers who would take a child just for variety's
sake. Then later, she ran from Ballast or Hurdy or others
equally dangerous. Even after she had learned the subtle
skills of manipulation, there was always another man to
avoid. Even Penworthy used her to solve his problems
within London.

She was tired of it. Tired of the games between men—
gentlemen or thieves. What about the women? What about
her? She was smart, capable, and more than a little canny.
Why could she not wield power just as effectively, just as
mercilessly as a man? What did they have, besides a pisser,
that allowed them to control her life?

The answer was clear. They had power. Money, influence, and their sheer numbers gave them the control. In order to become a force on her own, she needed at least one of the three.

She had no money, nor did she lead anyone except perhaps Nameless and his gang of boys. As for influence, she had nothing but a passing friendship with Wilberforce.

Wilberforce.

She slowly lifted her head, as her mind replayed her own thoughts. Who was Wilberforce except one of the most influential MPs in all of England? Penworthy and Marcus had already invested a great deal just to keep the man alive, and he did not even appreciate it. If ever there was political influence in one man, it was in Wilberforce. Nearly all the charitable projects in the rookeries bore his name. The elite spoke of him with reverence. If she could get him on her side, put his name to any one of her dreams for the rookeries, she could make an enormous difference there. She could create a school for the children and teach them a trade, something other than thieving and whoring. She could start a kitchen, providing food and warmth for those who need it. Or better yet, she could help find jobs, matching employers with workers, especially if she could guarantee the employees would be honest and respectable.

Possibilities spun in her mind, each of them more ambitious, more wonderful than the next. But could she do it? Could she get a crippled, old man obsessed with stopping slavery to throw his enormous influence behind her?

She did not know. But, by God, she would try.

With that in mind, she returned to the wardrobe, this time choosing a dress with more care than she had ever done in her life. After all, it had to be good enough to impress an evangelical MP.

CHAPTER 21

Marcus knocked ponderously on Lord Baylor's door, then let his gaze wander to Giles as the boy walked his horses. The grays were lively, easily dwarfing the child, but Giles was firm as he led them to a nearby park. He had orders to exercise the horses until Marcus finished his business with Baylor. But Marcus could not even begin his business until someone answered the door!

Turning back to the knocker with an impatient frown, Marcus pounded again. Would nothing go right this day?

He sighed, thinking that perhaps nothing had gone right since he had first met Fantine. Or perhaps he had that backward. Nothing had been right until the day she had sauntered into his life.

She loved him.

The words still echoed in his thoughts, filling him with a warmth and a wonder he could scarcely credit.

She loved him.

And he would marry her.

Marcus paused, surprised at himself. This was not the time to make such a decision. His father had spent three days fishing and another day in church before he finally decided to offer for his mother. How could Marcus suddenly resolve to marry while standing outside a murderer's door?

But he did. He would marry her.

His mother could think it ridiculous. Fantine was beneath both his dignity and his station. But of late, he had come to think such things were not all he once thought. After all, Fantine had no station and very little dignity, yet she sparkled in his thoughts and he had fallen completely in love with her.

Marcus froze, the knocker lifted in preparation of banging once again. He did not move. He did not even blink. He merely stared at the faded paint and let the shock wash through his system unimpeded.

He was in love with Fantine. Certainly he had said the words before. Had thought them on more than one occasion, but he now realized that emotion had been like a child's word. He loved her as he loved his toy boat or his favorite horse.

Except now, he felt differently. His love for her was so much more, so much deeper and truer. It was a man's love. One that would extend through the years, growing stronger with age, hotter with touch, and deeper than he could possibly imagine.

He loved her that much. More than enough to court social ruin by marrying her. Enough to risk life and limb and his mother's derision as well.

He grinned. Goodness, his life had gotten a good deal less bland of late.

He straightened his shoulders, suddenly more anxious than ever to be done with his errand. He wanted to rush home and tell Fantine the news. He loved her! And they would marry!

He did not fool himself that she would fall into his arms immediately. She was much too stubborn to be persuaded easily. But she would eventually fall to him. He was an excellent catch and besides that, she loved him!

He nearly danced a jig. Instead, he pounded one last furious time on Lord Baylor's door.

"Bloody hell," grumbled Baylor as he finally pulled open the door. "Can you not take the hint and go away?"

Marcus's eyes widened at the sight of Lord Baylor himself answering his door. "Where is your man?"

"On holiday," came the surly response.

Marcus nodded. It only took one glance inside to understand what was happening. Good Lord, the house was nearly stripped bare. Baylor had probably sold everything that was not nailed down. He clearly needed money. And power. He needed Wilberforce's seat. Given Baylor's connections, he could easily parlay that into a lucrative cabinet post that would tide him over until his inheritance came through.

As for the man himself, Baylor only confirmed the image of someone on his last respectable gasp. Though his clothing was immaculate, his stance was stooped and haggard. The man's cravat was impeccably tied, but the skin along his jowls seemed to hang sallow over his shirt points.

But lest he assume the man completely done in, Marcus chanced to look directly into Baylor's eyes. Not only were they alert, they were almost nervously focused. His gaze darted from Marcus to his clothing to the street and his curricle with precision.

It was a disconcerting sight, but then again, Marcus had always found Baylor somewhat disconcerting.

"Well, speak up, Chadwick," the man snapped. "I mean to go to White's, and I have no interest in standing about with you."

Thus recalled to his task, Marcus wasted no more time on pleasantries. "You need not rush," he said bluntly. "There will be no murder today. Wilberforce will not go to White's. I have come to allow you to escape with your reputation and honor, such as it is, intact. Leave for the Colonies by tomorrow dawn or I shall expose you in a public trial." He allowed himself a smile as he delivered the final blow. "Imagine what your father will do when he finds out. Disinherit you, I'm sure."

Baylor spent a moment gaping at him, then suddenly pulled himself together with a theatrical gasp. "Good God, you are mad! Chadwick, dear boy, I have not the slightest inkling of what you are talking about."

Marcus shrugged, suddenly weary with the whole affair. "Then a court of law will find you innocent." He gave Baylor a mocking bow and made to leave, but the man caught his arm.

"Wait! Wait a moment, please."

Given their position, Marcus had no choice but to stop while Baylor pulled his thoughts together.

"You have caught me at an awkward moment—"

"No doubt," Marcus responded dryly.

"I played rather deep and fast, last night—"

"And lost, I do not wonder."

Baylor sighed, his hand slowly relaxing against Marcus's coat. "I was trying to extricate myself from this situation. There is more to it than first appears." He took a deep breath and looked extraordinarily pathetic. "It would be a great relief to unburden myself to a friend. I do not wish to hurt Wilberforce. I never have. Oh, Lord!" He took a shuddering breath as he stepped backward into the dark recesses of his hallway. "Please, can you not help me?"

It was a good performance, if indeed Baylor was acting. If not, then the man was truly in horrible straits.

Marcus hesitated. Was Baylor weak enough to be manipulated by someone else? Someone more powerful, more canny? The answer was an absolute yes. A month ago, Marcus would have dismissed the thought immediately. Surely corruption in the British government could not run so deep. But Fantine had made him question a good many of his long-held beliefs. It was possible that Baylor was being used. But by whom and why?

"Please," pressed Baylor, "I am so frightened. Surely, as a gentlemen, you cannot stop at anything less than the full truth."

Marcus sighed. Gentlemen or not, the man was right. He had to explore this last ridiculous ploy to discover if there was a grain of truth somewhere in it. "Very well," he said dully. "Fifteen minutes. But if I suspect this is all a ruse, then I shall not wait. I will personally drag you to the magistrate without a second's thought."

"I understand."

And with that, Marcus stepped into the gloomy interior of the Baylor town house.

"Oh, thank God you are still here, Jacob," called Fantine as she rushed toward Marcus's coachman and carriage. "I hurried as fast as I could."

The man looked up from where he was hitching up the horses. "An' why would you be looking fer me?"

Fantine put on her most innocent, most beguiling look. "To go with you to get Wilberforce, of course."

The old man frowned, rubbing his grizzled cheek. "The master said I was to keep Mr. Wilberforce at the cottage, not take 'im anywhere."

Fantine sighed as she scrambled into the box. "But that was before we found out he needs to be moved. I am to take him someplace else. Surely he said something to you."

Jacob stroked his chin, regarding her with steady eyes. "'E did not say a thing about that."

Fantine released a curse of frustration. "Well, it is what we have to do. I do not care if he has forgotten to tell you, I am here now."

Jacob folded his arms across his chest. "Did you two 'ave another spat?"

"What we have," she responded curtly, "is very little time to get to Wilberforce. Please will you come on?"

He hesitated, and she feared she had overplayed her hand, especially when he narrowed his eyes, peering at her. "An' jes where are we supposed to take 'im?"

She answered without thought. "To my home in the rookeries."

"What?" he gasped, but Fantine was already speaking, cutting off his objections.

"I know it is risky, but there are things I must show him, things he must understand. That can only be accomplished in the rookeries."

Jacob just shook his head. "Sounds risky t' me. Wot about them other folks, Hurdy and Ballast?"

Fantine shook her head, lying to herself as much as Jacob. "It's quite safe. Hurdy's busy at White's, and it will take time for Ballast to round up his men." Abandoning her confident pose, she resorted to honest pleading. "I swear we won't stay long. He only needs to speak to Nameless and Louise. If he could hear their stories, then he will understand."

Jacob simply sighed. "I don't understand, but then it ain't my business to understand. If you're sure the master knows, then I'll drive ye."

"Absolutely," Fantine lied.

"Well, then," he said as he jumped into the box. "I suppose we best be going." He started the horses moving with a smart snap of the ribbons, his expression chipper in the sunlight. "It will take us a mite to get there. So how 'bout you spend the time explainin' wot 'e did to upset you so?"

Fantine shifted on her seat, surprised not only by the shift in conversation, but by the man's perception. "I am not upset," she said slowly.

He simply chuckled and reached over to pat her hand. "Aw, don't get all touchy on me, girl. I was just gonna offer ye a little fatherly advice, is all."

Fantine looked away, unaccountably startled by the gesture. Fatherly advice? When had she last had that? Never. Penworthy, though he was her father, had never stooped to giving advice. Commands were more his style, which perhaps explained why she never much listened to him.

But advice? The very thought was intriguing, and so she turned on the bench and allowed all her anger to pour out. "He is just so arrogant I want to tear his eyes out! He thinks I have no brain whatsoever."

Jacob simply laughed at her outburst. "I never did see two people so much in love muck it up so badly."

"Love!" Fantine exploded, not caring that her accent was slipping. "E 'asn't the slightest idea wot the word means!"

"'E doesn't, does he?" returned Jacob. "An' wot about you? Do you want to stay around, fight it out until the end? Or do you jes want to run back to your old life, gettin' knocked on the 'ead by Hurdy fer your troubles?"

"Of course not," Fantine returned hotly. But in a moment, his words began to penetrate. Minutes later, her pride gave way enough to realize he might be right.

"Do you think…" She paused, considering her words. "Have I been running from him? Fighting him out of—"

"Habit?" Jacob offered.

Fantine shrugged, unable to turn her mind from this path. She had been attracted to Marcus from the very first moment. He was everything she wanted and hated all at once—rich, handsome, titled. She had set out to humiliate him, to torment him, anything that would force him to reveal his true colors as a spoiled, pampered aristocrat. But he had not done that.

Or perhaps he had, and she had found him so noble that she could not resist him.

Yet, she still fought. Why, she had even told him she loved him, and in the same breath announced her intention to wed someone else. It was no wonder their road had been so difficult, no wonder he had tried to lock her up until they could speak at length without interruption.

In every moment, in every way, she had both wanted and fought him until neither of them knew which direction to turn.

And now, was she doing it again? Was she running away? It did not feel that way. For the first time, she felt as if she had a purpose, a determination to make a better life for herself and others in the rookeries. But she was not sure.

Was she merely using this as an excuse to avoid Marcus? To thwart him even when she wanted the same as he—to find a way through the muddle?

"Oh, Jacob," she cried softly, "I do not know who I am anymore. I do things, and I do not understand the reason."

"Do you love him?"

"Yes. But he does not love me."

Jacob shrugged."'E's a man and a nob. At the moment, 'e does not know his nose from his arse unless you show him."

Fantine shifted in her seat. "But how? What shall I do?"

"Ah, as to that, don't you women 'ave some secret potion or something that puts us all under yer thumbs?"

Fantine smiled, thinking of her actions last night. "I have already used it, and though he enjoyed it mightily, he seemed completely unaffected this morning."

"But you 'ave not given it enough time. 'E's still in that glowin' moment o' satisfaction. Give 'im a day t' start wantin' it again."

Fantine frowned, wondering if she indeed could be mistaken. Could Marcus truly love her? "I do not know, Jacob. He seemed so...so overbearing this morning."

"Ah, well, ain't I said 'e's a nob through and through? It takes them a mite longer t' understand. It be their pride, you know. Clogs up the brainpan."

"Do you really think so?"

"Absolutely. Now me wife and me, there was a courtship to remember..."

Jacob continued speaking, spinning delightful stories about himself and his wife, but Fantine could not keep her mind on them. There was too much to ponder, too many angles to consider.

Did Marcus truly love her? Had she been running from him? And how did this effect her plans for Mr. Wilberforce?

It did not, she finally decided. Whether or not she and Marcus worked out their differences, she still intended to become powerful in her own right. And for that, she needed the MP.

Marcus was bored. He had come inside to a room bare of everything except a case of brandy. He accepted the obligatory glass, though he never actually drank it, and stood staring at the threadbare carpet while Baylor blamed everything from the current government to his first nanny for his failures.

It was tedious and disappointing. One would think a man daring enough to assassinate Wilberforce would have more originality.

Still, Marcus had promised fifteen minutes, and for all that it seemed like fifteen years, he was a man of his word. Until Baylor made a fatal mistake.

In the middle of his recitation, in the middle of a word, no less, he suddenly whipped out a pistol and pulled the trigger.

Fortunately, for all his bored attitude, Marcus had seen it coming. Clearly, Baylor was not used to handling the weapon. His shoulders had tensed just before the fateful movement, his breathing had noticeably accelerated, despite his long speech, and, most telling of all, he had set down his brandy glass on the mantel and closed his eyes for a brief moment.

The shot went wide. Not because Baylor missed, but because Marcus dove sideways. While Baylor was still recovering, Marcus surged upward, easily wresting the weapon from the man's hand.

Then, weaponless and exposed, Baylor retreated to infancy. He cowered in the corner and whimpered all sorts of nonsense.

"Shut up!" Marcus snapped. The idiot had completely ruined his morning. Instead of running to the Colonies like any intelligent villain, Baylor had proved himself stupid as well as evil. Now Marcus had to take him to the magistrate and likely answer hours of annoying questions while Fantine no doubt grew angrier and more stubborn by the second. "What a bloody pain in the arse!" he cursed.

Then his skull exploded with pain, and the world went dark.

Marcus woke slowly. He was lying face down, his arms and legs tied painfully behind him, his head throbbing like the very devil. He must have been hit from behind, he realized slowly.

Then he cracked an eye just to be sure. Yes, he was still in Baylor's home, could even see his full glass of brandy on a windowsill a few feet away, just beyond reach. To one side, he could hear Hurdy and Baylor arguing in low tones, though the words were not clear enough for him to understand.

How long had it been? he wondered. No more than a few minutes, he guessed, though he could not be sure. He had little experience with being knocked on the head and trussed up like a Christmas goose. For all he knew, he could have been unconscious for a month or two.

Twisting with a strength born of anger, Marcus tried desperately to break his bonds. But they wouldn't budge. He was well and truly caught.

With a grimace of disgust, Marcus relaxed and tried to reason out his situation. But all he could think was that the situation was completely ridiculous. Here he was, incapacitated by a jackass before he had revealed his heart to Fantine. Good Lord, the way things were going, Fantine might never know he loved her!

When he got free he would kill Baylor with his bare hands. Meanwhile, Hurdy's voice was becoming clearer, rising in anger.

"One gent! I's been paid fer one nob, and I will no' do more until I get paid fer two."

Marcus winced, understanding the meaning. Hurdy would not kill Marcus until Baylor paid him more money. Thank God Baylor hadn't a feather to fly with.

"And I tell you again," cut in Baylor, "that it is only because of your bungling that Chadwick is here at all. Now clean it up or I shall be forced to take drastic measures."

Marcus rolled onto his side, trying to move quietly so he could view the combatants. What he saw was not reassuring. Baylor was clearly furious, his rabbity eyes so focused they seemed to burn pinpricks into whatever he sighted. As much as Marcus wanted to think Hurdy would not give in to such pressure, it was clear the criminal was considering Baylor's words.

"I begin to think you incapable of performing the simplest task," continued Baylor.

"Murderin' an MP is not a simple task!"

"Perhaps you have not the stomach for killing."

"Don't be daft," Hurdy snapped.

"Really? Prove it. Show me you can kill in cold blood. After all, Chadwick is your mess. He would not be here, accusing me of murder, if it were not for your bungling."

"My bungling!" returned Hurdy, his voice growing in irritation. "It's him and Rat. Ain't no gent smart enough to figure it out without someone on the inside. Has to be Rat." Marcus could hear the growing malice in the villain's voice and knew that Fantine's life was forfeit.

Unless he could change their minds.

"Do not be ridiculous," he said in his most superior tone. He had the satisfaction of seeing both of their heads snap around. "I used Rat plain and simple."

For a moment, Marcus thought he had convinced them. Hurdy was watching him, his handsome brow narrowed in concentration. Then he shrugged. "Ain't no difference. Stupid or treacherous, she's dead either way."

Then before Marcus could think of anything else, Baylor was pushing forward, his voice sharp and irritating. "Are you going to kill Chadwick or not?"

Hurdy sighed, grudgingly raising his pistol. "It don't pay to work fer gents," he muttered. "It don't never pay."

At that moment Marcus finally understood he was about to die. Up until that second, he had thought his title offered him some small security from the likes of Hurdy. Apparently, his protection was gone. And with him dead, there would be no one to warn Fantine that Hurdy was on to her.

"Wait!" he called, scrambling as best he could to an awkward sitting position. "Baylor, you cannot wish to kill me, right here in your mother's parlor! Think of what she will say if she sees the bloodstains!"

"Gawd," drawled Hurdy as he rolled his eyes. "As if that makes no never mind."

"It does," put in Baylor softly. "You cannot do it here."

"Wot!"

"In fact," continued Marcus, rushing to push his point. "You need not do it all. I can give you my seat in the House of Commons."

"Wot!" exclaimed Hurdy, confusion clear on his handsome face. Then he spun to Baylor. "Wot is 'e talking about?"

"That is what you want, is it not?" continued Marcus. "You want a seat, any seat. It would restore your pride, your status—"

"My income."

Marcus hesitated. "You have been promised a ministry then."

"Yes." Baylor visibly preened. "You did not think I was that clever, did you?"

Marcus shook his head. "No," he admitted, "I did not. But who would promise you—" He cut off his words. It did not matter who was silly enough to promise a lucrative ministry post to Baylor. The promise had been made.

"You need not kill Wilberforce," Marcus said softly. "You may have my seat."

Baylor took a single step forward, his eyes narrowed as he clearly considered the possibility.

"Aw, don't listen to 'im," said Hurdy. "'E's just talking so we don't kill 'im."

"True," pressed Marcus, "but I am a man of my word. I will cede my seat to you—publicly. And I will say nothing about any of this. Just release me."

"'E won't do it."

"You know that I will. I swear it on my honor as a gentleman."

It was a bizarre scene. Never before had his reputation been more important, his word as a gentleman more significant. Yet, he had never thought less of it.

He did not intend to give his seat to Baylor, no matter what he promised. The man was a murderer and a poor planner. This whole affair with Wilberforce had been ill managed from the start. There was no telling what nonsense Baylor would promote once he had political power. Marcus could not leave England in such a man's care.

So he traded on his reputation, promised Baylor the moon and the stars, and prayed that the man was stupid enough to take it at face value.

He was.

"Do not kill him."

Hurdy groaned, shaking his head in disgust. "Daft lords, idiot gents. If this is what working fer the upper crust means, then I do not wish fer it."

"Quit groaning. You have been paid to take care of Wilberforce. Go finish the job."

Hurdy folded his hands. "Not now."

"What?"

"Naw. I told you, I thinks you all daft."

"I do not care a fig what you think so long as you finish your task!"

"And I will, but only if you come along."

"What? You agreed to handle this yourself!"

"And I 'ave no wish to be brought before the magistrate for your crime. If you insist on keeping this nob alive"—he gestured disdainfully toward Marcus—"then I want you there with me. It's my only insurance that when 'e turns, you will be in Newgate right next t' me."

"Do not be ridiculous. Chadwick is a gentleman through and through. He would never go back on his word."

"Right. An' no mort would ever pay to 'ave another mort knocked off, either. So either you two ain't gentleman or gentlemen ain't wot you think they are."

Baylor shook his head, clearly frustrated with the man's stubbornness. Then he turned toward Marcus, his expression one of superior condescension. "They will never understand, will they, Chadwick? That is why we run the world and they run the docks." He drained his brandy glass. "Very well," he said to Hurdy. "Lead on."

"But you have no idea where Wilberforce is!" cried Marcus. Assuming Jacob had completed his task, the MP had not moved from the quaint cottage where he had spent the night.

It was at that moment that Marcus saw a truly evil sight. Hurdy turned toward him, lust and hatred combined on his handsome face in a way that was almost gruesome. "Ah, but there you are wrong. I 'ad a man waiting outside your 'ome this morning. 'E's a good man. Well able to follow Fanny and an old coachman."

Marcus straightened, a cold chill sliding down his spine.

"I know where Fanny took the MP. She went to her old rooms, right smack dab in the center o' the rookeries." His grin turned into a leer. "An' this time, she cannot escape me."

Marcus's mind raced. Fantine and Wilberforce in the rookeries? She could not be that reckless. But he knew that she was. After their argument this morning, running back to her home probably made sense to her. She was comfortable there, had friends, knew the best ways to fight or escape.

But why would she bring Wilberforce there? What possible purpose would that serve? He did not know. He only understood that he had to stop it if at all possible.

"There is no need for this," he repeated, this time focusing on Baylor. "There is no point in killing Wilberforce now. What about my seat?"

But Baylor ignored him, being too occupied with smoothing out a wrinkle in his coat.

"Come along, guv," grumbled Hurdy. "Fanny is slippery. I do not wish to give 'er any more time than necessary."

Baylor frowned as he pulled on his gloves. "Who is this Fanny?"

"Miss Fantine Drake," growled Hurdy.

"Ah," returned Baylor, but it was clear from his expression that he had no understanding of anything at all.

"Baylor!" Marcus cried, but they ignored him, and Marcus was left to curse in silence as they sauntered to the front door.

"Damn!" Baylor suddenly exclaimed. "I have forgotten my pocket watch. You get the carriage ready. I shall be out directly."

Hurdy obviously did not like this, but he left nonetheless while Baylor slipped back to Marcus, his voice low and urgent. "Are the ropes too tight?"

"Yes. Much."

"Good. You must forgive me, old chap, but I am afraid I am forced to keep you bound for just a bit longer."

"Do not do this!" Marcus begged. "Why commit murder when you can have my seat without risk?"

"But I'm not, dear boy. I accept your offer most gratefully," he said, his prominent gold tooth flashing in the sunlight. "But only after I have performed the daring rescue of Mr. Wilberforce, England's dearest MP! Oh, it shall be glorious."

Marcus groaned. To think the man had survived this long! Such stupidity was indeed criminal. "Hurdy will never allow it. He will kill you first, and then return here and kill me."

"Nonsense, dear boy. Those kind think nothing beyond their fee. All Hurdy believes is that I will pay him handsomely for the murder. He will not realize what is happening until he is being clapped in irons."

"He is not that blind!" Marcus invested all his energy, all his intensity, in his one statement, but Baylor was too caught up in his visions of glory to heed him.

"Bear with me, dear boy. And do not worry. I have no idea why Fantine Drake is involved, but I shall keep her safe as well." Then he stood up. "Too bad she is not an heiress. She will be ever so grateful for her rescue."

"She's more likely to put a knife in your gullet."

But Baylor wasn't listening. With a last cheerful wave, the man left his home. Marcus could do nothing but glare at the closed door and curse.

To think, he began this morning believing he was actually in control of the situation! But then, who could have guessed that the mysterious Teggie was an idiot?

CHAPTER 22

———◆———

Getting Wilberforce to come with Fantine was easy. After all, he knew she had been hired to protect him. He trusted her.

Convincing the lame man that he needed to climb three sets of stairs to her little room above the pub, on the other hand, had been hard. But she was charming and insistent, and in the end he managed to make it to her tiny space. She helped him to her one chair and offered to get him something to drink from downstairs.

Thankfully, he declined. He did not like strong drink, and she did not wish to leave him alone. So they settled into her room with an awkward silence. She knew it was time to speak. With Jacob in the alley keeping an eye on the street, she was entirely private with the MP. She must make the most of her opportunity now, while she still had the chance.

But this part of her plan was more than hard. Now, she attempted the impossible. She had to convince the MP to listen to her as he would a person of power and influence.

She began slowly, with soft phrases to soothe him. "You have been very patient, sir, and I must thank you for your forbearance. Unfortunately, I must ask your indulgence for just a bit longer."

"Do not worry, Miss Dela—er, Drake," he said, though his voice wheezed a bit.

"Please. My name is Fantine Delarive." If nothing else, she would do this under her own name.

He smiled. "Miss Delarive, then. I have been in much worse places. The cargo hold of a slave ship comes to mind. Still, I cannot help wondering at Chadwick. I cannot like that he has exposed you to these rough surroundings."

Fantine shifted awkwardly where she stood, wondering how best to respond to such a statement. She decided on being forthright and honest. "Actually, sir, Lord Chadwick had absolutely nothing to do with this. He still thinks you safely ensconced in that charming cottage."

Wilberforce straightened, peering again at her tiny room. "I do not understand."

"Sir, these are my rooms. The best I have had, in fact, for most of my life. You see," she said with a touch of pride, "they are clean and serviceable. Few rats. A job downstairs. I was very lucky to find it."

Wilberforce shook his head. "But—That cannot be. You are a gently reared young lady."

She restrained a bitter laugh. The one time she truly wished to be exactly as she was, her companion refused to believe it. "I am a bastard. My mother was an actress who made little more than a few quid per show. The only way for her to survive was by bringing men into her bed. Then I was born."

"Impossible," snapped Wilberforce. "You are being brought out by Lord Chadwick as a family friend. I cannot believe his mother would countenance such a person in society."

"I assure you, it is true. It is, in fact, Lady Anne's most generous understanding that has convinced me to approach you today." She stepped forward, knowing her next words were the most important, and she prayed God would give her the right ones.

"I have lived on the street, seen the horrors that are forced on girls and boys alike. I have been a liar, a thief, and once

I stabbed a man. It was only by God's good fortune that I found my father, and he was willing to help me. Otherwise, I would still be in the gutter doing anything I could to survive."

This time Wilberforce folded his arms across his chest and frowned at her. "You are a gently reared young lady. I have seen you be such on numerous occasions. This...this playacting does you no credit." He looked as if he were scolding a child, and Fantine wanted to scream at such willful blindness.

"I am not playacting, Mr. Wilberforce. At least not now. When I go about in society, however, I use my skills, learned painfully at my mother's knee. Later, Chadwick's sister and mother filled in the gaps."

"You cannot be serious."

"I have never been more serious in my life." Impulsively, she settled on the floor beside him, using her posture to be both submissive and imploring. "I was extremely fortunate. I found my father, and Penworthy was willing to help me change. But there are many who do not have so exemplary a parentage."

"Penworthy?" he gasped. He peered down at her, his frown growing deeper. "Yes, I suppose I see a resemblance. Around the eyes, I think."

"And in our singular determination to be heard, sir," she returned.

"Do not try my patience, young lady."

"Then do not willfully close your eyes to the truth," she returned hotly, abandoning her submissive posture. Shifting to the bed, she faced him eye-to-eye. He did not appreciate the change as he matched her glare with his own.

Good Lord, he was as blind as the worst of his class, willfully closing his eyes to what was literally right before his nose. But he was also a man of God, and perhaps that was how best to open his mind. Wilberforce saw her as a pampered, empty-headed young miss. Perhaps that would not change. First impressions were often the hardest to overcome.

But she had already sent a message to Nameless. He and his friends would be here any moment. Half of them had been chimney sweep boys. If their stories did not make the God-fearing Mr. Wilberforce weep, then nothing would.

"I want to introduce you to some of my friends," she said. "I do what I can for them, feed them when I have the funds, try to give them hope for the future when I do not. Perhaps you would also like meeting Louise. She is very young, but already she is considering life as a prostitute, and indeed, that is all that is open for her if she cannot continue her dance lessons."

Mr. Wilberforce merely folded his arms and looked at her, his expression thoughtful. "Why should I listen to them?"

"Because they will tell you how they live and what they expect. Then I will tell you how I want to help them. If we teach them, give them choices other than thieving or whoring, then it will be better for all of England. There could be less anger in the lower classes, you know. I need not tell you that alleviating that is the first step in preventing exactly what happened in France."

"The English people would never revolt against the Crown!"

Fantine bit her lip. No, she did not think they would.

But the upper crust seemed desperately afraid of the downtrodden souls. Their biggest fear was that the poor would revolt as strongly, as viciously, as they had in France. She was not above using such fear to meet her own ends.

"The poor are angry, my lord. You and I both know what horrors an angry mob can perpetrate."

He was silent a moment, glaring about the room as if it were to blame. She let him remain frustrated, stewing in his impotence. Then she spoke, giving him the answer as if it were his own idea.

"You can help them. Just by hearing their stories, you can show them that they can ask for help. Then we can work on a solution together."

"And if I refuse?"

She pulled at her lip. "I pray that you do not." She returned to her submissive pose, doing her best to look young, innocent, and so earnest it would soften his heart. "Please, I have prayed for someone to listen. Just once. Please?"

He was silent a long time, and Fantine held her breath waiting. Finally, she could stand it no longer and offered one last suggestion. She felt as if she were baring her soul in the most painful of ways, but it had to be done. If this were the only way, then she would do it. For Nameless and Louise.

"The priests say that God works in mysterious ways. Can He not work through me as well? Whether I am a mad debutante or a strange bastard, I am still part of God's kingdom, am I not? Will you not see what I can show you?"

In the end, the man raised his arms in a gesture of defeat. "Very well," he said, though it was clear he had little patience for this. "I will listen for an hour. But then I shall have to insist you take me to White's. My work is there, obtaining the votes I need for my bill. There is nothing here for me to see."

With that inauspicious beginning, Fantine brought in Nameless and Louise and many of the other people she knew to tell their stories. With each grimy face, with each angry or pathetic or thieving soul she brought in, she prayed to Wilberforce's God that this story would open the MPs head as well as his mind.

But it did not work.

By the end of the hour, he was as irritable, as anxious, and as willfully blind as before. True, he cared about the sufferings of the slaves. But there was no room in his heart for more.

She had failed.

"I am sorry, sir," she finally said. "I can see I have wasted both of our time."

"Oh, child," he said softly, and for the first time that day, she saw compassion in his expression. He reached out and touched her face, lightly, as a father would stroke the dirt from his child's face. "It is not that I do not believe their stories, but there must be priorities. God has sent me to end the suffering of the slaves. To divide my attention would damage both our causes."

Fantine pressed forward. "Surely you support what I wish to do here."

"And what is that?"

"To make a better life for them."

"They must do it on their own, as you have."

She shook her head. "It is not that simple. They need food, an education, the simple belief that they can."

Wilberforce merely frowned. "They must turn to God for that."

"They are turning to you."

"No, Fantine Delarive," he said softly, "they are turning to you."

And that, it seemed, was that. Wilberforce had his own cause. Now she had hers. "But how am I to help them?" she asked herself as much as him. "How do I build the things I wish for?"

Wilberforce merely smiled. "The way is simple. Find yourself a good husband—one who is smart, political, and rich. Then convert him to your cause."

She stared wordlessly at him. He spoke as if it were the easiest thing in the world. As if she had not just spent the last few hours determined to become a power in her own right.

But perhaps he was right. Perhaps she could use a rich, powerful husband. "But how do I get one?"

Then, for the first time ever, she heard the MP's laugh. It sounded hearty and strong in his frail body, and it was a wonder to hear it. "Surely, somewhere among your vast array of talents, you have learned how to charm a man?"

Fantine felt a coy smile pull at her lips. "Well, perhaps I have some knowledge of that."

"Then use it. Use whatever you have, whatever tool you can find. Pray daily, hourly if need be, and God will provide what you need."

Fantine twisted her hands in her skirt, still uncomfortable with such piousness. "You truly believe that?" she asked. "God will help me?"

"Yes," he said, his voice warm, "I truly believe that. As you said, God works in mysterious ways, even through a strange bastard or a mad debutante."

Looking into his eyes, hearing his powerful voice surround her, Fantine vowed to try and believe his words.

Then Ballast burst through the door.

Fantine was caught off guard. She had spent too much time in Lottie's safe home, and her thoughts now were centered on the future, not the present.

She should have known better, but it was too late. Ballast and three of his men burst through the door, catching her standing stupidly beside the MP, her knife across the room in a pile of Rat's clothing.

Wilberforce began to stand, but he was no match for the man who pushed him roughly back into the chair. Fantine was similarly cut off as she made a dash for her weapon. Ballast and his two remaining men surrounded her with a speed even she found surprising.

Ballast must have wanted her badly if his men were frightened enough to give their very best against a lone woman and a crippled old man.

So she straightened slowly, squaring her shoulders as she confronted Ballast. He looked as dirty and rumpled as usual, but this time his face had the added greenish cast of an old bruise finally fading. Fantine could not help smiling. She had known Marcus had hit him hard, but she had not realized how very punishing his fist could be to have marked Ballast for this long.

It was a gratifying thought.

Then the image was brought forcibly home as Ballast hit her solidly across the face.

She cried out as her head snapped back, and she fell, landing painfully, half across her bed.

Nearby, Wilberforce surged to his feet. "Stop it!" he cried

even as the brute near him laughed and pushed the MP back into his chair.

"Get up," growled Ballast at her.

Fantine rolled painfully into a sitting position. Her head throbbed, and she tasted blood. But she did not speak. Not yet. She was still evaluating the situation.

She had expected Ballast to talk with her a moment, rattle his saber, so to speak, before he degenerated into true violence. But he had not done that. In one vicious blow, he had wiped away any veneer of civility. In seconds, Miss Fantine Delarive was gone, and a mixture of Fanny and Rat surged to the fore.

Fantine forgot her lessons in civility, forgot everything but the need to survive. With it came a cockiness, a solid belief in her own invulnerability that was as much a defense on the street as a knife.

Especially since it was the only weapon she had.

"Where is my son?" bellowed Ballast.

Fantine felt her eyes narrow in disdain. "Wot?"

"My son! Sprat! I saw 'im get in th' carriage with you and th' daft an' 'e ain't been home since. You bring 'im t' me, or I'll slit yer gullet from ear t' ear."

"You mean t' do that anyways," she muttered. "An' besides, I don't know where yer bloody brat is."

This time she was prepared for his blow. She pulled back, avoiding most of the impact, but he still caught part of her cheek, adding another bruise to her already swelling face.

Lady Anne would never forgive her for allowing such a thing to happen.

Fantine frowned at the irrelevant thought, and then she stopped. Perhaps that was the answer, after all.

"'Ey! Careful with me visage," she cried, making a show of rubbing her jaw. "Loiday Anne—" She made a concerted effort to return to her cultured form of speech. "Lady Anne will be most perturbed if I appear with a distorted visage."

Ballast merely blinked and stared at her. Then, abruptly he burst into an evil laugh. "Jes listen t' Rat, boys. She thinks she's the bloomin' Queen o' England."

"No, I am not," returned Fantine smoothly as she gained her feet and smoothed out her gown. "But I am to be presented at Court soon." Then before Ballast could comment, she sharpened her gaze on him. "And so will Sprat, if you let me be."

It was a mistake. She should have stayed with pretending ignorance of Sprat's whereabouts. After all, there were dozens of ways a young boy could disappear in the dockside rookeries. But it was too late, and now she had to face Ballast's rage.

"Where is Sprat?" he bellowed. Then he raised his fist again, but Fantine was prepared. Ducking under his fist, she dove straight for one of Ballast's thugs. He was so startled, he did not fight her. He merely stepped aside, allowing her to fall flat on her face, into the pile of Rat's clothing.

Her hand curled around her knife.

"Get up!" screamed Ballast between obscenities.

Fantine stood, knife before her. She did not make the mistake of believing herself out of danger. She was still only one small woman against four large men. But at least her knife kept Ballast from hitting her again.

And that gave her enough time to reason with him.

"Yes, Ballast, I have your son. He is learning Greek and Latin and table manners. He is being taught how to talk and dress and read French. He is making his own future now, a better one than you could ever have."

"I don't believe you!" exploded Ballast, advancing on her. "Wot did you do t' 'im? Did ye kill 'im? Was 'e going t' cut you out of yer daft nob? Is 'at why?"

"He ain't dead!" she practically screamed at him."'E's going to 'Arrow."

"Don't lie t' me!" he bellowed. "'E ain't never gonna get t' Arrow, an' you and I both know it!"

He had stopped advancing, but his face was purple with rage. Fantine readjusted her grip on her knife, but she did not use it. She was still hoping to reason with Ballast.

"He will get to Harrow. You are supposed to get a letter from him soon. I swear it!"

She could see the struggle on the man's face. She saw the hope and the disbelief and the panic all wound together. She had always known he loved his son, but she had not realized just how much the boy's disappearance would affect him. Ballast was so twisted up with fear and hope for the boy, he did not seem to know what to do.

"You must trust me," she said softly. "He is safe and happy. He is getting an education. He will have a future outside of the rookeries."

She saw his emotions at war on his face as he tried to believe what she had told him. And she saw him lose his own fight. Ballast had lived too long in the rookeries. He could not trust in a better life for him or his son.

"I want me son!" he roared in a voice that seemed to echo in her head. Then he fell on her. She had the knife ready, and she worked it with as much skill as she could, but he was unstoppable in his fury. Finally she plunged the knife into his thick belly, while he pummeled her about the face and shoulders. She heard nothing, saw nothing, knew nothing but the furious rain of blows.

Then suddenly, he was gone, plucked off of her as if he had never been.

She looked up, her thoughts spinning. Had Marcus come to rescue her?

She first saw Ballast on the floor, his wound bleeding sluggishly. She saw Wilberforce, still pinned to his chair, but this time, not by Ballast's man, but by...Hurdy's man? The three thugs Ballast had brought with him were already on the floor, either held at knifepoint or knocked unconscious, being watched by more brutes. She dismissed all of them with barely a glance.

Her gaze was drawn to another man, a man in gentleman's attire who stood by Wilberforce and gloated.

Teggie. Or Lord Baylor, as she now recognized him.

Then, before she could comment, another man stepped into her line of sight. He was the one man more dangerous to her than Ballast. She had not thought him so at first, but then she looked into his green eyes. There was a dangerous glint in there, and no mercy whatsoever. Fantine bit her lip.

Hurdy. And he knew she had betrayed him.

Still, she tried to brazen it out, hoping against hope that she could slip through relatively unscathed. She smiled warmly as she struggled to her feet. "Thank God you are here."

"Do not thank me yet, Fanny."

She pulled her swollen eyes as wide as she could and tried to look innocent. "Why? What is wrong?"

He took a leisurely step forward, his expression almost serene. "Because I know, Fanny. I know you and th' daft were using me to stop Teggie—"

"No!" she gasped.

"O' course you were. I found Chadwick right at Teggie's doorstep threatening all sorts o' things." Then he stepped forward with an evil grin on his face. "I took care o' him—"

"No!" she whispered as a vision of Marcus's dead body filled her thoughts.

"Yes," he returned as he neatly pulled the knife from her slackened grip. "Now I'm going t' take care o' you."

Fantine tried to resist. She wanted to fight, but she had no heart for it. The thought of Marcus dead killed any hope she had for the future. For even the present.

He was dead.

They had done their best. *She* had done her best, but the odds were stacked too high against them. Marcus was dead.

"Bloody, pissing hell!"

Marcus cursed with fluidity as he struggled against his bonds. His wrists and ankles were raw from the fight. His nose was bleeding and his shoulder ached abominably from the two times he had managed to gain his feet only to fall painfully onto the body parts in question.

"Sink and pissing ant," he grumbled. He might even have knocked a tooth loose. What he had not done was inch one mote of dust closer to the door. Neither had he managed to loosen his bonds in the slightest.

That was when he heard it. A small creak as if someone or something stepped on a loose floorboard in the hall. It was not a loud sound, barely noticeable over his own muttered curses, but he heard it nonetheless, and he stilled immediately, his heart pounding in his chest, his breath too loud in his ears.

Was it Hurdy returned to finish the job? No, Hurdy would not bother to be silent. But it could be one of his men. More likely, it was Baylor's last remaining servant. No, wait. The man was on holiday.

It did not matter. Whoever it was, he was well and truly caught.

CHAPTER 23

It took some time before Fantine could straighten herself up enough to face Hurdy. It took even longer for her to try and find a handle on the situation to turn it to her advantage.

It took so long, in fact, that she could not do it. She could only sigh as Hurdy stood before her, lifting up her bruised face until he stared right into her eyes.

"You betrayed me. You were supposed to kill 'im." It was not a question.

"I told you I would protect Wilberforce until I met with Teggie." She glanced over at Lord Baylor. "My lord, would you be so kind as to open your mouth."

"I beg your pardon!"

"Do it!" ordered Hurdy.

"I will not." The man practically quivered in outrage.

Then something absolutely delightful happened. Mr. Wilberforce, a crippled old man, surged up and grabbed hold of Lord Baylor's hair, pulling it backward. Then he peered down into the man's mouth.

"Three gold teeth," he pronounced solemnly.

Fantine smiled. She had not even thought Wilberforce aware of their discoveries regarding Teggie.

In answer to her unspoken question, the MP turned to her. "Penworthy told me. I swear, it has been difficult counting men's teeth while discussing politics. Gave me a headache."

"I understand completely," responded Fantine, some of her equilibrium returning.

Unfortunately, Wilberforce's one comment was enough to wipe away Hurdy's lingering doubts. He now had absolute proof that she had been colluding against him.

"You will die horribly," he hissed in her ear.

Fantine's heart sank. She heard no reprieve in his voice, no room for manipulation. She had lost, and she knew it.

A dull sort of fatalism washed through her. She had no expectation of a daring rescue by Marcus. Hurdy had already "taken care o' him." But then she frowned. That did not necessarily mean he killed him.

"What exactly did you do to Chadwick?" she asked.

Hurdy grinned. "'E's dead. I sent my best man to finish 'im."

Fantine could only close her eyes against the stab of pain. Baylor, on the other hand, stiffened, pulling away from Wilberforce with a swift jerk of his head. "You did not!"

"Aye, I did," returned Hurdy. "'E'll be colder than stone by now."

"How dare you!" shrieked Baylor. "Why would you do such a thing?"

Fantine forced herself to open her eyes, forced herself to pay attention. She might not care for herself anymore. With Marcus dead, she had little heart for her own life. But Wilberforce was another matter. She still had a responsibility to save him.

So she clenched her teeth and tried to bring her thoughts into focus. Lord Baylor and Hurdy were quarreling, over Marcus, of all things.

"I told you to leave Chadwick alive!" he screeched.

"Well, 'e's dead. And now you ain't got a choice. You 'ave to kill Wilberforce, and it will be by your own 'and too. I will not be left to 'ang just because of your nonsense."

Then the strangest thing happened. Baylor actually seemed to preen. He puffed up his chest, his expression sly. "Perhaps it will be you who dies." Then he pulled out a pistol. Just one. Loaded, no doubt, with one ball. Against four men, not counting the lumped forms of Ballast and his men.

At least he had the brains to point it at Hurdy and not any of the hirelings. Still, he looked quite ridiculous standing there, a single weapon against so many.

"You see," he said to the room at large, "I have uncovered a most heinous plot. Unfortunately, I was not in time to save Chadwick or Wilberforce," and he swung his pistol to the aged MP. "But at least I was able to kill the famous dockside criminal and rescue the lovely Miss Drake." He pointed his gun back toward Hurdy as he smiled at Fantine. "Come along, my dear. I know this must seem terribly confusing, but I swear I shall explain it all to you."

Fantine considered going with him. At least by his side, she could keep him from shooting Wilberforce. But one glance about the room told her she need not worry. Two of Hurdy's men were already flanking Baylor and both had pistols. If the one did not get him, the other would. Lord Baylor would be dead before he could get off a single shot, and he was the only one who did not understand that.

She could not even summon up enough energy to feel sorry for him. "My lord, you are a fool," she said softly.

Then the door flew open, smashing Baylor in the face, flinging him backward. The reports of two guns went off, echoing loudly in the small room. The one was from Baylor and produced a massive hole right in the center of her door. The other was from the poor sod Baylor landed on, and went right through Baylor's chest from back to front.

Fantine did not have to see the body to know that Lord Baylor was dead. She was more interested in why the door had suddenly flown open.

But there was nothing to see. The hall seemed empty. Fantine's heart soared within her. She did not dare hope, but she did. Had Marcus come back for her?

Then she remembered that he was probably dead, and she had to blink away the tears. She could not hope for aid from her personal daft hero.

Finally someone stepped into the open door, and Fantine had no more time to spare for grief. It was an auspicious moment, a grand entrance, as everyone strained to see who was there.

"Louise?" Fantine gasped, horrified at the girl's colossally bad timing. The diminutive child was sauntering in on her toes, lightly carrying a tray of...soup?

"Wot?" came the girl's high voice.

It was only then that Fantine noticed the odd things. First off, the girl held the tray high, hiding her face. Fantine knew who it was, of course, because other than general size and build, Louise was the only child she knew who perpetually walked on her toes. The other thing she noticed was that the girl was dressed childishly, in clothes she must have rooted out of the bottom of her wardrobe. She could not have looked younger if she had put on nappies! Louise was nearing thirteen, but she looked seven at the most. And the face that twisted and turned from beneath the tray was so blandly innocent that Fantine knew the girl was up to something.

"Blimey," Louise called out in her most childish voice. "Oi can't see anything from behind this tray. Where are you, Fanny?"

"Right here," she said with a sigh. Then, after a curt nod from Hurdy, Fantine stepped forward. "Hold still or you will spill it. Louise! Louise, do not wiggle so. Louise!"

The soup went tumbling down, spilling scalding hot liquid all over Hurdy.

The criminal screamed while Fantine quickly grabbed the tray. Pushing Louise to one side, she began swinging the heavy wood with all her might. Hurdy went down, still bellowing from his burns. His henchmen were next as Fantine spun, searching for another target.

But there were none.

Instead, there was Marcus, alive and furious, right in front of her, striking brutes down one by one with all the fury of a rampaging bull. He was magnificent, and soon all she need do was step back and watch.

"Coo, he is good," whispered Louise. "Jes think wot 'e'd be like in bed!"

"Louise!" she cried. Then she tensed. Ballast was rising up, fury mottling his features, his men surging to their feet as well. Apparently they had been waiting for just the right moment to strike.

But again, Fantine's services were not needed. Marcus had seen them coming, knocking them down before they gained their feet. Those he could not catch were dispatched by Wilberforce, cackling in delight. "I may be old, but I am not completely useless, am I?" he cried.

Then he plopped back down in his chair, completely winded from his exertions.

Meanwhile Marcus spun, once, twice, and a third time as he made sure all the brutes were down. Suddenly there was the sound of many feet scrambling up the stairs to her door. Would this never end?

Fantine raised her tray. Marcus readied his fists. Even Louise lifted the empty crock of soup while Wilberforce once again struggled to his feet.

Jacob appeared at the door.

Marcus was barely able to pull back the blow aimed square at his coachman's face. "Jacob! Bloody hell, man, announce yourself first!"

The man stopped dead in his tracks, surveyed the scene before him, and paled to a pasty white.

"Cor blimey, my lord," he breathed, "you are good!"

Marcus did not answer. He merely returned his gaze to the floor, then stepped forward, and neatly cuffed one of Ballast's men who was struggling to his feet. "We need something to bind them with."

"No problem, guv," answered a high voice.

Fantine looked up to see Giles, Nameless, and a series of ebullient, dirty boys scurry in with long leather strips in their hands. It was not until they began tying men up that Fantine realized what they were using.

"Those are your reins."

"Aye," answered Jacob. "It was what we had on hand."

"You did fine," answered Marcus, his voice low.

Fantine had not realized how close he was, how very near to her body he was, until he spoke those words. She turned slightly, moving into his embrace without conscious thought, and he pulled her close.

"I thought you were dead." She breathed deeply, savoring his earthy scent, knowing it meant he was alive.

"I am very much alive, thanks to Giles. Thank God the boy cannot follow simple orders. After Hurdy and Baylor left, he crept in and cut me free."

She felt him touch her chin, tilting her head so he could see her face. She did not even remember her bruises until she felt him tense, anger and horror mixing in his expression.

"I am fine," she said softly. "Truly." Then she closed her eyes and buried her face against his chest, reassuring herself that he was well. "Hurdy said he sent someone to kill you."

"The man met with an accident," he whispered against her hair. "It would take more than Hurdy and Ballast and all the knives in the rookery to keep me from you."

Fantine swallowed, not at all surprised to realize her face was wet with tears. He was alive. She had been so afraid...

"Gawd, kiss her, already," cut in Louise, giving Marcus a little shove. "Are all the lords as slow as this one to take a lady?" she asked Wilberforce. "If so, then I 'ave a miserable life ahead of me." Then her voice changed somewhat, becoming more canny as she crossed to the MP's side. "Unless some kind stranger would pay fer just a few o' me dance lessons..."

There was more, of course. Louise would not stop pestering Wilberforce until he had given her thrice what she needed for a dancing career. But Fantine was no longer listening.

Marcus was kissing her, his touch strong, his passion seemingly as fierce as her own. He nearly crushed her to him, and yet she longed to be closer. He was alive! They were alive!

And she loved him.

"If she ain't 'is mistress by now, I wager five quid she will be afore the night's out." That was Louise again, her voice barely registering over the pounding of Fantine's head. But then Marcus drew back, his expression grave.

"No," he said softly. "She will not be my mistress."

Fantine tensed. He did not want her? Surely…

He must have read the panic in her eyes, because he pressed his finger to her lips, effectively holding back her pain for a moment. A bare second, but it was all he needed.

"I love you, Fantine. I want to marry you, if you will have me."

All her words stopped in her throat, and Fantine stared at him, caught between the sinking horror of a second ago and the sudden surge of elation now.

"Coo…" breathed Louise.

Then before Fantine could answer, Marcus suddenly buckled, his knees going out from under him as he sank to the floor.

"Marcus!" she cried, but she was stopped by Nameless's dirty face.

"Daft bugger," the boy said with a grin. "Don't 'e know 'e's supposed to be on 'is knees?"

Then Marcus shifted and glared at the boy. "You need not have kicked me! A simple word would have sufficed."

"Oi'll kick you again, if'n ye don't do it right."

"What?"

"Yeah," chorused the boys. "Do it proper, guv. Right now!"

Beside them, Jacob merely shook his head. "You best do it, my lord. They's a fearsome lot."

Marcus stiffened, making himself imposing even from his knees. "Would all of you please excuse us a moment so that I may be private—"

"Not wise, my boy," cut in Wilberforce. "We cannot leave until the magistrate arrives. The criminals might rise up again, you know. I could not risk your safety or that of the lady's."

"They are bound and gagged!" cried Marcus.

"Nevertheless…" returned the MP, apparently enjoying the scene as much as everyone else.

"Go on, guv. Do it." That was Nameless again, looking threatening as he readied another kick at Marcus's shins.

Marcus tried to stare him down, but the boy did not flinch.

"Enough, Nameless," Fantine cut in. "I have no wish for you to terrify him into…into…" She could not get the word out.

"Proposing!" supplied Louise cheerfully.

Marcus cleared his throat. He made to rise up onto one knee, but a single glare from Nameless was enough to make him change his mind. Remaining on the floor, he drew her hands up to his lips. "I wish that this were a more proper place and time," he said, casting an annoyed glance about the room, "but nevertheless, I know the truth now and will not turn from it."

He kissed first her left hand, then the right before continuing. "You have given me such joy. Such terror and wonder and anxiety as well, but mostly you have opened my eyes. You make me a better man, Fantine Delarive. You teach me things and see things I cannot fathom. I love you. Will you do me the greatest honor of becoming my wife?"

Fantine felt a rush of emotion surge through her. It could not be true. Marcus could not be proposing to her, could not be saying he loved her. And yet he was.

Then she bit her lip, remembering everything he said, hoping she had heard right. Then she frowned. "You want Fantine Drake, do you not?"

He shook his head. "I want you. Not Rat, nor Fanny, nor Miss Drake. I want you, Fantine Delarive, to be my wife. And so I shall say in front of everyone if you will have me."

She opened her mouth to answer, but before she could, Louise stepped forward, tapping her on the shoulder. "Remember to get everthing out in the open. Negotiate first."

"But—" began Fantine.

"Do it. A girl 'as to remember business."

Fantine hesitated. This was a glorious moment for her, one that she never dreamed possible. But a part of her did worry. It could not possibly be true…. "I have talked to Mr. Wilberforce," she began slowly. "About working in the rookeries. There are a number of things I intend to do here."

Marcus just stared at her, his eyes wide and uncomprehending.

"I want to help Nameless and his friends—"

The boys cheered.

"Then there is Louise and some of the other girls who want a real future—"

"'At's right, Fanny," piped in the girl. "Make sure 'e understands."

"You will not try to stop that, will you?"

Marcus still just stared at her.

"I want to do these things," she repeated.

Marcus nodded. He made to get up off his knees, but Nameless kicked him again, so he cursed and stayed where he was.

"Marcus?" she asked.

He merely stared at her. "Fantine, what has any of that to do with marrying me? A simple yes or no would suffice."

"But I do not wish you to stop me—"

Marcus sighed. It was clear his knees were beginning to pain him. "Good Lord, Fantine, you have half the rookery here telling me how to propose to you and kicking me when I have not got it right. What do you think they would do if I tried to lock you up somewhere? I would fear for my very life!"

"Yeah!" That was from the boys. They liked the idea of striking terror in a gent.

"So you will let me do as I wish?"

"Haven't I always?"

The change came quickly, but Fantine felt every split second of joy as it grew within her, coursing through her veins, until she felt as if she glowed with it. She dropped to her knees, embracing Marcus with all the strength in her body.

"I love you, Marcus."

"I love you, Fantine."

Their kiss was as passionate, as heartfelt as all the ones before, but this time there was an added dimension. There was shared wonder and the expectation of a lifetime of adventures to come.

Then at last they separated, and Marcus made to get to his feet.

"Not yet, ye don't," cried Nameless. "She ain't said yes yet!"

Marcus turned imploring eyes on her. "Please, Fantine, for the love of God, say yes, or I shall be forced to stay like this until my legs break off."

Fantine grinned, finally speaking the words out loud. "Why yes, my lord, it will be my greatest honor to become your wife."

Then they were mobbed by everyone who was not bound and gagged. The surge was so quick and so overwhelming that Marcus was forced to remain on his knees for a full ten minutes more.

EPILOGUE

◆

Marcus Kane, Lord Chadwick and Miss Fantine Delarive were married in St. Paul's Cathedral on April 1, 1807, with all the pomp and circumstance appropriate to the occasion. A particularly elegant bridesmaid added to the event by literally dancing up the aisle, charming everyone with her grace and style.

Beyond that, the event was characterized by a great deal of odd happenings. Guests were warned in advance not to bring or wear anything they would not wish to lose, and indeed, those who did not heed the warning found themselves lacking their jewelry in an amazingly quick amount of time, often before an army of small boys could usher them to their seat.

Mr. Wilberforce added his own personal blessing, his manner especially ebullient after passage of his bill banning slavery in the British Isles. It was rumored that his newest cause was the plight of chimney sweep boys.

Then, to the astonishment of a great many people, the bride announced that all their gifts would be sold to aid a charitable foundation designed to help children in the rookeries. The bride herself intended to run it! And if that were not enough, the young ushers then proceeded to pass around the collection plates demanding more "gifts" for the bride and groom.

One even threatened to kick the Duke of Ashbury!

Extortion notwithstanding, the bride was radiant, the groom handsome, and the champagne flowed freely.

Rumors that the couple escaped their wedding breakfast by climbing out of a second-story window carrying a sack of food were, of course, discounted as nonsense.

*Turn the page for an
excerpt from*

DEVIL'S
BARGAIN

The Regency Rags to Riches Series
Book Two

Jade Lee

I"Is this my room alone?" Lynette asked. "Or do I share?"

She detected a slight lift to his lips, but his eyes remained remote, his tone distant. " It is yours alone." Then he gestured to a doorway half hidden in shadow beside the bed post. " That leads to my bedchamber. I will thank you to knock before entering."

She stiffened, turning to him in shock. "I shall not enter it at all, sir! I am to be married, and I shall enter that state with my purity and my honor intact."

This time he did smile, though the expression seemed cold. He stepped into the room, folding his arms across his chest as he leaned negligently against the bedpost. "Your honor is not my concern. Your purity, however, shall be grossly torn by even the most lax standards."

His words shook her. He spoke as if it were a foregone conclusion that she would be dishonored. But what were her alternatives? She could not run. She had no money to return to Kent, and even if she did, her family had already left for her uncle's. They thought her safely ensconced in a nunnery. What would she say to them? That she had decided to take a jaunt to London? Alone?

Her reputation would be in tatters. She had to make the best of her situation here. So she lifted her chin, deciding to salvage her pride, if nothing else.

"Sir, you are offensive," she said stiffly.

He nodded, as if that, too, were a foregone conclusion. Then he abruptly sketched a mocking bow. " Please, allow me to introduce myself. I am Adrian Grant, Viscount Marlock, and this is my home."

"Your home," she echoed weakly as her mind whirled. Had she heard tales of the Viscount Marlock? Even in Kent? Was he the one with a reputation for debauching young girls? She could not remember. So she took refuge in good manners, dropping into a demure curtsy.

"Perhaps you were told that I shall be assisting your education," he drawled.

Lynette was trembling. She did not know why, but she felt the weakness in her limbs and was powerless to stop it. If only she understood what he intended. " You will find me a husband?"

"You will have a bridegroom and a rich one at that. Indeed my fortune and yours depend upon it."

She shook her head, denying everything he said. "But—"

He cut her off with a single raised finger. " Do you know what a courtesan is?"

She bit her lip, trying to decide how she should answer. Her father would have flown into a rage if she confessed the full truth: that she had eagerly listened for any drop of gossip about such creatures. So instead of a full confession, she chose a partial truth. " I only know what little I have heard. I am sure none of it could be true."

"Of course it could be true. That and a great deal more," he drawled, his amusement obvious. "No matter. You, my dear, will be taught very much like those wonderful creatures."

She gaped at him in true horror. Her a courtesan? " But I was told—"

"Listen to the rest, Lynette. You will become a Marlock bride. Like a courtesan, you will be beautiful, accomplished, and knowledgeable in a variety of pleasures. But you will also be loyal, gentle, and of course, presentable. And for this, some man—likely an older, experienced man—will pay a great deal to wed you. So that you may grace his table by day and entertain him in bed at night."

"But, I don't understand. Why would they marry me? When a... a courtesan's pleasures can be had—"

"For a few gems? Until the man becomes bored? Or the woman unpresentable?"

She nodded. That is exactly what she meant. Why would a man wed what can be had for a few pennies?

"Because a smart man knows the value of paying once

instead of monthly or at a lady's whim. Of tying a woman to him for the rest of his life—assuming she is the right woman—rather than for a few months. Of finding a bride who will nurse him kindly in his old age, rather than abandon him to seek her own pleasures."

"But you cannot promise that—"

"Of course, I can!" he snapped. " Because you will. Because I have done it six times before and my reputation stands on that promise." He stepped closer until he was looming over her, his breath hot on her face.

"My lord," she gasped, wondering what she could say to make him retreat.

"Will you be faithful to your husband?" he asked. " Will you please him at night, care for him in his dotage, even if he is a hundred years old with cold hands and rancid breath?"

She blinked, wondering why tears blurred her vision.

"Will you, Lynette?" he demanded.

"Yes!" she gasped, knowing that was the answer he wanted. Knowing, too, that it was the truth. For whatever reason she wed, she would not dishonor the man she married. " I could not break a vow made before God," she whispered.

He stepped back, his entire body suddenly relaxed, almost congenial. " Then I believe you shall be my best bride yet." He reached out, gently stroking her cheek with an almost paternal air. " You will fetch a high price indeed."

She jerked backwards, drawing her face away from him. "I don't understand—" she began. But he cut her off.

"Enough questions. It is all too new for you." Then he abruptly headed for the door. " There were be time enough after the initial evaluation."

That drew her up short. " Evaluation?" she asked.

But he was already gone.

———◆———

DEVIL'S BARGAIN

available in print and ebook

THE
REGENCY RAGS TO RICHES
SERIES

No Place for a Lady
Devil's Bargain
Almost an Angel
The Dragon Earl

Jade Lee, a USA Today bestseller, has two passions (well, except for her family, but that's a given). She loves dreaming up stories and playing racquetball, not always in that order.

When her pro-racquetball career ended with a pair of very bad knees, she turned her attention to writing. An author of more than 30 romance novels, she's decided that life can be full of joy without ever getting up from her chair